HOT NIGHT

SHANNON McKENNA

WITHDRAWN

HOT NIGHT

BRAVA

KENSINGTON PUBLISHING CORP.
http://www.kensingtonbooks.com

BRAVA BOOKS are published by

Kensington Publishing Corp.
850 Third Avenue
New York, NY 10022

All Kensington titles, imprints and distributed lines are available at
special quantity discounts for bulk purchases for sales promotion, pre-
miums, fund-raising, educational or institutional use.

Special book excerpts or customized printings can also be created to fit
specific needs. For details, write or phone the office of the Kensington
Special Sales Manager: Kensington Publishing Corp., 850 Third Avenue,
New York, NY 10022. Attn. Special Sales Department. Phone: 1-800-221-
2647.

Brava and the B logo Reg. U.S. Pat. & TM Off.

ISBN 0-7582-0564-3

First Kensington Trade Paperback Printing: October 2006
10 9 8 7 6 5 4 3 2 1

Printed in the United States of America

HOT NIGHT

Prologue

P irate gold. Coins and buttons, golden chains, orders of chivalry, glittering diamonds, glowing rubies, necklaces and rings and reliquaries.

Lucien's fingers tingled as he leafed through the museum journal. The softly gleaming Spanish gold that had lain at the bottom of the Caribbean for hundreds of years made today's take, lying in a tangled heap on the bed, look like cheap costume jewelry.

"I've found my next project," he said to the naked woman who stood in front of the window. "Come look at these pictures, Cammy."

The woman made no move to show that she had heard.

Lucien got up and uncorked the champagne, pouring it into the flutes that he had brought to the remote cabin just for the occasion. He carried one to the woman. "Camilla," he murmured. "To our success."

He chose a three-strand pearl collar from the pile of jewelry and fastened it around her neck. She shuddered at the contact.

Lucien kissed the angry marks on her back, where he'd pushed her down against the jewelry during sex. "You're so quiet. Something wrong?"

She wrapped her arms across her breasts, shivering. "You didn't tell me you were going to kill her."

Lucien kissed a scratch on her shoulder blade that still oozed blood. "Is that all?" he crooned. "Gertrude Bingham was a greedy old hag. She overworked you and underpaid you. She deserved what she got."

"But you shot her in the head." Camilla's eyes were haunted.

"I wouldn't have, if she hadn't burst in on us," he said calmly. "These are the risks, when you steal millions' worth of jewelry."

Camilla's chin shook. She put her hands over her mouth.

Lucien hid his impatience. "Come on," he coaxed. "The woman was over eighty. You saved her from a lingering decline into senility."

Camilla put her hand to her throat, as if the collar choked her. "So much blood," she whispered thickly.

"Don't think about it," he crooned. "Think about you and me, making love on our yacht."

Camilla grabbed him and clung to his neck. "I l-l-love you."

That was his cue. The knife shifted from pocket to hand, stabbed deep under her rib cage. Realization, betrayal, then death, in one brief instant. His ears roared with excitement as he felt life leave her body.

He let her sag onto the rug. Wiped his hands with her blouse. Removed the collar. Rolled the body up like a cigar. There was a tarp under the rug to make things simpler for the cleanup crew.

No muss, no fuss.

He dressed, then tossed the jewels into his suitcase, staring at Camilla's trussed remains with lingering dissatisfaction. The letdown had descended too soon. He already felt restless and out of sorts.

The only solution was to start planning his next diversion. Now.

He grabbed the museum journal and shoved it into the suitcase on top of the glittering snarl of gems.

Chapter

1

Silver Fork, Oregon
Nine months later

Abby Maitland rummaged through her bag again. And again. No house keys. Not possible. Not tonight. Oh, please.

She leaned her hot forehead against the door of her apartment and tried not to sob. The evening bag yielded up wallet, cell phone, and lipstick. Sheba meowed from inside as if she hadn't been fed in weeks.

Edgar, the blind date from the bowels of hell, rattled his car keys. "Makes it tough to invite me in for a nightcap, huh?" His voice was an oily ooze of insinuation.

Yeah, jerkwad. I'd only rather be dipped in boiling lead. She stomped on the words only for the sake of Dovey, her well-meaning coworker who had set up this date. She had freely agreed to spend an evening with this puff-toad, and it was classier to keep her mouth shut.

It wasn't really a blind date. She'd met him at a reception for a new exhibit at the science museum in Portland. He'd seemed promising; i.e., nice-looking and articulate. The flirtatious e-mail exchanges had been fun. The first hour of the date hadn't been bad.

After some wine, though, the illusion of wit and charm had faded. His face went red, he stopped listening to anything she said, his gaze dropped to her chest and stuck. By the time the food had arrived, she'd been casting around for a polite escape route. She should have called her car service then and there. She hadn't realized how drunk he was until he was driving her home. He'd scoffed at her offer to drive, of course, macho turd that he was. "I don't want any more company," she said, for the eighth time. "And you've had enough to drink."

"I did knock back a few. Can't drive back to Portland like this. You'll let me stay, won't you, dollface? I'll make it *so* worth your while."

Dollface? "In your dreams, Edgar," she said. "Get a room."

"Cool idea. Let's go check into that No-Tell Motel down on the highway." He swayed toward her. "Cheap, sleazy motels turn me on."

"Nope." She swayed back, to minimize the stupefying effects of his garlic-and-wine breath. Her landlady lived on the ground floor, but she was eighty, and would not appreciate being dragged from her bed just because Abby couldn't keep her purses organized.

"Break the kitchen window," Edgar suggested. He hefted her doorstop, a swirl of driftwood attached to a chunk of petrified wood.

"No!" Abby grabbed the doorstop, staggering under the momentum of Edgar's enthusiastic downswing. "Do not help! I'll deal with this problem myself. In fact, you can go. Now. Please. Feel free."

She fished out her cell phone and punched in the number of her friend Elaine, the only person besides Mrs. Eisley who had a set of keys.

Elaine picked up on the fourth ring. "Abby? What's up? You OK?"

"I'm fine," Abby said. "Sorry to call so late, but I was a ditz and locked myself out. I figured you'd turn the cell off if you were asleep."

"Um, well . . . I'm out."

"You're what?" Abby was startled. Shy, homebody Elaine was never out on a Wednesday night. Or any other night, for that matter.

"Out. Actually, I'm sort of, ah . . . involved, right now."

Abby's mouth worked for a moment, but she rallied swiftly. "Really? Whoo hoo! Good for you, girlfriend! I had no idea."

Elaine's giggle sounded nervous. "It's been a secret. I just met him recently. But later for that. Are your keys to my house locked in, too?"

"Yup." Abby recoiled as Edgar kissed her neck. His sour breath made her gag. She swatted him away. "Edgar, do you mind?"

"Abby, are you in trouble? Do you want me to call someone? Like the police?" Elaine's voice sharpened.

"I can handle the situation," she assured her friend. "Could you grab the Yellow Pages and find me a locksmith?"

"Coming right up."

Edgar chortled as Abby batted his hand away. He seemed to think they were playing a game, like an unruly dog hanging on to a stick.

"Abby? You still there?" Elaine asked anxiously.

"Hanging in there," Abby said grimly, rummaging through her bag. "Edgar, do you have a pen?" Edgar pulled a gold pen out of his pocket. Abby snatched it out of his hand. "Go ahead, Elaine."

"Let's see, let's see . . . oh, perfect. Night Owl Lock and Safe. It says, 'nighttime lockouts are my specialty.'"

"Great." She wrote the number Elaine recited on her thumb.

"Call me when you get inside," Elaine said. "If you don't call within twenty minutes, I'm calling the police."

"I'll call," Abby soothed. "Be ready to spill juicy details tomorrow."

She broke the connection and eyed Edgar with trepidation.

It was going to take some serious, hardcore rudeness to pierce his protective layer of self-absorption.

She sighed to herself. How squalid and depressing.

Zan was perched on the fence on Lookout Drive, wondering if that high, fast-moving cloud was going to hit the moon, when his phone vibrated. He checked the display. Unknown number. Lockout job.

Not tonight. He was in one of his moods. He was better off focusing on neutral things, like the moon on the ocean.

The vibration of the phone tickled his thigh. He didn't answer. He didn't feel like hauling his ass back down to the world of people. Their problems, their opinions. His family, for instance. Granddad and his brothers were constantly in his face, which was one of the reasons he was in this funk to begin with. Everybody telling him to change his coping mechanisms, his career, his whole goddamn personality.

Just thinking about it was getting him all wound up again. He focused on that smudge of stars on the horizon to chill himself out.

Hard to do, when the damn phone kept ringing.

Maybe he should phase out locksmithing altogether. He certainly didn't need the money. His computer consulting kept him busy. He kept his locksmith license current only because he enjoyed pitting himself against locks now and then. Besides, he didn't sleep at night. Nights could get long and boring. Sometimes he welcomed something to do.

But not tonight.

The caller gave up; the phone went still. He let out a sigh of relief and tried to get back into his groove, blissing out on the pulsing surge of the surf. Moonlit foam, in gleaming swaths over the beach. Full moon, clear night. Rare for the Oregon coast. He'd stay till dawn. The view was better than his computer screen, or the ceiling over his bed.

The phone buzzed against his thigh again. He resisted the urge to hurl the thing over the cliff, if only because he despised littering.

It kept ringing. He counted the number of rings stored in his short-term memory. Twelve. Curiosity started to poke at him. Sixteen, seventeen. Wow, someone was desperate. Or just stubborn. Nineteen, twenty. Aw, what the hell. He clicked TALK. "Night Owl Lock and Safe."

"Oh, thank God. Finally. I thought I'd misdialed."

A woman's voice. Low, husky. Sexy Southern accent. He was intrigued, in spite of himself. "Nope," he said.

He offered no explanation. After a puzzled silence she pushed on. "I'm locked out of my apartment. It's 2465 Tremont. Are you nearby?"

Tremont was just down the hill. He was about to say he'd be there in a few when a male voice said something loud but unintelligible.

"Stop it, Edgar." The sexy voice was muffled, no longer directed at the mouthpiece. "Keep your hands off—hey! Back off! I'm not—"

Thunk. The phone went dead.

Zan stared at it, hit the caller redial. Let it ring, eight times.

He felt jarred. Prodded by urgency. Like it was his responsibility to gallop off and solve this girl's problems with this dickhead Edgar. *Not my problem. Repeat after me. Not. My. Fucking. Problem.*

The litany didn't do any good. Something was revving up inside him, part knee-jerk chivalry, part curiosity. If he didn't make sure the Southern belle was OK, he would worry all night. If he then found out that something bad had happened to some girl on Tremont, he would blame himself and feel like shit. He had to make sure she was safe.

And find out if her face and body matched that soft, sexy voice.

He laughed at himself as he headed for his van. Maybe this was all about his poor neglected libido. His self-imposed celibacy was biting his ass particularly hard lately.

No point in analyzing it, though. A guy had to do what a guy had to do.

Chapter

2

Abby's shove knocked Edgar almost off his feet.

He caught himself against the porch railing and glared at her. "So that's the way you're going to be."

"You forced me to be rude to you, Edgar. I tried to avoid it."

"Try harder," Edgar said. "And give me back my goddamn pen."

His eyes had turned to glittering slits in his flushed face. Abby wedged herself into the corner of the porch and held out his pen. He jerked it out of her hand. Her phone, which had dropped to the floor in the scuffle, started to ring. She made a move to pick it up.

Edgar kicked it out of reach. "Go ahead," he jeered. "Bend over, sweet cheeks. It's my favorite position."

Her insides went icy cold. The phone kept ringing, but she barely heard it, with his crude words and ugly tone ringing in her ears.

Oh dear. She'd taken Edgar for a harmless jerk. He'd just mutated into something nastier. Her belly cramped. Elaine had said, what, twenty minutes before she called the cops?

A lot could happen in twenty minutes.

One last shot at pseudo-politeness while she psyched herself up to scratch and gouge. "The locksmith is on his way, Edgar. There's no reason to wait. Bye-bye."

He sensed her nervousness, and liked it. He oozed closer, until her back was pressed against the wall. "Scared, Abby?"

She forced herself to smile. "Nothing to be scared of, is there? Look, we're going to wake up my landlord if we keep yakking. He's a cop, and he works weird hours, so he won't appreciate being bothered."

"You're scared," Edgar repeated, delighted by the discovery. "Of me." He grabbed her wrists and pinned her to the wall.

She struggled, panic squirming in her belly. His face was slick with sweat. Oh, gross. It became unpleasantly evident that he was excited. She tried to remember tricks from the self-defense course she'd taken at the gym, but the only thing that came to mind were house keys. Good for eye jabbing, face raking and the like. Hah.

Edgar licked her neck. Her stomach lurched. She dragged in a deep breath and drove her spike heel into his foot, with all her weight.

Edgar howled. *Whap*, the back of her head smacked painfully into the shingled wall. "You *bitch*!"

"Let go of her," said a deep voice.

Edgar swiveled his head. "Who the fuck are you?"

Abby wrenched out of his grip, catching herself against the wall.

It was hard to follow what happened. It was dark, the stranger wore black, her eyes were watering, her head spun from the blow.

Edgar whipped around like a rag doll and flailed, facedown on the floor. The stranger sank down on top of him, twisting Edgar's hand behind his back, pinning his shoulder to the floor with his knee.

She blinked tears from her eyes, squeezed them shut. Tried again.

Yes, the man was still there, crouching on top of Edgar. He was real. Dark hair hung long and loose over a battered black leather jacket. Keen eyes studied her, thoughtful and curious.

He grabbed Edgar's hair, jerked his head up. "Apologize to her."

"Fuck you," Edgar wheezed. "I'll have you arrested, you scumbag piece of shit. I'll ruin your goddamn life!"

The guy let go of Edgar's hair and chopped the edge of his hand down onto the bridge of Edgar's nose. He shrieked. Blood bubbled.

"Wrong answer," the stranger said mildly.

Edgar made wet choking sounds. The man shot her a questioning glance. "Want to call the cops? I'll verify that he was assaulting you."

She shook her head.

"You want me to hit him some more?" the man prompted.

She forced sound past the lump in her throat. "If you could, ah, just make him go away, that would be great, thanks."

"OK." He yanked up on Edgar's hair. "This is your lucky day, pusbag. The nice lady doesn't feel like watching you get stomped. Which is better luck than you deserve. You should thank her."

Edgar made gurgling noises.

"Too bad," the man murmured. "Another lost opportunity."

Edgar shrieked as the stranger jerked him to his feet, hand still twisted up behind him. He doubled over, moaning as the guy hustled him down the stairs. Abby clutched the banister, white-knuckled.

The men were soon lost to sight around the corner of the house. The stranger said something in a low, intense tone. Edgar coughed and gasped in reply. A car door slammed. Lights came on, a motor hummed to life. The Porsche revved up and crushed Mrs. Eisley's pansy beds as it cut a corner out of the driveway and sped away. Silence.

She wondered if the guy was just a wishful hallucination.

The shadows in the bushes at the base of the stairs resolved into a tall, dark form. He climbed until Mrs. Eisley's porch light shone full on his face, paused, and waited. She got the sense that he was trying not to scare her. Letting her get a good, long look at him.

She couldn't have stopped looking if she tried. The guy was straight out of a naughty dream, the kind she woke up from hot and damp and achingly lonesome. Tall and solid-looking, sharp cheekbones, an angular jaw. His eyebrows were a slashing black line. His dark mane had the look of a long-ago haircut that he hadn't bothered to refresh. There was a tattoo on his neck. He looked hard, seasoned. Dangerous.

The kind of guy she'd sworn off for all time.

"Are you all right?" he asked her, his voice hesitant.

She clamped down on the hysterical laughter. "Yes, thank you."

His eyes flicked over her body. In the porch light, she could finally decipher the bright color. Not blue or gray. Topaz gold.

She looked down to check what she was wearing. The Diego Della Valle. Low-cut, slinky, short. She'd been regretting her outfit all night, the way Edgar had drooled over her cleavage all evening.

This was different. The stranger's brief, discreet once-over made her feel stark naked. She shivered, and let go of the railing to cross her arms across her breasts. She swayed, groping for the banister.

He leaped up the remaining stairs with pantherlike swiftness, grabbing her around the waist. "Whoa! Steady there."

"Sorry." Her hands fluttered. She had no idea where to put them. He was all around her. The only place to rest them was his shoulders, tangled in his hair, wrapped around his waist. Gripping his butt. Whoa.

He wore black cargo pants, covered with utilitarian pockets, all of which appeared to be in use. A gray T-shirt was stretched out across a broad, muscular chest. He smelled good, too. Like herbs. Rain on the earth, with faint accents of metal and woodsmoke and sea air.

"Here. Sit." He pulled her until she stumbled down two steps, and coaxed her into sitting down on the top step. "Put your head down."

She pressed her face against her knees as much to hide from those intense golden eyes as to recover from the head rush.

"How about you let me run you over to the emergency room?" he offered. "Your lips look kind of bluish."

Lovely. So she looked like death, too. "No, thanks," she mumbled.

"But he bashed your head against the wall." He reached around and touched her head. The contact gave her a tingling shock.

She leaned away. His hand dropped. "I'm fine, thanks."

She sneaked a quick peek at his tattoos as she struggled to her feet. On his neck was the swirling knotwork of a black Celtic cross. The one on his hand was a pair of crossed cutlasses. Pirate swords.

"OK, whatever," he said. "Just go slow, OK?"

They stood there looking at each other until his brows knitted in a puzzled frown. "Why are you looking at me like that?"

"I, uh . . ." She floundered. "I guess I was just sort of surprised to find you still here, after Edgar left."

His eyes narrowed. "Why wouldn't I be?"

She shook her head, embarrassed. "It seemed so improbable. A mysterious guy pops up at the eleventh hour, like Batman. He does his thing, saves the day, and whoosh, he disappears."

A faint smile touched his lips. "But I haven't done my thing yet."

What was that supposed to mean? Mrs. Eisley was deaf, and the night was dark, and she was shaking so hard, she could barely stand.

He backed down two steps, hands lifted. "I don't mean anything sinister. I just meant that I haven't done the job you called me for yet."

"Called you for . . . for what?" She was utterly lost.

"The locksmith. Remember? Your lockout?"

Her jaw dropped. "You're the *locksmith*?"

"Yeah." His sidelong glance was delicately cautious. "And, uh, exactly why is this so hard to believe?"

She looked over six feet and some odd inches of lethally gorgeous male. "I've never called a locksmith," she babbled. "I expected someone with a potbelly and a bald spot. In a blue coverall. Named Irv. Or Mel."

Smile lines crinkled around his stunning eyes. The topaz color was set off by inky lashes. "Sorry to disappoint you. My name's Zan."

He held out his hand, and she took it. His grip was warm and strong. "I see. Zan," she repeated inanely. "What kind of name is that?"

"Alexander," he said. "I was named for my dad. He was an Alex. I didn't like being Alex Jr., so I bullied everybody into calling me Zan."

She had no business being fluttery. He'd saved her from Edgar, and for that she was grateful, but he was still a black-leather-wearing über-alpha wolf, like all the bad news boyfriends in her checkered past.

He probably ate girls like her for breakfast. They all did. They all had. She had no intention of being eaten for breakfast, ever again.

Her naughty brain took that thought, twirled it around and had a party with it. She rummaged for her keys, remembered why he was there, and blushed. "Sorry," she said. "I'm kind of rattled."

"Of course you are." The locksmith knelt, pulling a leather pouch from one of his pockets. He pulled out a couple of metal tools and gave her a quick, assessing glance. "You still look pretty wobbly." He took her hand and placed it on his broad shoulder. "Lean on me."

Her fingers dug into his shoulder through the thick leather. She hadn't had anybody to lean on for so long.

She barely noticed what he did to her lock. It clicked open after a few seconds. He made a courtly gesture for her to enter. She lifted her hand away and walked in, wishing it had taken longer.

Seconds ticked by. She flipped the light on to break the spell. "Come on in." Her voice was pitched way too high. "I hope a check is OK."

"A check is fine." He stepped into her kitchen, eyes scanning the place with discreet curiosity. Sheba padded daintily over to his feet, sniffed his boots, and began to weave sinuously around his ankles.

Abby was startled. Sheba despised strangers, and she clawed strips out of the hands of anyone presumptuous enough to pick her up.

The locksmith picked her up.

"Careful," Abby warned. "She's twitchy. Don't let her scratch you."

"Oh, she won't. Cats love me." He stroked Sheba's downy back.

"Really?" she said wistfully. Her last would-be boyfriend had been violently allergic to Sheba. The affair had ended after that panicked trip to the emergency room. Cortisone shots really killed the mood.

"Never met a cat who didn't." Sheba purred and flung her head back over his wrist, baring her throat with sluttish kitty abandon.

Abby dragged her eyes away from the spectacle with some effort. "Thank you, by the way," she said.

He shrugged. "Just doing my job."

"No, not for the lockout. I meant for what you did with Edgar."

He looked uncomfortable. "No big deal. Don't thank me for that."

"Too late," she said. "Thanks anyway. It's a huge big deal to me."

He gave her a dismissive nod, followed by a long silence fraught with embarrassment. "I, uh, have to pay you," she repeated.

"Yeah," he agreed, rubbing expertly behind Sheba's ears.

"What's your fee?" she asked. "And is a check OK?"

He looked faintly amused. "You asked me that before."

Abby discreetly tugged her neckline higher. "Did you answer?"

"Yes." His deep voice was as soft as silk. "I said a check is fine."

She let out her breath slowly. "So what's your fee?" she repeated.

"Does your check have your phone number on it?" He stroked Sheba's fluffy belly. Her raucous purring seemed deafening.

Abby checked to make sure her hair covered her cleavage. "I usually don't—that is, I prefer—I mean, what for?"

"So I can ask you out." His playful dimple seemed out of place in that lean, dangerous face.

Her toes curled inside her pumps. A rush of excitement tightened her chest. "I thought this was a . . . a business transaction."

"It is. I just happened to ask for your number in the middle of it."

"Don't take this personally, but it's been a bad night," she said.

He nodded. "Of course. That's why I'm just getting your number, for now. I'll wait a decent interval before I call and ask you out."

Abby tugged her skirt over her thighs. "What's a decent interval?"

"Hadn't thought about it yet," he said. "A week? A couple days? Twelve hours? What do you think would be a decent interval?"

"Let's stick to business," she said. "How much do I owe you?"

He looked thoughtful. Sheba butted his hand with her fuzzy head. He stroked her obligingly. "That depends," he said.

"On what?" she demanded.

"On the client. If the dickwad in the Porsche had called me— what was his name? Edward? Edmund?"

"Oh. Edgar."

"If it were Edgar, I'd jack up the price as much as my conscience allows, which is a lot. Then I'd make him pay before I opened the door."

Abby was suspicious of that teasing dimple. "And why is that?"

He shrugged. "He could afford it. Plus, he'd been driving under the influence, which pisses me off."

"I'm not drunk," she said. "How do you know I wasn't driving?"

He rolled his eyes. "Yeah, like that meathead would ever let a girl drive his eighty-thousand-dollar penis substitute."

She shook with nervous giggles. "You have a point. I tried to get him to let me drive. The harder I tried, the faster he went."

"Dickhead," Zan commented. "Truth is, I wouldn't have come at all if I hadn't liked your voice so much. I just had to see who owned that sexy Southern drawl. Where are you from, anyway?"

Abby tried three times before she could make any sound come out of her throat. "Atlanta. But that's, ah, irrelevant. And inappropriate."

"Oh, don't mind me." His voice was silky. "I'm just stalling."

"I see that." She grabbed her checkbook. "What do I owe you?"

"But as soon as you write that check, I'll have to go away." His fingers dug into the thick fur of Sheba's belly. Her tail lashed wildly.

Abby wrenched her gaze away from the spectacle. "Stop stalling and tell me how much I owe you, Mr., er . . ."

"Duncan. Call me Zan." He pulled out a card and laid it on her counter. "I could cut you a deal. I always cut my friends a deal."

Abby's heart thudded heavily. It was a reaction to the adrenaline, she told herself. Not to the idea of being his, ah . . . friend.

"I appreciate the offer, but I'm really obligated to you already," she said. "Please, just tell me your fee. It's late."

His eyebrows lifted. "No phone number?"

"No." She poised the pen over the check.

He looked wistful. "OK. Make it for a hundred and twenty, then."

Abby slapped the pen onto the counter. "That's highway robbery!"

He blinked. "At least I didn't ask you to pay me in advance."

"You couldn't have! My checkbook was locked inside!"

"I never said I wasn't practical." His eyes gleamed. Sheba had abandoned herself, fluffy tail dangling over his arm like a feather boa. "I didn't mean to piss you off. I thought you didn't want to feel obligated."

"Sure, but there are limits!"

"I'll make a deal with you, then," he said. "Your lock is crap. Let me replace it with something decent. A Schlage, maybe. Parts and labor, plus the lockout, two hundred bucks. It's a great deal."

She tried not to laugh. "You are an opportunist."

"One seventy-five, then, parts and labor. I swear, you won't regret it. Call around, do a price comparison, if you want."

Sheba yawned hugely and stretched, in a state of utter bliss.

Abby flipped open her checkbook. This had dragged on long enough, and it was her own damn fault for encouraging him. "Who do I make this stupid check out to?"

"Make it out to Night Owl Lock & Safe," he said.

"Tomorrow I'm going to make some calls to see what the going rate is for a nighttime lockout," she said, scribbling the check.

"Be my guest."

She ripped it out of the book. "If I find that you've egregiously overcharged me, I'm going to call the Better Business Bureau."

"You do that," he said. "Then call me up and tell me what an evil, greedy, grasping bastard I am. Any hour of the day or night is fine."

She held out the check. "Take this. And put my cat down."

"But she loves me," he protested. "She's as limp as a noodle."

"Thank you, and good night," she said sternly.

He hesitated, frowning. "It's true, what I said about your lock."

"What would it cost to install a lock you couldn't get through?"

A slow smile curved his lips. "It would cost you a fortune to install a lock I couldn't get through. I'm good. Patient, thorough . . . tireless."

She broke eye contact and shook with nervous laughter. "My goodness. You certainly do have a high opinion of yourself."

"Yes." The word was spoken entirely without vanity.

She blew out a sharp breath. "What a night. First Edgar, now you. Just take your check, please." She pushed it across the counter.

Zan's smile had vanished. "I am nothing like Edgar," he said flatly. "I have nothing in common with that shit-eating insect."

"I'm sorry," she said, flustered. "I didn't mean to offend you."

"I don't want your apologies," he said.

She was at a loss for a moment. "Ah, OK. Thanks again for the—"

"I don't want your thanks. Most of all, I don't want your check."

"So what do you want, then?" The eloquent silence that followed her words made her feel like an idiot. "Oh, duh," she mumbled. "Set myself up for that, didn't I? Handed it right to you on a silver platter."

"A kiss," he said.

She blinked. "What?"

"That's what I want."

She put her hands over her hot cheeks. "Uh . . . whoa."

"Don't worry. No pressure. You don't have to kiss me," he assured her. "But you asked me what I wanted. I'm just telling you. That's all."

She was utterly flustered. "But I . . . I just can't."

"I know you can't. I'll live," he said. "You're just so pretty. You smell wonderful, and your voice makes shivers go down my spine. I'm talking about just a tiny, respectful, worshipping kiss. Like kissing the feet of a golden goddess. A sip of paradise."

Oh, he was diabolically, scarily good. She was spellbound by those seductive topaz eyes, that silk-and-velvet voice. Imagining how it would feel to be kissed like that. As if she were precious, unique. *Loved*.

She backed away, appalled at how tempted she was. "I'm sorry," she whispered. "I . . . I just can't risk that."

He nodded. "Of course not. Sorry. Shouldn't even have said it."

Damn. If he'd been churlish, that would have broken the spell. As it was, his sweetness threw her into terrible confusion.

He placed Sheba on the floor, gave her a farewell stroke, and rose to his feet. His gallant nod was almost a bow. He walked out. She stared at the blank rectangle of night beyond the open door.

She hurried out onto the porch. "Zan!" she called.

He stopped halfway down the stairs and turned slowly. "Yeah?"

She started down after him. "Don't you want your check?"

He shook his head. "I'd rather dream about my kiss."

She stopped on the step above his. He still loomed, inches taller than she. "That's, ah, not very good business," she told him.

"Nope," he agreed. "I'm sorry. I shouldn't have pressured you."

"Shhh." She put her finger against his lips. They were amazingly soft and warm. Something broke loose inside her, and tears flooded down.

His arms circled her, and suddenly she was draped over him, shaking with sobs. She lifted her head a moment later, sniffling. "Sorry," she murmured. "Bet this service isn't in your fee schedule."

"I don't want a fee from you," he said. "Get it through your head."

"Take this, then." She took his face in her hands and kissed him.

It was a careful kiss. Tender and charged with sweetness. She felt every detail intensely: the scent of his breath, the softness of his lower lip, his hot skin, the strong, elegant bone structure beneath her hands. His beard stubble was so long, it was no longer scratchy. It was soft.

She forced herself to pull away. Zan's head was tilted back, his eyes closed as if he'd received a divine benediction. His cheekbones were stained with color.

Her laughter sounded soggy. "Zan? Hello? You OK?"

He smiled, eyes still closed. "I'm in heaven."

"Oh, please." She swatted his shoulder. "Don't overdo it."

He opened his eyes. "I tasted tears on your lips. Made me blush."

"Oh." She wiped her eyes, her cheeks. "I'm, ah, glad you liked it."

He took a step down the stairs. "I'd better go. Right now," he said. "I can't keep up this perfect gentleman act any longer."

So don't. She forced the impulsive words back. "So it's an act?"

He backed down the steps. "Only since the dawn of mankind."

He turned the corner and was lost to sight. She listened to his vehicle pull away. Headlights rounded the curve.

She realized that her phone was ringing. The machine clicked on as she walked in. *"This is Abby. Sorry I missed you. Leave a message."*

"Abby? Are you home?" Elaine's voice was sharp with worry. "Pick up if you are, because I'm about to call the police."

Abby snatched up the phone. "I'm here," she said. "Relax."

"You got rid of the date from hell?"

"With some help, yes." She dropped limply into a kitchen chair.

"Help? What do you mean, help?"

"Edgar was slobbering all over me, which was gross, and then this locksmith materialized out of nowhere and, uh . . . beat him up."

"Beat him . . . good God, Abby!"

"Yeah, it was pretty special," Abby said fervently.

"So the locksmith saved you, then? How romantic!"

"Actually, it was really violent and scary," Abby snapped.

"I'm sure it was," Elaine soothed. "I didn't mean to be flip. You haven't sounded excited about a guy since you made up the List."

"Let's not get into my List tonight."

"OK. One last thing, though. Was the locksmith cute?"

Abby hesitated. "It doesn't matter if he's cute," she said heavily. "He's everything I've sworn at all costs to avoid."

"Ah," Elaine murmured. "The plot thickens."

Abby winced. "No, it doesn't. Please. I've suffered enough tonight."

"Tomorrow, then," Elaine said. "Oh, another thing. Would you bring my house keys to work tomorrow? I want to give a set to Mark."

Abby was startled. "Really? How long have you known this guy?"

"He asked for them." Elaine's voice was defensive. "I figured I'd just give him the ones I gave you and make new ones for you. OK? Don't worry. Really. It seems too good to be true, Abby. He's just so—"

The murmur of a masculine voice cut off whatever Elaine was about to say. She came back on the line a moment later. "Gotta go."

"OK. Thanks for calling. Have fun with Mysterious Mark."

Elaine let out an anxious, tittering laugh. "Sweet dreams of the yummy locksmith. Don't forget my keys. See you tomorrow."

"Right." Abby hung up, kicked off her heels and sank into the sofa. Sheba leaped onto her lap, covering her skirt with fluff.

This was not jealousy. She would be thrilled if Elaine found true love, or even just hot sex. Her coworker was a lovely girl, talented at her job as exhibit designer, but painfully shy when it came to men.

Abby had worked for years to get Elaine to believe in her own attractiveness. Now Elaine was giving keys to Mark, while Abby, with all her extensive dating experience, was home alone with her remote control, her cat, and a pint of Fudge Ripple for company. How pathetic.

She turned on the tube, surfed until she hit an old black-and-white film. A hardboiled detective, a fragile blonde in an evening gown. She stroked Sheba. Heavy purrs vibrated through her hands. It made her think of Zan's hands. The bold, expert way he touched her cat.

Back in her crazy period, she would've given that guy her number without hesitation. And waited breathless by the phone until he called.

Oh, get real. Probably she wouldn't have let him leave at all.

Not now. Her weakness for tattooed, leather-clad bad-boy wolf types had gotten her into no end of trouble. They'd crashed in her place without paying rent, run up her phone bill, used her car and wrecked it. After the third wreck, her insurance agent had begun to make insulting comments about her taste in men. She could scarcely blame him.

The blonde was getting agitated with the handsome detective, and Abby upped the volume to see what was bugging her.

". . . hired you to find my brother, not to listen to your disgusting insults!" the actress declared. "I demand to be treated with respect!"

Amen, sister, Abby thought, remembering the time she'd come home to find a pack of travel-stained bikers chugalugging tequila in her kitchen. Greg's buddies. And the time Jimmy had accused her of sleeping with her boss, followed her to work and attacked the poor guy. Skinny, timid Bob, with his glasses and his bald spot.

The final straw had been the night she was dragged out of bed in her panties by the police at 3:00 AM, only to discover that her then-boyfriend Shep had been hiding controlled substances in her attic.

She'd been so mortified, she'd left the state.

That was the ultimate wake-up call. The guys she went for when she followed her natural inclinations were one-way tickets to disaster, if not prison. The solution was obvious. No more yielding to impulse. She would run her love life strategically. The way a general ran a war.

She didn't want to live on the edge of disaster, as her mother had. Paycheck to paycheck, forever late on the rent for the cheap dives she lived in. Crawling into a bottle when things got too tough to bear.

Which had been pretty much all the time, toward the end.

She wanted better for herself. Beauty, security, respect. Nice things. Social standing. All that good, dull, respectable stuff. She'd worked hard to transform her life, moonlighting as a paralegal for years while slogging away on arts-administration internships.

Now she was the development manager at the Silver Fork Museum, and she was good at raising money. The museum had doubled its operating budget since she'd started working there.

She felt a glow of accomplishment when she thought about the Pirates' Hoard. It was the springboard for their new exhibit program, a trove of treasure from a Spanish galleon sunk off the coast of Barbados by pirates three hundred years ago and just recently rediscovered.

The Pirates' Hoard was a huge feather in her cap, if they made their crowd. It was a stretch, with that stiff quarter-million-dollar fee. A big, nail-biting gamble. She'd pulled the proposal together herself over a year ago, landing a competitive $1.2 million grant from the NEA to support the exhibition program, including funding for catalogs, wall text, mountings, a high-tech security system, etc., etc. It was an amazing coup. She was proud of herself. And this was just the beginning.

Abby had personally pulled in a lot of the money that had made the construction of the museum's new wing possible, though her boss, Bridget, the development director, would rather die than admit it.

Her career was on the rise—and she was going to make her love life conform to the same high standard or die trying, damn it.

To that end, drumroll please, she'd compiled the List.

The List was strict. No backsliding, no freewheeling. She dated clean-shaven, well-dressed men. No lost souls, rap sheets, or addictions. No martial arts freaks, guns, or motorcycles. Above all, no tattoos.

She only considered men with good jobs, nice cars, retirement plans, college degrees. Men who were conversant in politics, economics, art, men who had well-formed opinions about the relative merits of French and Italian cheeses; men who knew how to order wine.

On TV, violins swelled, and the detective seized the blonde and kissed her. Abby sighed. Three years of dating, and she had yet to find a man who fit the List who turned her on. Her coffee cup said that if you wanted to meet Prince Charming, you had to kiss a lot of frogs.

She was sick of kissing frogs. She wanted to kiss Zan Duncan. She shut her eyes, leaned back and unleashed her very lively imagination. Supposing that the hot buzz of attraction between them had gone further. If she'd resisted a little less, if he'd pushed a bit more.

Suppose he'd looked at her with those hot golden eyes until her flustered stammering petered off into breathless silence.

She jerked her chin at him, inviting him into the living room. He hesitated in the doorway, savoring the sweet agony of anticipation.

Like kissing the feet of a beautiful goddess. His remembered words made her chest ache with longing. He approached her, stroked her cheek, slid his hand under her hair. Exploring, marveling.

He caressed her jaw and cheek with his lips before fitting them to hers. A couch materialized behind her as he sank down in front of her. He slid his hands under her skirt, tugged her panties off, and bent his head, warm lips kissing and nuzzling, circling in a tightening spiral, closer and closer to her clit, taking his time. Making her wait—and wait.

Patient, thorough . . . tireless. She was a knot of tension, thighs clenched, as her dream Zan finally opened her, sliding his tongue into her slick, furled folds. First the pressure of his lips was a kiss, asking permission, then a feathery caress, and then the swirl of his tongue got bolder, circling her clit, fluttering with voluptuous skill—God.

Pleasure erupted, throbbing through every part of her body.

Oh, whoa. Her eyes fluttered open to the black-and-white flickering on the TV, her tears swirling it into a featureless gray blur.

Which was a pretty succinct description of her current love life.

She stared at the screen and wondered what Zan would think if he knew she was sprawled on her couch with her hand on herself, thinking about his eyes, his hands. His mouth.

The renewed jolt of excitement startled her. She squeezed her thighs together. Pleasure jerked through her, in wrenching spasms.

Wow. Just the thought of him watching her come was all it took.

Chapter

3

Lucien was irritated. He'd specifically told Elaine not to mention his name—or rather, his alias—to anyone, but here she was, babbling away to her girlfriend about "Mark." Brainless cow.

Elaine clicked her phone shut and gave him a tremulous smile. "Abby's going to bring that extra set of keys to work tomorrow," she said. "I can give it to you when we meet for dinner."

Lucien stretched luxuriously before reaching across the tangle of sheets to wind his fingers into Elaine's blond hair. He twisted, hard enough to make her gasp, enjoying her confusion before he kissed her and made it better. He pried the cell phone out of her cold fingers.

"Sweetheart. Did I or didn't I say not to tell anyone about us?"

Elaine's blue eyes got very big and began to blink nervously. "But that was just Abby! I had to tell her why I wasn't home at one in the morning on a Wednesday night, or she would've gotten suspicious."

"OK, OK," he murmured. "But even so, it's better if—"

"She's been trying to persuade me to let myself go, and thank God I finally have, and I knew she'd be happy for me, so I thought I—"

"Shh." He cut off her babbling with another hard kiss. "I said no one, and I meant no one," he said sternly.

Elaine's eyes overflowed. "I'm sorry." Her voice was a shaking wisp. "I'll tell Abby not to tell anyone. She won't if I tell her not to."

Yeah, thereby drawing even more attention to him. Perfect.

"Don't make a big thing of it," he said. "I don't want to risk what we have by letting the whole world in on it. And besides . . ." He placed her hand on his penis. ". . . secrecy excites me."

"Me too," Elaine breathed, stroking him.

Of course, her too. If he'd expressed a desire to dive headfirst into a festering dumpster, sweet, suggestible Elaine would bleat '*me, too.*' He forced a smile. "Who's Abby? I want to know about your friends."

Elaine brightened. "Oh, she's our development manager. She's fabulous. So smart and funny, and gorgeous, too. She's a wonderful friend. She's been here for three years, since Bridget fired the last . . ."

Lucien tuned out her empty chatter. He'd done his research on Abby Maitland, as he had for all of the museum's administrative staff. He had a thick file on Abby. The photos had intrigued him. So had her background check. Jailbird father, alcoholic mother, an arrest for drug dealing for which she was later cleared. Most interesting.

She'd put it all behind her, though. Come to the West Coast, put herself through school, made a new life for herself. Admirable.

She was very attractive, in a tall, buxom Amazon sort of way. Her checkered, problematic past made her a good candidate for his plans, but he'd studied a close-up of her face one night, and decided against it.

It was her eyes that had tipped the balance. Too wary, too cautious. She'd been around the block too many times. Lucien was very good at feigning normal emotions. Ninety-nine point nine percent of humanity never knew the difference.

Abby Maitland looked like she might be in that point one percent.

Besides, he preferred his lovers more physically delicate. The pretty blond curator, Elaine Clayborne, met that description. She was also more fragile, naive and trusting, and so dull, he was in imminent danger of death by boredom. He should have targeted Abby

Maitland. He'd have been able to maintain his erections better, at least.

"Is she seeing anyone?" he asked, cutting Elaine off midbabble.

Elaine floundered. "Ah . . . ah, no. Her date tonight bombed, so no possibilities there. I think this guy was one of Dovey's blind dates. Dovey's our development associate. He's always trying to fix Abby up with guys who fit her List."

"List? What list is that?"

"Oh. That." Elaine let out a nervous titter. "Well, actually, she told me about that in confidence, so I probably shouldn't—"

"I won't tell anybody." He looked deep into her eyes. "Trust me."

Elaine blinked rapidly. "OK. It's just that she's had man trouble in the past, so she's worked out strict criteria for the men she dates."

"Money?"

"Well, they do need to be financially comfortable. And she likes fine dining, theater, music, high culture. I tease her about her List, but with the trouble she's had, I really can't blame her."

"Interesting," he said.

And it was. The most interesting thing that Elaine had told him so far, in the three weeks that he had been fucking her. He filed that tidbit away, rolled on top of her, and got down to the task of feigning passion.

It was hard going. This project wasn't giving him the sexual buzz he needed. There was risk, and a vast profit margin, and the thought of stealing pirate gold appealed to him—but he didn't pull jobs like this for money. He'd been rich all his life, and filching jewelry and fine art from his friends' families' villas in Monaco ever since he was a bored, thrill-seeking teenager. Desperate for something to make his heart pound.

He'd slowly realized, as he grew up, that he was a little bit different from other people. He had a blank spot inside him. A sort of emotional deficiency. He'd learned to cover for it, there being absolutely nothing wrong with his intelligence or his instinct for self-preservation.

But if he wanted a thrill, he needed something very, very intense.

His parents were busy and self-absorbed. They'd never noticed a problem. Why should they? He was charming, intelligent, good-looking, a high achiever. He'd been groomed to run the philan-thropic arm of the vast, family-owned Haverton Corporation. He'd gotten the reputation for being the softie of the family, the bleeding heart who gave away money while the rest of the Haverton sharks slaved at making it.

The irony of that misconception secretly amused him.

He self-medicated as best he could. He'd tried drugs of all kinds, with mixed results. High-risk sports helped, bizarre and violent sex worked even better. Recreational murder was fun, too. Messy, though. He didn't like spoiling his clothes, and he was repelled by the smells.

His all-time favorite high was stealing. Nothing beat it, for pure buzz factor. His best defense against boredom. He wasn't afraid of pain or prison or death, but oh God, how he hated boredom.

If Elaine had been married to the museum director, if she were the director's teenage daughter, if the stakes were higher for some reason, seducing her might be titillating enough to be worth the bother. It was stimulating to convince his victims that he loved them. It gave the killing blow that much more punch. Ultimate be-trayal, and all that.

But not with Elaine. She had been so easy to seduce. She'd fallen in love with him almost instantly. Born victim. Big bore.

He rolled her onto her back and kissed her hard. He didn't know what passion felt like, but he'd seen enough movies to know what it looked like. His fingers tightened around her hair. Her startled squeak of pain had a salutory effect on his erection.

He pushed her head down toward his lap, nudging his penis against her lips until she opened to him. He shoved himself into the warm, wet recesses of her mouth, closed his eyes, and established the rhythm he wanted, his fists tangled in her hair. Slightly better, but she made such irritating noises. Elaine was not skillful at fellatio.

He wondered if Abby was better. He would bet the Pirates' Hoard that she was. The thought was very invigorating to his erection.

He imagined fucking Abby while Elaine was forced to watch, tied hand and foot. The image provoked a surprisingly powerful orgasm.

He smiled at the ceiling, stroking Elaine's thin, trembling back.

Keep driving. Straight home. Don't even think about going back to Abby's place to see if it was true—that she'd wanted him to take things one step further, and whee, off they'd go, down the slippery slope.

But the poor woman had just been assaulted. If he was really interested in getting involved with her—and oh, was he ever!—then he had to take things slow. Show her that he was one of the good guys.

What's a decent interval?

He laughed to himself. Dangerous question to put to a guy with a raging hard-on, sweetheart. Ten seconds, maybe?

Weird. He made a point of being sensitive to the fears of women who called him for late-night lockouts. He never came on to them, no matter how cute they were. But he hadn't wanted to make Abby feel safe. His instinct had been to back her up to the wall, follow up every advantage, and plunder all that sweet bounty. Maybe it was the effect of the fight, if one could call that a fight. He could have hammered that dickless clown in his sleep. It was his glands talking. If he saved the female from the saber-toothed tiger, that meant he got to fuck her, right?

He could've handled the situation with less force, but the sound of her head smacking the wall had severely pissed him off. He'd broken the guy's nose for sure, maybe sprained his wrist. Dickwad deserved it.

Hell of a first impression to live down, though.

Zan pulled up by the old factory building he and his brothers had bought and restored. Granddad and Zan's youngest brother, Jamie, shared the apartment on the first floor. His sister Fiona's room was there, too, though she'd been traveling across Asia for months. Free-spirited Fiona. It made him sweat to think of his baby sister wandering through the teeming cities of the world, but he couldn't chain her down.

His mother had lived on the first floor, too, before she'd boogied off to Vegas to have her midlife crisis in style. His other two brothers, Christian and Jack, had divided the second floor, although Jack was currently in hermit mode and preferred his eyrie up on Bald Mountain.

The top floor was Zan's lair. Arched windows reached from floor to ceiling on both sides. Exposed brick, hardwood floors, open spaces. He hadn't partitioned it, except for the bathrooms, since he liked one huge, breezy room. The kitchen was at one end, locksmithing equipment at the other. Then there was his work zone, his leisure zone with couches and TV. His motorcycles were parked in a corner. Lots of space left over in the middle to do tai chi. It was tough to heat, but what the hell.

He killed the motor and pulled out his cell, punching a few buttons that would permanently save Abby Maitland's number in his phone. He glanced up at the windows of his apartment.

Shit. That flickering light could only mean one thing. Granddad was awake, and was lying in ambush. He groaned. He didn't want Granddad to bust his balls tonight. He just wanted to sprawl on his bed, dick in hand, and think about that girl.

Those slanted, wary brown eyes looked like they'd seen a lot. She had amazing lips, too. Such a unique, sexy shape: the sulky swell of the bottom, the delicate contours of the upper. And that swirling swish of auburn hair, just like the girls in hair conditioner commercials. He'd always figured that ultrashine effect was computer enhanced.

Abby's hair was for real. He'd touched it. As soft as it looked.

And her body. Jesus wept. He didn't go for female bodies that were stringy and taut, aerobicized down to nothing. He liked them like Abby, tall and strong, but round, too. Full tits and a round, gorgeous ass. The seams of her stockings drew the eye upward to shadowy glories beneath the short skirt. His hand tingled with longing to stroke that luscious curve. He hadn't actually done it, but it had been a near thing.

His fantasy took on the form of a classic porn vignette. Horny locksmith comes to the rescue of hot babe, saving her from the evil bad guy. She invites him in, flushed with gratitude, and checks him out boldly, eyes lingering on his lips, then his chest, then his crotch. Her pink tongue flashes out to moisten her bottom lip . . . and whoa. He should save this one for the shower. Torrents of hot water and a soapy hand.

The fantasy played on, despite his efforts to squelch it. He pushed the low-cut dress down over her shoulders—just the lightest twitch should do it. Her tits would be propped up in some frilly bra. His mind hung up briefly on her nipple color scheme—pale pink, hot red, beige?

A light flicked on. *Damn.* The freight elevator rumbled open, revealing a tall, stooped figure behind the mesh gate. Granddad gave Zan a questioning jerk of his grizzled chin.

Zan sighed, and yielded to the inevitable. He got out and sauntered to the elevator. "Hey, Granddad. What are you doing awake?"

"A man don't need much sleep at my age. I just been thinking."

Always a dangerous development, Zan reflected as he stepped into the huge, battered elevator. "What made you decide to do your thinking in my apartment? I don't remember giving you a key."

Granddad glared out from under bushy eyebrows. The elevator began to creak and groan, hauling them up. "I got keys from Chris. Chris ain't so uppity about his precious privacy. You got some lip, kid."

"I'm thirty-six, Granddad," Zan said patiently. "I'm not a kid. And yeah, I know, Chris is the good grandson these days."

"Cut the crap." Granddad's voice was snappish.

The big doors ground open. Granddad had left the TV on. An old black-and-white movie flickered on the screen. "What have you been thinking about that's keeping you awake?" Zan shrugged off his jacket and sprawled on the couch. Granddad shuffled over to the fridge, returning with two beers that exhaled a fine plume of cold vapor from their open necks. Zan accepted his gratefully and took a long pull.

"You." The old man poised himself over the couch and thudded onto the cushions with a grunt. "I been worried about you, Alexander."

Zan leaned back, closing his eyes. When Granddad called him Alexander, there was a lecture in the offing. "Here we go again," he said.

"You been working too much," Granddad announced. "You hide in here all day, playing on that goddamn computer—"

"Working on the computer," Zan said, with rigid patience. "People pay me money to do it. I bill them. By the hour. Through the nose."

"Playing," Granddad insisted. "It's like Nintendo. Kids play them things until they don't know the difference between games and reality. That's you. You never see normal people. You're like one of those vampires on those TV shows. It ain't healthy, and it ain't normal."

Zan ran the icy cold bottle across his forehead. "I promise, I'm not a vampire," he said. "And you should be glad that business is good."

"Business?" Granddad waved his bottle around. He was getting all cranked up. "I'm not talking about business! I'm talking about your life! You make good money, and that's dandy, but it won't do you a damn bit of good if you don't have anything worth spending it on!"

"Why did you pick me to worry about?" Zan asked. "Why not Jack? He's more antisocial than I am. Or Fiona. The last call we got was from Katmandu, weeks ago. And Jamie's got a ring in his nose."

"Oh, that's just for his play." Granddad dismissed Jamie's nose ring with an airy wave of his hand. "And I do worry about all of you."

"Wow. Lucky us," Zan said drily.

Granddad blew a smoke ring, watched it dissolve. "Look at you! Thirty-six, and no girlfriend! It gets harder to snag a good woman, the longer you wait. You'd still look halfway decent if you'd get a haircut!"

"Look, Granddad, I'm too tired for this shit tonight—"

"You could shave, too." Granddad was on a roll. "You're letting yourself slide. Next thing you know, your gut rolls out over your belt, the crack of your ass starts to show, and that's it, boy. You're sunk."

Zan gave the lean, muscular body sprawled out in front of him an appraising glance. "I sparred with Chris last week, and slammed him so hard he's still not speaking to me. The crack of my ass isn't going to start showing anytime soon. And besides, I've had lots of girlfriends."

"And where are they? You tomcat around and scratch your itch, maybe, but you haven't brought any of them home to meet us!"

Zan snorted with laughter. His discreet, infrequent affairs could hardly be described as tomcatting. He thought about Abby, and lifted his beer bottle in a silent toast. "I'm working on it, I promise."

"Well." Granddad harrumphed. "Work harder. I ain't getting any younger, and I want to get me some great-grandbabies."

"Let Jack take the heat on the grandbaby issue. He's the oldest."

"I will, soon as I get my hands on him," Granddad said darkly.

"And I am going out during daylight hours this week," Zan told him. "I'm doing a job for the Boyles. Key job for the art museum. I'll have to interact socially, maybe even with women. Is that normal enough for you?"

Granddad stuck out his stubbled chin. "Smart-ass punk. Why the hell are you working for the Boyles, after what they did to you?"

Zan shrugged. "I've put it behind me. It's a job, like any other."

"Like any other, my ass." Granddad let out an explosive grunt of disgust. "You don't need money bad enough to subcontract from them two snakes. You don't need money at all, from what I can see."

Zan took a slow, meditative sip of beer. "I think Walt calls me for jobs because he feels bad about what happened," he said quietly.

"Bullshit," Granddad said, a shrewd gleam in his eye. "Walt calls you because you're smart. He needs smart people."

"He's got Matty," Zan pointed out. "Matty has a degree in electronic engineering. I don't have a degree in jack shit."

"Degrees don't mean nothing," Granddad scoffed. "You've got

more brains in your little finger than Matty has in his whole body, and everybody knows it. You watch your back, boy."

The door to the stairwell swung wide. An apparition in black leather, mascara and dreadlocks strutted in. His little brother, Jamie. Zan shut his eyes and groaned. "Who the hell gave you a key?"

Jamie brandished the diamond pick and tension wrench Zan had incautiously taught him to use some months back. "Don't need one."

"I didn't say to practice on me," Zan complained. "It's illegal."

"So have Chris arrest me. He'd have a ball." Jamie yanked open Zan's fridge and eyed the beer stash with disdain. "This stuff is horse piss, Zan. Want me to go downstairs and get you a decent beer?"

"Don't drink it if you don't like it. What's with your new look?"

Jamie popped open a beer, took a swig, and grimaced. "Horse piss," he muttered again. "My look is for my play, lamebrain."

"Play? What play?"

Jamie rolled his eyes. "Earth to Zan? I told you about the play, remember? The Stray Cat Playhouse summer stock season? They're doing *Romeo and Juliet*, and I choreographed the duels. Then last week, the guy playing Tybalt broke his leg parasailing, and the director asked me to fill in. I've been rehearsing every night for the past week, and this is the first time you've noticed my makeup job?"

"Oh, I noticed it," Zan said. "I just didn't think it was out of character, so it didn't occur to me to comment on it."

Jamie rolled his heavily made-up eyes. "Just for the record, I may be a weirdo, but I'm not the type of weirdo who wears mascara."

"Huh," Zan muttered. "That's a relief, I guess."

"Tybalt's a great part," Jamie went on. "All I do is swagger around and make trouble. Halfway through the play, Romeo slashes my throat with a beer bottle. I wish Fiona were here. She'd get a big kick out of it."

"I bet she would," Zan agreed. "Bloodthirsty demon that she is."

Granddad and Jamie exchanged meaningful glances.

"I, uh, ran into Paige at the Performing Arts Center today," Jamie said carefully. "She looks good. Seems to be doing real well."

Zan stiffened at the mention of his most recent ex-girlfriend. "Good. Glad to hear it. What does that have to do with anything?"

"My show opens weekend after next," Jamie said. "It would be a perfect opportunity to, ah . . . call her up. See a romantic play with her."

"You guys have been putting your heads together, haven't you?"

"You're in a rut, Alexander," Granddad added earnestly. "You need to get out. Meet some ladies. It's time to think about your future."

"You guys back off and mind your own business," Zan snarled.

They all stared into the TV. A blonde was pleading with a guy in a trenchcoat. He said something. She hauled off and slapped him. He planted a passionate kiss on her cupid's-bow mouth. The girl slowly stopped struggling and wrapped her arms around Trenchcoat's neck.

Yeah, right. That kind of move never worked in real life.

The cell rang. He fished through his pocket, eager for an excuse to disappear. Maybe Abby had gone to check her mailbox and gotten locked out again. This time in a filmy peekaboo nightie.

His bubble burst as soon as he answered. Just some dumb college kid down at the roadhouse who'd locked himself out of his car.

Boring as hell, but anything was better than staring at Jamie's and Granddad's disapproving faces.

"Gorgeous day, isn't it?" chirped the girl with pink spiked hair behind the espresso cart. "What'll you have, Abby? Your usual?"

Brilliant morning sunlight glinted off the studs that decorated Nanette's nose and brows. They hurt Abby's eyes.

"You OK?" Nanette's brows furrowed. "You look terrible."

"Gee, thanks, Nanette. Give me the usual."

"You got it." Nanette's hennaed hands worked efficiently. "I'll put chocolate-covered coffee beans on top. That'll give you a nice buzz."

"Hair of the dog that bit me. And make a decaf soy latte for Elaine, OK? Today it's my turn to provide coffee."

"Yeah, I saw her sprinting by here a couple of minutes ago," Nanette said. "She could use some coffee. She looked stressed out."

Abby dug into her purse for her wallet. Her eyes stung with exhaustion. She'd been too wound up to sleep, and had ended up watching the rest of the film on the Classics Channel. After the movie, she'd surfed late-night cable, anchoring herself in reality by consuming a pint of Fudge Ripple. She'd woken on the couch with Sheba draped across her neck, barely in time to shower and run for the bus.

Abby took a bracing sip of her espresso before heading into the museum. She had to stop launching her day with sugar and caffeine. The ice cream in front of the TV hadn't done her much good, either. Tomorrow she'd cut back to bran flakes, or else shop for a whole new wardrobe next size up. And she was no skinny Minnie as it was.

First things first, though. Proofread the gala journal to make sure no big-shot VIP donors' names were misspelled. Make a gazillion wheedling phone calls to remind trustees and Museum Council ladies to get their RSVPs in. Meet with the artists who were helping with the gala decorations, light a fire underneath their flaky artistic butts. Organize the volunteers to assemble and stuff hundreds of goodie bags with the gifts donated by local businesses and gala sponsors. Tally the money they'd pulled in so far, calculate how many more checks had to come in to reach their funding goal. Above all, she somehow had to avoid Bridget, her scary boss, in order to get it all done. Bridget was hell to work for, threatened as she was by Abby's talent. Bridget was also married to the executive director of the museum. Enough said.

To make things even more fun, the admin offices had moved into the new wing this week, so everything was in boxes. It was the worst possible timing, right before the gala, but one could argue that it was Abby's fault they were moving at all, since she was partly responsible for the budget surplus. She did try to look on the bright side of things.

Abby slipped into Elaine's office. Elaine was on the phone. "Yes, fettucine alla boscaiola, and grilled swordfish . . . stuffed mushrooms, and the garlic calamari. For dessert, the panna cotta. Garlic-rosemary focaccia, and Prosecco . . . yes, and add a twenty-five percent gratuity for the delivery person. Same address as last night, please . . . yes, nine o'clock is fine. Charge it to the usual account. That's great. Thank you."

Elaine hung up the phone and turned. Abby's cheerful greeting stuck in her throat. Elaine was lovely as always, in her fragile blond way, but she did not have the euphoric glow of sexual fulfillment.

She looked pinched. Haunted, almost.

Abby hid her dismay and set Elaine's coffee down, rummaging in her purse. "Here are your house keys, as promised. So how about this secret lover? Did Mystery Mark let you sleep?"

Elaine's gaze slid away from hers. "Not much."

"A romantic dinner for two, huh?" Abby persisted. "Good for you. Who did you order that sexy meal from?"

"Oh, that's Café Girasole. My mother has a corporate account." Elaine looked sheepish. "I just call up and pretend to be Gwen, Mom's secretary, ordering dinner for Mom. No one ever calls me on it."

Elaine's mother, Gloria Clayborne, was by far the richest woman in town. Abby could well imagine that no one called Elaine on it. That had to be at least a four-hundred-dollar meal from Café Girasole, the trendiest restaurant in Silver Fork. "Yum. Here's your decaf soy latte."

"Thanks, Ab, you're a sweetie, but Mark already made me one."

"He made you coffee?" Abby said approvingly. "Good man. He gets points. Did he make you breakfast, too?"

"No, he made me a decaf soy latte," Elaine said, stressing every word. "He bought decaf espresso, he foamed the soy milk, he even sprinkled it with cinnamon. He remembered how I took my espresso from the first coffee bar we went to together. Every tiny detail."

Abby blinked. "Wow. That's, uh . . . that's really special."

"I know." Elaine looked nervous. "Um, I have to ask a favor, Abby. I promised Mark I wouldn't tell anybody about us. At least not until his divorce is final. So I would appreciate it if you kept it to yourself. I shouldn't even have told you last night. He was so mad."

Mad? At Elaine? Who could be mad at Elaine? It was like being mad at a baby bird. "Divorce?" Abby prodded gently.

"I can't tell you the details until he's comfortable with it. Please don't be mad, OK? He won't even let me park near his house, he's so paranoid. He makes me park in a garage five blocks away."

"Of course not. Don't worry," Abby said heartily. "My interest won't go away. But Elaine . . . you look kind of peaked. Are you OK?"

Elaine sank down into her chair, her translucent eyelids fluttering. "He's, well . . . I'm not used to . . . oh, never mind."

Abby stared at her, eyes narrowed. "What aren't you used to?"

Elaine looked strangely lost. "I don't know," she murmured. "It was so perfect, the first week. Then I started feeling, um, odd. The things he likes, they're a little, well . . . extreme. And then last night, after he got mad, after you called, it got really, uh, strange."

Abby was open-minded about sex, but not when it came to the fragile Elaine. Her protective instincts bristled up like gun turrets on a tank. "Define strange," she demanded. "Please be specific."

Bright spots of color stained Elaine's cheeks. "It's hard to describe," she said primly. "It was a mood thing. Just, ah, darker."

"Rougher? Did he hurt you?" Abby's belly clenched.

"Oh, no! It was more, ah, psychological than physical."

"Head games," Abby said grimly. "Big pig. Thumbs down."

"You're overreacting." Elaine's voice shook. "I can't expect a guy to be perfect, right? There are always adjustments to make."

Abby shook her head. "No, honey. Some things you should take for granted. Like him being gentle and respecting your feelings."

Elaine would not meet her eyes. "Don't lecture me, please."

Abby counted to five, lips tight. "I just worry about you, honey."

"I appreciate your concern, but a woman's got to take chances, right?" Elaine's smile was shaky. "Isn't that what you always tell me?"

"Within limits," Abby specified. "As long as you're having fun."

Elaine looked childlike and uncertain. "I don't know. Fun isn't the right word for it. It's more like being terrified. Or jumping off a cliff."

"Ouch," Abby said sourly. "Woo hoo. Sounds like a real party."

Elaine didn't seem to register her sarcasm. "He's so gorgeous. I never thought such a handsome guy would be interested in me."

Abby prayed for patience. "Elaine, you are beautiful. Top ninety-ninth percentile beautiful. For God's sake, get it through your head. Women would kill to look like you. You're being safe, at least, right?"

"Yes, Mother," Elaine said demurely. "Don't worry. Things will be better tonight. We just had a weird moment. A mood thing. No biggie."

Abby declined to comment. Weird moment, her ass. Mystery Mark was a big fat loser, her instincts screamed it, but Elaine had to find out the hard way. Like Abby had. God knows she had no right to judge.

Still, she worried. In fact, her skin was practically crawling.

"Let's grab lunch tomorrow, at Kelly's," Abby said. "You don't have to tell me details. All I'm interested in is how you feel. OK?"

"OK," Elaine said reluctantly. "It's not like you think, Abby. He's so romantic. He saw the Pirates' Hoard last year when it was in New York. You know that Flemish medallion with the gold scrollwork and the sapphire cabochons? He says they're exactly the color of my eyes. He wants to make love to me while I wear that necklace. Isn't that sweet?"

Abby grunted, unimpressed. "He could buy the reproduction from the museum gift shop and play out his fantasy for two hundred eighty-five bucks rather than . . . How much is the Pirates' Hoard insured for?"

"Forty million dollars." The clipped voice from the doorway made them both jump. Bridget stalked into the office. "With two weeks to uncrate this installation, you ladies have more urgent things to do than titillate each other with sexual fantasies." She turned a fishy glare upon Abby. "I need an update of your progress on the gala today at noon."

Abby floundered. "But . . . but I already have a noon meeting with the volunteers who are putting together the goodie bags, and then I—"

"Rearrange your schedule. I'm meeting with an important donor at one." She swept out, leaving a suffocating cloud of Joy in her wake.

Great. Now she had to make another ten frantic phone calls to schedule another time for the volunteers' meeting. A typical day on Planet Bridget. Abby took a desperate swig of espresso and hustled into her office. The phone was blinking. She grabbed the receiver. "Yes?"

"Abby? Dovey's holding for you on line two," the receptionist said.

God forbid he had another blind date. Dovey was determined to find her Mr. Right, and much as she appreciated his efforts, today was not the day. "Put him through," she said. "Dovey? Are you there?"

"I am! And how is my lovely Abby today?"

"Not so lovely, I'm afraid. I'm swamped, and Bridget's cracking the whip big time. Where are you? Can I call you back later?"

"This will take just a minute. How was your date with Edgar?"

"Train wreck," Abby said, shuddering. "Bloodbath. Total carnage."

Dovey clucked his tongue. "This may seem strange, but I'm glad to hear it, because I've found a much better candidate! Hetero, forty-three, handsome, intelligent, single—that is to say, divorced—"

"Divorced?" It made her think, uncasily, of Mysterious Mark. Brrr.

"Three times. The wives' fault. Bitches, all three. Apart from that, he fits every requirement on the List, right down to liking cats!"

Abby took a gulp of coffee. "Let's not get ahead of ourselves." Dovey was so excited, she hated to tell him how unenthusiastic she felt. No matter how Listworthy this guy was, he wouldn't have anything on a hunkadelic locksmith. "What does he do?" she asked dutifully.

"He's a psychotherapist," Dovey said. "I can personally vouch for his financial solvency, love. You could balance the budget of a small country with the money that I've paid him in the last few years."

Abby stared out the window as she doodled on her desk calendar. "You're sweet to think of me, Dovey, but can't we give it some—"

"Just give me permission to give him your number," Dovey pleaded. "Then just lie back and let destiny take its course."

"That sounds alarming." Abby fidgeted, fishing for an excuse.

"Pretty please?" Dovey wheedled. "He could be your date to the gala. I've already sold him a ticket. And he'll look great in a tux."

She doodled some more, stalling. "What's his name?"

"That means yes, right? His name is Reginald Blake. You'll love him. He's perfect. I'll call him up right away. Ciao!"

Abby hung up, and noticed that the locksmith's number was still on her thumb. Her shower had faded it. Before she knew what she was doing, she had rewritten it on her thumb in fresh, wet black ink.

Yikes. She watched the ink dry, alarmed at herself.

It was normal to have fixated on Zan. He'd saved her from an awful fate. He was also drop-dead gorgeous. There was probably a name for this in the psych manuals; the Something-or-Other Syndrome.

A List-approved date was the perfect way to distract herself from this silly infatuation. Tonight, even. Why not? She ran her love life. She did not let it run her. And having a date for the gala would be nice.

Her eyes wandered to her desk calendar. Her doodles practically leaped out at her. Zan Duncan. Zan Duncan. Zan Duncan.

His name was emblazoned all over the month of June.

The chocolate-covered coffee beans Nanette had given her caught her eye, still wedged into the recesses of the plastic coffee lid. She pried them out, popped them into her mouth and crunched them up.

One had to take life's little comforts wherever one found them.

Chapter

4

It was cold in Mark's bedroom.

Elaine shivered, struggling against the strips of the silk scarf that bound her wrists and ankles to Mark's bed. That scarf had been one of her favorites. A gift from Abby. She hadn't wanted it ruined, but Mark hadn't listened once he'd started to rend. Mark didn't listen very well.

Hah. Was that ever a stunning understatement.

The coverlet was wadded into a scratchy bulge beneath the small of her back. Mark had left her there and wandered downstairs a half hour ago. At one point, she heard him talking on the phone in what sounded like Spanish. Then she heard the muted hum of the TV being turned on. The TV, for Christ's sake. She struggled harder, and made as much noise as she could, which wasn't much with the scarf tied over the gag in her mouth. She tried not to cry, but she'd never had much luck at that when she felt hurt and abandoned.

Tears kept sliding down, tickling her face. She tried to blot them on the pillows. Her nose was blocking up with snot. What an alluring picture she'd be once he finally decided to pay attention to her.

A woman's got to cut loose and take some chances sometime, right? God, had she really said that?

Within limits. As long as you're having fun, Abby had replied.

She struggled harder for breath. She was not having fun. She'd been in a state of dazed incredulity since this affair began, she'd been excited, titillated, dazzled, but she had never had one ounce, not one pinch, not one speck of fun. She never relaxed with Mark. Never.

She was too afraid of him.

She knew herself, after years of therapy. She knew her weak spots and her defects like the back of her hand. She might have no clue how to overcome them, but damn, did she know them. And she knew that this was not fun. She should not be afraid of Mark. Not if this was true love.

Then again, she was afraid of everybody. Her own mother, her own boss, who wasn't she afraid of, other than maybe Abby?

She was so pathetic. How typical, that she had to be bound, gagged, screwed, and forgotten to get a clue. Tears of shame oozed out.

It had been so exciting, finally having an affair, like normal women did. Actually having sex, after all those depressing years without. Good sex, too. At least at first. For about a week, it had been perfect. Then something strange had crept into it, so gradually.

It had gone rotten from the inside. As usual, she hadn't wanted to let go of her fantasies. She waited until they were wrenched away, like a bandage off a scabbed wound. So that it hurt as much as possible.

Last night she'd started facing reality. Tonight, she had no more doubts.

The most awful thing about it was that she'd consented to this treatment. She had no one but herself to blame for being so eager to please. She'd even bought rope, at his request, so that they could play his games at her house. She was a willing accomplice to his cruelty.

Her therapists said that her problems with men were a direct result of her problems with her father, issues of abandonment, blah-blah, tell her something new. She understood the dynamic. Now all she wanted was out. She wanted to fly away. To be somewhere else, someone else. She wanted out of this bed, out of these silken ties.

She couldn't run away to Spain with this man, as she had promised him. He would destroy her. He was destroying her now.

Mark appeared, silhouetted in the door to the bedroom, still talking on his cell phone. His voice was so beautiful, speaking Spanish. It still thrilled her, even bound and shivering. The light behind him lit up the bulb of the glass of wine in his hand. It glowed like a chalice full of blood. The Cabernet she had ordered to accompany their meal.

She shuddered, so deeply she felt like it should shake the bed. Mark clicked his cell phone shut and flipped on a row of the muted track lighting recessed into the paneled rafters of the bedroom. He wandered over and stared down at her. He put something in his mouth, chewed it as he stared. He washed it down with wine.

Snacking, while she lay here gasping vainly for breath.

More tears welled up, blocking her nose. She started to choke.

Mark sipped his wine, his eyes moving slowly over her body. Wretched as she was, she was still stupefied at how beautiful he was. Chin-length dark blond hair waving around a Greek god face. That broad chin with the sexy cleft, the cruel sensuality of his full mouth. And his body. So amazingly strong. He could immobilize her with one hand. Had done so, in fact. On many occasions.

"You're beautiful," he said. "I bought those sheets because I imagined you glowing like a pearl, black satin as a backdrop. Perfect."

His voice was dreamy and absent. Elaine writhed and mewled for air. She was starting to panic at her complete inability to communicate with him. She began to flail wildly. His penis had started to lengthen, but as her movements grew more frenzied, his smile faded. He put his glass of wine on the bed stand and climbed onto the bed, straddling her.

He trapped her wrists. "Stop," he commanded. "You'll leave marks on your skin. I don't want that. That's why I used silk."

She heaved ineffectually beneath him. He frowned into her wet, staring eyes. "You're upset," he observed, his voice puzzled.

No shit, Sherlock, she wanted to shriek, through wads of silk.

Mark peeled the scarf off the bottom of her face and plucked the damp, wadded cloth from her mouth.

She gasped in huge gulps of air, coughing. Mark lifted off her, snagged the wineglass, and held it to her lips, tipping Cabernet into her mouth. What didn't slosh down over her chin hit her dry wind-pipe, and she choked and gasped, tears of humiliation streaming down her face.

Mark kissed her tears away. "Why are you crying? You're beauti-ful like that." He licked the wine that dribbled down her chin.

"You left me like this to watch TV. And talk on the phone. Like you'd forgotten me," she blurted. "I couldn't breathe. I was scared."

He frowned. "You can't expect me to pay attention to you every second of the day, love. Did you buy your ticket today?"

She nodded, docile as a cow. She had to tell him that she'd changed her mind about going, but a nervous little voice inside her whispered that maybe now wasn't the best time for that announce-ment, bound hand and foot, with Mark sitting on top of her. He was so heavy.

"First class, for Barcelona." Her voice was a cracked whisper.

He kissed her eyelids. "My driver will take you to the resort. You wait there, shopping and getting a tan, while I finalize my divorce. Then I come to you a free man. And we start our life together. In paradise."

She tried to speak, but he continued without noticing.

"You told me you wanted to fly away from it all," he said. "I'll send those photographs to my contact in Spain. He'll arrange for an EU identity card and passport. Spanish citizenship. Your name will be Elena in Spain. Beautiful like you. My sweet Elena."

"Mark," she faltered. "I . . . I—"

"You can forget all of it. Your parents, the hospitals. Everything painful in your past. You'll be free."

Yeah, tied hand and foot? She opened her mouth, but he kissed her deeply, his tongue thrusting into her mouth, blocking the words she wanted to say. She jerked away, feeling suffocated.

"Mark, untie me. Please," she begged.

"No," he said. "Can't risk that. You're mine now."

"But my arms are asleep," she protested. "I have pins and nee-dles in my hands. It hurts. And I have to use the toilet. Please, Mark."

"Should have left you gagged," he muttered. He yanked open a drawer in the bed stand and took out a small knife. A flick of his wrist, and the blade snicked out. The knife flashed between his dexterous fingers as his gaze moved over her body. As if he were considering . . .

No. Don't think it, she told herself frantically. She was imagining things. He would never . . . no. It was unthinkable, so she just wouldn't think it. "Please," she whispered.

He severed the ties with four slashes of his knife. Elaine rolled into a shivering ball, still wearing knotted bracelets and anklets of green silk. "If you need the bathroom, go," he said. "Don't make me wait."

She rolled off the bed and fled down the hall to the bathroom. It was filled with mirrors, a luxury she didn't appreciate tonight. She looked pale. Bluish, like skim milk. Her eyes looked huge and staring.

Scared half to death by that weird emptiness she'd glimpsed in his eyes while he was holding that wicked looking little knife.

She shoved open the window and leaned out, checking escape routes. Second story. Sheer drop. No porch roof, no drainage pipe, no handy tree. The probability of hurting herself was very high. Besides, she was stark naked. Her clothes were in the bedroom with Mark.

Calm down already, she told herself. She was just dramatizing, like she always did. She could imagine Gloria Clayborne's reaction if her daughter were found wandering around town naked at night, babbling about a secret sadist lover. Mother had been very clear about how important it was that Elaine not embarrass her again. She had to keep it together, or it would be back to the loony bin for Lainie.

It was hard to say which prospect frightened her more. Her mother's fury and scorn; the loony bin; or Mark, staring down at her naked, immobilized body. Twirling that knife between deft fingertips.

She splashed cold water on her face. She was imagining things, working herself into a state, as always. She tried to undo the knots, but they'd been pulled too tight. They were as hard as little rocks.

She would go in and assert herself, for once. Thanks, Mark, for the new identity, but she was sticking with her old one. She flung her hair back, straightened her back, and started toward the bedroom.

But the strips of silk tied to her ankles trailed behind her like a dog's leash.

Abby speared a plump truffle ravioli on her fork, and stared into her plate. The pasta was adorned with a dusting of grated truffle. The elegant decor, the muted clink of silver on china, the discreet, attentive service: it was just right. She sipped her wine and tried to concentrate on what Reginald was saying. Her face felt like a rubber mask.

Reginald stopped in mid-monologue and stroked his goatee. She wondered if the white streaks over his ears had been put there by a hairdresser. They were so improbably symmetrical, suspended in a thick, swept-back scaffolding of hair gel. Like Dracula.

What an ungracious thought. The guy had done nothing wrong, other than be pompous and boring. Since when was that a crime?

"Are you all right?" Reginald's baritone voice oozed sensitive concern. "You seem distracted."

"Do I? Gee, I'm sorry." Abby attempted to wrench her mind into focus. It was like wrestling alligators in a mud pit.

"Intuition is my stock in trade," he said. "I'm a psychotherapist, as Ludovic must have told you. Nothing escapes my notice."

"How nice for you." Abby speared another ravioli with a jab of her fork and put on a bright, interested smile. "Who's Ludovic?"

Reginald smirked. "You must have known Ludovic for a long time if you still use the nickname 'Dovey.'"

"Dovey? Good Lord. You mean Dovey's real name is—"

"Ludovic has decided that he must leave his past behind, and with it, his nickname. A name that represents self-destructiveness."

Abby searched for a coherent response to that, but Reginald sailed smoothly on. "If you consider yourself his friend, call him by his real name, which represents both his essential, core self, and also the supremely realized future self toward which we all aspire."

Wow, that was a big chunk to chew on. "But Dovey never—"

"I can't say any more without violating the doctor-patient bond of confidentiality." Reginald stroked his goatee, a Freudlike gesture.

"Uh, of course. All I meant was, Dovey never even told me that—"

"Ludovic's former persona often dominates his behavior." Reginald gave her a knowing smile. "Setbacks, slipups, they're all part of the process of growth, Abby. As I'm sure you know."

"But he never once even mentioned—"

"But can one ever plumb the depths of another person? Their dreams, their dark desires? No matter how close we might feel, another person is a foreign country. Even one's most intimate . . . beloved."

She eyed him with mounting alarm. "Uh . . ."

"But oh, the thrill of the unknown." Reginald's eyes fixed on her with what she guessed was meant to be a seductive gaze. "No quest is more compelling than the frontier of the Beloved Other. Verdant jungles . . . thrusting mountains . . . precipitous chasms . . . more wine?"

She stuck out her glass. "God, yes," she muttered.

"I feel like an explorer tonight." Reginald filled her glass with an experienced twist of his wrist. "With such an attractive woman."

"Uh, thanks." Abby gulped her wine, and persisted in trying to finish her sentence. "But all I was saying is, if Dovey—"

"I can't permit our conversation about Ludovic to continue, Abby." Reginald's tone turned stern. "My professional ethics forbid it."

Abby closed her mouth with a snap. Reginald reached over to pat her hand. "Sorry to be abrupt, but I would so prefer to talk about you."

"That's nice," she said tightly.

"Oh, yes." Reginald did not seem to register her discomfort. "Such a beautiful, mysterious woman makes me curious." He eyed her bosom.

"Oh, really?" She hated her brain dead, two word replies, but it didn't matter. This guy didn't need any help carrying on a conversation. He could hold up both sides all by himself. Abby stabbed the last ravioli and stuck it into her mouth. She was going to need all her strength.

"Ludovic told me a lot about you," Reginald said. "He told me that you had a very, shall we say, colorful past, romantically speaking."

Abby's fork clattered loudly onto her plate. "Oh, did he?"

"I was fascinated." Reginald took a big bite of his steak and eyed her hungrily as he chewed it. "I'm bending my own rules by being here tonight, you see. It's a bit dodgy, to allow one of my patients to fix me up, but Ludovic had told me so much about you, I just couldn't resist."

"I, ah, see," she said stiffly. She was going to have a stern little talk with Dovey. The very second she got home.

Reginald's smile displayed large teeth. "Don't be embarrassed," he purred. "We all have our dark sides. It's the shadow play of light and dark, the contrasts, the secret, hidden places, that creates the sizzling heat of sexual attraction between a man and a woman."

Reginald licked his shiny lips and smiled. He had the smug look of a man who was dead sure he was going to get laid tonight.

She was being slimed. Classy restaurant or skeevy dive, the effect was the same. The prices on the menu didn't change a thing.

Reginald edged his chair closer and laid his clammy pink hand over hers. "I'm not afraid of your dark side, Abby," he crooned, lifting her hand slowly toward his lips.

Oh, no. This was one frog she was not going to kiss. Screw politeness. She wasn't even waiting for the dessert cart.

She yanked her hand away, dabbed at her mouth with her napkin, and sprang up. "Thanks for dinner, Reginald. I've gotta scoot."

Reginald looked blank. "Huh?"

"Bye." She gave him a brilliant smile and headed straight toward the headwaiter's podium. "Could someone call me a cab, please?"

"Abby." Reginald grabbed her arm. "What did I say? Did I offend you in some way?"

She wrenched her arm out of his grip and pushed out the door. "I need to go home," she said. "I have a headache."

Café Girasole was on the water. The boardwalk was right across the street. Fortunately, it was crowded with people on this clear June evening, so she was in no danger of repeating last night's stupidity.

Reginald hurried out after her. "I'll take you home, Abby."

"Cab's fine, thanks," she said crisply.

"I'm so sorry you're not well," Reginald persisted. "You should have said something earlier. I'm expert in several different massage styles, you know. Ten minutes of my Black Serpent technique, and you'd be ready for anything." He leered as he groped for his keys.

Unbelievably, the guy still had no clue. It boggled the mind.

"Thanks, but I'll pass," she said. "'Night, Reginald."

"But I . . . wait a minute." Reginald dug in his other pants pocket. He tried his jacket. He tried them both again. He peered into the BMW. The keys were still in the ignition. He tried the door. It was locked.

Abby tamped down the giggles. It seemed cruel to have so much fun at his expense. "It happened to me last night. Maybe I jinxed you."

The laughter in her voice made his head whip around. "Every superstitious belief has its roots in psychological fact," he said icily. "I conduct the activities of daily living with heightened mindfulness. Locking my keys in my car is a sign that other forces are at work."

Abby's mirth faded. "Meaning? What other forces?"

Reginald spoke slowly, as if to a dull child. "Certain people create chaos wherever they go. What an ignorant person might refer to as a jinx is, in fact, just contact with a nexus of chaos and negativity."

Abby forced her mouth to close. "It was a joke," she said slowly. "Do you know what a joke is, Reginald? Do I need to explain it to you?"

Reginald frowned. "Sarcasm is unbecoming."

She could practically hear the clicking sounds as her vertebrae stacked themselves up. "Are you implying that I actually jinxed you?"

Reginald shrugged. "Ludovic led me to understand that your past was one chaotic, unpredictable disaster after another."

"So it's my fault you locked your keys in your stupid car?"

"You're oversimplifying," Reginald said loftily. "It's very complex."

"I have not even *begun* to oversimplify, you pompous butthead!"

"No need for hostility." Reginald looked much more cheerful, now that he'd whipped her into a frenzy.

"You call me a nexus of chaos and negativity, and then say there's no need to be hostile?" Her voice was getting shrill.

Reginald looked down his beaky nose. "You have a problem with anger management, which doesn't really surprise me. Please control yourself long enough for me to find a professional to open my car."

She was opening her mouth to tell him exactly where he should stick his anger management when the switch flicked inside her. *Ping.*

A professional to open my car. A shiver went through her.

Oh, no. She'd be better off going home, turning on the Classics Channel, getting out the Fudge Ripple and a nice big spoon. Being a nexus of chaos and negativity was way too stressful for a working girl.

She tapped Reginald's shoulder. "I know a locksmith."

He pushed a button on his phone and frowned. "How's that?"

"I was locked out last night. Call this number." She held up her thumb. "If you're not afraid of getting sucked into my nexus, that is."

Reginald rolled his eyes as he punched the number into his phone. She held her breath as he waited for it to ring.

"Hello?" he said. "I'm locked out of my car. In front of Café Girasole, on the boardwalk. Do you know it?" He listened. "How quickly can you arrive? Ten minutes? Very well." He switched off the phone.

A wave of heat climbed into Abby's face. Her cab was on its way, and with it, her last opportunity to cheat fate and act like a grown-up. The locksmith was trouble at best, heartbreak and ruin at worst.

But she just had to know if he was as mouthwatering as she remembered. Maybe it was just a flush of fluttery gratitude for being rescued that had beautified him to her.

Ten minutes felt like forever. She ignored Reginald and stared at oncoming headlights. She hoped Zan would get there before her cab. It would be awkward and embarrassing to justify not hopping right in.

A shiny black van pulled over next to them. Zan was at the wheel. He killed the engine and sat there for a long moment, staring at her.

"What the hell is he waiting for?" Reginald grumbled.

Zan got out. His gaze swept over her brief dress. Spaghetti straps, plunging neckline. She shivered, brushed hair out of her mouth, and turned her back to look out at the ocean, her face very hot.

It wasn't a flush of gratitude. He was monumentally gorgeous.

"I take it a check will be acceptable?" she heard Reginald ask.

"I prefer cash." Zan's voice was bland.

"But that's inconvenient for me. I promise, my checks are good."

"The bank doesn't care about promises," Zan replied.

Reginald sputtered. "But I don't have a hundred in cash on me at the moment! Be reasonable."

"I'm reasonable," Zan said mildly. "You're free to call someone else if you prefer. If not, there's a bank machine around the corner."

Reginald stomped away, muttering.

Abby leaned on the wooden railing and lifted her hot face to the breeze. Zan's gaze felt as palpable on her skin as a physical touch.

"Is he the reason you wouldn't give me your number?" he asked.

A sound came out of her, part laughter, part sob. "No! Just a blind date. Not that it's any of your business."

"Maybe you should rethink these blind dates, sweetheart," he said. "Maybe it's time that you opened your eyes."

His fresh scent was so different from Reginald's cloying cologne, which had made her throat tickle. "I didn't ask for your opinion."

"I know," he said. "It's chilly out here. You can wait in the van for Prince Charming, if you like."

"Thanks. I'm fine out here," she said.

"You're shivering. No wonder, going out at night in a slip."

She was stung. "This is a Versace! It cost me two weeks' salary!"

"Two weeks' salary wasted." He looked her up and down. "Save your money and buy yourself a sweater, baby."

Her knees weakened at the lazy appraisal in his eyes. "Stop it," she whispered.

"Stop what? I'm not doing anything."

"Stop . . . stop vibing at me," she blurted.

"Sorry, beautiful. It's the one thing that I cannot control," he murmured, moving closer. "You're cute with your hair up, you know? I usually prefer girls' hair down, but I like those swirly wisps." He twirled one of her wisps around his finger. "You've got color," he went on, his voice velvety. "Are you blushing? Or do you have a fever? I swear, you'll get pneumonia dressing like that. Not that I'm complaining."

Every individual particle of her body was anxiously aware of how near he was. Every hair stood on end. "Smart-ass," she said shakily.

"That's what they tell me," he admitted. "Since I was a baby."

Looking into his face made her feel like she was going to topple over backward. "You're looming. Stop it. It makes me nervous."

"Don't worry. Your stuffed shirt will be back from the bank machine in a minute to protect you. Relax."

"I'm not tense. And I don't need protecting." She stretched up to peek over his shoulder to see if Reginald had reappeared.

He wasn't there, but the cab was. She turned to tell Zan goodbye.

He cupped her jaw, his thumb dragging delicate circles over her cheek. "Forget about him." He brushed a wisp of hair out of her eyes.

"Who?" she breathed, as he leaned closer.

His smile widened in triumph. He cradled her face in his hands. The leather of his jacket creaked as he leaned forward.

His lips were sensitive, coaxing. Velvety soft. Startled pleasure flashed through her body. His arms closed around her, his lithe body pinning her against the railing. He tasted wonderful. Coffee, a hint of mint. So warm and solid, vibrating with energy. She wanted to wrap herself around him and squeeze, but she was melting into taffy.

He stepped back. The void between them seemed to ache.

A couple was getting into her cab, laughing and smirking. The cab pulled away. They stared at each other. His eyes were so dilated, they were almost black. He gripped her shoulders. "You can't let him touch you," he said. "Tell me you're not going to let that guy touch you."

She opened her mouth to say she would never let a gasbag idiot like that touch her. The concept was too complicated to verbalize in her melted-taffy condition. He leaned forward to kiss her throat. "Promise me," he urged, under his breath. The plea was breathless and ragged.

"I promise," she whispered.

"I take it you two have met?" Reginald's voice was glacial.

Zan's hand dropped. Abby locked her knees, hoping they would bear her weight. "Ah, yes," she said distractedly. "I locked myself out last night, remember? He was the locksmith who opened my door."

Reginald squinted. "You didn't tell me that you knew this man intimately before you gave me his phone number, Abby."

"Actually, I, ah, don't," she admitted.

"Ah. This kind of promiscuous behavior is exactly what I would expect from someone suffering from your pathology."

She was so rattled by Zan's kiss, it was hard to follow the through line of Reginald's insults. She focused on Reginald's face, then wished that she hadn't. She hadn't noticed just how unattractive his beady dark eyes were. Squinched into a furious frown, they seemed rodentlike.

"So it's not a coincidence?" Zan pitched his voice just for her ears. "You gave him my number on purpose? Wow. I'm touched."

"This disgusting impulse to have a sordid liaison with a stranger is symptomatic of the larger chaos of your life," Reginald said. "I'm sorry to have witnessed this, Abby. It's painful to me. But I'm glad to know the truth about you before I got embroiled. Thank you for that, at least."

"Disgusting and sordid?" Zan sounded remarkably cheerful. "I've been called lots of things, but I do believe that one's a first for me."

"I wouldn't have touched you with a ten-foot pole anyhow, so piss off, Reginald," she said.

Reginald blinked. "Temper! You're projecting your frustration over your own lack of self-control onto me. In my professional opinion, you would benefit from intensive psychotherapy, specifically targeted at your rage problem and your sexual addiction. A pharmaceutical approach might be in order, as part of a multimodal treatment plan."

"Sexual addiction?" Her mouth worked. "You . . . you *jerk*!"

"How about you guys thrash out the psychiatric treatment plan after you pay me?" Zan's voice sounded faintly bored. "That way I can open up the car and we can all call it a night. OK?"

Reginald pulled out his wallet and wrenched out a wad of money. Zan shoved it into his pocket. He pulled a toolbox out of his van and crouched beside the car. Reginald hovered over Zan's shoulder as he pulled out a wedgelike object and a long pronged wire.

Zan frowned up at him. "I can't work with you breathing over my shoulder," he said. "You're blocking my light. Give me some space."

"Do not scratch my car," Reginald said.

Zan raised an eyebrow. "Back off, if you want this thing opened."

Reginald backed away. Zan inserted the wedge between the window and its seal, easing the wire rod delicately under the window, probing with small, precise movements, his face calm and faraway.

She couldn't keep staring like this. She had to call a cab, get a clue, disappear. She turned, looked at the ocean, tried to breathe.

She heard the muted pop of a car door opening, and cautiously turned around. Reginald crouched over the car door, checking for scratches. Zan packed his tools up and looked over at her. "Your date's a big loser, sweetheart," he said. "Get in. I'll take you home."

Reginald nodded, as if his worst suspicions had been confirmed. "Just as I thought. Classic case of sexual addiction. How sad."

Abby looked at Reginald's beady, avid eyes. He licked his lips. They gleamed, red and moist, between his mustache and beard.

She looked at Zan, waiting patiently beside his van, his face calm and watchful. His long hair blew across his face in the breeze. He opened the passenger side and beckoned her in, inclining his head.

The gesture was so graceful and courtly. As if she were a queen, being handed into her carriage.

Reginald tsk-tsked. "You'll never overcome your shadowed past if you continue to yield to your darker impulses," he admonished.

Zan's lips twitched. Abby hurried to the van and clambered in.

Chapter

5

Abby crossed, uncrossed, recrossed her legs. Clasped her hands, unclasped them, wrapped her arms across her chest, sat on them.

"Put your seat belt on, please."

Zan's voice was gentle, but she jerked three inches up off the seat.

He gave her a cautious, sideways peek. "What are you so uptight about? Is it your shadowed past? Our disgusting and sordid liaison?"

"Don't start," she warned. "Don't tease me. I'm too wound up."

"Look, if you feel the urge to yield to your darker impulses, give me fair warning so I can pull over in time, OK?"

"Very funny," she snapped. She wrestled with the seat belt. "That pompous creep. Do you know what he called me?" She swiveled to face him. "A nexus of chaos and negativity!"

Zan made a low choking sound. "Come again?"

"He thinks it was my fault that he locked his keys in his car! He thinks I literally jinxed him! Rat-faced, butthead bastard!"

"Wow. That's, ah, awful," Zan said. "So rude. Just horrible."

"Don't make fun of me, if you value your life," she warned him.

"God, no," he said hastily. "Wouldn't dream of it."

"Just because my love life is a blasted wasteland doesn't mean that I'm a curse to everyone I get near." She tried to control the quaver in her voice. She didn't want to look the part of a weepy, crazy girl whose life was one chaotic, unpredictable disaster after another.

She didn't recognize the street they were driving on, which gave her a fresh jolt of adrenaline. "Where are you taking me?"

"Home," he said calmly.

"I don't know this way home!" Her voice vibrated with tension.

"I'm taking the scenic route. Lookout Drive, and we can look at the bay. The moon might even be peeking through the clouds. You can tell me about your monster date. Get it all off your chest." He gave her an inscrutable glance. "After all, it's not every day a person gets accused of being a nexus of chaos and negativity."

Her giggle was so waterlogged, it was more of a gurgle.

"I mean, that's not just an insult," he continued. "That's a mega-galactic insult. You should have told me back at the restaurant. I would have pounded that rat-faced butthead for you before we left."

"Thanks, but once was enough. I don't really approve of indiscriminate butthead pounding. Unless it's absolutely necessary."

"Neither do I," he agreed. "In last night's case, it was."

"Oh, come on. Once you made Edgar stop groping me, you could have passed on the nose bashing, and the wrist twisting, and the—"

"Nope. He bonked your head. How is your head, by the way?"

"Ah, it's just fine, thanks," she said. "But he—"

"He's lucky I didn't break his neck."

His flat, uncompromising tone took her aback. "You don't know me, Zan," she said warily. "What do you care if my head gets bonked?"

"I just do." He turned into the viewpoint as the moon sailed into a cloud window, flooding a patch of ocean with light. He parked the van. "I think an insult on that scale calls for a burger and a beer."

"I just had artichoke bruschetta, grilled eggplant, and black truffle ravioli. I don't actually need any more calories for about a week or so."

Zan pondered that. "Wow," he said. "Sounds fancy."

"It was," she said fondly. "It was marvelous. The only worthwhile thing about the evening. I adore that restaurant. Do you like Italian?"

"Well . . . I like SpaghettiOs," he offered. "That's Italian, right?"

He had to be yanking her chain. "Uh . . . you're joking, right?"

"I just pour a can of cream of mushroom soup on top of just about anything, stick it into the oven, and I'm good to go."

She studied his solemn expression. "You *are* joking, right?"

"Dead serious. Speaking of food, I had a ham sandwich and a pickle about twelve hours ago."

"Twelve hours! You must be starving!"

"Yeah," he admitted. "Would you accompany me to a burger joint? Maria's Bar and Grill is good, if you don't mind going back down to the boardwalk. I'll buy you a Coke, or something innocuous like that."

Abby stared out at the ocean. Long-term personal goals, she told herself. She'd wasted enough time on dead-end relationships.

But he'd been so gallant, to rescue her from Reginald. To say nothing of saving her sorry butt the night before, from Edgar. The least she could do was have a Coke with the man. What was the harm?

Unless it made her start pining after something she just couldn't have. She turned to Zan and opened her mouth to tell him to take her straight home, but his smile flashed in the shadows before the words could form. So gentle. So seductive. So incredibly attractive.

"Just a Coke, sweetheart," he said. "Who's gonna know?"

Back off. Take it easy. Don't shoot yourself in the foot.

The litany repeated in Zan's head as they pulled into the parking lot, but his frantic self-censorship was choking off all conversation, leaving him tongue-tied, like a nervous little boy.

He'd been tempted to fake like he was some big gourmet, but by the age of thirty-six, a guy should know better than to lie about himself to impress a woman. He wouldn't have been able to pull it off anyhow. Chris could have, or Jamie, with their highbrow tastes in food and beer.

Then again, maybe he'd overdone it with the SpaghettiOs crack. He had a tendency to be contrary. Or so he'd been told.

Nope. Honesty was the way to go. When he got hungry, he ate whatever presented itself. It just never occurred to him to be picky.

"Here we are." He immediately kicked himself for that scintillating conversation starter. She looked nervous, too, twiddling with the strap that barely held her dress on her body. That outfit was sexier than the one she'd worn the night before, which was saying a great deal.

He wrenched his gaze away. "Shall we?"

He headed around the van to open her door, but she'd jumped out on her own. He met her coming around the van and ran smack into her.

He steadied her. She was so warm and resiliant and soft, under the smooth fabric of her slip. Dress. Whatever the hell it was. He felt her shiver in reaction to his touch. He stared into her face, transfixed by the shiny loose locks of hair that had fallen forward to frame her chin.

Everything about her was so fine-grained and smooth, every exquisite detail. She shimmered and glowed. As if he'd captured some mythical creature in an enchanted forest, like a unicorn, and persuaded it to come to a bar and have a beer with him.

She smiled, and the gleam in her eyes broke the spell. She was all flesh-and-blood woman, with those full, sensual, gleaming lips.

He wondered how that lipstick would look smeared all over him.

"Let's go," he said hoarsely.

Maria's was crowded. He spotted a booth in the back and made for it, keeping a hand on Abby's elbow as they wove through the crush.

Abby looked around. "They're staring at me like I have two heads."

He couldn't hold the words back. "It's not your two heads they're staring at, sweetheart."

She gave him a narrow look. "Yeah, my super slutty dress. I know you hate it." She slapped her purse down and slid into the booth.

"I don't hate it." He slid into the opposite seat. "I'd like it just fine in the privacy of my own bedroom."

Abby looked down, drawing her lower lip between her teeth.

The waitress swung by. "What'll it be for you folks tonight?"

"Cheeseburger deluxe, medium rare, fries and a beer," he said.

"Just a Diet Coke for me," Abby said.

"You got it." The waitress plunged back into the crowd.

Zan's eyes fastened hungrily on to Abby again. He wished he were dressed better. She started tucking up the hair that had fallen down around her face. Raising her arms did interesting things to her bosom.

She twisted a lock into place, and another tumbled down to take its place. "You're staring," she accused.

"That happens, when a woman with a body like yours goes out in public dressed in an incredibly expensive slip," he observed.

"Oh, stop going on about my dress, already. You're bugging me." A wisp she'd just tucked slipped down again. "Damn."

"Why don't you just take it all down?" he suggested.

"You told me you liked it up." She stabbed a hairpin in.

"Sure, I like it." He glanced around. Dozens of pairs of male eyes slid innocently away. "So do eighteen other guys."

Her lips tightened and she began plucking out pins, slapping them down onto the table. She unwound the coil, pulled it forward, and draped it over her tits. "Happy now? Am I decent?"

It only made her look that much more tousled and seductive.

Their drinks arrived, and Zan waited until the waitress was gone to reply. "You look beautiful, Abby," he said.

"How do you know my name?"

"The stuffed shirt called you Abby when he was lecturing you about your sexual addiction and the dark shadows of your past. Besides which, it was printed on your check."

Her cheeks reddened. "Which you still have not taken. Speaking of which, you did overcharge me! A hundred and twenty, my butt!"

"I did not overcharge you," he said.

"You charged Reginald twenty dollars less and you didn't even ask for his phone number!"

He laughed and picked up a hank of her hair, shifting it under the light to admire the glimmering red highlights. He caught a tantalizing whiff of her perfume. "Yeah, but Reginald called at 9:48 PM, and you called at 11:39 PM. Big difference in base rates," he countered.

He let go of her hair. It settled, featherlight, across her wrist. He touched the soft skin of her wrist with his forefinger. Her rosy lips parted, breath quickening. She wanted him, he exulted. He could feel it. She started to say something and choked the words off as his finger slid into her cupped palm. Exploring velvety, secret inside places.

He shifted uncomfortably on the hard wooden seat.

His heart hammered. She was softer than anything he'd ever touched. The waitress chose that moment to bring him his burger.

He withdrew his hand with a sigh, uncapped the ketchup and dumped some on his fries. He opened his burger, glopped some more on.

"What kind of cheese is on your burger?" Abby asked.

The question puzzled him. "Damned if I know."

"Lift up the bun. Let me see," she directed.

Bemused, he lifted up his ketchup-smeared bun.

"Ick," she commented with a shudder. "That presliced processed stuff tastes like wax. Why didn't you ask for Tillamook, or Gruyère?"

The question stank of a trap, but he could think of no way to evade it. "Never occurred to me," he said stoically. "Never would have. Are you sure you don't want something to eat?"

"How are the fries?"

"Don't know yet. Help yourself," he offered.

She plucked one from his plate, dipped it into ketchup, and popped it into her mouth. He was relieved at the approval on her face.

French fries might not be much to go on, but they were a start.

Abby was floating. The sensual heft of Zan's jacket felt wonderful over her shoulders, even though it hung halfway down to her thighs.

They'd reached the end of the boardwalk, where the lights began to fade. Beyond the boardwalk, the warehouse district began. They'd walked the whole boardwalk, talking and laughing, and at some point, their hands had swung together and sort of just . . . stuck. Warmth seeking warmth. Her hand tingled joyfully in his grip.

The worst had happened. Aside from his sex appeal, she simply liked him. She liked the way he laughed, his turn of phrase, his ironic sense of humor. He was smart, honest, earthy, funny. Maybe, just maybe, she could trust herself this time.

Their strolling slowed to a stop at the end of the boardwalk.

"Should we, ah, walk back to your van?" she ventured.

"This is where I live," he told her.

She looked around. "Here? But this isn't a residential district."

"Not yet," he said. "It will be soon. See that building over there? It used to be a factory of some kind, in the twenties, I think. The top floor, with the big arched windows, that's my place."

There was just enough light to make out the silent question in his eyes. She exhaled slowly. "Are you going to invite me up, or what?"

"You know damn well that you're invited," he said. "More than invited. I'll get down on my knees and beg, if you want me to."

The full moon appeared in a window of scudding clouds, then disappeared again. "It wouldn't be smart," she said. "I don't know you."

"I'll teach you," he offered. "Crash course in Zan Duncan. What do you want to know? Hobbies, pet peeves, favorite leisure activities?"

She would put it to the test of her preliminary checklist, and make her decision based on that. "Don't tell me," she said. "Let me guess. You're a martial arts expert, right?"

"Uh, yeah. Aikido is my favorite discipline. I like kung fu, too."

She nodded, stomach clenching. There it was, the first black mark on the no-nos checklist. Though it was hardly fair to disqualify him for that, since he'd saved her butt with those skills the night before.

So that one didn't count. On to the next no-no. "Do you have a motorcycle?"

He looked puzzled. "Several of them. Why? Want to go for a ride?"

Abby's heart sank. "No. One last question. Do you own guns?"

Zan's face stiffened. "Wait. Are these trick questions?"

"You do, don't you?" she persisted.

"My late father was a cop." His voice had gone hard. "I have his service Beretta. And I have a hunting rifle. Why? Are you going to talk yourself out of being with me because of superficial shit like that?"

Abby's laugh felt brittle. "Superficial. That's Abby Maitland."

"No, it is not," he said. "That's not Abby Maitland at all."

"You don't know the first thing about me, Zan."

"Yes, I do." His dimple quivered. "I know first things, second things, third things. You've got piss-poor taste in boyfriends, to start."

Abby was stung. "Those guys were not my boyfriends! I didn't even know them! I've just had a run of bad luck lately!"

"Your luck is about to change, Abby." His voice was low and velvety. "I know a lot about you. I know how to get into your apartment. How to turn your cat into a noodle. The magnets on your fridge, the view from your window. Your perfume. I could find you blindfolded in a room full of strangers." His fingers penetrated the veil of her hair, his forefinger stroking the back of her neck with controlled gentleness. "And I learn fast. Give me ten minutes, and I'd know lots more."

"Oh," she breathed. His hand slid through her hair, settled on her shoulder. The delicious heat burned her, right through his jacket.

"I know you've got at least two of those expensive dresses that drive guys nuts. And I bet you've got more than two. You've got a whole closet full of hot little outfits like that. Right?" He cupped her jaw, turning her head until she was looking into his fathomless eyes.

Her heart hammered. "I've got a . . . a pretty nice wardrobe, yes."

"I'd like to see them." His voice was sensual. "Someday maybe you can model them all for me. In the privacy of your bedroom."

"Zan—"

"I love it when you say my name," he said. "I love your voice. Your accent. Based on your taste in dresses, I'm willing to bet that you like fancy, expensive lingerie, too. Am I right? Tell me I'm right."

"Time out," she said, breathless. "Let's not go there."

"Oh, but we've already arrived." His breath was warm against her throat. "Locksmiths are detail maniacs. Look at the palm of your hand, for instance. Here, let me see." He lifted her hand into the light from the nearest of the streetlamps. "Behold your destiny."

It was silly and irrational, but it made her self-conscious to have him look at the lines on her hand. As if he actually could look right into her mind. Past, future, fears, mistakes, desires, all laid out for anyone smart and sensitive enough to decode it. "Zan. Give me my hand back."

"Not yet. Oh . . . wow. Check this out," he whispered.

"What?" she demanded.

He shook his head with mock gravity and pressed a kiss to her knuckles. "It's too soon to say what I see. I don't want to scare you off."

"Oh, please," she said unsteadily. "You are so full of it."

"And you're so scared. Why? I'm a righteous dude. Good as gold." He stroked her wrist. "Ever try cracking a safe without drilling it? It's a string of numbers that never ends. Hour after hour, detail after detail. That's concentration." He pressed his lips against her knuckles.

"What does concentration have to do with anything?"

"It has everything to do with everything. That's what I want to do to you, Abby. Concentrate, intensely, minutely. Hour after hour, detail after detail. Until I crack all the codes, find all the keys to all your secret places. Until I'm so deep inside you . . ." his lips kissed their way up her wrist, ". . . that we're a single being."

She leaned against him and let him cradle her in his strong arms. His warm lips coaxed her into opening to the gentle, sensual exploration of his tongue. "Come up with me," he whispered. "Please."

She nodded. Zan's arm circled her waist, fitting her body against his. It felt so right. No awkwardness, no stumbling, all smooth. Perfect.

She was undone by his gentleness, his teasing humor, his big, gorgeous, yummy body. She couldn't wait to peel that T-shirt off him and take a good look at those hard, ropy muscles.

Her hands tingled, thinking of touching his hot skin, running her fingers through the cool silk of his hair and over the rasp of his beard stubble. She was so dazed, she didn't even register the sounds from behind the building.

Zan stopped, stiffening. Those were bad sounds. She heard blows, gasps, shouts. A bloodcurdling screech, choked ominously off.

Zan shoved her back. "Wait. I'll see what the hell is going on."

Abby grabbed his arm. "Forget it. I'm sticking with you."

He started to object, but she just hung on to his arm and peered over his shoulder as he rounded the corner.

It was a scene from a nightmare. A crowd of guys circled around two men who were fighting. The onlookers jeered and howled. The two men waved broken bottles at each other. They were drenched with blood. One feinted to one side, tripped the other when he fell for it, and lunged, slashing at his throat. Blood spurted. Abby shrieked.

Zan sucked in a harsh breath. "Holy fuck, that's . . . *Jamie*!"

He hurtled into the melee, breaking through the ring of onlookers, and dove at the two men locked in a bloody embrace on the ground.

Everyone started yelling. Five guys leaped onto Zan. Abby backed away, hand clamped over her mouth to choke off the terrified mewling sounds. *Don't panic, you stupid bimbo ditz.*

She wanted to wade into the fray like that chick from *Alias*, save Zan with a few kicks and karate chops. But there were over fifteen guys in that heaving clump of men, and she was no TV ninja babe. Zan was on his own. The best she could do for him was run for the cops.

She kicked off her sandals and sprinted for the boardwalk while she fumbled for her phone. Her feet barely touched the ground.

Chapter

6

Someone grabbed Zan's arm before he could slash it down across the throat of that shithead and smash his trachea into pink mush. He bellowed as fury gave him the strength to wrench it free to try again.

Someone landed a blow to his face, someone else grabbed him from behind. In that moment of confusion, a ton of bricks hit him in the back and splatted him facedown on the ground.

He bucked and heaved. Someone sat on his legs, someone else on his feet, someone else on his ass, and then the whole fucking pack was sitting on top of him, squeezing the breath out of his lungs so he had to stop yelling and struggle for air, which made it possible to hear someone screaming his name. Two someones. His brothers' voices.

". . . fuck is wrong with you, man? Chill out!" *Jamie.*

"Calm down, Zan. Do you hear me? Zan? Stop fighting." *Chris.*

Jamie. That first voice had been Jamie's. So Jamie wasn't murdered. His throat was not slashed. He was alive. He was OK.

The red haze in Zan's head began to subside, and his muscles went limp. He started shaking so hard, the guys on top of him had to be shaking too, like they were perched on a volcano about to blow.

He realized that the shaking was laughter, or maybe tears.

Nah. Call it laughter. If tears and snot were mixed with the blood streaming out of his nose, the fifteen guys sitting on top of him would never need to know. His body shook harder.

Jamie. His smart-mouthed, scrappy baby brother. God.

"Yo, Zan. Earth to Zan." Jamie's voice vibrated with tension. "Do you hear me? Get off him, Martin. Move your ass."

"No fucking way. This freak practically killed me. I'm sitting on him till the cops get here."

"OK, let me put this another way." Jamie's voice was underlaid with steel. "Get the fuck off him, or I'll knock out all your teeth."

The crushing weight on Zan's back reluctantly shifted. Then the other various weights lifted themselves off. Someone shoved him, not gently, onto his back. He blinked, eyes burning with grit. He stared up at the grotesquely backlit circle of faces. They contemplated him with cautious dread. As if he were some sort of gigantic, mutant cockroach.

His brother Christian helped Zan into a sitting position, and wiggled his nose, which hurt like hell. "Hold your head up," Chris directed. "Or the blood will go down your throat."

I know that, Zan wanted to say, but his talking apparatus wasn't functioning. His body still vibrated at a screamingly high pitch. He was so zinged, he could have floated right up off the ground.

"Use your sleeve. It's all bloody anyway," Chris said. "Jesus, Zan. You scared the living shit out of us."

That crack found Zan his voice again. "Me? I scared the . . ." His voice trailed off into a harsh crack of laughter. "I scared *you?* I see my baby brother getting his throat slashed, and I'm the one who—"

"I told you!" Jamie bellowed. "How many times do I have to tell you about the fucking play? You're as thick as a brick wall! I choreographed this fight!"

Zan blinked at him stupidly. "Oh. Ah . . . shit."

"Yeah! Shit! We called a fight rehearsal tonight, but the dancers already had booked the practice rooms at the performing arts center, so I just brought them here. Figured I couldn't bother anybody here. Ha!"

"Did it occur to you to warn me that you planned on simulating your own murder in front of our building tonight?" Zan snarled.

"I thought I had!" Jamie yelled back. "If you'd get your head out of your ass and listen to what I say, you'd have figured it out! I told you, I'm Tybalt, right? I told you about getting my throat cut! This is Martin, who plays Romeo. Anton here is Mercutio. Me and Mercutio have a big fight, and I stab him to death, and then Romeo here freaks out and kills me. And the rest of these guys are various henchmen for the mob fight."

Zan's head had begun to throb. "Who hit me?" he asked.

Chris looked sheepish. "Uh, that would be me. Sorry."

Zan looked around at the bizarre assortment of guys. Half of them had dreadlocks, spiked hair, piercing, Goth makeup. The rest of them were clean-cut, dressed in jeans and polo shirts. He focused on the one he'd jumped, the one who had simulated slashing Jamie's throat.

He shivered. *The guy he had almost killed.*

Romeo's face was wet with sweat. He was spattered with fake blood, and his eyes slid nervously away from Zan's gaze. Probably he had just an inkling of how close he'd just come to death. Poor bastard.

Zan turned to Chris again. "Thanks," he said quietly.

Chris nodded, his face somber. "Way too fucking close," he murmured, pitching his voice for Zan's ears. "You were this close to another murder rap. You need to chill out. You scared me bad."

"Yeah," Zan said hoarsely. "I scare myself." He looked up at Romeo. "Sorry," he muttered. It was all he could think of to say.

Romeo's eyes darted around at everyone but him. He nodded, tried to speak, and failed. His Adam's apple bobbed.

Zan tried to struggle to his feet, but his legs shook under him. He might have fallen if Chris and Jamie hadn't grabbed him by the armpits and hauled him upright. He searched for something to say.

"Uh . . . nontraditional casting, I take it?" he ventured.

"You bet." Jamie's habitual cheerfulness had reasserted itself. "Guess we don't need to worry whether the fight looks realistic, right?"

"Right," Zan said sourly. "No worries. Put your minds at ease."

"It's a cool production," Jamie went on, warming to his subject.

"The Montagues are tight-assed preppies, and the Capulets are punk-goth wackos. We've got an acid rock band to play the Capulet party that Romeo and Mercutio crash. The scene is miked. It's going to be a blast."

"That's nice," Zan said faintly. He contemplated Jamie's blood-drenched costume. It made his stomach roll. "That stuff looks real."

Jamie's blood-spattered face split into an evil grin. "Yeah, don't it though? Look here." He indicated a plastic bulb that hung inside his jacket. "All I have to do is squeeze this, and . . . voilà!"

An arc of blood shot out of a tube attached to Jamie's throat, splattering liberally across Zan's face, shirt and jeans. Assorted Montague and Capulet goons giggled and snorted.

He looked at them. The laughter petered out into nervous silence.

"Gee, sorry," Jamie said, but the gleam in his eyes was supremely unrepentant. "Didn't know that tube was pointed straight at your face."

Anton cackled. "I hope that shirt's synthetic," he said. "Fake blood stains, big time. Your jeans are pure cotton. They're, like, history."

Zan swallowed back a savage and inappropriate response. His ruined jeans were the least of his problems.

The biggest problem was . . . it hit him, and another jolt of adrenaline assaulted his shredded nerves. "Oh, fuck me. Abby!" He looked around wildly. "Did anybody see the girl who was with me?"

"What girl?" Chris said. "I didn't see any girl."

"I was with Abby." Zan lurched around the corner of the building, heart hammering. No Abby. Only a pair of flimsy spike-heeled sandals, lying in the gravel. Zan scooped them up and stared at them in blank dismay. "She's disappeared."

"Smart woman. I don't blame her," Chris said. "I'd disappear too, if I saw my date pull a stunt like that."

"Oh, would you shut up?" Zan snapped.

Jamie poked the delicate sandals dangling from Zan's hand, making them sway. "Left her shoes and bolted, just like Cinderella."

"She ran across three gravel parking lots in her bare feet," Zan said. "She must have been terrified."

Chris heaved a philosophical sigh, pulled out his cell phone and punched in a number. "Hey. Ricky? It's Chris Duncan. Yeah. Did some girl call in a homicide down on the wharf? Yeah . . . I'm on the scene. It's not a real fight. It's a theatrical thing, for the playhouse . . . yeah. My little brother's in it. Fake blood spurting . . . uh-huh, tell me about it. Hey, do me a favor. The girl's my brother's date, so tell them to be really nice to her, OK? Give her a cup of tea, a ride home? OK? . . . Thanks."

"A girl? You were bringing a girl here? Wait till I tell Granddad!"

"Don't bother," Zan said through gritted teeth. "She probably never wants to see me again, after all that blood."

"Oh, shit." Jamie looked dejected beneath his spattered gore. "Don't tell me I derailed your love life the minute it got going. I can go with you, if you want. I can explain that we were just—"

"Christ, no," Zan cut in. "For God's sake, don't try to help me. You look like something out of a zombie splatter film."

"So do you, buddy," Jamie observed cheerfully. "The difference is that your nose is genuinely mashed into bloody paste, and mine isn't."

Zan declined to respond as he stumbled for the elevator.

Abby's sore feet throbbed, despite the hot bath and soothing ointment. She tore herself away from the vacuous reality show and shuffled to the kitchen. She'd hauled out all her comfort props: flannel pajamas, afghan, cocoa with marshmallows, bunny slippers, the New Age CD that usually put her practically into a coma, all ocean waves and bird cheeps. Nothing worked. There was no comfort to be had.

She stung all over, as if she'd been slapped. She was so rattled, so humiliated. The cop who brought her home had tried not to smirk while he explained to her what had happened. How stupid she had been.

She'd done it again. Made a public ass of herself because of a sexy man. A fight rehearsal for a theatrical production, for the love of God. Unbelievable. At least it had been real enough to fool Zan, too, though that wasn't much comfort. She would never forgive him for that interval of agonizing fear, thinking he could be bleeding to death in a warehouse lot. She'd felt so useless and weak. She was pathetically glad that Zan was OK, but the feeling lingered on, like a bruise.

She thought of the brandy, but dismissed the idea. She never drank when she was alone. Particularly not when she was miserable. A stiff drink took the edge off, but that led to the land of bad, sad, awful things. Watching her mother all those years had taught her that much.

Of course, lots of paths led to the land of bad, sad, awful things. She seemed to be mapping out new, original paths to it every single day.

She wished she could call Elaine, but she didn't want to piss off Mysterious Mark and ruin her friend's evening. The only weapon left was the Fudge Ripple. She was going to expand right out of her clothes, but so what? Who was she trying to stay slim for?

She rooted through the silverware drawer for her ice cream spoon. The rap on the door made the silverware sorter leap out of her hands. Utensils crashed and tinkled to the floor. She stared at the door, her heart tripping so fast she thought she might faint.

She peered out the peephole. Zan's somber face, battered and swollen, gave her a jolt, keen and painful. Anger and hopeless longing.

He looked through the door, as if he could see right through it into her eyes. "Abby. Please open the door. We have to talk."

"No, we don't," she called back. "Go away, Zan."

"No," he said. "Not until we talk."

It occurred to her that he could open her lock in seconds.

He knocked again. "Please, Abby." His voice was soft, pleading.

She wanted to open it so badly. Why did she never want what was good for her? She propped her forehead against the door and started sobbing silently. It was so freaking hard to do the right thing.

When the tears finally eased off, she mopped her eyes on the sleeve of her bathrobe, figuring he must have left. She peeked out the peephole. Gone. The disappointment that flashed through her was wildly irrational. She yanked the door open to make sure.

He was sitting on the steps. She dragged in a startled breath.

He looked around, and rose to his feet. "Hey, Abby." He took a step toward her and held out her sandals. "These are yours."

She took them, stared at her dangling footwear. "Thanks."

"Your feet all right?" he asked.

Her swollen feet throbbed. "Fine." She yanked his jacket off the hook by the door and thrust it at him. "Here. We're even. Good night."

"I'm not going until we talk," he said.

"I'm not in the mood to talk," she said.

"So I'll wait until you are in the mood," he said. "I'm patient."

"Yeah," she said bitterly. "You told me that. You told me a lot of things. Maybe you should just go home and get some sleep."

"I never sleep at night," he told her.

"Oh. Well, fortunately, that is not my problem. So go do whatever it is that you do at night, if you don't sleep. Bye."

"You have to let me explain," he said.

She held up a warning hand. "Oh, no need for that. The nice patrolman explained it all to me. While trying not to laugh in my face."

He winced. "I'm sorry."

"Huh. Me too." She looked more closely at his face. His nose was puffy, his eye swollen half shut. "You look awful," she said bluntly.

His mouth twitched. "Yeah. My brother popped me a good one to get me under control."

"How lovely. What pleasant siblings you must have. This would be the brother who's in the Shakespeare play? The fountain of blood?"

"No, the fountain of blood was Jamie, my youngest brother. The one who punched me was Christian, the next to youngest."

"So you had two brothers involved in the fake massacre. Is this a form of sibling rivalry? Do they play this kind of trick on you often?"

"I actually have three brothers," he offered. "There's Jack, the oldest. I have a little sister, too. Her name's Fiona. She's twenty-five."

"I shudder to think of what your family gatherings must be like."

He smiled briefly at that. "Hey, so do I, sometimes."

She didn't smile back, and the silence grew heavy and cold.

"Abby," he said. "Please. I didn't know about the fight rehearsal. I had a terrible scare, too, and I feel just as stupid. Forgive me. Please."

She stared up at the moon. "Maybe you have no idea what I went through. First, I witness a gruesome murder. Then I see you dive into the middle of it. I leave you to get help, and feel like garbage because I couldn't save you. I was sure you were dead, or dying. And then, I find out that it's just a big, funny joke, and I am the butt of it."

"No, Abby," he pleaded. "Nobody thinks that."

"I'm glad that you weren't killed. Don't get me wrong. But it was tough, you know? First, the horror, and then I get to feel stupid, too."

He rubbed his face, gingerly. "God," he muttered. "I'm sorry. I don't know what else I can say, except that I bet it was worse for me than it was for you. I practically killed an innocent guy tonight."

An explosive sound, half bitter laughter, half sob, burst out of her. "God, Zan. Is that little detail actually supposed to *comfort* me?"

He drew in a sharp breath and turned away, leaning on the porch railing. He rested his face in his hands. She wanted so badly to soothe and pet him, it hurt. Finally she reached out and touched his nose with her fingertip. "Does it hurt?" she asked hesitantly.

"Yeah," he said gruffly. "But I'll live."

"I'm glad," she quavered. "I'm really, really glad of that."

"Oh, Abby." He reached for her.

She lurched away. "No. I do not want to see fountains of blood, or watch a man I care about jump into a knife fight! Forget it! No more!"

"Abby, try to understand," he pleaded. "I didn't know—"

"Oh, I'm great at understanding," she said bitterly. "That's what's ruined my life so far. I'm drawing the line now. A thick, black line."

"But he was my brother!" Zan protested. "I did what I had to do!"

"Of course you did. I don't fault you for it. You were very brave. Your brother is lucky you care so much. But I just cannot deal. So I've made my decision." She took a deep breath. "You don't fit the profile."

His eyes narrowed. "Huh? What the fuck is the profile?"

She steeled herself. "I don't want adventures like this in my life. Ever again. Therefore, I need to stay away from a certain type of man."

"Type?" He looked bewildered. "What type am I?"

She shook her head. It was so hard to verbalize this kind of thing. "It's . . . the black leather, the tattoos, the fighting, the whole lifestyle."

"What lifestyle? What the hell do you know about my lifestyle?"

"I know what I need to know. You live in an abandoned factory—"

"Abandoned? Abby, my apartment is not a—"

"I want a normal life!" she yelled. "I want a normal man, a normal car, a normal house! Nice things! And I don't want to have to feel guilty about wanting them! I'm entitled! It's not too goddamn much to ask!"

"Yeah? Edgar? Or Reginald?" Zan flung back at her. "Is that who you want to see when you roll over in the morning and open your eyes?"

She winced. "No. But I don't want the kind of thing that happened to me tonight. I know for sure that I don't want that."

His throat bobbed. "You surprise me. I wouldn't have taken you for a judgmental, materialistic bitch. You look so warm and real."

Ouch. She flinched back. "You'd better go," she whispered.

"Oh yeah. I'm going. Sweet dreams, Abby. I hope you find what you're looking for. Because it's exactly what you deserve." He turned and ran down the stairs.

"Zan!" she called, prompted by God knew what crazy impulse.

He looked back over his shoulder. The look in his eyes broke her heart. "I'm really sorry," she faltered. "I didn't mean to hurt you."

"So don't make it worse." He disappeared into the dark.

Chapter

7

Zan shifted his sore shoulder against the big driftwood log. The sun had burned the mist off the beach. The heaving surges of white noise were supposed to stun him into a state of zenlike tranquillity.

That was the theory, anyway.

He'd been lying on the sand dune for hours, waiting for zenlike tranquillity to descend. Every muscle in his body ached. Coffee would be good, so would a shower, but he couldn't face a lecture from Granddad, or advice from Chris, or teasing from Jamie.

He tried to be philosophical about it. You win some, you lose some, fuck 'em if they can't take a joke. But it didn't feel like a joke.

The phone in his jacket buzzed. He squeezed his burning eyes shut and pulled it out. Matty Boyle. He rubbed his sore face and stared at it. He was supposed to do a master-key job for them today. He had no excuse for not answering. He hit the button. "Hey, Matty."

"Just wondered if you remembered the museum job," Matty said.

"Have I ever forgotten to show up for a job I'd contracted to do?"

"Don't get huffy," Matty said. "Come by the office before, OK?"

He didn't want to deal with Matty in his current mood. "What for?" he demanded.

"Um . . . we figured, someone who looks like you would be better off introduced." Matty laughed heartily. "Just, you know, a formality."

Zan's blood rose to a quick boil. "You want me to pass on this gig? If I'm too scruffy for them, they can all go fuck themselves."

"Whoa! Calm down! I don't mean that!"

"Never mind, Matty," Zan said wearily, ashamed of his outburst. "Sorry. I just had a really bad night. When do you want me there?"

"How about we go over to the museum before lunch? I want to talk to you about something important. A business proposition."

"I'll come over now," Zan said. "You're at the office?"

"Yeah, but I wanted to—"

Zan clicked the phone shut. What a pain in the ass.

Matty and Walt Boyle only called him to do jobs for them to ease their guilty consciences. He tried to be polite, for his late father's sake. Alex Duncan would have wanted his son to forgive, but distant, tight-lipped courtesy was about the best that he could do.

Matty had been part of his life ever since preschool. Matty's dad, Walt Boyle, had been a college buddy of Zan's father. They'd been planning to open a security business together, Duncan & Boyle, until Zan's father had been shot to death in the line of duty.

Zan and Matty had played together and fought together like brothers, until that fateful night eighteen years ago. He wondered if Matty ever thought about that night. Maybe he'd blotted it out. Drugs were a quick solution to Matty's many problems. He'd certainly been in orbit the night that he stole the Porsche from the Silver Fork Resort parking lot. He hadn't told Zan where he'd gotten the car when he'd swung by to show it off, though Zan should've guessed.

Zan hadn't, though. He'd climbed in and gone for a ride.

He still had nightmares about the guy they'd hit. Woke up groping desperately for the wheel as the car spun out. Seeing the man's terrified eyes, hearing that sickening thud. Blood on the windshield.

Matty had freaked and run, leaving Zan alone to sprint through the rain looking for a phone. Zan had been the one to sit on the street, crying and holding the guy's hand. It had taken a fucking eternity for the ambulance to get there. Too long. The man had died.

Matty left him holding the bag. For the theft, the accident, even the baggie of coke in the car. It had been so easy to pin on him. Zan's prints were all over the wheel, while Matty had worn gloves to nick the car. Matty said he'd just gotten wasted and passed out, at home. That he didn't remember a thing. And Matty's dad had backed him up.

It hadn't turned out as badly as it might have. Zan had been seventeen, young enough for a juvenile charge. Walt Boyle had pulled all the strings he could, probably out of guilt. Zan had come out of the situation with no more than a few months of community service.

Except that the guy who owned the Porsche had been on the scholarship board. Zan lost the scholarship that would have sent him to MIT. This misfortune coincided with Mom getting laid off from her accounting job. Chris had been fourteen, Jamie eight, Fiona barely six.

His plan had been to work for a year or two, get a degree some other way. He'd gotten licensed as a locksmith, and never stopped working long enough to go back to school. The computer consulting had been a late-night hobby gone wild that had evolved into a career. Work he enjoyed. It had turned out OK, in the end. He had no regrets.

He'd been furious with the Boyles for years, but he'd slowly let it go. And when Walt Boyle had started calling him to subcontract key jobs, he'd decided to interpret the gesture as a tacit apology.

So he took their jobs. Not always, but now and again. It was never any fun, though. The Boyles made him tense. Father and son both.

He left his bike outside Boyle Security and went in. Matty jumped up from his perch on the buxom blond receptionist's desk.

"There he is! The man himself!" Matty was in one of his jolly moods. He clapped Zan heartily on the back. Zan stifled a yelp of pain. Fifteen Montagues and Capulets had stomped that exact spot last night.

"Jesus, what happened to you?" Matty asked. "You look like shit."

Zan gritted his teeth. "Long, boring story. Another time."

"Sure thing, my man. Come on into my office."

Zan followed him in, looking around hopefully for a coffee machine. Matty perched on the edge of an unnaturally neat desk. His face was plumping up around the neck, and his hair was thinning over the temples. Matty gave him a fixed smile until Zan started to twitch.

"What is it, Matty?" he demanded. "Is something up?"

"Nah. Hey. Remember how we used go up to my dad's cabin on Wilco Lake when we were kids?" Matty asked. "Playing pirates?"

Zan stared at him for a moment. "That was a long time ago."

Matty's fingers drummed against the desk. "Want to go up to Wilco Lake this weekend? Do some fishing, just for old times' sake?"

Holy shit. Zan was caught so off guard, he couldn't think of a ready excuse. "Sorry, Matty, but I can't," he said. "I've got, uh, plans."

Matty's cheerful rictus of a grin was starting to creep him out. "Oh yeah? Some weekend getaway with a hot babe, I bet, huh?"

Yeah. In my dreams. Zan was too whipped to think of anything more plausible. "Something like that," he muttered lamely.

"I knew it! Who's the babe? Anyone I know?"

"Too soon to say," Zan countered. "I'm playing it cool."

Matty's smile soured. "Yeah, you always did. And the girls just ate that shit up. The rest of us losers had to make do with the leftovers."

Zan was unnerved. "What is bugging you, Matty?"

"Nothing." Matty's smile came back, bigger than life. "I've got an idea I want to run past you. You know we're securing the museum?"

"You subcontracted me to do the key plan. That's why I'm here." Matty missed his irony. "Do you know about the Pirates' Hoard?"

"Treasure from a sunken Spanish galleon? Yeah. Sounds cool."

"Yeah. It's amazing. I want you to take a look at how we're securing that exhibit. Chuck Jamison will show you how the stuff works. He's one of the engineers that's doing on-site setup. Just tell him you're interested in his gadgets, and you won't be able to shut him up. Analyze the security weaknesses for me, and then write me a report."

Zan was baffled. "But I don't specialize in museum security. That's your department, not mine."

"Yeah, sure, but it's the same mindset, see? You attack computer systems, uncover their weaknesses, analyze solutions, and offer to share them with your victims for a price, right? Isn't that how it works?"

"That's one way of putting it," Zan said cautiously.

"And you make a bundle at it, right?"

"I do OK," Zan hedged, his income being none of Matty's business.

"Well? There you go! We're using some cool stuff. Electro-magnetic presence sensors, gravimetric and piezo-seismic detection, infrared, state-of-the-art video surveillance software. I want you to apply that pirate mindset to the whole thing. Look at it as if you want to steal the loot yourself, you get me? I need feedback from someone who thinks outside the box. That's you, man. Zan the pirate. Just like old times."

Compliments from Matty made him feel like he had ants in his clothes. "I'm swamped," Zan said cautiously. "I've already got more work than I can handle. Call somebody who knows what the hell he's doing."

"Name your price," Matty said.

Zan was taken aback at Matty's dramatic tone. "Huh?"

"I'll pay you. Really well. I'm talking the big bucks, dude."

Zan studied the tense, smiling grimace that was stamped onto Matty's face. "What is up with you? Are you in some kind of trouble?"

Matty laughed and loosened his tie. "Oh, nah. Nothing. Work stress, you know. Business is, ah, booming."

Zan's eyes flicked over Matty's blank, antiseptic desk. It didn't look like a work space at all. His own work lair at home was a huge table, a mass of disks, CDs, manuals, diagrams, flowcharts, professional journals, invoices, wires, electronic bits and pieces, heaped and snarled together under a bar of powerful hanging lights, with his big black swivel chair thronelike in the middle. "Ah. I see," he said. "You should, uh, relax."

"Yeah, I know. Look, don't turn me down yet. Just consider it, OK? Please? As a personal favor to me?"

Matty's face looked strangely desperate. Zan hesitated. "I'll think about it," he temporized. "Maybe I could take a quick look."

"Great, great," Matty said, beaming. "Lemme take your picture."

This kept getting weirder and weirder. "My what?"

"For a security ID at the museum. If you're going to be around the Pirates' Hoard, you need to be on the grid. That stuff's insured for forty million bucks. Go stand by that white wall, facing forward, OK?"

Zan obliged. Matty held up a digital camera, snapped a shot. "OK, now turn to the side. The right side, OK? And push your hair back."

"A mug shot? I thought you'd want to downplay the tattoos."

Matty snapped a photo. "Another favor. Don't say anything about this, OK? This is my idea. I want to show Dad I'm being proactive."

Matty's problems with his dad was another sore spot that Zan didn't want to touch. He nodded. "Won't breathe a word."

Abby clicked her cell phone shut and checked her watch again. Elaine was twenty-five minutes late for their lunch date. Very strange.

Abby washed some aspirin down with diet Coke and peeked at the long list of work calls she had yet to make. She couldn't linger much longer. It had been insane to make a lunch date today, but she'd been so worried about Elaine, and the museum was no place for confidences. Not with Bridget charging around on a permanent power trip.

Maybe Elaine had forgotten. Abby should have tracked her down to confirm, but she'd been so busy, she hadn't looked for her.

The unease in her belly sharpened into worry, laced with guilt. She punched Elaine's number into her cell phone.

Elaine entered the restaurant as it started to ring. Abby's relieved greeting trailed off into a silent gasp. Elaine looked awful. Eyes pinkish and swollen, lips discolored by fever blisters. Her hair was scraped into a messy ponytail. Her slender form was lost in a flapping gray gym suit.

"I know, I know. I look like a walking corpse. You don't have to tell me." Elaine dropped her phone on the table and sank into a chair.

Abby studied her with worried eyes. "Are you sick?"

Elaine shrugged. "Sorry I'm late. I just rolled out of bed now."

"Did you call in sick at work?"

Elaine shook her head, looking dazed. "I just . . . forgot to go."

Forgot? With a forty-million-dollar exhibit to uncrate? Abby's worry sharpened. She gave Elaine a hug. "What's wrong, sweetie?"

Elaine pondered the question, eyes blank. "Um . . . everything?"

Abby beckoned the waitress, making a coffee pouring gesture. "Everything's awfully big. Let's break it down, OK? Big things first."

Elaine didn't appear to follow Abby's cheerful patter. "I woke up thinking about you. What you told me, about your mother drinking, your dad in jail. Truth is, it's not all that different from how I grew up. I mean, I was filthy rich and all, but my dad ran out on us too, and thank God for that, because he was a . . . well, just thank God, that's all. And my mom, well, she just . . . she can't stand how I'm so . . ." Her voice trailed off into a tight, strangled squeak.

"How you're what?" Abby prompted her, alarmed. "What can't she stand, honey?"

"The stuff that hurt you when you were a kid? It made you stronger." Elaine's voice shook. "Not me. What happened to me made me weaker. And I hate myself for it. I just can't stand it anymore."

Elaine put her face into her hands and dissolved, shoulders vibrating. The waitress, who had been about to approach the table with a pot of coffee, stopped and gave Abby a terrified glance.

Later, Abby mouthed. She scooted her chair and put her arms around her friend. "God, Elaine. Is it Mark? Shall I kill him for you?"

Elaine fished for the napkin. "I'm such a mess," she mumbled.

Abby shoved it into her hands. "Did he hurt you?" she demanded.

Elaine dabbed her eyes. "Uh, not really. Depends on what you mean by hurt. He's careful not to mark my skin."

Abby shuddered. "Jesus, Elaine. What have you got yourself into?"

"I don't know." Elaine's voice sounded lost. "It was so perfect at first, and then it just went off. I get scared that I'm boring him, and the more scared I am, the more boring I get. I feel smaller and smaller, and I get tongue-tied . . . and I say stupid things that make me cringe, and when he makes me do things, I don't have the guts to say no."

Abby stroked Elaine's hair. "Ditch him," she said.

Elaine's laugh was soggy. "I tried last night. Couldn't get the words out. And the further it goes, the smaller I feel, and the less I can—never mind. And then this morning . . ." Her voice trailed off.

Abby was maddened. "What did he do this morning? Talk to me!"

"No, not him. I got a call from the investigative agency."

"Huh? What investigative agency?"

Elaine smiled wanly. "Background checks. Every man who's ever gotten within ten feet of me. Heiresses always have to be on their guard for fortune hunters. Mother never believed a guy might be interested in me for my own sake. Maybe she's right," she concluded dully.

Abby suppressed the urge to say something sharp. "That's enough of that bad attitude," she said bracingly. "So? Your mother ran a background check? And you just got the results? So what were they?"

"No, Mother never knew about Mark. It was secret. But last week, I was feeling weird, so I called the detective myself."

Abby waited while Elaine blew her nose. "And?" she demanded. "What did the detective tell you, for God's sake?"

"That Mark doesn't exist," Elaine whispered.

Abby was bewildered. "Come again?"

"The name he gave me. Everything about his past. It's all a lie. I'm such an idiot. I should have known." She buried her face in her hands. "Now I've got to confront him. I can't make myself do it."

Abby grabbed Elaine's cell phone, punched in the address function, selected M. There he was, Mark. "I've got no problem talking to him," she said hotly. "I'll just say hey, you lying, sadistic piece of shit, my buddy Elaine never wants to see you again, so fuck off and die already. How does that strike you for a blow-off line?" She hit CALL.

It started to ring. Elaine snatched the phone away. "I'm the one who has to say it, or it doesn't count. Really. I'm working up my nerve."

Abby calculated the chances of Elaine finding her nerve by tonight. "You shouldn't see him alone. You need moral support."

"In case I cave?" Elaine tried to smile, but the results were painful. "I've got to do it myself, Abby. I've got to stop acting like a doormat. It's just that he's so charismatic, you know? And I'm so not."

Abby's nails dug into her palms. It drove her nuts that she couldn't convince Elaine of her worth. She wanted to kill Mark. Puppy-kicking, kitten-stomping bastard.

"Oh, my goodness. Elaine? Is that you?"

Elaine flinched. Her hand flew up to cover her blistered mouth. It was Marcia Topham, an important member of the museum council. Her many-chinned face was a caricature of dismay.

"Hi, Marcia," Elaine whispered, trying to smile.

"Elaine, darling, you do not look well!" Marcia pronounced the words loudly, with relish. "Does your mother know you're not well?"

"I'm fine," Elaine said hastily. "Really. Just a touch of the flu."

"Then why aren't you home, in bed? Have you seen a doctor? When your mother hears about this, she will be very upset!"

"No need to say anything to her." Her voice quavered. "I'm fine."

Marcia leaned to embrace her. Elaine shrank back. There was an awkward moment while the older woman straightened up huffily.

"Sorry," Elaine whispered. "The flu. I don't want you to get it."

Abby hastened to create a diversion. "Mrs. Topham, I'm so glad I caught you! You were next on my list to call! You are planning to come to the gala, aren't you?"

Marcia Topham turned to Abby, blinking. "The gala? Of course."

"Oh, thank goodness," Abby babbled. "I was beginning to worry. I still hadn't gotten your RSVP, you see, and I wanted to make sure that you and Mr. Topham get primo seating right up front, so I—"

"I'll send the check today." Marcia turned her plump back and minced out, every part of her body radiating offended dignity.

"Oh, shit," Elaine moaned softly. "Marcia's one of my mother's biggest spies. When my mother finds out . . . she'll kill me."

"Finds out what?" Abby protested. "That you went out of the house without makeup? That you're feeling under the weather?"

Elaine shook her head. "You'd have to know my mother."

"I'm glad I don't," Abby said crisply. "Never mind your mother. Concentrate on ditching Mark. Can we celebrate afterward?"

Elaine let out a short, bitter laugh. "What, a suicide watch?"

Abby was shocked. "Elaine," she said when she found her voice. "Don't say things like that. Not even in jest. It's not funny."

"Yeah," Elaine said dully. "Sorry. It would be nice to have company. I won't be much fun, though. I'll probably cry all over your—"

"Your place?" Abby broke in, cutting her off. "Mine? Or out?"

"My place, I think," Elaine said. "I doubt I'll be up for going out. You're sweet, Abby. A good friend. Better than I deserve."

Abby mimed tearing out her hair. "Arrgh! When am I going to break you of saying stuff like that? It drives me freaking nuts!"

Elaine winced. "Sorry," she whispered.

"You deserve the best, honey." Abby emphasized every word. "You are pure gold. Remember it while you're giving that slimeball the boot."

"I'll try. Really." Elaine pushed back her chair. "I'm sorry, Abby. I can't eat. I'd better go to the beach, to think up what to say to Mark."

"Grind that jerkwad into the pavement with your heels," Abby urged her. "Make him wish he'd never been born."

"Yeah. Right." Elaine shot an unsteady smile over her shoulder and pushed out the door. Someone jostled her. She stumbled back. The woman who had run into her said something rude and shoved past her.

Abby sucked in a pained breath. Elaine was too fragile to deal even with normal, everyday rudeness. Let alone a scary sexual sadist.

The gravity of Elaine's problems had put her own into perspective. She started back to work, relieved to see Nanette's espresso cart on the corner. Nanette's hair was rolled into a checkered pattern of knobby buns. A green jewel was pasted to her forehead, and a hole in her spandex bodysuit displayed a matching jewel in her belly button.

"Nanette, your look gets more interesting every day," she said.

"Hi, Abby! This is the 'priestess of the cursed temple.' Like it?"

"It's, ah, very colorful," Abby hedged. "Make me a triple, please."

"Sure thing," Nanette said, as she got to work. "Everything OK?"

"Why wouldn't it be?"

"For you do lie upon the cheek of night whiter than a pearl in an Ethiope's ear," Nanette said earnestly.

Abby squinted at her. "Huh?"

"Oh, don't mind me." Nanette packed espresso into the machine, looking embarrassed. "I meant, you look kinda pale and washed out."

Abby dug money out of her pocket and paid her. "Thanks. You're great for my ego, as always," she said wryly. "What's with the poetry?"

Nanette twirled her nose ring. "I'm doing a Shakespeare play at the Stray Cat Playhouse," she confided. "Sometimes I get carried away."

The mention of Shakespeare and the Stray Cat Playhouse made Abby writhe with remembered shame. "That's great," she said with forced enthusiasm. "Espresso and Shakespeare. Cool combination."

"You bet. Take it easy." Nanette handed her the cup.

With Elaine gone, work was going to be even crazier than usual.

She had to write up the honorees' and the board of trustees' speeches for the gala, and the welcoming remarks for Peter, the museum director, plus find someone to deal with the door that wouldn't close in the new exhibit hall, and the water damage from the leak in the new foyer.

She shoved open the offending exhibit hall door, and—oh God. She rocked backward. She had to be hallucinating. Not possible.

She peeked again. It was Zan. He looked so big and vivid in the empty room. Battered and dangerous, like a pirate after a battle, with all those scrapes and bruises. Maybe he was stalking her.

He turned. Whoops. Busted.

His eyes widened. "Holy shit! What are you doing here?"

His surprise looked genuine. So he wasn't stalking her. She felt almost piqued. "I work here," she said. "I'm the development manager."

"You never told me you worked at the museum." The words sounded almost accusing.

"We never got that far," she said. "We got sidetracked by, ah . . ."

"Sex and violence?" he finished for her.

She rolled her eyes. "What are *you* doing here?"

"I was supposed to do the master key plan for your offices, but the boss-lady doesn't like my looks." He jerked his head toward the conference room door. "I have that effect on women a lot these days."

Bridget's voice penetrated the door. ". . . in your bizarre choice of subcontractors! The image of our organization is at stake, you know!"

Matty Boyle's smooth voice overrode Bridget's strident protests.

Abby winced. "Oh dear. I'm really sorry."

"I don't blame her. I'm having a bad hair day. Or maybe it's the two black eyes," Zan mused. "Whatever. I'm getting used to it."

Bridget flung open the door and looked him over, lip curling.

"I'll just leave," Zan offered. "I don't want to freak anybody out."

Matty Boyle hurried out after her. "But Zan has worked for us for years," he protested. "He's skilled, reliable—"

"So make him cut his hair and dress properly," Bridget snapped.

"Nobody makes me do anything, ma'am," Zan said. "I'm a free agent." He flashed her a grin that looked demonic with his black eyes.

"I don't like his attitude," Bridget said icily.

"I don't like being discussed in the third person," Zan commented. "If you don't like my attitude, tell me, not him. I don't need an intermediary."

Bridget bristled. Matty stepped between them, his hands raised. "He's the best man for the job," he said. "I'd stake my life on it."

Zan blinked. "God, Matty. It's just a key job, not brain surgery."

"Shut up," Matty hissed, eyes fixed on Bridget's face. "Give him a chance," he pleaded. "We'll lose valuable time finding someone else, and we're under the wire, with the gala coming up next week."

Bridget harrumphed. "If your father will vouch for him—"

"Oh, he will," Matty Boyle assured her. "I promise, he will."

"In that case, Abby, show this, ah, *person* around the offices, and explain our security needs to him." Bridget spun and clicked away.

Abby's heart gave a frightened skip. "Bridget, I'm swamped," she called out after her boss's retreating back. "Can't Jens or Cathy—"

"Jens is busy with the layout for the wall text, and Cathy's busy with the exhibition catalog. Don't waste my time complaining." The door of the exhibition hall slammed shut. Abby's face went hot.

"Wow," Zan said. "That woman must be hard on your health."

Abby's eyes dropped. "I handle it."

Matty Boyle cleared his throat. She'd forgotten he was there. He was looking at them with odd intensity, eyes darting from her to Zan.

"Do you guys know each other?" he asked.

"Yes," Zan said.

"Not really," Abby said simultaneously.

They looked at each other. Zan shrugged. "Whatever," he said.

"Huh," Matty Boyle said slowly. "I'll head back to the office, and you can get started. Let me know if you have problems."

"Sure," Zan said. "Later, Matty."

The silence lengthened after the door fell shut behind him.

"What?" Abby demanded. "What's that weird look about?"

Zan shook his head. "This is a strange gig. Matty's acting even weirder than usual, your boss is a hysterical hag, and then there's you."

She folded her arms over her chest. "What? What about me?"

"You keep throwing yourself in my path. It makes a guy wonder."

"I am not throwing myself in your path," she said. "The offices are this way. Let's get this over with."

Abby wove through cubicles. Her body tingled with a hairs-on-end awareness of Zan's presence. She turned a corner and ran into Cathy, Bridget's assistant. Zan smiled. Cathy did a double take, and stared.

"If it's any comfort, if I'd known you worked here, I wouldn't have taken the job." Zan pitched his voice just loud enough for her to hear.

"That's absolutely no comfort to me," she said.

"We passed that watercooler before." Zan's voice was cautious. "People are starting to look at us funny. Let's go to your office."

"Fine," she muttered.

The only chair she had to offer was piled with files. She grabbed an armful. His arms slid beneath hers.

"Allow me." He deposited the load on the last bare patch of floor.

"Thanks." She sank into her chair.

He sat down, and waited. She looked out the window, at her telephone, at her lap. He just sat there quietly, being gorgeous and charismatic. "I . . . I haven't thought about the key plan at all," she said.

"How about you just tell me about the office?" he suggested.

"Good idea," she said, relieved. "What do you want to know?"

"Basic stuff. How many employees work here? Who owns the building? How big a janitorial staff do you have, and which rooms will they need access to? Get me a floor plan of the offices."

Abby groped for a piece of paper. "With the support staff, we've got about twenty people. Bridget and Ambrose and Peter will want keys to everything. Cathy should have a set, she's Bridget's assistant. Then me and Jens and Dovey, we all work weekends . . . oh, and Trish is always the first to arrive, so she'll need—wait. Let me think about this."

"Ah," he said. "So what you're saying is, you've got no idea."

"I've been busy," she snapped. "Doing my job. I'm out of my mind with the gala preparations and this new exhibit."

"You mean the gold from the sunken Spanish galleon?"

She was startled. "You know about the Pirates' Hoard?"

Amusement flickered in his eyes. "I read the arts and entertainment section of the paper, just like normal people do."

"Oh. Ah, that's good," she floundered.

His mouth twitched. "Don't be fooled by my disreputable appearance. I do know how to read."

"Don't be ridiculous. I just didn't take you for a museum type."

"Nope," he said. "You didn't take me at all. Cruel Abby."

"You're making me nervous on purpose," she accused him.

The laughter in his eyes infuriated her. "Let's get back to the key plan," he said mildly. "It's like a flowchart, with different levels. Grandmaster, master, submaster, area master, and slave keys."

"Sounds like a kinky sex game," she heard herself say.

The words echoed in the heavy silence that followed.

Zan stared down at his boots and blew out a long breath. "Don't wave red flags if you don't want the bull to charge you, sweetheart."

"It just . . . popped out. I have this nervous talking thing," she said. "Which is your fault. The nervousness, I mean."

"Yeah, right. Everything's my fault." Zan rolled his eyes. "Let's get back to the key plan. Since you have no idea what you want, I suggest you tape a piece of paper on every door, and every time people go through a door, they initial the paper. I come back in a couple days, we count the initials, see who needs access to what. Sound OK?"

"Oh." She swallowed. "So, ah, this is going to take a while, then."

"Yeah." Zan's mouth tightened. "Look, Abby. If this is too uncomfortable for you, I'll just leave. Matty can find someone else."

Abby's eyes slid away and focused on her desk calendar.

Oh God. She'd forgotten about his name, scribbled all over it. His number, too, in the margin. Circled. Curlicued. *Hearts,* for God's sake.

Adrenaline zinged through her. She wanted to cover the doodles, but they were all over the place. She would need six hands.

"I don't even know why we're having this conversation," he said, with soft bitterness. "Why am I torturing myself? It's so damn stupid."

He looked down, focused on the desk. He froze, eyes widening.

Abby covered her hot face with her hands. Seconds ticked by.

"Wow," he said. "This is an . . . ah, interesting development."

"It's not a development." The pressure of her fingers made red dots twirl in her eyes. "It's just doodles. You've been on my mind lately."

She peeked under her hand. He had leaned forward to trace the heart drawn around his phone number with his fingertip. "I did that once," he said. "It was eighth grade. I had a crush on Amy Bristol. She was a ninth grader. A foot taller than me, on the girls' volleyball team. I didn't have a chance. I wrote her name on everything. Even my body."

His voice was caressing. He hooked a lock of her hair with his finger, let it slide the length of his hand. "So you've got a crush on me."

She lifted her shoulders in a mute, helpless shrug.

"I remember how I felt when Amy Bristol would walk by in the lunchroom," he said. "My heart pounded, and my head roared, and my knees wobbled. I would have lain down and let her use me for a carpet."

She dropped her hands and forced herself to look up at him.

"Funny, how things work out," he said. "That was pretty much the way I felt about you, too."

His wistful tone made her want to howl. "I'm sorry. I just can't—"

He held up his hand. "If you're looking for sympathy about why you're blowing me off, you're talking to the wrong guy."

She bit her lip. "Fair enough."

He slowly moved around the desk, placing his warm hands on either side of her neck. "Maybe I don't make the cut when it comes to boyfriend status, but I do turn you on, hmm?" He caressed her jaw.

"If you're so mad at me, why are you fondling me?" she asked.

"Because I can. You haven't stopped me, have you?" His hands slid down to cup her breasts. Her nipples hardened instantly.

She covered his hands with her own, but she didn't pry them off.

"I could crawl under your desk right now, and inaugurate your new office with my tongue," he suggested. "I bet you'd like that."

"This is . . . way out of line," she quavered.

"That's the point, Abby. That's what you want, isn't it? Dickheads like Edgar and Reginald are fine for posh restaurants, but when bedtime rolls around . . ." His teeth grazed her throat. ". . . you want the big bad wolf to eat you up."

She twisted, trying to meet his eyes. "Stop it. You're scaring me."

"So? Being good will get me nothing. But being bad . . ." He leaned down and bit her neck. ". . . might get me everything."

She shivered at the hot kisses he pressed beneath her jaw, down her throat. "This is my place of work. That door is not locked."

"I know, baby. I'm the one who was supposed to make you a key. But guess what? I don't care. I'm the big bad wolf, remember?"

"Not here." Her voice was strangled. "Just stop it. This instant."

Zan took his hands off her, backed away and walked out.

Chapter

8

Greedy, horny rat bastard. It never failed.

Matty was so used to being angry at Zan, the emotion had worn a groove in his mind. The feeling was so familiar, it was almost comforting.

He parked in the lot, yanked the emergency brake up.

So he was going to get Abby, too. The instant Zan saw something Matty wanted, he just reached out and took it. It had started in school. Matty would bust his ass to get a girl to notice him; she'd take one look at Zan, and forget Matty existed. But Abby was no pimply thirteen-year-old. Abby was a trophy woman. That body, that face, that smile.

He'd been jerking off to Abby fantasies ever since Boyle Security got the museum job. There was no point in asking her out until he had his ace in the hole—five million bucks. He'd planned it all out. Once he got his cut, he would start to court her. In a low-key way, nothing flashy, but with a style and confidence that he'd never had before.

Then in walks Zan, looking like something the cat dragged in, and the stupid bitch starts to stammer and blush. Just like all the others.

Probably Zan would follow his usual pattern. Fuck her for a while, get bored, and dump her. But Matty had gone out with some of Zan's leavings before. All they ever wanted to do was sob on his shoulder and pump him about Zan. Who was he with. Why did he leave them. What did he really want. Boo-hoo. With five million bucks, he should be able to get a woman Zan Duncan hadn't already fucked.

The bastard had always lorded it over him. Taller, smarter. Girls slobbering over him. Fucking scholarship to MIT, while Matty had been so stoned senior year, he'd barely graduated. Dad had shoved that comparison down Matty's throat until he'd practically choked on it.

He'd put a stop to MIT with the Porsche incident, though he barely remembered doing it. Sometimes he wondered if it was just a story his dad made up to make him feel like shit. Then he'd see the look in Zan's eyes. Nobody talked about it, but nobody had forgotten, either.

And look at them now. Matty the fuckup, with an engineering degree his dad had bought for him, kept like a bug on a pin under Dad's eye, where he couldn't do any damage. And Zan, on his fucking high horse. He'd created a consulting career out of nothing. Made good money, too, if rumors were true, and he didn't have to kiss anybody's ass for it. Even Walt Boyle respected him for pulling that off.

Above all, Matty would never be able to forgive him for that.

It's just a key job, Matty, not brain surgery. Yeah, fuck you, too, buddy. No matter how much Zan made, no way had he scraped together five million. Not that Matty would be able to flaunt it, of course, but still, just knowing it was there would change everything. His secret riches would make his balls tingle all the time. Even if he couldn't tell the women, they would sense it. It would change everything.

He pushed into the bar of Jodie's Roadhouse, two towns down the coast from Silver Fork. He pressed his hand against his waistline, to ease the ache. He felt it all the time, when he was sober. Some things made it worse, like thinking about Zan, or Dad. Lucien made it worse, too. The way the guy looked at him, like Matty was some kind of idiot.

The most legal cure for that feeling was bourbon. It turned the ache into a hot, tingling burn. He was not the asshole in this equation, he reminded himself. He was an equal partner in this enterprise.

Yep, there he was, bent over his drink, being discreet. Matty hunched into his suit jacket. Trying to look unmemorable, not that he had to try that hard. He wove through tables, trying not to jostle anyone, and sat next to Lucien. He opened his mouth, but the words didn't come, and he missed his chance to open the conversation.

"It's stupid to insist on meeting here," Lucien said. "We have nothing to talk about. You do your job, I do mine. Simple, right?"

"Uh . . . right." Matty swallowed hard. "It's just that, um . . ."

"You're having trouble doing your job?" Lucien took a meditative sip of his whiskey. "That's not what I want to hear, Boyle."

Matty signaled the bartender, jerking his head toward Lucien's glass. No reason to be nervous. This guy was not God. He was just a guy. "Not exactly," he said. "It's just a matter of timing. The guy started the job at the museum today. But I still need to persuade him to—"

"Find someone else for your fall guy, if this one won't behave."

Like it was so fucking easy. The bartender splashed bourbon into his glass. Matty waited for the guy to move away before he replied.

"But Zan fits the profile. He's a hermit type, works nights, owns guns. The quiet nerdy guys who keep to themselves are the ones who freak out and start eating people's livers, right? And if he does this job, he'll generate evidence against himself, so it's a foolproof—"

"Stop congratulating yourself if it's not working," Lucien said. "Offer him more money."

Matty floundered. "But . . . but he doesn't care about money."

Lucien looked blank. "Offer him more until he starts caring."

"Yeah. Uh, the problem with offering Zan more money is that I can't offer him anything implausible. He's smart. He won't fall for it."

Lucien's appraising eyes darted over Matty, judging and dismissing. "Be smarter," he said.

Rage twisted in Matty's innards. How he hated him. For being so fucking tall. For not having a bald spot and a monkey on his back.

Lucien sipped his drink. "Five million dollars," he murmured. "You guaranteed me you could handle this."

"Uh, yeah," Matty said. "I just wondered if we could adjust the timing, just until I get Zan in the bag."

Lucien's grin was sharklike. "It's too late to turn back."

"I didn't say that," Matty said hastily. "I just wondered if we could be a little bit flexible—"

"No." Lucien's eyes were bright chips of ice. "There is no wiggle room. You have to do your part." He drained his glass.

Matty struggled for words. Something like *who died and made you God, fuckhead?* Instead he stammered, "Oh. Uh, OK. I'll do what I can."

"You do that."

"So it's going well from your end?" Matty tried to sound jovial.

"Things always go well for me," Lucien said. "It's only when I associate myself with incompetent idiots that there are any problems."

Matty forced out a chuckle. "Elaine's set to run away with you?"

"Keep your voice down, you idiot," Lucien hissed.

"Uh, sure. Sorry," Matty said, in a whisper. "One thing, though. What if Elaine gets cold feet? She doesn't strike me as the adventurous type. She might start missing her mother."

"She won't," Lucien said quietly.

"How can you be sure?" Matty argued. "I mean, unless she's in on the scheme. Once she hears about the heist, she'll figure out—"

"She won't."

Matty stared into those strange eyes. The cold spot in his stomach spread. It got too big and too deep to be warmed by the bourbon.

Like a reflex, he latched on to the thought about the five million dollars, looking for the sweet, salutory buzz the fantasy gave him.

It didn't work.

"Are you sure you want to know?" Lucien asked softly. "Once you know something, you can't unknow it."

Too late. It hadn't been hard to convince himself that Zan deserved what he got, but Elaine had never been anything but nice to
him. He wanted bourbon, or something stronger. Something to turn
his brain soft and fuzzy, so he wouldn't have to speculate about why
Lucien was so sure that Elaine wouldn't give him any problems in
Spain.

He shook his head.

"That's wise." Lucien touched his hand, and smiled as Matty
flinched. "Five million dollars," he said. "No going back."

Matty nodded, like a robot.

"Don't waste any more time with these stupid meetings," Lucien
said. "Find a solution to your problem, or you'll find yourself knowing a lot of things you don't want to know. Do we understand each
other?"

Another robotic nod, and Lucien looked away.

Matty slid off the stool and fled. He'd been dazzled by the five
million bucks. He'd wallowed in the fantasy of making Zan pay. But
Elaine? He hadn't bargained on this feeling. This fear.

He thought of the way Abby had looked at Zan. The anger that
flooded him was therapeutic. He steeled himself. Too bad about
Elaine. After all, he would never hurt her himself. It wasn't his fault
if—

Never mind. He had to find another bar, another bourbon.

Five million would go a long way toward easing a sour stomach.

Sullen dusk turned slowly to drizzling night. Zan waited outside
the side door of the new museum wing. Like a devoted hound,
eager to lick the foot that kicked him. First he entertained himself
by listing all of the more constructive things that he could be doing
with his time. That subject exhausted, he moved on to all the stupid
things he'd ever done in his life, and how waiting in the rain for
Abby measured up.

Nothing came close. He'd never done anything so deliberately
self-destructive. He'd made mistakes, sure. Errors in judgment,
based on pride or inexperience. But this was like driving off a cliff.

Anyone familiar with the concept of gravity had no excuse.

His mind kept circling a series of contradictory facts. One, he didn't measure up to her standards. Two, this humiliated him. Three, he turned into a sex fiend every time he touched her. Four, if he didn't have sex with her soon, he was going to go off like a bomb. That scene in her office had burned up every last scrap of self-control he had.

So here he was, lying in wait. He just couldn't wait to get insulted again. Like a junkie desperate for his fix. That mouth, that body, that voice. But it wasn't just her beauty. It was that wild, floating feeling. She made the world feel huge and infinite. Even when she pissed him off, it felt different than garden variety anger. It was wild, molten.

Like the sex would be.

The door opened. His body snapped into red alert. She stepped out, held up her hand to test the rain. Her stance changed as she saw him, looking, graceful, and wary like a deer about to give flight.

He should try to look nonthreatening. Hah. Who was he trying to kid? He took a deep breath, fired up the engine, and rolled down his window. "How are you getting home?"

"The bus," she said. "I take the 12 down Edgemont Road. Sorry, Zan, but I've got to run. The last one leaves at—"

"Get in," he said. "I'll give you a ride." *Yeah. The ride of your life.*

The rain dampened her thin blouse, making it cling. "What happened today doesn't mean anything has changed, you know."

Divert, distract, dazzle. Zan gave her his most charming grin. "You have this magic way of making a guy feel good about himself."

"Just trying to be clear," she murmured.

"You're clear. You're also shivering and getting soaked. Get in, Abby. We can have this conversation in my van, where it's warm."

She looked suspicious. "And what conversation is that?"

"Oh, you know. The one about how I have to stop bugging you because your mind is irrevocably made up. Remember?"

She almost smiled, but stopped herself. "You smart-ass."

"Or would you prefer to skip that conversation?" he suggested. "We could always have it later on."

Abby let out a snort of laughter and climbed in. The stadium inside him exploded in wild, crashing applause.

"Were you waiting for me out here all this time?" she asked.

"Nah," he said. "I just get off on loitering in tow zones in the rain. What the hell do you do in there so late?"

"My job," she said austerely. "All the things I should have been doing while you were fondling me and talking dirty to me."

"Aw, come on. You didn't let me do that for five hours." He hesitated. "Although I would be glad to."

She snorted. "Oh, please."

"Is that a challenge?"

"It is not," she said coolly. "Maybe this is a bad idea. You can leave me at the bus stop. We don't have anything more to talk about."

"Sorry," he said meekly. "I thought we were going to skip this part of the script. You can always blow me off later."

Abby avoided his eyes. She was nervous. He pulled out onto the street and racked his brain for some topic that didn't lead directly to sex. "Why do you take the bus?" he ventured. "Don't you like to drive?"

"I don't have a car. I'd have one in a second if I could."

"What's the problem?"

"Can't afford the insurance," Abby said glumly.

He pondered this. "You can afford Versace and an apartment on Tremont, but not car insurance?"

Abby looked away from him. "My insurance is special."

Now he was genuinely curious, not just fishing for a neutral topic. "You're killing me, sweetheart. What's so special about your insurance?"

"Three wrecks is what's special about it," she muttered.

He whistled softly. "Whoa. You wrecked your car three times?"

"No. Not me," she specified. "I wasn't driving. I wasn't even in the cars at the time. In fact, I didn't even know the cars were in use."

Her words brought up ugly memories: bent metal, broken glass, blood. He shook them away. "I'm glad you weren't in those wrecks."

"Three times," she said grimly. "Three cars, totaled."

"And the drivers weren't—"

"Insured? Nope. Not a one of them," she said.

He waited patiently for her to go on.

"They were my ex-boyfriends," she explained, twisting her fingers together. "I've had some real winners, in my time."

"Three cars." His voice was neutral. "Three different boyfriends. Wow, sweetheart, what are the odds? That's some karma."

"It sure is. So I take the bus," she concluded. "The ironic thing is, I'm a really careful driver. I've never even gotten a parking violation."

"Is it just that they were bad drivers?" he asked.

"Oh no. They were just plain bad. My taste in men has always gotten me into trouble."

"Yikes. Looks like we're about to end up smack in the middle of one of those conversations I was hoping to avoid."

She shook her head. "I'm not trying to push your buttons. I can't tell you how many times I loaned them money, or bailed them out of jail, or provided alibis, or whatever. Time after time, using my credit cards, forging my checks, wrecking my cars, God knows what else."

"I see," he said, turning onto her street. "So that's why."

"Yeah, I guess it is," she admitted.

He glanced at her. Her face was tight, fingers white from the leather strap wrapped around them. Like she was bracing herself.

"What did your folks think of all these bad boyfriends?" he asked.

She shook her head. "I don't have any folks."

He was incredulous. "No one?"

Abby looked away without answering. A stark silence followed.

He thought of Fiona. How suspicious he'd been of the guys who'd trailed after her ever since she was twelve, and too cute for her own good. He even pulled that crap on Mom, and she was pushing sixty. No one who didn't deserve the precious women in his family would get within a hundred feet of them if he had anything to say.

No folks. It sounded so bleak. His family drove him crazy, but he couldn't imagine the world without them. The aching loneliness he felt for her made his throat tighten. "Just one thing I want to know."

She flinched. "What's that?"

"If you've got these bad news ex-boyfriends, how do you sleep at night with those cheap, garbage locks on your door?"

Abby's eyes widened. "I . . . but I don't—"

"Let me put in some decent locks. I'll waive the fee, just charge you for the hardware. Good locks are the least of what you need."

"Why would you do me any favors?" she asked guardedly.

"I don't know," he admitted. "It just comes to me, baby."

"I'm not a baby," she whispered. "I don't need to be looked after."

He parked outside her apartment and slid his hand around the back of her neck. "It sounds like you could use some looking after."

She turned away, sniffing. "Thanks, Zan. It's a sweet offer. I really appreciate the thought." Her voice had a telltale quaver.

"Is that a yes?" he demanded.

She fished a tissue out of her bag and dabbed her nose. He wished he could read her mind. Or his own. He couldn't tell if this sweet, protective routine was just a clever ploy to coax her into bed, or if he was just lying down and begging her to walk over him with cleats.

Or some perverse combination of both.

"This weekend, then," he said. "Saturday. You're off Saturday?"

Her laugh sounded wet and tearful. "God, you're like a pit bull."

"I'm not going to let this go," he said. "I want you to have new locks. How about Sunday? You'll be home for sure on Sunday, right?"

She stared down at her twisted fingers.

He'd been formulating his proposition all afternoon, refining it, practicing the delivery. He was shooting for seductive and masterful, since she seemed to go for that. He couldn't wait to cut out the mental masturbation, get her clothes off, and start with the orgasms. A few of those and they could discuss the situation more rationally.

"Are you going to ask me in for coffee, Abby?" he asked quietly.

She shook her hair back. "Yes, Zan. I am."

"Pass me those photos," Neale said.

Lucien handed over the photos of Elaine to Neale, privately marveling at how homely the man was. As a rule, Lucien surrounded himself only with attractive employees, male or female. Henly and Ruiz both fit that requirement nicely: Henly with his thick, Teutonic good looks; Ruiz with his sinuous, muscular body, black hair, flashing dark eyes.

Henly and Ruiz were just brute muscle, though. Good with guns and knives, but both lacked Neale's technical and computer skills. It was worth putting up with the man's puffy, froglike appearance.

Neale squinted at the pictures with professional disdain. "Chick looks like shit in these."

"Of course," Lucien said. "ID and passport photos always do."

Neale set to work trimming them. "What did the Boyle on the Butt of Humanity have to say at the afternoon rendezvous?"

Lucien took in a deep drag on his cigarette and remembered Neale's other big drawback. He liked to chat.

"No surprises," he said. "Just that he's incompetent. A sob story about how he can't get his pet fall guy into place fast enough."

Neale glanced up sharply. "Will that be a problem?"

Lucien shook his head. "Boyle is his own fall guy. He's the only one who doesn't know it. If he incriminates more people along the way, that's fine with me. You didn't think I was going to leave an idiot like that breathing to testify against us, did you?"

Neale blinked. "It did seem kinda weird."

Lucien blew out a lungful of smoke. After a minute, he noticed that Neale was just sitting there staring at him. "What's the problem?"

"Just, ah, wondering if you're gonna waste me, too."

"No," Lucien said. "Your death would serve no purpose. Unless you plan on fucking me over. And you're not going to do that, are you?"

"Oh no," Neale said hastily. "No way. Why would I do that?"

"Why, indeed?" Lucien said silkily. "So put your mind at ease, Neale. Get back to work." He waited for Neale to recommence working.

Neale cleared his throat. "Makes me nervous when you watch."

"Cope," Lucien said.

Neale was silent for almost three blessed minutes, printing out the license templates and transparencies before he started up again.

"Thought you had a date with little Miss Please-Don't-Hate-Me-Because-I-Am-Beautiful," he said.

Lucien exhaled a lungful of smoke before replying. "She can wait."

Neale's chuckle was unpleasantly oily. "Yeah. That bitch would beg, roll over, and walk on her hands if you told her to."

Lucien did not bother to negate the man's more or less accurate impression. "It's tedious," he said, in a distant voice.

"I wouldn't mind," Neale said dreamily. "Telling them pussies what to do and then having them just do it. No back talk. Mmm. Makes me sweat, just thinking about it."

Lucien grimaced. "Please don't sweat when you're near me."

Neale chuckled appreciatively, and examined his handiwork. "I don't like the way this came out," he complained. "The font on the security pattern is too big. Looks stupid as hell."

Lucien glanced at it. "It's fine. It doesn't have to be perfect. No one will ever present this license as an ID. It's just a prop."

"Oh. Well, I'm a perfectionist, you know. I like to do good work."

"Of course you do," Lucien soothed. "You're a skilled professional. That's why I always call you."

Neale was mollified. He worked for a few minutes before starting the annoying chatter again. "Elaine doesn't strike me as the brightest bulb, either. Is she going into the shredder at the end of this gig, too?"

"You ask too many questions," Lucien said.

"Yeah, I know. Is she?"

Lucien's cool, inscrutable smile was his answer.

"Ah." Neale chewed on his fleshy lower lip. "I was wondering . . ."

Lucien sighed inwardly. "Yes?"

"Since you're gonna waste her anyhow, I wondered if me and Henly and Ruiz could, uh . . . you know. Seems a shame, to toss it all away without sampling the goods. Waste not, want not. I got that from my thrifty grandma Bergen. Cheapest old bitch who ever lived."

Lucien stared at him, expressionless. Coils of smoke rose from the cigarette in his fingers, wreathing him in an eerie, moving cloud.

"I mean, don't worry about it if it's a problem," Neale added quickly. "I just meant, for bonus perks, for hazard pay, or—"

"I'm sorry, Neale," Lucien said gently. "I don't know if that will be logistically possible. Timing, and all that. We'll see how things go."

Neale let out a resigned sigh. "Thought it wouldn't hurt to ask."

Lucien's cell phone rang. The display informed him that it was Elaine. So it was not in the cards that he was to have a moment's peace this evening. He heaved a sigh and hit TALK. "My love," he crooned.

"Mark?" Elaine's voice trembled, as always. He'd begun to find it intensely irritating. "I have to t-t-tell you something."

The stutter put him on his guard. "What's the matter?"

"I've come to a decision," she whispered.

He was startled. He hadn't thought her capable of an actual decision. "You make it sound as if it's a matter of life and death."

"It feels like that," Elaine said. "I'm afraid that I . . . oh God, this is hard. These weeks have been amazing. But I have to, um . . . end it."

Genuine surprise left him wordless. He thought fast, redistributing resources, rescheduling his evening.

"Mark?" Her voice was tremulous again. "Are you OK?"

"No." His voice was a toneless rasp. Pain, torment, anger. He knew how these scenes were supposed to go.

"I'm so sorry, Mark," she whispered.

"You told me you loved me." Betrayal, shock, horror, he manufactured them all on the spot. "You lied to me?"

"God, no! I meant it! It's not that. It's just that we're, ah . . . not right for each other. The things you want from me, ah, they're too—"

"If you want me to change, I'll change." Fervor roughened his voice. "Give me another chance. You can't do this. I won't accept it."

Hitching sobs came through the phone line. "I'm so sorry, Mark."

She didn't get it. "I won't accept it," he repeated. "Are you home?"

"Yes, but I don't want to—"

"I'll come over. We'll discuss this in person. It's cowardly to dump me on the phone after everything we've been to each other."

"Mark, I . . . I know everything."

He was stunned into silence once again. "Excuse me?" he said. "Know what? What the hell are you talking about, my love?"

"Your fake identity." The words came out in a little sobbing rush. "I had a background check done. I know."

He blew out a silent breath as he stubbed out the cigarette. This was the closest thing to alarm that he'd ever felt. "I'll be right over."

He hung up and stared at his reflection in the window. The wavy hair, the beard, it had to go. "Change of plans," he said. "We're getting out of this house. Don't leave so much as an eyelash. Henly?"

Henly grunted from the couch. "Yeah?"

"Get the clippers. You have to cut my hair, and then clean it up. Carefully. Vacuum the house. Clean the bathroom after my shower."

"I ain't a hairdresser or a cleaning lady," Henly grumbled.

Lucien gave him a thin smile. Henly scrambled hastily to his feet. Neale held out the IDs. "Want to check these before I pack up?"

"Destroy them." Lucien stripped off his shirt. "Change of plans."

Neale stared at him, his mouth a slack, heavy O. "Already? Aw, what a waste." He stared down at the ID card. "Just as well, though. Don't like these photos. Poor little bitch looks like a fuckin' corpse."

Lucien snickered as he shook his hair loose. "Fancy that."

Chapter

9

Zan stared at Abby's legs as he followed her up the stairs. Sheer brown hose with seams up the backs. He'd never cared much about stockings before, but tonight the detail struck him as intensely erotic.

"Don't stare," she said.

She hadn't even turned to check. "How do you know I was—"

"Don't bother to deny it," she said.

"OK," he agreed easily. "I don't deny it."

She unlocked her door and flipped on the light. His mind went blank, staring at the fine, creamy silk blouse. The way it crumpled around the curve of her waist where it was tucked into her skirt.

He struggled to remember his clever plan of action.

She threw up her hands. "Yeah, I know, I know!"

"Huh?" He was bewildered. "Know what?"

"Yes, I do own a jacket! One of them even matches this skirt. But I was running late this morning. So don't get on my case about it."

"I wasn't thinking about your jacket," he said.

"Oh." She looked away, embarrassed. "Well, you're always bugging me about my clothes, so . . . I'll just make that coffee, then."

He looked at her feet. Black, spiky-heeled, pointy-toed fuck-me pumps. "You sprinted for the bus in those shoes?"

"There's a technique to it," she murmured. "Your choices are French roast, Kona, Ethiopian, or Italian espresso. I also have decaf."

He tried not to laugh. "You know me well enough not to ask me questions like that. Choose for me. Be the expert. Dazzle me."

Abby's eyes narrowed. "Do not patronize me, Zan Duncan."

Sheba padded daintily into the room and promptly leaped into his lap. Zan buried his hands in her fur, grateful for something to occupy them. Sheba's small body vibrated with throaty purrs.

Abby scooped some coffee into a fancy little glass pot and sat down at the kitchen table across for him. She crossed her legs and arms so tightly, she looked as if she were tying herself in a knot.

"So," she said. "You wanted to talk. This is your chance."

She was so tense. He wished he could make her laugh, but he wasn't up to being a clown tonight. He placed the cat gently on the floor and stroked her arched back as she glared at him indignantly.

"You're a great little kitty, but we've got to finish this cuddle session later," he told the cat gently. "I promise, I'll make it up to you."

Prrt. Sheba stalked out of the kitchen, unmollified.

He took a deep breath and reached across the table, holding out his hand. Abby looked at it. "Take my hand," he urged softly.

"What are you going to do with it?"

"I'm going to hold it," he said.

She stared at his hand for a long moment, and unwound one of her arms from across her chest. She held it hesitantly out to him.

He seized her hand. It was cool and slender, trembling as he closed his fingers around it. He stroked the network of violet veins at her wrist with his forefinger. "I have a proposition to make," he said.

"Oh dear. Here we go." She tugged her hand. He wouldn't let go.

"Hear me out," he said. "I know you've ruled me out as a potential boyfriend, so never mind that. I'm suggesting something different."

Her eyes went big with alarm. "I don't think I even want to know."

He reached out with his other hand to touch the deepening rose of her cheek. So amazingly soft and fine. "Yes, you do," he said simply.

She dragged in a hitching, broken gasp as he ran his finger across the gleaming curve of her lower lip in the wake of her pink tongue. Then the upper one. He could do it forever. Rosy and moist and inviting.

"Something's happening between us," he said. "It's very strong. It won't go away just because it's inconvenient for you."

He felt her breath quicken, warm against his wrist. "I don't want to complicate my life," she said, sounding lost. "I'm trying so hard."

"I don't want to complicate it either," he said smoothly. "The arrangement I have in mind is extremely simple."

She turned her face away and put her free hand up to touch her hot cheeks. "I see where this is going."

"Yeah. I know you do," he said. "You've been thinking about it as much as I have. I want to be your secret lover, Abby."

She tugged her hand away from his and wound it around her middle again. "That doesn't sound simple. That sounds complicated."

"Nothing simpler," he said. "I'll be your boy toy. I'll come to your bed at night, when no one's watching. Just play with me, Abby. Toss me away when you're done. I'm very tough. I won't get my feelings hurt."

She stared at him. "But that's ridiculous. I can't do that."

"Why not?" He captured her hand again. "It's the perfect setup. Private, secret. Nobody knows about it, nobody has opinions, or makes judgments, or asks questions."

She closed her mouth, frowning slightly as she considered it.

"Nobody has any expectations," he went on. "Least of all me. You don't have to introduce me to your friends, or tell me when you'll be home from work. You don't have to calculate me when you're making dinner plans. You don't have to buy me a birthday present. Simple."

"But I don't—"

"It doesn't have to interfere with your hunt for the perfect husband, either. When it's over, it's over. It'll be like it never happened."

The teakettle's low warble rose quickly to a shrill wail, but Abby seemed frozen in place. He moved to deal with it himself, and she jolted to her feet as if waking from a dream, lunging for the kettle. Boiling water splashed onto her hand. She dropped the kettle with a gasp.

Zan sprang up and took her hand, examining the red spot. He turned the cold water on and held her hand beneath the stream. "Now would be the proper time to announce that I have a clean bill of health," he said evenly. "No STDs, ever. Always had safe sex. Just so you know."

"Ah . . . me too," she said distractedly. "I haven't . . . I haven't been with anyone in a really long time."

"How's the hand, baby?" he asked gently. "Need some ice?"

"It's OK," she whispered. "Don't worry about it."

He kissed her wet hand. "So? What do you think of my idea?"

She pulled her hand away and dabbed it on a tea towel. "Wouldn't it make you feel used?" Her voice was small.

He breathed down the burst of startled laughter that shook him before it could make him jittery and emotional. He had to stay icy cool for this to work. "Sure. So? What's your point?"

"You don't mind that? Because I would, if I were you."

"Hey, it's your average guy's ultimate fantasy," he said. "Having a gorgeous, classy woman use him for sex. Squeeze me dry, baby."

"You're not an average guy," she said.

"No, I'm not," he admitted. "Let me show you just exactly how far from average I actually am."

"And you didn't answer my question, either. If you felt used, you'd get angry with me. I think that you're just pretending to—"

"Hold it," he said curtly. "One of the perks of being a secret lover is that you're exempt from this kind of cross-examination about emotions. That kind of stuff is for boyfriends, fiancés, husbands."

She winced. "Ouch. I didn't mean to cross-examine you."

Back off, bonehead. Lashing out wasn't going to earn him points.

This was tricky. He wanted to please her, and he wanted to punish her for putting him into a box. He wanted to strip her bare, to get so deep inside her mind that he could exploit all her secret desires. He wanted her in thrall to pleasure. He wanted total power over her.

Wow. Yeah, it would appear that he was angry at her.

"I didn't mean to snarl at you," he ventured. "It's just that there are some things you just can't ask of me if we want this to work."

She turned away. "I'm not sure if I want it to work. Not if it means giving up any kind of emotional interchange."

He was helpless to deny it. "You can't have it both ways."

"Then I'd better not have it at all. Not if it means keeping my mouth shut and letting you just . . . fuck me." She got up, walked to the window, and stared at the darkness. "Thanks, Zan. But no thanks."

He struggled to express it in some way that didn't sound offensive. "No. I didn't mean that. I just meant . . . we have to keep it light. Lengthy discussions about our feelings would kill it."

"Huh. I don't feel very light right now," she said bitterly. "But oops, look at me. Already breaking the rules by mentioning my feelings."

He made a frustrated gesture. "That's not what I meant, Abby. I just want us to stay in the moment."

"And have sex," she said.

"Yeah," he agreed. She gave him a look, and he threw up his hands. "OK, then. Wild, crazy, awesome sex. The best you've ever had."

She snorted. "Oh, for God's sake. You are such a guy."

"Not much I can do about that." He walked to the window and stood behind her, stroking her shoulders. The fine silk snagged against the hard spots on his hands. Time to wrest control back from the bad-tempered beast and try the seductive and masterful routine again.

He nuzzled his nose into her hair. "Picture this. A day in the life of a woman with a secret lover. She goes about her day like always, work, lunch, shopping, friends. But she has a secret—her lover comes to her at night. He knows she's awake, no matter how late it is. She's so eager, she's already naked and wet, thinking about other times, other nights."

"My goodness. You think a lot of your own ability, don't you?" The words were tart, but her voice had a telltale quiver.

He circled her waist, gripping that deep curve over her hips. "He knows it, though," he went on. "He can smell that sexy woman scent. She's so ready, she's about to come just from thinking about his touch."

She exhaled a shuddering breath. He let his hands slide over her hips. "He covers her, warming her body with his." He kissed her throat, skimming teeth across the delicate tendons. "His cock is as hard as steel. Dripping, just from thinking about doing his duty. And then . . ."

He let his voice trail off. Abby twisted around and gave him an accusing look. "And then? Don't tease."

"I wouldn't," he promised.

"So?" She prodded him with her elbow. "What does he do?"

"Whatever she needs," he said simply.

She elbowed him. "You can do better than that."

"Oh, that's just a beginning." He rucked up her skirt until his fingers found velvety skin above the edge of her hose. "It depends on her. If she needs him to be gentle, rocking and sliding inside her until she melts into hot liquid, he's all for it. If she needs to be mounted from behind and ridden long and hard, that's great."

"Oh, God," she whispered. "This is crazy."

"But you like it, hmm?" His fingers found the perfect warm under-curve of her bottom, and explored it. So smooth, so round.

"Sure, I do, but . . . this is a fab fantasy, Zan, and it's really turning me on, but it's as unrealistic as hell."

He smiled against her hair. "Yeah? What makes you think so?"

She covered his hands with her own. "What about you?"

Her nipples were so tight, tickling his palms through her bra, her blouse. He felt dizzy. "What about me?" he muttered. "I'm in heaven."

"No, I mean, what about your feelings, your moods? What if you're tired, or pissy, or sad? How can you guarantee—"

"Shhh," he murmured, cutting her off. "Let me worry about my moods. They're not relevant. Not in this scenario."

"I don't think so," she said. "I don't think it's possible to—"

"Believe me, it is." He placed her hands on the windowsill.

She swiveled to stare at him. "What are you going to do?"

"Shhh," he soothed. "I'm going to finish telling you about a day in the life, and you have to concentrate so you can really get it."

She made a sound between a giggle and a sob. "Oh, I'm getting it."

"Good," he said. "Open your legs. Just a little bit."

"This is making me nervous," she murmured.

"It's also making you hot." He nudged her foot. She made a soft, uncertain sound as she widened her stance for him. He slid his hands under her skirt and lifted it up. Lace-trimmed sheer white panties showed off more than half of her rosy buttocks. He stared at her for several moments, hands trembling, before he dared to speak.

"Where were we?" he began again, stroking her curves. "Oh yeah. If she needs every inch of her body licked before he makes love to her, great. If she needs him to dominate her, he'll rise to the occasion. If she feels like being pleasured by her love slave, he's got a long, strong tongue and he knows how to use it. If she needs him to push her to the edge of reality, he'll do it. There's no limits. No end to the pleasure."

She jerked and whimpered as he ran a fingertip across the shadowy cleft between her buttocks, then fluttered it delicately along the humid seam of her labia through the sheer panties. The faint, glancing touch made her responsive body vibrate in his grasp.

"The one thing that she can count on always being the same is that he won't get tired, and he won't get bored," he said. "Whatever she wants, that's the grand prize. Making Abby come . . . and come . . . and come." He circled his other hand around her from the front. She gasped and wiggled as he cupped her mound, exploring the damp, springy softness of the curls against the lace. "Wow. Just feel you. All wet."

She shook with helpless, breathless giggles. "Ah, yeah. Duh."

Her laughter choked off as he peeled her panties down, tugging them over the sleek length of her legs. He lifted one foot out, leaving the panties to cling to the other ankle like a frivolous lace garter.

"Every morning, the only clue she'll have that he was there is the mess. Sheets crumpled; love bites on her breasts, her thighs. His scent, all over her. That's how she'll know he's not just a figment of her imagination." He teased a finger into the warm, moist tangle of curls from the front and coaxed her tender folds open, seeking the damp, slick warmth inside. "Oh, Abby. You're so incredibly sweet and soft."

"You're putting a spell on me," she accused him.

"She'll think about him all day, squeezing her legs around that hot, turned-on ache, thinking about her yummy secret," he went on. "She'll lose sleep, and it'll be a big distraction from her job, but she's a very skilled professional. No one will notice."

He thrust a finger into her body, and followed all the subtle cues: her shivering, her hips pressing back against him. He caught her clit tenderly between two fingers. It was like picking a lock, the expanded awareness taking over his brain that allowed him to visualize the inner workings of a lock mechanism. With Abby, it was different. Deeper, hotter, a sensing of heat and energy. An instinct of where and how to press, to squeeze, how hard, how fast. The mix of her hot, rich perfumes intoxicated him. He let two fingers delve into her, insisting.

Almost there . . . and yes. There she went. Gorgeous. She cried out, and he almost came in his pants then and there, imagining how it would feel when the sucking pull of her sex was clamped around his cock, not his fingers. Her legs around his hips. Her arms around his neck. The two of them, fused. This was fucking madness. He'd just given the woman permission to dump him when she got bored with him. He'd be an idiot to start seeing stars now, but his hands were too busy exploring the cloudlike softness of her body to worry about it; his lips too busy discovering all the various textures of her skin, her hair. Her chest heaved, her hair dangled over her face.

"So what'll it be, Abby?" He pulled open his belt, unbuttoned his jeans. His cock sprang out, desperate for action. "What's your fantasy?"

She dragged in a long, shuddering breath and shook her head.

"You want me right here? In your bedroom? Shower, table, floor, rug, couch, whips and chains, whatever, baby. I'm about to explode."

Abby turned and shook her hair back off her face, lips curling in a dreamy smile. She lifted her skirt, just high enough to reveal the puff of dark ringlets on her mound. "It would be fun to make you explode."

"Don't jerk me around." He grabbed her shoulders and pushed her back against the kitchen wall, harder than he meant to. "Tell me."

She cupped his face with both hands. "I want *your* fantasy."

He was too turned on to puzzle out what the hell she wanted from him. "So you want to be gobbled up by the big bad wolf? I'll fuck you right here up against the wall, if that's what—"

"No, goddamnit!" She shoved him. "I want *you* tonight. Get me? Not some fake fantasy gigolo who vanishes into smoke. *You.*"

His arms dropped to his sides. He stared at her, at a loss. He sensed danger. The kind that could rip him apart. He licked his lips. "That's not the deal," he said carefully. "That's not how it works."

"That's how *I* work," she said.

His hands shook. He'd never felt so charged every touch and glance alive with secret meaning. *Get over it.* He was a toy for her. A fantasy fuck. He was getting dragged under.

He clung to his anger like a lifeline.

She reached out and pulled him closer to her, running her hands greedily over his chest, over his belly. She gripped his cock. "That's how *I* work," she whispered again. "Give it to me, Zan."

"That's not fair." He shook his head. "You ask a lot, Abby."

"I give a lot, too." She flipped off the light. Light filtered in from outside: streetlamps and the eerie, shifting shadows of car headlights. Just enough light to see shapes in the velvety darkness, the delicate oval of her face, the shadowy pools of her eyes. He was intensely aware of the complex perfumes of her body, her hair. Her sex, on his hands.

She sank down in front of him and took his cock in her hands. His face went hot. He felt fevered, blushing like a boy as she caressed his aching shaft with soft, cool hands. Her warm breath was a caress in itself; so was the wafting brush of her hair, swirling around his

thighs, soft as a silk scarf. The touch of her lips, teasing, stroking—
the wet flick of her flirtatious tongue around the head of his cock,
and then, oh. God. *Yes*. She sucked him deep inside, into the scalding vortex of her mouth.

Suckle and swirl, glide and pull. The room dipped and swung
like a reckless carousel. He gripped her hair. "This is not . . ." He
swallowed to control the wobbly rasp. "I wanted to go down on you
first."

"Too bad," she said. "Too late."

She ignored his clutching hands and resumed driving him into a
frenzy. It was too good. The explosion was already gathering force.
He stopped her, cupping her face. "I want to be inside you when I
come."

"I want to make you come right now, like this," she told him.

He gazed into the perilous shadows of her eyes. She stared back,
unabashed, swirling her tongue around the head of his cock.

The intimate silence was ripped apart by the phone's shrill ring.

They froze. One loud, buzzing ring went by, then another.
Another. He touched her cheek. "Do you need to—"

"No way. Not in a million years. The machine can get it."

The answering machine clicked. They waited, frozen with renewed shyness while her own cheerful outgoing message played
out. *Click*.

"Abby?" It was a woman's voice, high and quavering. "It's Elaine.
Abby, are you home? Please, please pick up if you are, because
I'm—"

The rest of her soft, anxious words were covered by Abby's
smothered exclamation. "Oh God! I forgot all about Elaine." She almost stumbled over her feet lunging for the phone. "Elaine? Are
you OK?"

"Oh, thank God you're home."

The machine kept recording their conversation. This crisis was
going to break the mood for sure, so Zan shoved his dick back into
his jeans. It was an uncomfortable fit. He slid down the wall onto the
floor, dropped his head into his hands, and listened.

"What's happened?" Abby asked sharply. "Did you talk to Mark?"

"Yes," Elaine whispered.

"And? Did you tell him where he could stick it? Did you tell him to go to hell? Did you tell him what your detective told you?"

"I told him I knew, and that we were through. But it didn't take."

"Didn't take?" Abby's voice rose, in pitch and volume. "What do you mean, didn't take? It's not something that takes. It is, or it isn't!"

"I know, but he just wouldn't accept it," Elaine quavered.

"Did he bully you? That son of a bitch. He did, right?"

"He's coming over." Elaine's voice broke. "I don't know how strong I can be if he's right in front of me. He makes me feel so stupid, and I—"

"Hang on. I'm coming right over," Abby said.

Zan reached up and flipped the kitchen light on. Abby cast him a quick, apologetic look. He lifted his shoulders, tried to smile.

"No, it's OK." Elaine said. "Nobody can do this for me. I'll call you after, and we'll celebrate then. I just needed to hear a friendly voice. And I wanted someone to know what was happening, in case . . ."

Abby and Zan both waited for the rest of that trailing sentence.

"In case what?" Abby burst out. "Elaine, talk to me! Do you actually think that you're in danger?"

Elaine hesitated for a long moment. "Oh, of course not," she murmured. "That's absurd. There's no reason for him to . . . no. Not at all. Don't worry. Oh God, that's him at the door. I'll call you back."

"Don't let him in," Abby pleaded. "At least wait till I get there!"

"I gave him keys, remember? I can't keep him out. Wish me luck."

"Elaine, stop!"

The connection broke. Abby slammed down the phone, yanked it up again, dialed. She slammed it again. "It's on voice mail. *Damn* it."

She tried to button her blouse, but her fingers were trembling. Zan got to his feet and buttoned it for her. "Your friend's in trouble?"

"Man trouble. She had him investigated and found out he's using a false name. Probably everything he told her about himself is a huge lie." Abby gave him a nervous, pleading glance as she dialed. "Look, I'm sorry to run out on you," she began. "But this is an emergency, and I—"

"You need to go be with your friend," he said. "Of course."

"I can't let him push her around." Her voice shook. "Elaine's fragile. This guy scares her. Hell, he scares me, and I'm tough. I have to call a goddamn car service because I don't have a goddamn car, and I'm really sorry, I don't mean to be rude, but you're going to have to—"

"I'll take you," he said.

The phone clattered into its cradle as she looked up, eyes hopeful. "Oh God," she said softly. "Would you?"

"Put your panties on," he said. "Let's go."

Chapter

10

Lucien shut the car door and looked around the exclusive neighborhood. The perfume of wet grass tickled his nose pleasantly. The breeze felt chilly on his shorn head. He ran his hand over it. Too severe. It would take weeks before he got the look he liked, but he was grateful to be rid of the blond waves. He preferred things to be tidy.

That was why he was here, after all. To tidy things up.

He'd thought of everything. He'd scrubbed himself until he was raw. His clothes were new, worn for the first time tonight. His rubber-soled shoes had been splashed in a puddle and wiped to remove any stray carpet fibers from house or car. Leather gloves and a plastic raincoat completed his ensemble. He'd drawn the line at a hair net.

He stood at the bottom of the porch, carefully wiping off his shoes, then walked up and fitted Elaine's keys into the lock.

Elaine stood in the hallway, phone in hand. He wondered how he ever could have found her attractive. She looked like a sickly, terrified mouse, right down to the pinkish nose, twitching with nervous fear.

He pulled the door shut. She shuffled backward. "Who were you talking to?" he asked.

"Abby," she blurted, backing into the dining room. "I told her everything. She's coming over right now. You'd better go."

His last doubts evaporated. Shame that he had to hurry, in case her friend really was coming over. He preferred to take his time.

Her eyes were glazed with fear. She was more perceptive than he'd given her credit for. "You . . . you c-c-cut your hair," she faltered.

"I'm a new man," he said soulfully. "Hoping for a new chance."

Elaine stumbled back a step. "N-n-n-no. I d-don't think so."

A bag lay on the dining room table. A coil of rope stuck out of it, still in its packaging. "Is this the rope I asked you to buy?" he asked.

She turned a strange color, like an eggplant. "Um, no. I mean, yes, but I've decided that I don't like those kind of games."

He hefted it, checked the length, assessed the thickness of the cord. "But you consented. I could be forgiven for being confused."

"It's not the sex," she burst out. "It's what the detective told me."

"Detective?" He looked wounded. "You had me investigated?"

"My family is wealthy. Whenever I get involved with someone, I have him checked out. It's common sense, nothing personal."

"So you never trusted me." He felt genuinely hurt.

"You're a fine one to talk! You lied to me from the beginning! Who are you really, Mark? And what the hell do you want from me?"

He picked up the rope, letting the plastic shopping bag drift to the floor. For a moment, he was tempted to tell her the truth, just for the entertainment value. Time was pressing, though. He took a step closer.

"Nothing at all," he said, with complete honesty. "Not anymore."

She could retreat no farther. She was backed up against the dining room table, trapped. Her mouth began to quiver and blur. "Mark, I've got to ask you to just please, please go. I don't want you here."

He ripped the package of rope open with one wrench of his black-gloved hands. "Just a kiss?" he crooned, pinning her against the edge of the dining room table. "A good-bye kiss?"

She shook her head frantically, eyes darting from the rope in his hands to his face and back. "D-d-don't," she stuttered.

He uncoiled a short length of rope, stretched it out taut between his hands, and brought it down behind her head so she was trapped in the loop. "Tell me you love me," he ordered her.

She began to wiggle like an eel, eyes dilated with terror. "Mark . . . I can't do this. I can't. I don't like to play with—"

"Tell me you love me," he insisted. "Were you lying before?"

"No," she whispered. A tremor racked her body.

"No? Then why not tell me?" he coaxed. "One last time?"

She swallowed repeatedly, eyes squeezed shut. "I . . . I love you," she said, in a broken whisper.

There they were, the magic words he was waiting for. The wave was cresting, the moment of no return.

Lucien licked his lips and smiled. She finally realized. Her eyes went huge, but before she could inhale to scream, the wave broke.

He wrenched her around so her back was to him, looped the rope around her neck, and jerked upward with a violent surge of brute force.

Snap. Her neck broke.

He held her directly under the chandelier, turning himself into a makeshift gallows. His muscles vibrated with superhuman strength while life left her body. It rushed through him, like a flock of invisible birds. A storm of roaring noise inside his head. He fed on it as he held her high, like a trophy. He felt so strong, so savage. Hungry and fierce.

Then it was gone, the tension broken.

Ah. That had been good. One of the best he'd ever had.

He let his arms relax and let her crumple to the floor, legs splayed, mouth slack. He was careful to position her so that her bladder and bowels would continue to void right beneath the chandelier.

Lucien rose to his feet, feeling refreshed. He wiped his gloved hands on his pants and studied the chandelier, calculating lengths.

Then he shoved the table back, uncoiled the rest of the rope, and got briskly to work.

* * *

Abby pressed her feet against the floor of the van as if there were accelerator pedals beneath them and jammed her fists against her mouth. Zan kept his mouth shut and drove fast, taking shortcuts she never knew existed. She'd been braced to deal with surliness, but Zan wasn't surly. He was helpful and concerned. Very classy of him.

"Turn left onto Margolies Drive," she directed.

There was no unfamiliar car parked in Elaine's driveway. Just Elaine's gold Renault. Lights blazed in the windows. Abby leaped out of the van and ran across the lawn, heels ripping the wet turf. She leaned on the buzzer, beat the door with her fists. "Elaine! Are you in there?"

No response. Every second that passed, the silence got more ominous. Zan walked up the steps. "Calm down," he said gently.

"How?" she demanded. "How can I? Her lights are on. Her car's here. Mark was walking up to her door with her house keys in his pocket exactly"—she checked her watch—"sixteen minutes ago. She knew I was coming over. Why would she not answer?"

Zan shook his head.

Abby dragged her cell phone out of her purse and dialed 911.

The dispatcher answered. "Hello? I'm Abby Maitland," she blurted. "I'm outside a friend's house at 1800 Margolies Drive. I think she's in trouble inside. I have reason to believe her boyfriend might have hurt her. Could you send somebody? Yes, of course I'll remain at the scene . . . hurry. I'm really scared . . . yes. Thank you."

She turned back to the door. It stared back, like a flat, dour face.

Zan sank down to his knees, penlight clutched between his teeth, unrolling a leather envelope. He picked out his tools and set to work.

"Is that illegal?" she asked.

He slanted her a quick, ironic glance. "Of course it is," he said, around the flashlight. "You'd rather wait for the cops?"

"God, no," she said quickly. "Please continue. And thanks."

"Don't thank me," he said. "I have a really bad feeling too."

A couple of minutes, and the lock snicked open. Zan pushed open the door. The silence oozed out, wrapping around her. Abby propelled herself into the house. Zan grabbed her arm. She turned to see what he wanted. He was holding out his hand.

Tears welled into her eyes at the gesture. She took his hand and clung to it. They crept into the house together.

The place felt empty, in spite of the lights. Cold sweat trickled down her back as she peered through the arch that led to the living room. The huge grandfather clock ticked with stolid regularity.

"Elaine?" she called up the staircase. "Elaine!"

No answer, but she was no longer expecting one. The door to the dining room was ajar. The silence resolved into a faint, rhythmic sound.

Creak-creak. Creak-creak.

Then the smell registered, faint and bad and very out of place.

Zan's hand tightened around hers. "Abby, wait," he warned.

Too late. She'd barely touched the door, but it yawned open as if flung wide by a ghostly butler. The chandelier dazzled her for an instant, and all she noticed was disarray: the gleaming table shoved up to the wall, a chair knocked over, a plastic bag on the floor.

Zan gasped, and yanked her back against himself.

Elaine hung from the chandelier, head lolling at an impossible angle. *Creak-creak, creak-creak,* the rope squeaked at slow, deliberate intervals as she swayed. Her jaw gaped. Her eyes were terribly empty.

Abby's heart imploded in her chest.

The interval of time that followed felt like a frantic nightmare. They sprang into action. Zan wrenched the table over beneath Elaine's dangling body, wood shrieking against wood, and leaped onto it. Abby kicked her shoes off and followed him, supporting Elaine's limp body while Zan sawed desperately at the rope with his pocketknife.

As if hurrying could help. They knew Elaine was beyond help; the empty eyes and the improbable angle of her head were proof of that.

Still, it was unbearable to see her like that.

Zan scooped up Elaine's body and passed the knife to her. "I'll hold her while you finish," he said. "The rope's about to go."

Abby sawed through the last few strands of nylon, and Elaine sagged into Zan's arms. He crouched, supporting her head, lowering her tenderly onto the tabletop. He checked for a pulse. Checked again.

He straightened her limbs gently and looked up. He held up his hand, helped Abby down off the table. Kept a tight hold on her hand.

They stared down at Elaine's inert body. Abby shoved her fist against her mouth so hard, she tasted blood.

Zan closed Elaine's eyes. "Her neck is broken. It was quick."

Abby squeezed her eyes shut. "We were supposed to get together and celebrate her liberation tonight." She took Elaine's hand. It was icy. Elaine's nails, usually precisely manicured, were bitten to the quick.

That painful detail was too much. Sounds started coming out of her. Rough, hurt animal sounds that she could not control.

Suddenly she was in Zan's arms, held too tight to breathe, wet face squished against his hard chest. She just hung on.

"Could you give us more to go on, Ms. Maitland?" Ken Cleland, the homicide detective, fiddled with his pen, a frown on his long, tired face. "A first name that's just an alias isn't going to get us far."

Abby placed her coffee mug on the desk, wrapped her arms across her middle, and leaned over them, trying to breathe into the cramp. "It's all she told me," she said. "It was a secret affair. She made me promise not to mention him to anybody. At least not until his divorce was final."

"Ah." Cleland tapped his pencil against his notebook, a habit that was starting to drive her nuts. "Well, that's helpful."

Abby did not appreciate his ironic tone. "Talk to the detective who did the background check," she said. "He's sure to have more details."

"And that detective's name is?"

Abby gritted her teeth. "I don't know."

Tappety tappety tap with the pen. "Ah," Cleland said. "I see."

"Her mother would know," she said. "Elaine said that they've done background checks on her boyfriends before."

"Very well. Good." Cleland made a note. *Tappety tap tap.* "And so. Anything else you remember? Anything at all?"

"Just that this guy is really good looking, and into bondage games," Abby said. "His number's on her cell. I saw it."

"If we ever find her phone, we'll look into it," Cleland said, with weighty professional patience. He turned to Zan and studied the bruises on his face. "You didn't know Elaine Clayborne personally?"

"Never met her," Zan said. "I was just giving Abby a ride."

"Keep in mind that breaking and entering is a crime."

"I'm aware of it," Zan said evenly.

"We're not going to give you a hard time about it, considering the circumstances," Cleland said. "I just had to say it."

"He was perfectly justified!" Abby's voice began to shake. "And he did it as a favor to me, so it's not his fault. Blame me, not him."

"We're not blaming anyone." Cleland's voice was weary. "It's just that it's against the law, and therefore to be avoided."

"I understand." Zan gave him a bland smile. "I don't plan on doing this again any time soon."

Cleland stared at him, recognition dawning on his face. "Wait a minute," he said. "Aren't you Chris Duncan's brother?"

Zan nodded, resigned.

"So you're the one who crashed that fight rehearsal last night?"

"That would be me," Zan said stoically. "The town clown."

Cleland grunted. "The son of one cop, and brother of another? You should have known better than to contaminate the scene like that."

Zan looked down at the floor. "I know," he said. "I'm sorry. We didn't think. We just had to make sure that it was too late to help her."

"Hmm." Cleland turned to Abby. "So you must be the one who called in the murder and riot on the wharf yesterday. You're famous."

Abby swallowed over the angry lump burning in her throat. "How nice. And this is relevant exactly, uh, why?"

Cleland attempted not to smile. "Not many can say they called in two separate homicides, two nights in a row. That's got to be a record."

"I'm so glad it amuses you," Abby said icily. "Personally, I would have *so* preferred to spend both evenings differently."

"I'm sure you would have," Cleland murmured. "Well, that's about all. We've taken your prints for comparison, so you folks can go home now. Thanks for your help. Try and get some rest."

A thread of panic stirred inside Abby. Things were slipping in the wrong direction. "You will look for Mark?" she urged. "He's the killer, Detective. He was walking in the door when I was on the phone with Elaine. Listen to the message on my machine, if you don't believe me."

"We'll check out every angle," Cleland said. "The evidence techs are doing their job." He handed them business cards. "Call if you think of anything else. Go on home now."

Zan took Abby's elbow and tugged her up onto her feet. "Come on, sweetheart," he said gently. "Let's go home."

The van was deathly silent as Zan drove Abby home. He tried to think of something comforting to say, but in the face of such bleak, horrible tragedy, everything felt weak and trite and stupid.

He felt hollow and shaking himself. The last time he'd seen a dead body was that horrible night eighteen years ago.

Before that, it had been Dad. Laid out in his best blue suit.

The experience did not improve upon repetition. He felt like shit, and he hadn't even known that poor girl. He knew how Abby felt. He remembered it all too well. He hadn't been able to breathe for weeks.

He glanced over at her. "Are you OK?" he ventured. Weak, trite, stupid, it didn't matter. He had to say something.

She turned those big desolate eyes on him and shook her head. She wasn't OK. Big fucking surprise.

He pulled over in front of her apartment, and they sat in the dark while he pummeled his useless brain for something he could do to help. "Have you got someone who can stay with you tonight? A girlfriend?"

Her face crumpled. "Elaine was my best girlfriend."

He winced. "Oh, shit. Abby. Baby. Please, don't."

"She was so sweet, Zan. So gentle. She didn't deserve that."

"No. I'm sure she didn't." He pulled her into his arms.

She hid her face against his shoulder. "I'm going to hunt this Mark down and rub him out of existence," she said, her voice muffled.

That didn't strike him as either a safe or a practical idea, but now was not the time for lectures. "Of course," he murmured. "You do that."

He nuzzled her hair and contemplated his next move. He still didn't have an answer to his question, and he was afraid to ask again while she was crying. "I'll walk you up."

She mopped at her eyes and nodded, groping for the door handle, missing it, groping again. He reached across her and released it for her.

"Sorry," she muttered. "My hands are just so shaky."

"Mine too," he admitted.

She grabbed his hand and held it. Her fingers were cold, but her grip was strong. "It is not either shaking. You seem as solid as a rock."

"Seem being the operative word," he confessed.

She lifted his hand to her lips and pressed her face against it.

The heat that flared along his raw nerves was laced with guilt. This was no time to think about sex, but Abby's lips were so warm. His body surged into instant, painful readiness. There was no reasoning with a guy's dick. No sense of timing, no class, no conscience. No clue.

"Would a glass of brandy help?" she asked.

He floundered, having lost the thread. "Help what?"

"The shaking," she said.

Warning bells jangled, but still he curled his fingers around her hand, kissed it. He rubbed it against his cheek. Worshipping something beautiful was the only thing that could let him breathe again.

"It might," he said hoarsely.

He followed her up into her apartment. This time she left the kitchen dark and went straight into her living room, turning on one small, red-shaded lamp. She pulled a bottle of brandy out of a cabinet, poured some into two snifters she took from a rack hanging above it.

She handed one to him, and he stared into it, mesmerized by the amber liquid in the bulb of glass. He thought of the glasses in his cupboard at home. Mismatched juice glasses, decorated with cartoon characters. It had never occurred to him to buy glasses specific to a particular beverage. Stuff tasted the same, no matter what you drank it out of. Milk, beer, orange juice, Coke, a glass was just a way station on the path from bottle to gullet. One he often skipped.

The brandy expanded in his nose, burning a line down into his torso to meet with the fire in his groin. He wondered if little details like brandy snifters actually mattered. Could be. Anything important to Abby must matter. She could convince him that the sky was green, that the sun rose in the west. She could take him so far from himself, he might not even recognize himself when she was done with him.

And she would be done with him. That was the kicker. He knew how this would play. The sex would burn them alive, and then she would feel guilty and ashamed. She would hate herself for doing it, and she would hate him too, for having taken advantage of the situation.

And that would hurt. That would really suck the big one.

The plan had been so clear before Elaine's phone call. So simple. A light, sexy game he could play while keeping his feelings armored.

They were in a parallel universe now. The events of this night had stripped his armor away and left him naked and shivering, with a big target painted on his chest.

Abby sipped her brandy. "Cleland wasn't taking me seriously."

He shrugged uncomfortably. He'd gotten the same impression.

"I saw it, after that crack about the riot. I lost all credibility. I'm just a crazy girl who makes up far-fetched stories. Ha ha, very funny."

"Cop humor," he offered. "They see awful stuff like this a lot more than we do. They do whatever they have to do to cope."

She gave him a narrow look. "Oh, yeah?"

"Yeah," he said. "My dad was like that. My brother is, too."

She shrugged, looking so vulnerable, it hurt to think of leaving her alone. He tossed back the last of the brandy, took a deep breath, and tried his burning question once again. "Have you got someone you can call to come be with you tonight, Abby? You shouldn't be alone."

She shook her head. "No," she said. "No parents, brothers, sisters, aunts or uncles or grandparents. I had good friends back in Atlanta, but I've only been in Silver Fork for three years. It takes decades to make the kind of friends you can call at four in the morning. Elaine is it—" She stopped, swallowed hard. "Was, I mean. Elaine was it, for me."

"Oh." He fumbled for words, but there was nothing to say.

She pried his empty glass from his hand and flicked a button on the stereo. Music began to play, a throbbing pulse of bass and percussions, the plaintive wail of a soprano sax. She set his empty glass next to hers on the shelf and put her hands on his shoulders. "How about you, Zan? Could I call you at four in the morning? Is it against the rules to call a fantasy secret lover, or do I have to await his whim?"

"It's not a game anymore, Abby." His voice shook with the strain of not reaching out and taking what she was offering him.

"I don't think it ever was." She leaned against him. He barely breathed, conscious as he was of the swell of her breasts, her fragrant hair tickling his nose. "I'm in deep space, Zan. Pull me back to earth."

Unwinding her slender arms from around his neck, pulling away from her lush heat, was the hardest thing he'd ever done. He held her at arm's length. "I can't," he said miserably. "I'm sorry."

She stiffened. "Oh. I . . . I see."

His fingers tightened. He felt desperate. "No, you don't."

She wrenched herself away. "Is it such a big turnoff, then?" Her voice trembled. "Me being so weepy and sad and needy?"

"No! I'm weepy and needy, too! I want this as much as you!"

"Then take it! God, Zan. Of all nights to play hard to get!"

"I'm not playing," he told her grimly. "You are dangerous, sweetheart. You would end up hating me for taking advantage of the way you feel tonight."

"That's not true!" she protested. "I know what I—"

"If you were my wife, or my girlfriend, we would already be in bed, comforting each other. Reminding each other that we're alive, and life's still good. But I'm not. I'm just . . . I'm just some guy that you . . ." He trailed off, swallowing hard. "I don't know what the fuck I am to you."

"You're the one I want tonight," she said. "Isn't that enough?"

"No," he snarled. "I don't know you well enough to guess how you'd feel in the morning. I swear, it's not for lack of wanting you." He glanced down at the bulge of his erection. "Take a look, if you doubt me. My sincerity is visible to the naked eye."

She made a wordless sound, then shook her hair out of her face and straightened her shoulders. The gesture looked so lonely and brave, it made the lump in his throat burn like a hot coal. "Go, then," she said.

"Abby," he tried again. "I'm sorry that I—"

"Please don't." She held up a hand. "I understand. You're trying to do the right thing. That's admirable. So do it and go."

He stumbled backward toward the door. "Yeah. I'm, uh, gone."

Abby's face contracted. "I'm sorry. I didn't mean to sound harsh. You don't deserve that. Thanks for driving me there, for letting me in, for . . . for cutting her down. For all of it. You really stood by me tonight. I don't know what I would have done if I'd had to face that alone."

"You don't have to thank me," he said thickly.

She shook her head. "You've been nothing but good to me tonight," she whispered. "I won't torture you anymore. Go home."

"Damn it, Abby. You're the one who—" He stopped himself. *Who shoved me into this box.* She didn't need to be lectured or scolded.

She covered her face with both hands. "Go away, Zan," she whispered. "Please. Don't make me beg."

He felt like a cruel, clumsy jerk, but what could he say to her? Sleep well? Take it easy? Later, babe?

He slapped the door open and ran down her steps on legs that shook. He leaped into the van, peeled out onto the road, laid down hard on the gas as if he were escaping from something. But he wasn't escaping. The feelings kept building up: the relentless fist squeezing his throat, the queasy rolling sensation in his gut, the sense of impending disaster. There was no running from them. They kept pace with him.

The mellow buzz of the brandy had transformed into a burning pain in his chest. His face was clammy, his hands ice cold, the street in front of his headlights wavering dangerously. He usually just swept unwanted feelings under a rug, but there wasn't room under the rug for this. Not after seeing that poor girl dangling from a fucking chandelier.

He barely pulled over in time. He hung out the door, clinging to the handle, and retched into the gutter. Just dry heaves, after the brandy. There was nothing else to come up. The steak sandwich he'd eaten for lunch was long since burned into energy, the energy long since spent. The painful, jerking convulsions didn't stop. It took him a few stupid, confused, soggy minutes to realize that he was crying.

Oh, God. He hated this. He wasn't even sure what he was crying for, old stuff or new. It was all the same goddamn thing. Sitting helpless on the street in the dark, holding the hand of a dying man. Blood draining into the gutter. Babbling anything that came into his head that might be comforting, just in case the guy could hear him.

Like anyone could hear with a hole that big torn into his skull.

And just in case he wasn't feeling bad enough, suddenly he was looking down into Dad's coffin, hearing cheesy electronic organ music playing in the background, choking on the sickly smell of lilies. Dad's waxen face, his sunken eyes. The hole in his chest plugged with mortician's putty.

He wore the red silk tie Zan had gotten him for his birthday. It was the color of arterial blood. The bullet hole lay just beneath it. Right through the heart. The shot that had killed him instantly.

The way Elaine's rope had killed her.

Now he got to add this girl and her chandelier to his gallery of death images. Like he needed another one to round out his collection.

It was such a sad, stupid waste. Christ, he didn't even know that poor girl, but he couldn't stop shaking. Just as well Abby couldn't see him. This would shoot his seductive yet masterful mystique all to shit.

He sat there with his hands over his face for a half hour before he dared to drive. He wanted to run back to Abby, but not to comfort her. He wanted the comfort for himself. He ached for it; to lose himself in her body, to hang on tight and feel how strong and vibrant and alive she was. Those long, lovely limbs, wrapped tight around him.

Holding him together, so he wouldn't fly apart into space.

Chapter

11

Abby lifted the golden Agnus Dei reliquary carefully out of the crate with her white-gloved hands, shaking off the nest of shredded paper. As exhausted, burned out, and sad as she was, the object made her gasp with awe. It was in the form of a golden book with St. John the Baptist depicted on the cover, encrusted with precious gems. Inside were wax pellets made from paschal candles and consecrated oil.

She'd just finished writing status reports on a set of stunning silver-gilt tableware designed to grace the table of the aristocratic ship's officers on the doomed galleon. Before that, she'd been unpacking gold and silver coins, minted in Spain, Portugal, and all over the New World.

Elaine could have waxed eloquent for hours about the history and significance of each object. She would have gone crazy for this stuff.

The thought made Abby's insides clench. Elaine had designed this exhibit: the lighting, the wall text, the order. Studying notes written in her fussy cursive script made Abby's throat ache constantly.

Abby rubbed her brow with her sleeve so as not to soil the white cotton gloves. Uncrating an installation was time-consuming and laborious work, and she had no curatorial skills to speak of. She was pure administration. But Nancy, the museum curator, needed all the help she could get with Elaine gone, so here Abby was.

"Hey, Abby. You're going to have a slice of that pizza we ordered, aren't you?" Dovey asked. "You haven't eaten for twelve hours."

Abby tried to smile into Dovey's anxious face, though just the thought of pizza made her stomach curl up and try to hide. "I have to do the status report on this reliquary. Then I'll have a piece, I promise."

Bridget swept into the room and looked Abby over with a critical eye. "You should eat," she lectured. "You're as white as a sheet. You cannot permit yourself the luxury of collapsing, you know."

Abby blinked. "I haven't permitted myself any luxuries at all lately, Bridget," she said. "You've changed. Are you leaving?"

Bridget tugged at the blazer of her elegant suit. "Dinner at the Inn on the Wharf with some of the ladies on the Museum Board. Work, work, work," she said, sounding put upon. "It never ends."

Abby and Dovey exchanged glances. Dovey fled the room, looking like he was about to swallow his tongue.

Bridget pulled out her compact and dabbed at her makeup. "I expect to see the exhibit uncrated and the condition reports done by morning," she announced. "We simply must pick up the pace, people."

Abby gave the pile of crates an assessing look. "No. Even if we all worked all night, we wouldn't get it all done tonight."

Bridget's eyes widened. "So? With the gala less than a week away, we're going to have to face a few all-nighters! I'm not at all impressed by your attitude, Abby! You're being self-indulgent. Moping about. Starving yourself. Snap out of it, for goodness' sake. You're not the only one upset by this unfortunate event."

"Upset?" Abby repeated, incredulous. She got to her feet and brushed paper shreds off her jeans. "*Unfortunate?*"

"Good heavens, yes." Bridget frowned as she retouched her lipstick. "Elaine's timing couldn't have been worse. Of all the ghastly times to pick, less than two weeks before the gala—"

"Timing? Are you nuts? She didn't 'time' this! She was murdered!"

Bridget's mouth twitched with distaste. "Must you be so dramatic?"

"News flash, Bridget," Abby said. "Murder is dramatic."

Bridget rolled her eyes. "Yes, we've all heard about Elaine's phantom lover, who no one ever heard of or laid eyes on, who walked through a locked door, forced her to hang herself, and then vanished without a trace. Please, Abby. It's so soap-opera-ish."

Abby's face turned bright red. "What are you implying?"

"Don't bellow." Bridget pulled a bottle of perfume out of her purse. "When the truth is in doubt, the obvious explanation is usually the right one. Not the complicated, improbable one."

"I wasn't aware that the truth was in doubt," Abby said, through clenched teeth. "The situation looked pretty obvious to me."

Bridget gave her a pitying look as she dabbed perfume on her throat. "Elaine was depressed and lonely, and it got the better of her. Very sad, but common enough. Nothing mysterious about it, I'm sorry to say." She dropped her perfume into her purse and snapped it closed. "Now I really must hurry." She ran her eyes over the heap of crates. "And I suggest you rethink your need to sleep tonight."

Bridget marched out. Abby stared after her, breathless with shock. It hadn't occurred to her that her story would not be believed.

She shook herself, walked over to one of the big windows, and leaned her hot forehead against the glass. There was just enough light left in the twilit evening to see the billowing mass of fog beyond the cliff.

What Bridget thought would not affect the big picture, Abby told herself bracingly. Bridget was stupid. Her opinion was unimportant. The truth would be revealed in due course. It had to be.

Abby closed her eyes. The image was burned so deeply into her mind. Elaine's lifeless body, swaying back and forth, her eyes empty.

"I thought I might find you here."

She gasped, and spun around at the sound of Zan's deep voice. She was flustered by a tangle of contradictory feelings: embarrassment and terror, and beneath it all, a shiver of secret delight.

Zan was clean-shaven, his hair was combed behind his ears. The elegant bone structure of his face was so striking with no beard stubble to obscure it. "What are you doing here?" she blurted.

"Looking for you," he said gravely. "Are you OK?"

She did not feel the slightest urge to tell polite social lies to Zan. "Nope," she said baldly. "Pretty awful, actually."

He looked pained. "I guess it was a dumb question."

"Not at all," she assured him hastily. "I appreciate the thought."

He scrutinized her with a deliberate intensity that made her squirm. Wishing she had something prettier on than the loose, low-rise jeans and the sloppy beige cotton sweater. Her messy braid, her wisps.

"You look good with no makeup," he said.

She hooted with laughter. "I look like death warmed over."

Zan shook his head. "You're too pale, yeah, but that's not it." He leaned closer. She could smell his aftershave. "Your skin sort of glows with nothing on it. I like the freckles, too. You look sweet. More . . ."

"Washed out?" she offered, as he hesitated.

He paused. "I was going to say vulnerable."

"Hmm," she said, dubious. "What's good about vulnerable?"

He brushed her cheek with the backs of his fingers. "If you have to ask, there's no point in telling you."

She tried to laugh. "How did you get in? The museum's not open."

"Your colleague, that chubby bald guy, let me in." He pushed a lock of hair behind her ear. "Sorry I didn't call. After the way things went the other night, I didn't feel in any position to comfort you."

"That's OK," she whispered. "I don't blame you."

"I do," he said. "I should have called."

"So why did you come here tonight?" she asked.

"You stood me up. You told me I could install some decent locks. I went to your apartment and waited. Then I figured I'd find you here."

She was startled. "Oh, wow. But that was a million years ago, Zan. I forgot all about it."

He looked hurt. "Aw. But I already fronted money for the parts."

She looked at the stack of crates, glanced at her watch, and rubbed her stinging eyes. "Maybe some other time."

"No." His voice was hard. "You need good locks, and you need them now. Not later, who knows when." He glanced at his watch. "It's already eleven thirty, for God's sake. You've been here since when?"

"About six this morning. But I—"

"I'm not going to sleep until you have locks on your door," he said. "Besides, it's raining, and buses don't run down Edgemont on Sunday. I'll give you a ride home, and install your locks now."

"But I have to help uncrate this exhibit," she protested.

"And I have to take care of Abby," he said quietly. "You're tired, baby. Get your purse. We're out of here."

It was high-handed of him. She should put him in his place.

She looked at the stack of crates with a sigh. She'd been there almost seventeen hours. She'd stayed till three thirty the night before.

Nancy and Dovey had both urged her to go home hours ago, but she'd been so afraid of the flat, sad silence at home. Work was better.

But Zan's coaxing smile was magnetic. Her toes were tingling.

"I'm not sure what I would be agreeing to, if I let you take me home," she said. "I'm a basket case, Zan. I don't want any surprises."

Zan lifted up one of her hands and rubbed it against his cheek. "Do you want me to promise to be a good boy?" he asked silkily.

Good in what sense? She let him rub her hand against his cheek, enjoying the thrill of uncertainty. "Your face is so smooth."

His smile went rueful. "Enjoy it while you can. I'll have stubble again in ten minutes." He kissed her fingertips. The raw, volatile man who had shoved her away, told her she was too dangerous, was gone.

Her lighthearted, flirtatious, seductive secret lover was back.

"So you've decided I'm not so dangerous after all?" she asked.

He stifled a laugh. "Oh, you're plenty dangerous, sweetheart," he said. "It took me days to work up my nerve."

"Oh." She was suspicious of the dancing glint in his eyes.

"So?" he said. "What do you say, Abby? Shall I promise to be a good boy? Or do you want to take your chances?"

She took a deep breath. "I . . . I guess I'll take my chances."

It wasn't working.

Lucien stubbed out his cigarette and flung himself back onto the bed. He stared up at the ceiling. Sheets of paper crinkled beneath him. His notes for the new plan. He swept them irritably to the floor.

Nothing he'd come up with so far seemed plausible. He might have to cut his losses and pin the whole thing on Matty Boyle, but that felt so flat. A junkie zero like Boyle didn't have the brains or the balls to execute a job like this, and the police were smart enough to figure that out for themselves. Besides, since Elaine's death, Boyle had begun to degenerate. He might not controllable for much longer.

The chime that indicated a cell call from an employee sounded. He glanced at the display and hit the decode button. "What is it, Ruiz?"

"Hey, boss. I'm tailing the locksmith. Thought you might want to know that he went to the museum and picked up that other chick, the tall one with the long hair and the pointy tits who worked with Elaine."

"Abby Maitland?" Lucien sat bolt upright in the bed.

"Yeah. I followed them to her place. They're up there now. Guess she needs consoling." Ruiz let out a short, ugly laugh. "Wish it was me."

"Stay on them," Lucien ordered. "I'll send Henly. Put a GPS tag on his van. I want to know where they are at all times."

"Hey, can I stick with Pointy Tits and let Henly have the—"

"Shut up and do as you're told." Lucien snapped the phone shut.

Unfamiliar emotions churned inside him as he imagined the locksmith "consoling" Abby Maitland. He pictured Abby whimpering in various acrobatic sexual positions while the locksmith pounded lustily into her beautiful body. Dirty slut. Just days after her best friend's death. How could she? He felt almost indignant. Aroused, as well.

He examined the emotion he was experiencing, and concluded it might be jealousy. Interesting, since it was accompanied by such an intense erection. He should arrange to be jealous more often.

He opened his pants and massaged his penis as he considered the scenario. Abby, seduced and then framed by her best friend's killer. The locksmith, betrayed and murdered by that greedy, naughty whore.

The locksmith was now fucking a woman that Lucien had decided that he wanted. Which made it so much more personal. More visceral and emotional, more juicy and *sexual*. It all made sense to him now.

Yes. Abby and the locksmith would be the key to the new setup, which meant he had to approach her quickly. No time to stage an elaborate series of chance meetings, as he'd done with Elaine.

If what Elaine had said was true, then money and status would be the way to get Abby into his clutches. Lucien punched up the cell phone number of Ludovic Hauer. He'd met that comical man some months ago in Boston. Hauer had been beating the pavement for corporate gifts, and it had fallen to Lucien to deal with him. It was his job to pass out money to all the grubby hands that were held out for it.

His heart thudded as the phone rang. His palms were actually moist. He'd never compromised his real, official identity before.

"Hello?" Ludovic Hauer responded. "Who is this?"

"Mr. Hauer? This is Lucien Haverton, of the Haverton White Foundation. We met at the foundation headquarters in Boston some months ago. Your development manager, Abby Maitland, had submitted a grant proposal to fund education and public programming to accompany the 'Pirates' Hoard' exhibit . . . do you recall?"

"Oh! Of course!" Hauer sounded puzzled. "What can I do for you?"

"I'm sorry to bother you on a Sunday evening, but I was passing through your area by chance, and I thought you might be pleased to know that the foundation has awarded the grant. One hundred and twenty-five thousand dollars."

"Oh!" Hauer floundered. "Ah . . . ah, this isn't one of my friends playing a practical joke on me, is it?"

Lucien chuckled amiably. "No, I assure you, I'm the genuine article. Would it be possible to meet with you and your staff on Monday?"

"Oh, God, yes!" Hauer gushed. "Oh, this is fantastic. Whenever you like! Would you prefer earlier, or later? Nine? Ten? What's more convenient for you?"

"Early is fine, as long as I don't inconvenience your staff," Lucien said genially. "I know it's a busy week for you all. I understand your fund-raising gala coincides with the opening of your new exhibit next week. I don't suppose there are still tickets available?"

"Oh, we would be ecstatic if you could attend! Oh my God, I can't wait to tell the others! You made my night! Thank you!"

"Perfect. I'll arrange it when I meet you all on Monday." Lucien chuckled again. "It will be up to you to introduce me to some attractive dancing partners, Mr. Hauer. Don't let me be a wallflower at the ball."

Hauer twittered with delighted laughter. "Oh, call me Dovey! I have the perfect girl in mind already! Gorgeous, intelligent, scintillating, elegant! You'll be dancing up a storm! Have no fear!"

"I won't," Lucien said silkily. "I can hardly wait. Till Monday, then."

A few more mindless pleasantries, and the thing was done. He was committed. He hung up the phone. Risky to use his own identity, but he had to bait the trap, and what better to bait it with than his own rich, cultured, extremely attractive self? On the plus side, he wouldn't have to slink around in fear of being recognized, as he had with Elaine.

He pulled out his phone and dialed another familiar number. "Hello, Lucy?" he said. "It's Mark. About that order that I canceled?"

Lucy paused, suspiciously. "You better not have changed your mind, Mark. That girl's already busy with another job."

"Oh no, this is for something else. I need a new girl. Long, straight auburn hair, five seven, a hundred thirty pounds, C-cup, brown eyes. I'll FedEx you photos tomorrow. I need her in three days."

"I'm not sure if I have anyone in my stable who would be a half-way decent match! I can't make promises without seeing the photos."

He sighed. "How much do you want, Lucy?"

"That's not the issue!" Lucy snapped. "I have standards to maintain. I can't do things half-assed. It's dangerous for us both."

He named a sum, triple what she'd originally charged him for the girl who had been in place to double for Elaine on the plane trip to Spain. Lucy made an impatient huffing sound. "Send me the goddamn photos," she snapped. "I'll tell you if this is doable when I get them."

Lucien hung up the phone. He had no doubt that Lucy would come through for him. He was one of her best-paying customers.

Abby was better for this drama than Elaine. With her checkered past, the arrest, the drug dealer ex-boyfriend, she was already compromised. Yes, Abby was a bad, bad girl. He found the thought stimulating. He resumed stroking himself, and his pace quickened. The swirl of images. Elaine. Abby. Gleaming gold. Streaming blood.

He spent himself, shuddering and gasping in a long, violent, marvelous climax.

Perfect. Take the gold . . . while he fucked them all.

Chapter

12

Abby felt jittery and shy when Zan pulled up and parked in front of her apartment. What had happened to Elaine sat between them, dark and hulking and heavy, killing all possibility of light conversation. She wanted so badly to feel something good. Zan was the only person on earth who could do that for her. That gave him so much power.

"Well?" he prompted. "Come on. Let's go do it."

She tried to smile when she let him into the apartment. "Coffee?"

He hoisted a bag onto the table. "I'd like the Kona, please."

She slanted him a narrow look. "Are you making fun of me?"

His dimple flickered. "Tiny bit."

She turned away before she could turn the color of a tomato, and grabbed the teakettle. "I'll just get to work on that coffee."

"Pick your color, so I can get to work." He pulled two boxes out and laid them on the table. "Your choices are brass or antique brass."

She peeked at them. "Regular brass looks fine."

He boxed up the other one. "I'll drill a hole in your door for the deadbolt, too. How long have you lived here with no deadbolt?"

"I've lived here for three years," she said. "My landlady is in her eighties. She's not much of a handyman."

He grunted, and crouched down in front of her door. Sheba leaped up and laid her front paws against him, purring ecstatically.

He scratched behind her ears. "Your cat is great, and I like her fine, but you'll have to get her out of my way for a while."

"Of course." Abby grabbed Sheba and carried her into the bedroom, hoping that the animal would not express her displeasure all over Abby's favorite shoes. Sheba took things like this so personally.

She stopped in the doorway and shamelessly ogled him while he worked. Those broad shoulders, tapering gracefully down to that lean waist. That taut, lovely ass made her want to grab and squeeze. The way the fleece pullover clung so lovingly to his deltoids, the way his faded jeans fit on his strong, muscular thighs. Ah. It was criminal.

She spooned the coffee into the French-press pot and poured boiling water over it. The leather jacket hung on a chair right in front of her. She suppressed the urge to lift it to her face and inhale.

He unscrewed her doorknob and took it apart, dumping pins and springs into his hand. His sleeves were pushed up, revealing muscular, ropy forearms. Dark hair lay sidewise and silky across them. Broad wrists. Long, graceful fingers. She wanted to memorize every detail.

She wanted to see what he looked like naked.

He turned, and caught her staring. "Everything OK?"

"Why wouldn't it be?" She pushed the plunger down on the coffee and poured him a cup. "Cream or sugar?"

"Black," he said. He reached for the cup. She shrank back.

"Calm down," he said. "You're not passing raw meat through the bars of a cage to a starving tiger, Abby. It's just me, Zan."

"Don't be ridiculous," Abby mumbled. "I'm just nervous."

He took the cup. Their fingers touched, and a tingle rippled up her arm and down her spine, fizzing through her whole body.

He took a cautious sip. "Whoa. Strong."

"That's how I like it," she said.

The dimple flickered in his cheek again. "I'll keep that in mind."

"Is it too strong? You sure you don't want cream or sugar?"

"I can take it strong," he assured her.

Were they still talking about coffee? God, what a cream puff dork she was, getting all goofy over a few smoldering glances. Her fingers tightened around the handle of her cup. Coffee splashed on the floor.

His eyebrow tilted up. "Easy does it."

Abby hurried to clean up the mess. They finished their coffee in a charged silence. Zan put his cup in the sink.

"I have to go out to the van to take your locks apart, pin them up to the new keyways," he said. "Then I'll cut your keys and brush them."

"OK." Abby rinsed his cup. She didn't trust herself to look at him.

"Want to come watch?" he asked.

She hesitated, tempted. Everything he did fascinated her. But that would be a stupid, fatuous thing to do. "I have things to do here."

"Suit yourself." He disappeared out the door.

Abby sagged over the sink, heart pounding. She grabbed the phone, turned off the ringer. She pulled her cell out of her purse and turned it off, too. She raced on rubbery legs to the bathroom.

She studied herself critically in the mirror as she stripped and pinned up her hair. She'd always wondered how it would be to have those dramatic shadows under her cheekbones, like a prima ballerina.

Well, she had them. Whoop-de-do. She'd looked better before.

Taking a shower made her feel terribly exposed, with Zan outside. Still, no way was she going to face an evening of . . . well, of whatever, with four days' worth of stubble on her legs. She tried to be quick, but she couldn't forgo the scented lotion, and she just had to tweeze those pesky hairs that blurred the line of her eyebrows.

She cast a longing look at her nail polish and makeup.

Nope. Too obvious. Too desperate. She had to shoot for casual. *Oh, done already? Gosh, that was quick . . . more coffee? Or should we just rip off our clothes and start with the crazed monkey sex right now?*

Control, she lectured herself. Keep it together. If she couldn't keep herself from having sex with him, the next best thing was to do it under controlled circumstances. An uncommitted fling. Secret, private. Break the tension, burst the bubble, lift the taboo.

Think about something other than poor Elaine and her rope.

She clenched her teeth at the stabbing pain that accompanied that thought. Zan was a fabulous diversion. A distraction of mythical proportions. She would relax, and indulge—and then, maybe, the crush would defuse and take its proper place in the grand scheme of her life.

Why not? She wasn't engaged, or involved with anyone. Her future husband would never need to know. In fact, there were a whole lot of things her future husband would never need to know.

She wrapped herself in a towel and scurried for the bedroom. Her lingerie collection was vast, and it took a cooler head than hers to make such a vital decision. She rummaged, flung, and discarded. Black and red, too slutty. Lime green or purple, too goofy. White, too virginal. Flowers, bows, polka dots, stripes, thongs, no and no and no. *Argh.*

There it was. The apricot stretch lace chemise and matching panties. She struggled into them. The chemise functioned like a bra, the stretchy fabric more or less containing her boobs, though she still jiggled and bounced. She dragged on the same jeans and baggy sweater as before, to conceal her wild attack of grooming.

He was waiting in the kitchen when she hurried in.

"Oh, dear. I'm sorry," she babbled. "Have you been waiting long?"

He looked her over. "A bit," he said. "Took a shower?"

Busted. "How'd you know?" she demanded.

He smiled. "There's a perfumed cloud coming from the hall. You look all rosy and moist, and you smell delicious."

She blushed furiously. "Sorry I made you wait."

"No trouble," he said. "Can I ask you something, Abby?"

He stood up and took a step closer. Her pulse leaped. "What?"

"My heart's racing like crazy," he said. "And I'm having a hard time breathing. Does your coffee usually have that effect?"

"I . . . I don't think that coffee is supposed to have that effect."

"Maybe it's the sweater," he suggested.

Abby shook with nervous giggles. "This thing? This is the most unsexy article of clothing that I own, Zan."

"You mean, you turned your whole wardrobe inside out just for me?" His grin turned wicked. "Babe. I'm touched." He handed her six shiny silver keys. "Here. I made you some spares. For your landlady."

Her hand closed over them. They were hot from his hand.

"Try them out," he urged.

Abby stepped outside and fit the keys into the new locks. They snicked open easily. Zan stood on the other side of the door. Smoldering at her. "Thanks," she said breathlessly. "What do I owe you?"

"Nothing," he said. "My treat."

"Don't be ridiculous." She hurried into the kitchen and grabbed her purse, rummaging for her checkbook. "I can't allow you to—"

"Don't start." He grabbed her, wrapping one arm around her belly and pressing her back against him. "If you write that check, you will hurt my feelings. Be gracious. Say, 'Thank you, Zan.'"

She opened and closed her mouth, helplessly. His warmth was so delicious and all-encompassing, it scattered her wits. "I . . . but I . . . but I never even paid you for the lockout, and it's not—"

"Thank you, Zan." His voice was steely. "Three little words."

She blew out a long breath. "OK," she whispered. "Thank you."

"That's better. You're welcome." He pressed his lips to her throat, kissed his way tenderly down the curve of her neck. His touch left an ecstasy of tingling goose bumps in its wake. "You want me."

His words were not a question. She nodded.

"Where do we stand?" he asked. "Same ground rules? Secret fling under cover of darkness? No past, no future, no strings, no regrets?"

She gave him another jerky little nod.

Zan's hands tightened on her arms. He spun her around to face him. "So what's tonight's fantasy? Place your order, sweetheart."

She gazed into his eyes. "I can't play sexy games with you tonight," she confessed. "I just need you. I need to feel good, Zan.

I've felt so bad ever since . . . oh, I know we're not supposed to talk about how we feel, but I can't seem to—"

His kiss cut off the rest of what she was going to say. It melted into a formless, wordless swirl. His kiss was a wild assault upon her senses. He wanted to devour her, and she wanted to be devoured.

She kissed him back with all the pent-up, aching hunger that she had denied for so long, devouring him in her turn. He bent her back over the kitchen counter, pushing her legs apart. The bulge at his crotch pressed against hers in a slow, sensual grind that brought her instantly to a state of wet, whimpering readiness. She dug her fingernails into his shoulder, gripped his butt.

Her feet touched the floor, but only for a moment. He tugged her swiftly down the hall into her dark bedroom, pushed her through the door before him, tossed her down onto her rumpled bed.

The light from the hall outside backlit him, turning him into a huge, forbidding shadow. She reached for him, but he whipped her arms up over her head and kissed her again, spreading her thighs and pressing his weight against the ache of longing between her legs. She sharpened her own rising pleasure with every desperate, writhing wiggle.

He lifted himself off and whipped off his shirt. She reached for the bedside lamp, but he grabbed her and flipped her onto her back again.

She protested. "Let me turn it on. I want to see you."

"Too bad." His voice was rough and breathless. "You said you wanted to feel good, right? This is all about feeling, Abby. Not seeing."

"But I—"

"Shhh." He undid the buttons of her jeans and peeled them and her panties off with one long swipe. He tossed the sweater up so it bunched under her chin, exposing her breasts, compressed in the tight, sheer stretch lace chemise. "Dear God," he muttered. "Look at you."

She swatted at him. The restless heat building inside her made her furious, prickly, and crazy. "This isn't fair. If I don't get to look, then neither do you, damn it," she snapped. "Don't tease me."

He pushed her legs open. "Try and stop me," he taunted as he slid down the length of her body. His hot breath tickled her thighs.

She broke out in shivery goose bumps. She was going to freak out, fall apart, go nuts. She fought him, swatting at his head. "Hey, not fair! No fancy foreplay. I'm out of my mind. I'm not in the mood for—"

"I don't care. You're wet and yummy. I want to taste your lube."

Nothing she did could stop him. She flailed and batted at his head and massive shoulders, she yanked on his hair, but he did as he pleased, held her effortlessly in place and put his mouth to her.

His tongue explored her slowly at first, sliding up and down the length of her exquisitely sensitive folds, then thrusting deep, lashing and lapping. He suckled her clit, fluttering his tongue against it with relentless skill. The delicious assault went on and on, until he finally thrust two fingers slowly inside her, pressing and squeezing just . . . so . . . and she wound her fingers into his hair and screamed as pleasure overtook her, pulsing and throbbing through her body.

Oh. So that's what it's all about, she thought, as she drifted back. Her eyes fluttered open. She licked her lips, tried to focus her eyes. She'd had orgasms before. Good ones, too. But never anything like this.

"Whoa," he whispered. "That was sweet."

"Yes," she whispered.

He jerked her body down so her bottom was hanging half off the mattress, folded her legs up, and unbuckled his belt. The sheen of sweat on his shoulders gleamed. She surged up onto her elbows, eager to see every detail, and reached out to him. "Let me turn on the light."

"No." He pushed her back down, jerking her chemise up over her breasts. He pulled a condom out of his pocket, ripped it open with his teeth, and sheathed himself one-handed. "I like it dark. It works for me."

"But I want to see you," she protested.

He swallowed her protest with a savage kiss and prodded the thick, blunt head of his penis against her slick folds, nudging himself inside. His face tasted like her. "Forget seeing. Just feel, Abby. Feel me."

Yeah. Right. Like she had any choice. She gasped, digging her fingers into his shoulders as he pushed himself slowly inside her.

Oh, wow. The man was huge, and it had been so very long.

She was just starting to think that with a little wiggling, she might accommodate at least some of him when his muscles bunched, and he rammed himself inside her. She sucked in a sharp, strangled breath.

He stopped, panting. "Damn. Did I hurt you?"

Overgrown lout. She sank her teeth into the thick muscles of his shoulders.

"Ow!" He jerked away, and pinned her with his hand over her throat. "You are a fucking hellcat! What was that about?"

She licked the salt tang of his sweat off her lips. "Get off me!"

"Too late." His voice was low, breathless, and unsteady. "I can't."

"That *hurt*!" She thrashed beneath him, trying to fling him off. It was like trying to move a steel girder. "You bastard!"

"I'm sorry. Stop fighting. I'll make it good," he insisted. "I'll fix it."

Being trapped infuriated her. "Yeah, right! Get *out* of me!"

"No." His voice was flat and obdurate. He shifted his weight, folding her so that her knees were shoved against her chest. He pulled himself partway out as he rolled his thumb tenderly around her clit.

She whimpered, as he surged, very slowly, back into her again. Circling, swirling, deep. Stirring her around. Out, and again. And again.

She flung herself back, head thrashing back and forth at the huge fullness sliding and pressing and rubbing, all around, teasing the sweet, shivery hot spots into a throbbing chaotic blush of pleasure.

"Move with me." His voice was pleading. "Let me make it right."

She stared up into the impenetrable shadows of his face, trying to breathe, but her lungs seemed to shake. She wrapped her arms around his neck, her legs around his waist. Dug her fingernails into his skin.

"Oh, God, yes," he muttered, gathering her tightly into his arms.

It got better with each sinuous stroke. Hotter, slicker, easier. Soon he was thrusting deep, swirling himself around all the pleasure points she knew of and waking up a lot more she'd never known were there. Working her into another shimmering molten eruption that came from some deep inner place that she had never known.

Chapter

13

"The next one's for me."
The words penetrated her sensual daze long after Zan had spoken them. She opened her eyes. Neither words nor tone sounded like a request for permission, but he didn't move until she nodded.

No more of those lazy, licking, calculated strokes swirling over her pleasure points. It got very intense, very fast. He held her down and belabored her with hard, frenzied, slamming thrusts. It felt wildly, scarily good. She'd never been much for rough sex before, but she was yelling, clawing; she was going to have bruises, but she didn't care.

He shouted hoarsely as his pleasure tore through him.

They lay there, flattened. It slowly occurred to Abby that she couldn't breathe. She pushed on Zan's chest. He rolled onto his side.

The rush of air into her lungs made her dizzy. She sat up, dazed. Her mind blank. Her body a throbbing mass of sensation. Glowing, sore. Zan rolled off the bed, took off the condom, walked out.

He was back a few moments later. "I'm sorry," he said.

She squinted at his silhouette, baffled. "What? Why is that?"

"I promised you a perfect sexual fantasy. And then I lost control."

She started to shake with laughter. "Oh God."

"What?" he growled. "What's so funny?"

She curled her knees up to her chest and hid her face, but it was too late. She was laughing too hard to stop, and then the laughter tipped over the top and became tears, and the tears swelled into the torrent she had not been able to cry since Elaine's death.

And then, a flash flood. Damn. Of all times to totally lose it.

Zan made a horrified sound. He climbed onto the bed and hugged her tight against his hot body. "Jesus, Abby! Was it that bad?"

She shook her head, still sobbing silently. She couldn't get her throat under control to reassure him. "No. It's not that. It's just . . ." She lifted her hands helplessly. "Everything. It's crashing down on me."

"Great." His voice was wry. "And I'm the wrecking ball?"

"No." She patted his hair, then smoothed it again because the thick, strong, silken texture of it felt so good. "Not you. You're great."

He hugged her harder, pressing his face against her shoulder.

"I'm sorry, too," she said. "I know I'm not supposed to get all intense about my feelings. It's against the rules—"

"Fuck the rules."

She blinked at his curt tone, startled. "Um . . . isn't it a bit early in the game to be saying that?"

"Fuck the game, too."

She wiped her tears away and studied him with renewed caution. "I'm, uh, not sure what you mean, Zan."

He flung himself onto his back, pulling her down on top of him. "We came up with those rules before all hell broke loose," he said. "Before the thing with Elaine. They feel fake and contrived to me now."

She lay limply on the solid expanse of his chest, breathing in his hot, salty scent as he kissed her fingertips. His lips were soft and warm.

"Let's leave all our baggage and our bullshit behind. At least for tonight," he pleaded. "Let's just take a break from it, for God's sake."

She felt like she was made out of cream custard when he kissed her like that. She wiggled on top of Zan's big body, wallowing in a flush of guilty happiness. She crossed her arms over her chest and propped her chin on them. "If we're suspending the rules, does that mean I get to turn on the light? Or are you too bashful?"

He flicked on the bedside lamp. The burgundy paisley silk lampshade cast a reddish glow. "I'm not bashful. Anything you want."

She regretted her request when the light revealed the mess she'd made of her bedroom. Zan looked at the lingerie draped, heaped, and flung on the bed, the nightstand, the vanity. He plucked a lace bustier off a bedpost. "Wow. Did a bomb go off in your underwear drawer?"

She hid her burning face against his chest. "I had a hard time deciding what to put on after my shower," she confessed.

His voice was careful. "No wonder I had to wait so long. It must have been a difficult decision. Did I compliment you on your choice?"

"Um, not yet," she said.

"Sit up, then. Let me get a good look at that thing."

He rearranged her so that she was sitting up, straddling his belly, and peeled the sweater up over her head. He stared at her, and sighed.

She felt intensely self-conscious. The sheer chemise shoved up over her nipples had the effect of making her feel twice as naked as if she were completely bare. Her breasts felt fuller, hotter, under the heat of his regard. As if he read the thought, he reached up and caressed them, and his touch sent lovely, ticklish shivers of wild delight that all culminated in a blooming heat between her legs. He cupped the lush underside with reverent hands. "Your body is incredible," he said.

"Thanks," she said bashfully. "Yours is pretty superdeluxe too. Although I still haven't really gotten a good look at you naked yet."

He jerked his chin at her, lifting his hands. "Be my guest."

She clambered off him. He put his arms behind his head and stretched. It took a conscious effort not to let her mouth drop open.

Everything about him was perfect. Lean, pantherlike angles and tough, ropy muscles. His body looked streamlined and lethally strong.

She trailed her hand down over his powerful chest, petting the sweep of silky black hair that trailed down the flat, hard belly.

His jeans were half off his hips. His penis jutted past his belly button. Wow. He was enormous. She'd felt him in her mouth, she'd felt him inside her, but seeing was believing. A twining network of purple veins were distended and ropy along the length of his shaft. The slit in the glans was weeping a gleaming pool of precome onto his belly. She touched the tip, swirling her fingertips in the liquid and exploring the grooves, the softness, the hardness, the heat of him with her slick hand.

He gasped and arched off the bed. "God, Abby."

"Wow. Look at that big boy," she murmured. "No wonder it hurt."

He winced. "Sorry. I should have taken it slower."

She squeezed him in her hand until she could feel his heartbeat. "Mercy. Do you buy your condoms in a novelty shop?"

He put his hand over hers, gasps of pleasure jerking out of his throat. "Stop it," he complained. "You make me feel malformed."

"Oops. So sensitive," she murmured.

He groaned under her swirling hand. "I'll say."

"I can't believe you're ready again," she said. "We just finished the most outrageous sex I've ever had in my life, what, ten minutes ago?"

"I want to do it all night long," he said. "I never want to stop."

"It's too soon," she told him. "I'm still shaking from the last time."

"Then stop petting my cock," he said. "Or the matter will be taken out of your hands. In approximately three seconds."

She pulled her hand away as if he had burned it.

Zan tucked his penis into his jeans and yanked an ivory lace corset out of the bedclothes. "Wow. It's straight out of a wet dream." He rubbed it against his face. "The virgin bride. Blushing and trembling."

"She better be, if she's about to be deflowered by that rude brute."

He sat up on his elbows, an odd, uncertain look on his face. "Is my brute so terribly rude, then?"

She hesitated. "He's a bit of a shock, at first," she said primly. "But he definitely improves upon acquaintance."

His eyes narrowed. "Huh. Well, my rude brute stands at the ready, whenever you want a second introduction." He plucked a satin thong from under his shoulder and rubbed it against his cheek. "While you recover, you can entertain me by modeling your lingerie collection."

She cackled. "Oh, please. Get real. Like I'm going to put my clean lingerie on after we . . . after you—"

"After I made you all juicy and wet?" He lunged for her, and she skittered back off the bed, giggling. "Leave the panties off," he said. "But put on the stockings and this one. Wow." He held up a flowered silk teddy. "Sensual, but not too far from innocence. Better yet . . . that one." He got up and snagged a burgundy velvet bustier trimmed with black lace off the vanity. He tossed it at her. "Sensual and light years away from innocence. Here." He flung a lace-trimmed stocking after it.

She tried not to laugh. "That? Oh, please. I'll look like a whore from a brothel in the Old West."

"Go for it. I love make-believe."

She started to giggle. "This is not to wear, Zan. This is to laugh at. My girlfriends in Atlanta got it for my going-away party. As a joke."

"I love your Atlanta girlfriends," he said. "I want to meet them. I promise the end result will be worth your trouble. Indulge me."

She looked up at him, still giggling. That dimple quivering in his lean cheek, those white teeth. God, it felt good to be silly again.

She didn't want to break the spell by being a wet blanket. If he wanted her to play clown in that silly saloon girl outfit, she would do it.

"Do you want to sit for this? Or lie down on the bed?" she asked.

He leaned against the wall and gave her a devilish grin. "I'm too restless. My jeans are too tight anyhow. I'd probably injure myself."

She let her gaze wander boldly down to the thick bulge at his crotch. "Give yourself some air, if it would make you more comfortable," she said. "You're the client in this fantasy brothel. This show's for you."

His grin flashed again. "If you say so." He unbuckled his pants. His penis sprang out, swaying heavily before him. He took himself in hand and squeezed his fist around the swollen bulb. His flushed penis gleamed as if it had been oiled. "Get to it. I'm drooling in anticipation."

She dragged her gaze away and examined the problematic garment. "This thing is complicated," she complained. "It's got hooks and laces, too. Plus, it's too small, and it's scratchy, and I can't breathe, and my boobs spill over the top."

His eyes gleamed with excitement. "You're breaking my heart."

"OK, OK," she grumbled. She peeled the stretchy apricot chemise over her head and threw it at him.

He caught it one-handed, never taking his eyes off her body. "Stop," he said. "Turn around," he said. "Very slowly."

She lifted her arms, spun like a jewelry-box ballerina. "Like this?"

"You are so fucking beautiful, Abby."

"Oh. Uh, thanks." Now would be the time to be vampy and mysterious, but the smile on her reddening face was distinctly goofy.

She struggled with snaps, laces, and frills of cheap, scratchy black lace with fingers that buzzed. It was as difficult as she had anticipated to get the thing onto her body. The sheer effort involved made her break out in a sweat. She struggled with the laces.

"You're going to have to help me with this part," she grumbled.

"I stand ready." He let go of his penis to salute her. It swayed and bounced.

She dissolved into silent giggles. "Stop making me laugh, Zan."

His face took on an expression of mock hurt. "I'm so sorry if my rude brute is so comical. There's nothing I can do about my uncontrollable lust. It's cruel to make fun of me."

"Um, yeah. Right. I'm so sure." She turned her back to him. "Pull those laces tight, please. And tie them for me."

He grabbed the laces, pulling them back so hard, she was yanked back, flat and breathless, against his hard belly. "Hold my cock between your thighs while I do it."

She sucked in a startled breath at the sudden change in tone. The hard club of his penis prodded the back of her legs. He nudged and slid his entire length snugly into the clasp of her thighs.

"You're so wet and warm," he muttered thickly. "Hold on, let me tuck myself up farther, so I'm touching your pussy lips . . . yeah. That's perfect. Now squeeze me tight." He grasped her hips and began to slide his penis back and forth. It rubbed tenderly against her labia. "Squeeze harder," he directed. "Don't worry about squeezing too tight. I like it. Sweet and hot and hugging me. Squeeze . . . yeah. That's great, baby."

The rough urgency of his voice; the delicious, slick caress of his penis brushing teasingly along the length of her labia but never penetrating, never giving pressure: it was sweet torture. He found the rhythm he liked, and she pulsed and squeezed, gasping for breath, and so hot and trembling with excitement, she could barely whimper.

But she couldn't quite get herself off. She strained for it, but never quite got there. It eluded her, and she sensed that he was doing it on purpose. The energy rose and fell, rose and fell. Higher each time. Driving her nuts. She reached down to touch herself.

"Please, Zan," she whispered. "Please."

"OK," he soothed. "Shhh. You're doing great. I've got you, Abby. Trust me. I'll take care of you."

And finally his hand slid down, into the damp curls, seized her clit tenderly between two long, sensitive fingers, and pressed. Tender, but firm, rubbing her right exactly where she needed him to.

"Squeeze harder, Abby," he encouraged her. "Right now. *Now.*"

That push, his touch, his words, unlocked the tension of all that desperate effort, and it erupted like a fountain deep inside her, sobbing and throbbing and spreading, wider, sweeter, softer. She sank, boneless, to her hands and knees, aftershocks fluttering through her.

Zan crouched behind her, pulling her onto her knees and nuzzling her neck. "You OK?" he murmured.

She nodded, and he pulled her to her feet, hands under her arms. He turned her to the wall and wrenched the laces of her corset tight.

"Good God, Zan," she protested. "I can't breathe at all!"

He tied them in a bow with a flourish. "There you go," he said with evident satisfaction. "Get on with the show, babe."

She was astonished. "But you just reduced me to jelly!"

"Too bad." He grinned wickedly. "I still haven't come yet. I won't for a while. It ain't over till it's over, and we've only just begun. So stop chattering and get the rest of your outfit on."

He reached out, tenderly arranging her boobs so that the bottom swell was held in the cups of the bustier, though her tight brown nipples peeked cheerfully out of the frill of black lace. "I'm the client in this fantasy brothel," he said. "What I say goes."

She blinked. "The Dominator strikes again?"

"Whatever works. I'm just following the path of all these hot, creamy, yelling and screaming and clawing multiple orgasms. I've counted three so far—just counting tonight, of course."

He leaned down to tongue her nipple while his hand slid up her thigh. "You like it when I make you come like that?"

She nodded, her voice too thick to speak.

"Then put your goddamn stockings on. Let me do my thing."

She gazed at him for a few seconds. "You're not playing this dominator game just to turn me on," she said slowly. "It turns you on, too, doesn't it? Like crazy. Admit it, you bossy, arrogant bastard."

"Ooh." He whistled. "Bull's-eye straight to the heart. OK, I admit it. Now that you've found me out, do I have to bend you over and fuck you into submission to get you put those stockings on?"

It took all her nerve to break eye contact with him. She stepped into the middle of the room, feeling like she stood in the middle of a stage. His eyes were the spotlight. Excitement pulsed heavily through her. She was so primed, just squeezing her legs together would get her off. It could also make her faint dead away. A fate she hoped to avoid.

She bent down, trying to be graceful, and picked the stocking off the floor. No way could she balance on one foot in her current jelly-legged condition, so she dragged out the stool that sat in front of her vanity. She perched on it and gave him an uncertain glance. "With this outfit, I should be wearing lots of slutty makeup," she said.

"I told you. I like you better without." The gleam of humor was gone from his face. His brow had a sheen of sweat, and his face was set in lines of tension. He was gripping his cock. "Take down your hair."

She plucked out the clip that held up her wispy, careless bun and unraveled her day-old braid. "If I'd known I'd be entertaining such a demanding, ah, client, in my boudoir tonight, I would have fixed it better," she said. "Blow-dryer, hot rollers, shine enhancer, the whole shebang." She unraveled the strands of the braid, arranging it over her shoulders. "It's fuzzy and kinky from being braided all day."

"It's fine, just like that," he said. "Perfect, in fact. I prefer it."

She perched on the stool, picking her foot up daintily, and worked the stocking onto her hands.

"Turn to face me," he said. "And spread your legs. I want to see everything. All those pretty long pink flower folds, opened up for me."

She scooted around and slowly parted her knees. Her face was tingling. She felt like they were swimming in a pool of hot honey.

He knelt in front of her, stroking himself. "Wider," he said.

She opened herself, lifting one leg up high to roll the stocking over her foot.

"Put that foot on my shoulder," he ordered.

She hesitated, and he seized her foot in his big, warm hand and pressed hot, hungry kisses against the sensitive, ticklish arch, making her shiver with giggles. Then laid it against the hard muscles of his shoulder. She felt his hot sweat through the delicate nylon fabric. He slid the tip of his finger between the folds of her cleft, swirling his finger up to circle the taut, engorged point of her clitoris. Around and around.

She flung her head back and moaned. He slid his hand lower, thrusting one finger deep inside her. Then two. Up to his knuckles, pulsing in and out while his thumb worked her clit. She stared down at his wet, gleaming fingers as they slid out of her, and back in.

She felt dizzy. Head whirling, hot and woozy. "I can't take this," she said faintly. "I'm falling apart. I'm going to pass out."

"You will take it," he said, thrusting deep again. "And you won't fall apart. You'll explode."

She flung her head back, wanting to flail and writhe, but she was trapped, poised on the stool with one leg up on his shoulder, stuck on the prong of his hand. Clutching his shoulders just to remember which way was up. Gravity seemed suspended. Every direction seemed like she would be falling, falling endlessly if she let go. "Oh, please, Zan."

"Put on the stocking, Abby."

His voice seemed to come from very far away. She flung her head back and slowly rolled the stocking over her thigh while the tension built again. She fumbled with the garter straps. Zan smoothly reached out and fastened them for her. His fingers glistened with her juice.

She looked around for the other stocking. Zan scanned the room for it. "Maybe it's on the bed."

"You mean I have to walk?" She tried to laugh, but there was no breath behind the sound. "I can't walk. I can hardly breathe."

He hoisted her up to her feet and tossed her facedown onto her bed. "Get up on your hands and knees," he said. "Arch your back, ass in the air. Look for that stocking. And take your time about it."

She hoisted herself onto her knees, trembling as his shadow fell over her and his hands fastened onto her hips, forcing her legs wider.

"Stop playing with me," she pleaded. "I'm ready, I'm primed, I'm all yours. Just make love to me. Any way you want. Just go ahead."

"Not yet. My job is to say when. Wow, look at this. Your cunt is shining. It's the most amazing pink, like an exotic tropical flower. I love how those hot pink and crimson bits pout out of it. I want to lick them and suck them all. Find that stocking, Abby."

"Oh God, you are so stubborn," she snapped.

He dragged his teeth across her buttock, nipped her till it stung, then licked the tingling spot. "I know. I'm terrible. Everyone says so."

Her arms wouldn't support her anymore. She crumpled down, face and chest to the bed, and rummaged through the heap of intimate wear until she found the black stocking. His fingers opened her, thrusting, delving. She crumpled the stocking in her hand, whimpering with each skillful stroke, and gasped, disoriented, as he rolled her over.

"You're so hot," he whispered. "And your eyes, God. Your pupils are huge. Midnight forever. So sweet. I am going to melt you down."

"You already have," she said.

He lifted up her leg, sinking to his knees, and helped her slowly roll the stocking on, pull it up, hook the straps.

They looked at each other for a long, wordless moment. A muscle twitched in his jaw.

"What do you want from me?" she asked.

"Everything," he said.

He stood up. His penis bobbed in her face. The tip dripped with need. He didn't have to say what he wanted, because she wanted it, too. She slid off the bed to her knees, drunk and floating. Reached for him.

She took him eagerly into her mouth, making love to him with lips and tongue and all the passionate intensity he'd unleashed in her. Her emotions were in a tangle of anger and excitement. She was desperate for the release that he gave her. Furious at his controlling arrogance.

She wanted to bring him to his knees.

She clenched her trembling thighs together, poised right on the edge of another orgasm even while she pleasured him. He was making harsh sobbing noises. She wanted to make him scream and thrash, to come in her mouth and collapse limp and defeated in her arms. She felt his balls tighten, the skin go taut and salty. She sensed the violent pulsations of his muscles, the gasping sounds of pleasure—but he didn't ejaculate.

He wound his fingers into her hair and pulled her away. "Wait."

She almost wept with frustration. "For what? Dear God, Zan, give over already! Let go! Why won't you let yourself come?"

"Not yet." He pulled her up and tossed her up on the bed again, then lifted both legs and folded them high, so she tumbled onto her back. He plucked the condom from the nightstand and rolled it over himself. "Inside you." He thrust heavily inside her.

It was still a snug fit, but she was glowing with pleasure, and his entry was the delicious final detail that completed her delight. With every rhythmic surge and drag, it got better, lashing lovely wave upon wave of squirming hot pleasure through her. She wound her legs around him, digging her nails into his buttocks, meeting each thrust with her own and dragging him deeper. Demanding everything he had.

Triumph exploded inside her chest as he finally lost his iron grip on himself. He gathered her into his arms, and his powerful body hammered into hers with savage ferocity. She felt lithe and feral, dazzled by the strength and reckless courage her passion gave her.

She could hold a raging storm in her arms and call it her own. She was strong enough, brave enough. It was hers. He was hers.

He exploded with a guttural shout. His hips pumped and heaved against her, shoving her up the bed until she was scrunched right up next to the headboard. He collapsed across her body, gasping for air.

Minutes later, he lifted his head. "I didn't make you come again."

He sounded so forlorn, she burst out laughing, as much as she could with his weight pinning her chest to the bed. "As a matter of fact, you didn't," she said lazily. "Shame on you, you selfish bastard."

"No, really," he said dolefully. "I ruined the whole vibe. All that intense, complicated buildup, and then whoosh, I just blew it."

She wrapped her arms and legs around him and squeezed. "You did not blow it, you idiot. But if you really feel like you can do better, you can always try again."

His head lifted instantly. "Really?"

"Not now," she amended. "I'm exhausted, so I hope you have nothing more to prove tonight."

"You do have a whole lot of lingerie," he pointed out.

She slanted a cautious look at him. "Yes. And?"

"It's going to be quite a job, working though all of it. Playing out completely different fantasies for each outfit, of course."

"Oh, of course," she murmured.

"That is to say, we shouldn't wait around too long to get started again," he added, after a studied pause.

She melted into giggles. They sprawled together on the tangle of lingerie, limp and blissful. Zan raised his head again. "I'm starving."

"I'll make a deal with you," she said. "If you unlace this thing and run me a bath, I'll make you a sandwich and pour you a glass of wine."

"Deal," he said, sliding limply down the length of her body and jolting onto his knees to the floor. "Two sandwiches? Please?"

"OK. Ham and cheese on sourdough?"

"Heaven," he said.

She made sandwiches naked. It felt so intimate. She knew she shouldn't be so toe-curlingly happy, it was stupid, but she couldn't help it. She was bouncing, humming, touching her aching, tingling self with wondering hands. Astonished that her own familiar body could contain that much pleasure. Her chest felt so full, she could hardly breathe.

She came into the bathroom balancing a bottle of wine, glasses and a plate heaped with sandwiches and fruit. Zan sat stark naked on the edge of the tub, which was filled with perfumed white bubbles. He'd left the lights off, and lit all of the candles she kept in the bathroom.

"Ah. How lovely," she said. "Thank you. You really went all out."

"We're switching gears, after the Old West brothel fantasy," he said. "Now you're the pampered queen of the universe and I'm your adoring sex slave. I stand ready to peel you grapes, and lather you up, and clean all those little hard-to-reach places with my tongue."

She set the plate down and handed him a glass of wine. "That sounds like hungry work," she commented. "Want a sandwich first?"

"Good God, yes." He grabbed one and tore into it as she wound her hair up. She stepped into the tub and sank down with a sigh.

He frowned. "Aren't you going to eat?"

"I think I might," she said thoughtfully. "I haven't been able to eat ever since Elaine . . . since the other night. It's like there's a brick wall where my stomach used to be. But it seems to be gone."

He knelt down by the tub and held a half sandwich up to her. "Have a bite, then," he said. "You should eat."

She smiled and accepted it. His pampering made something go soft and fluttery in her chest. He peeled oranges and hand-fed her, putting juicy chunks into her mouth. Then he peeled her grapes. How sweet. Not that she'd ever particularly minded eating the skins, but it was a lovely thought. She took a sip of her wine and made a gesture of invitation. "Want to get in here with me? There's room. It's a big tub."

"Hell, yeah." He got into the bathtub and leaned back facing her. His bulk raised the floating bubbles to Himalayan proportions. He arranged himself, twining his legs with hers. The fragrant steam, the sweet bubbles, the water, the soft flickering gleam of the candles refracting through their glasses of pale white wine, the pop and drip and gentle slosh of water created a hot, sensual cocoon of intimacy.

Abby studied the lines and angles of his face as he leaned his head back against the tub. His dark hair clung to the white porcelain. The position revealed all the sensual curves of his Celtic cross tattoo.

She ached with curiosity, but they weren't supposed to ask questions. No past, no future, those were the rules. The words popped out anyway. "Does your tattoo have some specific meaning?"

He ran his hand across his neck. "Oh yeah. This is a relic of my wild youth. I got it when I was twenty-three. It's a memorial for my dad."

Her smile faded. "Oh. Is he . . ."

"Yeah, he is," Zan said. "Years ago. He was a cop, like my little brother Christian. He got called into a domestic dispute. The guy was threatening to shoot his wife. Ended up he shot my dad, instead."

"That's awful," she murmured. "I'm so sorry."

He shrugged. "Yeah. To get back to the tattoo. I had a fuck-you attitude toward the world at that time, for various reasons not worth going into. I was on a cross-country motorcycle trip with a friend of mine, and we stopped in a tattoo parlor in New Mexico, and dared each other to get tattooed. He got his girlfriend's name put on his ass."

She giggled and took a sip of wine. "Wow. Risky."

"I thought so, too. I picked this out of the tattoo artist's catalog. It reminded me of the time Dad took us to Scotland, to show us where his folks had emigrated from. So this . . ." He stroked the tattoo. ". . . is in honor of my dad. And in memory of that trip." A rueful look flitted across his face. "Try to explain it to my mom. She was beside herself."

She smiled as she pictured the scene, wondering what his mother was like. Her eyes fell on his hand, curled around the stem of the glass.

"What about that one?" she asked.

He glanced down at the crossed cutlasses on his hand, and his face tightened. For a moment it seemed as if he wasn't going to answer.

"That's the first tattoo I ever got," he said finally. "Matty Boyle and I got those when we were thirteen. It was a private joke between us. We used this symbol when we played pirates together as kids. That was how we signed our secret coded notes, that sort of thing."

"The Matt Boyle who works with the security company?"

He nodded. "We grew up together. His father was my dad's partner on the police force, way back when."

She tried to picture Matt Boyle's hand, but the man had never left much of an impression on her, other than his constant, obsessive smiling. "I don't remember seeing a tattoo on Matt's hand."

"You haven't," Zan said. "He had it removed. Laser surgery."

"Ah. But you never . . ." She trailed off, sensing a tension from him that made her wonder if she was putting her foot in her mouth.

"Nope. I left mine," he said. "I left them both. If I had to do it over, I admit, I wouldn't put a tattoo on my neck again. It's more trouble than it's worth. It's a red flag for a lot of people. You, for instance."

She winced. "I never said that—"

"But there's no point in taking it off." His voice was resolute. "Who you are is a sum total of where you've been. If you're embarrassed about it, if you try to deny it, you're just cutting off your own strength."

Blood rose in her face. She thought of all the things in her past that she would be glad to deny. His words made her feel judged.

Which was very unfair, she told herself. Zan knew nothing about her past, other than what she'd told him. He was talking about himself, and she was being silly and oversensitive.

She tossed back the last of the wine and got up. He studied the length of her body as the water trickled over her skin. "That's a fine philosophy, but sometimes where you've been is nobody else's damn business," she said. "What if people judge you because of it?"

His shoulders jerked in a careless shrug. "What if they do?"

"You don't care?" she insisted.

He shook his head. "I don't give a flying fuck."

She remembered how he'd faced down Bridget's rudeness without a speck of self-consciousness. "You must feel so free," she said.

He lifted his glass to her, unsmiling. "As a bird, sweetheart."

He drained it and set it down. His tone was so uncompromising. It made her feel pushed away. "Bully for you, Zan," she said.

She got out of the tub and hurried back to her bedroom.

Zan joined her seconds later, naked and dripping. He grabbed her from behind, dragging her against his body with a hard jerk.

"What is it, Abby?" he demanded. "Did I say something wrong?"

She shivered as he pressed pleading kisses against her ear. "I'm sorry. I'm just . . . it's late, that's all. I really should get some sleep."

He stiffened. His arms dropped. "Am I being dismissed?"

"No!" She spun around without thinking at all, and grabbed him tightly around the waist. "No! God, no, Zan. I didn't mean that."

His arms went around her again. "So I get to stay the night? I get to wake up with you in your bed? You sure about this, babe?"

Here she went, speeding right past yet another point of no return. Screw it. She'd barreled past so many of them, she scarcely noticed them go by anymore. She nodded, hiding her face against his wet shoulder. Water trickled down her body from his sopping hair. She couldn't resist. No one could expect it of her. He was so big and warm and solid, and his arms were so strong. She might even actually sleep, if Zan held her. His erection prodded her thigh. Then again, maybe not.

She dried his hair until it stuck out every which way, and dried his body with long, sensual swipes of the terrycloth.

"That's nice," he said dreamily. "Like a big tongue, licking me."

Zan flung the towel away. He scooped the lingerie off the bed and onto the floor with one careless sweep of his arm and flipped off the light. He swept her into his arms and laid her on the bed. He pulled the clip from her bun, unwound it and fanned the hair out over her pillow.

She heard the telltale sound of a foil package ripping.

She propped herself up onto her elbows. "Zan. No way. It's only a couple of hours till dawn, and I have work hell ahead of me tomorrow!"

He pushed her thighs wide and settled between them. "Too bad, sweetheart. You knew it would be this way. If you let me stay in your bed, I fuck you all night long. No rules, no limits. I warned you."

He slid down her body and started kissing her mound.

She giggled. "Don't you ever rest? What have I gotten myself into?"

"Big trouble." His tongue licked and probed, making her squirm. "If you play with fire, you have to accept the consequences."

Like she needed to be lectured about consequences. She would have laughed if she could, but she could only whimper and gasp.

He unraveled her with his lashing, thrusting tongue, drawing out her slick, lubricating liquid, then slid up and pushed himself slowly inside. Abby clutched his shoulders and gave in to the feel of that big phallus, massaging her slippery core. His kisses. Savoring her, slowly, endlessly. She would think about consequences later. She didn't need to go looking for them. They always found her in the end.

In the meantime, she wouldn't think about it. There was no point. With Zan all over her, she couldn't think at all.

Chapter

14

The sound of the shower woke Zan. He knew where he was without opening his eyes. Abby's sweet, woodsy scent was all around him, the sheets redolent with her subtle perfume.

He stretched and discovered a warm ball of fur curled up against his back. Sheba batted him with a sheathed claw, and rearranged herself, draping her tail across his neck. Long hairs tickled his nose.

The bedroom door opened and Abby came in, damp and glowing, swathed in a thick terrycloth robe. She looked tense.

"Good morning," he ventured cautiously.

"Hi." She hurried to her dresser without looking at him and rummaged busily through a drawer. "My alarm didn't go off, so I'm really late. Excuse me, but I have to run like a crazy woman."

He gently unwound the cat's tail from his neck, sat up, and looked at the clock. It read 7:16 AM. "What time do they expect you?" he asked.

"I should have been there hours ago, with that installation to uncrate. To be truthful, I should have stayed the whole night. Um . . . there's towels in the linen closet, food in the fridge. Help yourself. Make coffee, if you want. I'll get mine on the street." She pulled lacy underpants on underneath the bathrobe, sat down at the vanity, and started in on her stockings. She avoided his gaze, cheeks pink.

"Abby?" he said. "After everything that happened between us

last night, you still have to put your underwear on under your bathrobe?"

Abby looked worried. "I'm sorry, Zan. It's after seven, and Bridget's going to rip my head off. I turned off my cell phone and switched the ringer off my house phone last night, too. I have a feeling I'm going to pay for it in blood. The real world is crashing down on my head, that's all. It's nothing personal."

She went to her dresser and pulled out a frilly white confection of a bra. She hesitated, then let the bathrobe slip off and puddle to the floor. She faced him, looking bashful and demure, in lacy French-cut panties and lace-topped thigh-high hose. "Is that better?"

He feasted his eyes on her naked breasts, their high, pointed tops, the lush underswell as round and luminous as big pink pearls. Blood rushed to his groin, raising the sheet up like a tent pole. "Yeah. Much."

Abby's gaze flicked nervously away, as if she didn't want to see her effect on him. She struggled into her bra and hurried to the closet.

Zan slid his hand under the cover and gripped his turgid cock while Abby systematically hid her sexy body in the armor of a tailored business suit. The show was that much more erotic for its unselfconsciousness. Abby had no idea of the effect she had on him as she wiggled into her blouse, shimmied into a straight brown skirt, shrugged on a jacket. She was in too much of a hurry to notice or care.

She slipped on brown suede pumps and forced a comb through her wet hair. She looked at him, biting her full, sensuous lower lip. "I'm as white as a ghost. I have to put on some makeup. Excuse me."

She disappeared out the door, leaving a flat silence in her wake.

She was going to hide the luminous, freckled sweetness of her face beneath a professional mask, just like she'd hid her body from him.

He had an overwhelming urge to get one final look at her before the mask went on. The feeling bordered on panic. He leaped out of bed and followed her, slapping the bathroom door open.

Abby sucked in a sharp breath and smeared the mascara she was brushing onto her lashes. "Ouch. You scared me!"

"Sorry." He leaned on the doorjamb and studied at her. She hadn't gotten far in the process. Just the mascara. She fixed the smear in the corner of her eye and frowned. "Zan? What? Is something wrong?"

There was nothing he could say that wouldn't sound both mentally unbalanced and hysterically insecure, so he just shrugged. "I wanted to watch."

She put her mascara wand away. "You might have asked."

"Not my style," he said, without thinking.

She snorted. "Yeah, I noticed that. It's hard to miss."

He'd set himself up for that. She was slipping away. It scared him. Last night had been too intense. He'd overdone it. Spooked her. He had to wrench her mask away and get underneath the professional armor. Quick, before her walls were so thick, he would never find her again.

His lovely, sweet, wanton Abby. He wanted her back. *Now.*

Their eyes locked in the mirror. Her eyes widened with primitive feminine wariness as she gauged the look in his eyes and realized that she was trapped. He reached for her, spun her around to face him.

She went rigid in his arms. "Oh, Zan, I swear, I'm so late—"

"Just one kiss," he said, his voice soft with pleading. "One sweet, sincere kiss before you put your lipstick on, and then I'll be good."

She looked at the erection that prodded her thigh, and laughed. "Excuse me, but you do not look like you'll be content with just a kiss."

"Give it to me, and we'll see." He pulled her close and kissed her.

Her lips trembled beneath his, and the magic bloomed, twining them into a single pure impulse of desire. If he ever had a strategy, he forgot it. His hands wound into her wet hair and his mouth plundered the minty depths of her mouth, and he tore the silk blouse open, pearl buttons pinging on the tile floor, hungry to bury his face in those tits, propped up so high and proud in the frilly, shell-like cups of her bra.

He dragged the skirt up over her hips, slid his hands over the soft round globes of her ass, and gripped the gusset of the panties. He used the wad of damp lace to caress her cleft, rubbing it over her clit.

She moaned, clutched at him. He'd gotten his wish. She couldn't resist. She opened like a flower when he sought the slick secret flesh of her pussy, fingers sliding past soaked panties to slip inside her. He could make her respond. He had at least that in his favor.

God, it was the best thing on earth, getting Abby off. Her cunt clenched around his hand, and gasping sobs wrenched out of her parted lips with each spasm. It made him feel like a god.

Nothing short of a cataclysm could have stopped him from fucking her at that point. The condom he'd stashed on the radiator the night before was still there. He tore it open with his teeth, rolled it on himself, and turned her to face the mirror. "Watch me, Abby."

She lifted her head. Her face was dewy with a sheen of sweat, her mascara already smudged, her hair clinging to her face. He bent her over the sink, wrenching the panties down her legs until he lifted out one foot, still clad in the elegant suede pump. He kicked her legs wider, placed her hands on either side of the sink basin. "Hold on tight."

"Oh my God, Zan," she moaned. "This is insane."

He spread her, nudging his cock between her pussy lips until he was lodged in her tight opening. "Look into my eyes," he said. "Watch."

She cried out at the slow surge of his body into hers, but she didn't look away. It was lucky he'd already made her come, because he wasn't going to be able to make this last. It was too good, this stunning, disheveled woman with her panties around her ankle, bent over for him, sobbing with eagerness as he drove his cock into her slick depths.

He was gone. Lost.

He clutched her as pleasure jolted through him, his face pressed between her shoulder blades, his fingers digging into her hips.

Slowly, he realized he was putting too much weight on her. She was wobbling on those heels, shaky and unstable. He pulled his cock reluctantly out of her clinging body and stepped back, disposing of the condom. Abby lifted her head and glanced at herself in the mirror.

Her eyes widened, horrified. "Oh, dear God. Look at me."

He'd succeeded in trashing Abby's professional armor. But he hadn't calculated how she might feel about it afterward. *Yikes.*

"You look gorgeous," he offered. And knew, the same instant, that it was exactly the wrong thing to say.

She recoiled. "Don't touch me," she hissed. "I am wrecked! You ripped my blouse, you . . . you pig! I have to wash, change, and redo my hair and makeup, all in about ten seconds, and *you*"—she pointed an accusing finger, before which he retreated meekly backward out the bathroom door and toward the bedroom—"are not going to seduce, torment, or assault me again, in any way! Is that understood?"

"Yes, ma'am." He thudded down on her bed, chastened.

Abby kicked her shoes off and peeled the panties off her ankle. "While I'm at it, I might as well tell you right now that your dominator routine is fine for fun consensual sex games in the privacy of my bedroom, but if you ever try that crap on me again in normal life, you're going to find yourself tied in a freaking slipknot. You got me, buddy?"

He watched, fascinated, as she wrenched off the blouse, counted the missing buttons, and flung it to the floor with a grunt of disgust.

"Ow," he said cautiously. "You don't mean my, uh . . ."

"Yes!" She stepped out of her skirt and flung it at him. It hit him in the face. "I do mean your, uh! Speaking of which . . ." She scowled at his cock, which was swelling enthusiastically for her striptease, in total disregard for her furious harangue. She flung up her hands. "Oh, for the love of God." She scooped his jeans up off the floor and hurled them at his head. "Put that thing of yours away before you hurt yourself."

She tore off the stockings and bra, and stormed out to the bathroom, naked and magnificent in her towering rage.

He struggled into his jeans when he heard the bathroom door open minutes later. She marched in and made a shooing gesture. "You. Out," she said crisply. "I do *not* need an audience."

He crept off to the kitchen, abashed.

Abby came out two minutes later in a new outfit, a hot, sexy little red number, complete with red pumps. She looked perfect and utterly impenetrable. She tossed a purse on her shoulder. "I'm off."

He waited hopefully for something about when they might see each other again. Or some indication that he was welcome back at all.

Nothing. She just put her hands on her hips and looked stern.

"Do you want a ride to work?" he attempted. Maybe he could find an opening to ask her out to dinner on the way.

"No, Zan, you've helped my working day along quite enough already," she said. "I'll take the bus, thank you very much."

Ouch. He winced.

She walked out, and looked back. "Zan? You're a bad, dirty dog."

"And?" he said warily. "I sense a corollary in that statement."

She hesitated. "And last night was amazing." She spun around and left, heels clattering loudly down the stairs.

He stared out the open door, bemused. Well, hell. It wasn't what he'd been hoping for, but at least it wasn't a definitive fuck-off-and-die.

He rubbed his scratchy chin, wondering if a secret lover was authorized to stash a razor and toothbrush in the bathroom. He probably shouldn't push his luck. He'd shoved it to the limit already.

He flipped on his cell phone and checked out her apartment. Her furniture was nice, but not extravagant; dolled up with colored throws and funky, eclectic artwork. Medium TV, budget DVD player. Nice stereo. Big CD collection. Her desk was a messy heap. He didn't snoop. He didn't want to start off anything so important with bad karma. Things were weird enough lately, what with Elaine's mysterious death.

He had to proceed very carefully. Abby was the one. He felt none of his usual diffidence that had made him hold himself back from the other women he'd been involved with. He'd been with some lovely women, but their manipulations had made him feel nervous and suffocated. He'd always cut bait and run, in the end.

Of course you don't feel manipulated, bonehead. She's not sussing you out as a potential husband, his pesky devil's advocate reminded him. He was just a roll in the hay. A fuck in the dark. No need to maneuver him into position, no need to ask him where he thought this relationship was going. She already knew.

Nowhere.

The thought stung. He distracted himself by wandering into her bedroom. It looked like a tornado had torn it apart. He peeked into her closet. Just as he'd thought. The girl must spend every dime she made on clothes. He buried his nose in the dress she'd worn the day of the Romeo riots. Her perfume clung to it. It made him instantly hard.

He heard a meow, and pulled his head out of the closet. Sheba was seated on her haunches, regarding him with a disapproving air.

"You plan to rat me out to Abby that I sniffed her clothes?"

The cat's tail twitched back and forth. She meowed imperiously, trotted to the door, meowed again. He followed her to the kitchen, where she sat down next to her food dish and looked at him expectantly.

"I bet she fed you before I woke up," he said, rummaging through the cupboards. "This is blackmail. I can see it in your eyes."

Sheba wrapped her tail around herself and said *Prrrt.*

He found some dry food and poured it into her dish, then set himself to the task of making some coffee. It was more complicated than it should have been. Six different kinds of coffee beans, for fuck's sake.

He settled on the French roast, ground the beans, dumped them in the little glass pot, poured boiling water over it as he'd seen Abby do.

He had to convince her that he was husband material. He felt so alive, burning with energy. He'd been reborn as an omnipotent pagan sex god. No, Abby was the goddess, and he wanted to humbly worship at the shrine of her sex with his hands, his tongue, his cock, for hours.

Every night of his life.

He wanted to make her laugh. To brush her hair. Bring on the romantic clichés, he couldn't get enough of them. He wanted to frolic on a beach with her, throwing a piece of driftwood for their dog. Twine on the couch with her, watching sappy movies. Soak with her in a hot tub. Travel with her. Bring her breakfast in bed. Know what she'd dreamed about as a child, what her childhood had been like.

He felt like a veil had been torn off his face. Light was streaming in. He'd been wearing a veil so long, dull sameness had started to feel normal. Ever since the Porsche. He'd never quite come back from that.

He poured some coffee and took a gulp. Wow. Good. He could get used to this. Strung out, even. He was already hooked on Abby's sharp sense of humor, the freckles on her skin, the dazed look in her eyes when he made love to her. Her laughter. Her wanton, earthy sexuality.

He didn't even know who he was anymore. A few days ago, he could have said who he was, no hesitating. He was a free man, he spoke his mind, he paid his debts, he met his obligations. He took orders from no one. He'd prided himself on those qualities. Thought it was so damn important not to be jerked around or controlled by anyone.

The thought came on him in slow, imperceptible increments, the way the sky got paler at dawn. Why not meet her halfway? Why not?

The more he thought about it, the more straightforward it seemed. He wanted Abby. She was a classy woman who enjoyed the finer things in life. It was logical that he make an effort to provide them for her. He was more than capable of doing so, financially. He'd just never cared enough about any woman to demonstrate the capacity.

Money was meant to be spent. What better cause?

He could even spiff up his look, if she liked. The long hair, for instance. It was far more about laziness and inertia than it was an expression of personal style. His hair just grew so damn fast.

He could shave more often, too. Buy sharper clothes. Cultivate more expensive tastes. Fancy coffee. Wine. Foreign cheese. No problem.

Maybe he should start by planning her a gourmet dinner. He could ask Jamie or Chris for advice, if he could handle the teasing.

Hmm. Then again, maybe it would be smarter just to look for a nice lady clerk and charm her into giving him advice about what fine foods and wines went with what. He'd get candles, dessert, fruit. Champagne.

His cell rang. He checked the display. Matty. He was in such a good mood, he didn't even curse. He hit TALK.

"Hey, Matty. What are you doing up so damn early?"

Matty paused, suspicious of his cheerfulness. "Zan? Is that you?"

"Yeah, sure, it's me. Who else would answer my phone?"

"Oh. Well, uh, I was just wondering if you'd given any more thought to that consulting gig I offered you last week. Remember?"

He had opened his mouth to tell Matty to find someone else when it occurred to him that it was an excuse to see Abby again. Today.

Aw, what the hell. It wouldn't hurt to take a look at the security setup. He wouldn't bill Matty for his time, of course, since he didn't know fuck-all about museum security, but it felt right to mark such an important day with a gesture of forgiveness and reconciliation.

"OK," he said. "I'll come in and take a look, if you want."

"You will? Really?" Matty sounded flabbergasted.

"Sure. Later on today, though," Zan amended. "First I have to order a gourmet meal to surprise my girlfriend." It was insane to spill private business to Matty, but stating it out loud made it seem more real.

"Girlfriend? No shit! Who is she? Anyone I know?"

"Yeah, you do. She works at the museum. Abby Maitland."

Matty was silent for a long moment. "Uh, wow," he said finally. "Good for you. She's, ah . . . hot. Since when has this been going on?"

"It's new," Zan admitted. "Just a couple of days. She's amazing."

Matty grunted. "Yeah. I just bet."

"Anyhow. Gotta run. Lots to do," Zan said. "Call you later." He hung up, took a swig of coffee, and switched his cell phone off.

He needed concentration today. No locksmithing calls to distract him, no Matty hounding him about this damn project. Or Chris or Jamie or Granddad, calling to bug him out of sheer habit.

Jewelry was a classic way to demonstrate that a man's intentions were honorable, he reflected. It was too soon for a ring, but that left earrings, bracelets, necklaces. Whew. He'd never been in a jewelry store in his life, but today was a day for new experiences.

Matty struggled up the dune, his legs trembling. It wasn't that the incline was that difficult. He was simply too drunk. He'd been at least half drunk ever since he'd heard about Elaine. When he was fully drunk, he could convince himself that she'd offed herself, like everyone was saying. He'd contemplated it himself often enough. Just didn't have the balls to follow through. When he was half drunk, though, the hole in his belly told him that the suicide story was pure, stinking bullshit.

Fully drunk was way preferable. Didn't do much for his coordination, though. Or his wind.

He stumbled over the crest of the dune, panting. There they were, waiting for him amid sand grass and shreds of fog. Lucien and Ruiz, one of his musclebound goons. The dark, wiry, shifty-eyed one.

Ruiz noticed his approach, and nudged Lucien. "Yo, boss, check it out. The human pimple's finally showed up."

Matty had a brief but vivid fantasy of killing Ruiz. Slowly, making him squeal and beg before the final, bloody killing blow.

Lucien looked Matty over. His face looked different with his hair buzzed off, but those eyes were as soul chilling as ever. "You look like shit, Boyle. You're late. And you're drunk. Are you keeping it together?"

Matty nodded. "Sure. I printed up those photos." He dug them out of his pocket. "The neck tattoo, and—"

"Give them to me." Lucien held out his hand.

"The only one I don't have is the crossed cutlasses tattoo on his hand," Matty babbled on. "It's not like I could take a picture of Zan's hand. But I know exactly what it looks like, and I could reproduce—"

"Shut up, Boyle. I don't care about his hand."

Matty stared at him, his mouth opening and closing helplessly.

Lucien smiled thinly. "Gloves," he said. "I will be wearing gloves."

"Duh," muttered Ruiz, giggling to himself. "Gloves. Fuckin' cretin."

Matty swallowed. "Yeah. Gloves. Of course."

"Of course," Lucien echoed gently. "So? You said on your phone that your locksmith friend is finally in place? This is good news."

"He's coming in to the museum today to look over the security plan," Matty said. "He's supposed to study it and write me a report."

Lucien nodded. "Good. Find a way to have him seen on the security cameras near the museum on the night of the heist. That bank machine across the street, maybe. Get him to take out money."

"But it would be stupid for a thief to stop at a bank machine just before a heist," Matty said doubtfully.

"So? They'll think he's stupid. Do we care?"

"No. It's just that he's, uh, not. Stupid, I mean. No one who knew him would ever believe that Zan would be dumb enough to—"

"The man is not a genius," Lucien said impatiently. "He works nights breaking into cars. Ordinary men make mistakes. Particularly when they're breaking the law. Trust me on this. Sadly, stupidity is the rule, not the exception, Boyle. You, of all people, should know this."

Ruiz exploded again into muffled wheezing laughter, hands over his face, shoulders shaking. The fuckhead. "Whatever," Matty muttered.

Lucien got to his feet. "This dawn rendezvous has been pleasant, but I have to run. I have to spiff up for my appointment with Abby Maitland. Convenient, that she's spontaneously gotten herself embroiled with your locksmith. She makes a much sexier villain than Elaine."

Ruiz made a lewd, piglike sound of appreciation. "Yeah. Mmmm."

Matty looked wildly from one to the other. "What do you mean? What the hell does Abby have to do with anything?"

Lucien blinked. "I had to come up with a new scenario."

"Abby's not part of this!" Matty bellowed. "Leave her out of this!"

Lucien stared at him, and started to laugh. "You're in love with her? That's funny." He slapped Matty's back hard enough to make him stagger. "Women are dirty sluts, Boyle. Abby Maitland more than most."

"I don't want her involved! She's innocent!"

"Innocent?" Lucien chucked. "You wouldn't say that if you'd seen what Ruiz saw from the tree outside her window last night. Ruiz, show Boyle your photos. The one where she has his dick in her mouth is my personal favorite. Ruiz even put it on my Palm Pilot. Here, take a look."

"No." Matty stumbled back, slipping and falling on his ass in the damp sand. "Fuck you. I don't want to see them. Keep away from me."

"Oh, but they're excellent pictures," Lucien urged, holding the thing out to him. "Ruiz is quite a talented amateur photographer. Some of them are even kind of artistic. Take a look. It'll strengthen your resolve. You would not believe what those two got up to last night. They were at it for hours, literally. Your friend fucks like a world champion."

Matty pulled out his flask, took a swallow of bourbon. He wiped a trembling mouth. "He's not my friend," he said.

Chapter

15

Abby practically ripped all the tendons in her ankles in her mad dash for the bus. Those Pollini pumps were great, but not for sprinting.

Her alarm clock hadn't gone off because she'd forgotten to push the button down. After last night's final torrid episode, she'd drifted off without a thought for the following morning. She could have slept till nine. Till noon. She terrified herself. It was unthinkably irresponsible.

Her workday began as inauspiciously as she had feared. Trish looked up from the reception desk, her eyes huge and dramatic. "Boy, are you ever in the doghouse, Abby!" she said with unseemly relish.

Abby smiled with forced calm. "Good morning to you, too, Trish."

"Bridget wants you in her office right away," Trish called after her.

Bridget was in a white rage. "Ah, Abby. How kind of you to grace us with your presence. Don't bother to sit down. You don't have time."

Abby froze in the act of sitting, and awkwardly straightened up.

"I see you opted to take it easy last night," Bridget went on. "Cathy saw you leave shortly after I did. With that alarming fellow with all the hair. I do hope you had a pleasant, relaxing evening?"

Abby clamped down on a surge of disproportionate anger. "Yes, Zan was kind enough to offer me a ride home."

"A ride home," Bridget murmured. "Hmph. Really."

Abby sealed her lips and stared the older woman straight in the face. Bridget sniffed when it became evident that Abby was not going to babble an apology. "In any case, I was in at six-thirty. I expected to find you here. I also expected to see a great deal more progress uncrating the exhibit. I tried your phone, no answer. I tried your cell, it was off. And then, only days before the biggest fundraising event of the year, you have the gall to waltz in to work at"— she glanced at her watch—"eight nineteen AM. I simply cannot tell you how disappointed I am."

"I'm sorry, Bridget. I—"

"Up until now, I assumed that you were dedicated to your job," Bridget said. "Today, I was forced to question my own judgment."

"It won't happen again," Abby said tightly.

"Oh, it most certainly will not. In fact, it *must* not. You cannot afford any more lapses, Abby. Have I made myself quite clear?"

"Very," Abby said, through clenched teeth.

"Good. Please go and confer with Dovey. We have a very important emergency meeting with the head of the Haverton White Foundation. Dovey can brief you." Bridget looked at her watch. "You arrived just in time." She shot Abby a chilly glance. "They awarded us a very nice grant, you might be interested to know."

"Oh. Ah, that's . . . that's good," she faltered.

"Yes, isn't it? How nice of you to care. You may go." Bridget swung the chair around to face her computer. Abby was dismissed.

She made her way toward Dovey's cubicle. No point in feeling sorry for herself. This situation was the result of a long series of stupid choices, starting with the night Zan let her into her apartment in exchange for a kiss. The sweetest, most heart-softening kiss of her life. Just thinking of it made her chest go hot and squishy, and her throat get tight. Then there was the unconscious choice of not setting the alarm clock. And to be totally honest, she hadn't really tried to stop Zan when he jumped her in the bathroom this morning.

She'd just gone bananas, not thinking or caring about missing the 7:42 bus at the corner of Edgemont. Then there were the choices last night, which had culminated in the most marvelous lovemaking of her life.

She shivered. The man's sex appeal brought her to her knees.

Literally. She reached down to touch her sore knees. Oh, Lord. Rug burn. She bent down outside Dovey's cubicle to assess the damage.

What a ditz, to wear a miniskirt after a night like that, but she'd dressed in such a hurry. The red marks were very visible through the sheer stockings. She would just hope nobody looked at her knees today.

She was in danger of getting canned. She should at least have the grace to be stressed about it. Instead, she was crying for terror and joy because she was in love.

In love. It knocked the wind right out of her. She was euphoric. She wanted to sneak into the ladies' room, call Zan on her cell and tell him to talk dirty to her while she smothered her giggles.

"Abby! Finally!" Dovey's round face popped out of the opening of his office cubicle. "I've been trying to get a hold of you since last night! Whatever possessed you to turn off your cell phone today, of all days?"

"Oh, for God's sake, Dovey, not you too—"

"I'm so excited," Dovey chattered on. "Aside from the coup of pulling in that monster grant, the real prize is the man himself!"

"Huh?" She shook her head, bewildered. "Who?"

"Your future husband, silly! Handsome, cultured, filthy stinking rich, single . . . and already waiting for you in the conference room!"

She blinked at him. "Waiting . . . who's waiting for me?"

"Lucien Haverton! The man of your dreams, with whom you are about to have a fateful encounter, as soon as I spiff you up! He got here early, you see. He invited me to fix him up with a dancing partner for the gala. Can you guess who I suggested? Take a wild guess."

"Oh, dear." She stared at him, appalled. "You didn't. That is so skeevy and inappropriate, Dovey! There's grant money involved!"

"But it's the chance of a lifetime!" Dovey towed her down the corridor. "I'm so pleased with myself, my buttons keep popping off!"

That, of course, made her think of this morning's silk blouse debacle. Her face flamed. "You're a sweetheart to do this for me, but this guy's a big-shot donor, and I'm really not comfortable with—"

"Yes, you have to do your usual schtick." Dovey threw his arm over her shoulders and gave her a squeeze. "The modest reluctance routine is very much to your credit, but we don't have time for it right now. The future calls, cupcake." He hustled her into the ladies' room and grabbed her purse. "Let me see what lipsticks you've got in there."

"Dovey, this is the ladies' room. You're not supposed to be in here."

Dovey gave her a pitying look. "Oh, you fuzzy little duckling, you." He pulled a lipstick out of her purse and peered at the end of the tube. "Russian Red. Naughty slut. Perfect for that hot red suit. Pure sex, in a streamlined package of slick professionalism. You'll look like a Bond girl. All you need is a red Jag convertible and a little silver gun."

Dovey shoved the lipstick into her hand, and Abby painted her mouth violently red, her mind racing for an escape route.

A feigned attack of nausea, maybe? An epileptic seizure? She didn't want to be offered to this guy on a silver platter. She wanted Zan. Morning, noon, and night. She was in love. The deed was done. All the rich, handsome, eligible bachelors on earth could sit on it and spin.

She took a deep breath. "Dovey, I'm—"

"Late," Dovey said. "Late, my pet, for a hot date with destiny! Shoulders back, chin up, tits out! Atta girl!" He pulled open the door to the conference room and shoved her inside.

Ouch. This time Dovey kicked her under the conference table. Abby rubbed her bruised ankle. Dovey shot her an agonized glance. She sat up straighter and dragged herself into focus by sheer brute force.

"...so impressed with the innovation of the exhibit program," Lucien Haverton said. "This place is an ideal setting for high-end touring exhibits. The foundation has a long tradition of supporting innovative thinking, and that's what's happening here, people."

Wow. They were getting some serious strokes. She should be feeling gratified, proud. Maybe even contributing to the conversation.

But the scene left her cold. It just didn't seem real. The man struck her as a robot with a recorded message coming out of his mouth. It was creepy. All she could do was keep that frantic smile glued on her face and count the seconds until she could run screaming.

It didn't help that Peter, the executive director, was here too. He was a distinguished old gentleman with a cane and a white beard, who usually treated her with condescending indulgence. Today, he kept shooting her disapproving looks. Bridget widened her eyes when Abby once again missed her cue to take a turn kissing the man's ass.

"We are so honored by this gesture of support," Bridget gushed. "I was thrilled when Dovey called. It's wonderful that the foundation . . ."

It all faded into a faraway babble again. Abby stared across the swirling grain of the mahogany conference table. The room was so new, it still smelled strongly of fresh paint. The smell made her head ache.

She sneaked a peek at Lucien Haverton. He was everything Dovey had claimed. Tall, broad, lean, built. Classically handsome, well spoken, attractive voice, patrician bone structure. If she'd created a composite sketch of a man who embodied her List, Lucien Haverton would be it.

His brown hair was cut surprisingly short for a guy who clearly was not balding, but the severe style looked good on him. He wore a suit that must have cost three months of her salary, and he wore it well.

And she could care less. After Zan, every man looked dull. After the way Zan's hot topaz eyes had scorched her last night, Lucien Haverton's bright blue ones looked cold and calculating. Too close-set.

". . . so excited that you'll be here for the gala! Particularly since this contribution puts us so close to our funding goal for the season!"

"Oh, really? How much are you short?" Lucien asked.

Bridget looked expectantly at Abby. Abby tried to fish out of her short-term memory exactly what had just been asked. "Uh . . ."

"About fifteen thousand," Dovey inserted smoothly. "That is, if all goes as we confidently project for the gala."

"Well, then," Lucien said, his voice genial. "I'll buy a table for ten for the staff of the Haverton White Foundation, for twenty thousand dollars." He glanced around at them in the startled silence that followed. "If you're all in agreement, of course," he added. "That's not a grant from Haverton White, though. That's my own personal donation."

"Oh . . . my goodness," Bridget said, her voice faint.

"That is so generous, Mr. Haverton," Peter said. "I'm overwhelmed."

"Only if the lovely Ms. Maitland will promise me a dance, however," Haverton said, with a broad wink.

Dovey looked at her expectantly. Bridget blinked, startled, and followed suit. Peter smiled benevolently. She looked wildly at everyone in turn. This was weird. Nobody but she seemed to notice how creepy and manipulative and inappropriate the man's suggestion was.

They were all leaving her ass out dangling in the wind. *Yikes.*

Abby coughed violently, and lunged for the pitcher of water on the tray. She poured herself a glass, spilling a puddle of water over the table. "Excuse me," she whispered. "Got something in my throat."

Haverton rubbed his chin. "I'm so sorry. I didn't mean to put you on the spot, Ms. Maitland. It was very clumsy of me. Forget I said it."

"Oh, no!" Abby forced a smile. "A dance would be, uh, great!"

Dovey and Bridget rushed to fill the uncomfortable silence that followed. Abby tuned the chatter out, refilling her glass. Her mind was wrenched back into the conversation by Elaine's name.

". . . Elaine Clayborne, our assistant curator. Yes, the poor girl. It was just so tragic," Peter was saying in hushed tones.

"I'm so sorry." Lucien's voice was appropriately subdued. "I heard she was a lovely young woman. A suicide is so difficult to accept."

"It was not a suicide!" Abby's voice cut sharply across their decorous murmuring.

There was an awkward pause. Lucien's brow rose. "I beg your pardon?"

"Elaine was murdered," Abby said. "It was not a suicide. Don't think for a minute that it was."

Lucien flicked a puzzled glance at Dovey, who cleared his throat. "Abby? Let's leave that unhappy subject alone. It's not relevant to—"

"It offends me when people say Elaine killed herself! I was the last person to speak to her, and her sadistic, murdering pig of a boyfriend was walking up to her door right before she died! He *killed* her!"

"Abby!" Bridget exclaimed. "Control yourself! You are shouting!"

Abby looked around, at Bridget's outraged face, at Dovey's tight, apologetic smile, Peter's horror, Lucien Haverton's mild puzzlment.

She was suddenly struck with the futility of her yelling and carrying on. These people didn't care about the truth, and she couldn't force them to. "I'm sorry," she said dully. "I was out of line."

"I'm the one who should be sorry," Lucien said. "I seem to have struck a nerve. It's the last thing I wanted. I feel like an idiot."

"Certainly not!" Bridget patted his hand. "I'm sorry for this unpleasantness." She shot Abby a venomous glance. "Abby, may I speak to you in private?"

Oh, yay. Public execution time. Abby got to her feet, deliberately avoiding Dovey's anguished gaze, and followed Bridget out of the room.

Bridget whirled around outside the door. "You *idiot*! Do you have any idea how much money the Haverton White Foundation is giving us?"

"Certainly. I put together that grant proposal myself. I put them all together, Bridget. Every last one of them. Haven't you noticed?"

"I do not appreciate your sarcasm!" Bridget snarled.

"It's not sarcasm," Abby said flatly. "It's just the truth."

"Oh, really? And you think that entitles you to behave like a spoiled, whiny child? I expected professional behavior from you!"

A red haze rose up before Abby's eyes. "Bridget, do you even care that Elaine was killed? Other than the inconvenience, of course?"

Bridget gasped in outrage. "How dare you say that?"

Abby shrugged. "I was just wondering."

Bridget's thin face was red and mottled with fury. "You know, Abby, I think it's time for you to polish up your resume. I don't think the Silver Fork Museum needs your services anymore."

"How long will it take Peter to figure out who really pulled in these grants?" Abby asked. "How long before it all shrivels up on you?"

Bridget's nostrils flared. "Get out of here," she hissed.

Abby dashed the tears away when she got outside, ashamed of her outburst. She was not helping Elaine with this show of bad temper. Now she might have paid for her lack of self-control with her job.

She was so blurry-eyed, she ran into a man on the street. She veered away, muttering an apology, and realized that it was Lucien.

He clasped her shoulders tightly. "Ms. Maitland? Are you OK?"

She almost laughed in his concerned face. "Not really. But there's nothing anyone can do about it, so please don't worry about it."

"I am so sorry about what just happened," Lucien said. "The last thing I wanted to do was to cause you friction with your colleagues."

"It's OK. No biggie." She dug in her pocket for a tissue. He handed her a crisp, folded handkerchief with LH appliqued on the corner. She dabbed her eyes with it. "It wasn't your fault."

"I'm terribly sorry about the loss of your friend," he said. "It must drive you crazy, that people are taking it for a suicide."

His exaggerated sympathy made her feel vaguely embarrassed. "Thanks," she muttered. "And yes. It does."

"Can I take you to breakfast? As an apology for my clumsiness?"

She was so scrambled, she couldn't think of an excuse. "Uh . . ."

"There's a lovely little café a few blocks away."

She pulled herself together and found her voice again. "I'm sorry, Mr. Haverton, but today is a crazy day. I don't have time."

"Coffee, then? There's a bar up the street," he wheedled. "Please. It might help to talk. I'm a very good listener. And call me Lucien."

She hesitated. The man was trying to be nice. To say nothing of the fact that his foundation had just given a huge chunk of money to the museum. Being pleasant to him was part of her job description.

She nodded. "Thank you. That would be lovely."

He took her arm, and she was walking down the street with him as if they were a couple. That did not feel good. Unease squirmed in her midriff, as if Zan were sure to see her and draw the wrong conclusion.

Oh, please. She was being silly and paranoid. Zan had no official claim on her. Not yet, at least. And even if he did, this was work. A cup of coffee and a schmooze with an important donor. No biggie.

She ordered her usual and dusted it liberally with cocoa powder before they sat down at one of the little tables near the window. Lucien stared at her quivering confection as he sipped his own black coffee.

"Wow. That looks good. What is it exactly?"

She took a sip, embarrassed. "Triple espresso with whipped cream and a shot of vanilla syrup. Frivolous, I know, but this is probably my breakfast and my lunch. So I'd better make it count."

He reached across the table and took her hand, to her dismay. "So tell me what happened that night," he said. "You say you spoke to your friend minutes before her death?"

She pulled her hand back, ostensibly to pry out a packet of sugar, though the vanilla syrup made it sweet enough by far. "Yes, I did. She'd just broken up with her sadistic jerk of a boyfriend, and he was on his way into her house to bully her right when I called. I got there less than twenty minutes later, and she was already dead."

He dragged in a sharp, harsh breath. "Oh, dear God. I didn't know you were the one who found her. That must have been terrible."

"Yes," she said quietly. "It was."

Lucien stared so intently into her face, her gaze skittered away from his bright blue eyes. "And the police? Aren't they investigating this boyfriend? You would think that he would be their prime suspect."

"You would think," she said wearily. "But they don't know who he is. Neither do I. In fact, no one but me even knew that the guy existed."

"I see. So you have no proof that this man exists? None at all?"

"Not yet," she said grimly.

His eyebrows shot up. "Oh? So you have a plan?"

She rolled her eyes. "I wouldn't go so far as to call it a plan. But I'm not going to let that bastard get away with killing my best friend."

He regarded her with admiring eyes. It made her squirm. "That's courageous, Abby. Have you considered that it might be dangerous?"

"I can't be bothered to worry about that," Abby said. "Maybe I'll get scared when my brain starts functioning again."

He chuckled appreciatively. "Can I help?"

She was disconcerted. "How? With what?"

He gave her a modest shrug. "I have resources and connections that I could put at your disposal. You shouldn't have to face this alone."

I'm not all alone. I have Zan, she wanted to yell. "Ah . . ."

"Do you even know what this man looks like?" Lucien asked.

She shook her head. "All I know is that he's really good-looking."

Lucien's mouth twitched. "Well, that narrows it down somewhat."

"I suppose." She gulped her coffee and got up. "It's kind of you to offer to be my white knight, Mr. Haverton, but I hardly know you."

"I would love to know you better. And it's Lucien. Please."

Oh, great. This was all she needed. "Lucien, then," she said. "I'm flattered, but it's a bad time. And I have to get back to work."

He got up. "I understand. I'll walk you back to the museum."

Argh. Abby wanted to tear out her hair. She simply could not get rid of this man, but it was professional suicide to be rude to him.

"Gee. That's not necessary, but thanks," she murmured.

She tried to keep a safe distance from him on the sidewalk, but sure enough, he veered toward her and grabbed her arm again. She gritted her teeth. One block. She could make nice for one little block.

"I'm only in town through next weekend," he said. "I know it's not the best time to request the honor of escorting you to the gala, but I doubt I'll have another opportunity." He gave her a winsome smile. "All I want is the pleasure of your company, a few dances. Conversation."

They stopped in front of the museum steps. Abby gazed at him, intensely uncomfortable, her mouth working. "I, uh . . . uh . . ."

"May I have your card?" he prompted.

"I suppose." She dug one out of her purse. He pulled out his Palm Pilot, entered her number and held the device up right in front of her face. A button clicked, and a bright light flashed, blinding her.

Abby yelped and jerked back. "Did you just take my picture?"

He grinned. "Of course. It'll pop up on my display when you call."

Yeah, like she was going to do that any time this century. "Oh. Wow. Very cool," she said weakly. "Isn't technology fun?"

"Here, take a look." He held out the device. "It's a good one."

She peeked at the photo. She disliked it. Her eyes were wide and startled, and her mouth hung open like a blithering half-wit, the lipstick so red and shiny and scary. "Wow. That's . . . that's nice," she faltered.

"Please. Just think about my invitation." He plucked a card out of his pocket and pressed it into her hand. "And if you ever need to talk to someone, just call me. Day or night." He lifted her hand to his lips.

"Thanks," she said. "I really don't think that—oh, dear."

He kissed her hand. Slowly, flirtatiously, seductively.

Abby snatched her hand away and backed up, almost tripping on the steps. "Have to run," she babbled. "Thanks for the coffee. Bye-bye."

She pulled out her cell phone as she raced through the foyer, and desperately punched in Zan's number. She needed to hear his voice.

The cell service informed her that the requested client's phone was either turned off or out of range.

That unhappy news made her burst promptly into tears.

"So what we've got here, see, is basically a network of detection and control sensors using electromagnetic energy to create an invisible protective cocoon around each object," Chuck Jamison explained. The man's eyes were alight with enthusiasm behind his thick glasses.

Zan nodded as he gazed at the jeweled golden candelabra perched on its pedestal that Jamison was currently securing. He was fascinated with the technology in spite of himself. "Matty mentioned infrared, too," he prompted the other man.

"Oh, hell, yeah. We've got infrared barriers that are resistant to dust, weather, misalignment. We've got piezo-seismic sensors to detect microshocks, inclination, contact. We've got gravimetric detection that senses variations in weight." Chuck leaned closer to Zan. "They had a hell of a budget for security. We pulled out all the stops," he confided.

"I can see that," Zan said. "Amazing stuff. Can I take a look at the software?"

"Oh, sure," Chuck said cheerfully. "Come on up to the—"

"May I help you with something, Mr. . . . . ?" an acid voice broke in.

"Duncan," Zan supplied, turning around. It was Abby's bitchy boss, Bridget, looking down her pointy nose at him. He almost told her to call him Zan, but the lofty disdain on her face changed his mind. She could call him Mr. Duncan, if she called him at all. He shrugged. "No."

Bridget scowled. "Whatever the nature of your interest in this exhibit, it is not yet open, Mr. Duncan. You're not authorized to be here. Please go." She gave him a skintight, fuck-you-very-much smile.

Zan thought about explaining how Matty had asked him to look at the security, but it wouldn't sound any more plausible to this vinegary harpy than it had to Zan himself. Besides, Matty had said to keep it secret. So Matty would just have to smooth his way before he tried this shit again. "OK," he said easily. "Is Abby around here someplace?"

Bridget's mouth tightened until it puckered like a shriveled apple. "I have no idea where she is," she said icily. "Off somewhere pursuing her own mysterious agenda, no doubt."

Whoa. That sounded like a serious can of worms. He nodded politely, smiled at Chuck Jamison, and walked out of the exhibit hall.

He briefly considered slipping into Abby's office and waiting for her, but people were sneaking curious glances at him. He would be noticed. Making trouble for Abby at work would not help his cause.

He made his way out through the original museum, glancing at familiar installations about the history of Silver Fork, explanatory text typed onto yellowed index cards that were unchanged since his middle school field trips. He fingered the velvet box in his pocket.

He was so pleased with what he'd found for her. He was itching to give it to her now, but probably it would be better to wait until after dinner. He'd decided that it had to have Abby written all over it, plus be unique, extravagant, and have some personal significance to the two of them. He'd found it in a shop window, and waited on the sidewalk for almost forty minutes for the jeweler to open his shop.

He'd known it the instant he saw it. A gold pendant in the shape of an old-fashioned key. The head was an elaborate cloverleaf pattern that looked like Celtic knotwork, and each of the leaves was adorned with a small ruby. Real rubies, not the kind that were cooked up in a lab. They looked like glowing drops of blood.

The price made his palms sweat, but so what? Courting a woman was expensive. Part of the process of natural selection. No time to get stingy. A flash of red caught his eye. His heart thudded, his chest tightened. He bounded toward the entrance and skidded to a stop.

Who the *fuck?* There was a guy draped all over her. Tall, spoiled frat-boy good looks, expensive suit, shit-eating grin. His arm was twined through Abby's. He was dragging her so close, they were hip to hip.

And she wasn't pushing him away.

The scene wound down into slow motion, every gesture exaggerated. The guy whispered in her ear. Abby blushed. She pulled out a business card. Frat Boy tapped her number into his phone and took a picture of her. More laughter, more simpering flirtatious bullshit. He showed her the picture. How cute. Ha-ha. He gave her his fucking business card. She tucked it carefully into her purse.

The sound and air and light and heat were sucked right out of the world, leaving him in a sickening ice-cold vacuum alone, watching Abby and Frat Boy giggle and flirt through a horribly clear wall of ice.

Don't freak out yet. Abby was a beautiful woman. Every man she met must put the moves on her. It didn't necessarily mean that she—

Frat Boy grabbed her hand and kissed it so passionately, it looked like he was sucking on it. The heat inside Zan rose to the boiling point. Abby broke away, laughing, and ran for the door, her color high.

Zan didn't even know why, but he retreated behind the Norfolk pines before she got the door open. She scurried past without seeing him.

He doubled over for a second, eyes squeezed shut, trying to suck breath into his lungs. He slunk out as soon as he could move again.

He sat in the van for a long time, slumped over the steering wheel. This was his own fault. Whipping himself into a romantic frenzy while Abby carried on with her hunt for the perfect husband. Christ, it hurt.

Last night was amazing. That's what she'd said, word for word.

And here he'd been behaving as if she'd said *I love you.*

Chapter

16

Abby noticed the envelope late that evening, when she passed by her office to grab her purse. It was just a plain white envelope with her name typed on it, but the very simplicity of it, the deliberate way that it was propped up against her coffee cup, struck her as ominous.

She opened it with caution. It was typed in capital letters.

IF YOU WANT THE TRUTH ABOUT ZAN DUNCAN CALL THE NUMBER
BELOW ASK FOR JOHN SARGENT SIGNED A FRIEND

Abby sank into her chair, legs rubbery.

Her colleagues didn't know about Zan. Bridget was suspicious, but she knew nothing about Zan, nor was she constitutionally capable of writing something without punctuating it. Dovey was smart enough to guess, but he would never play coy about something important.

The "truth." What could it be? A jealous ex-girlfriend? Illegitimate kids to support? A wife? She stared at the note as if it were poisonous. She didn't want to know what John Sargent had to say if it was going to kill this soft, hopeful feeling that had been huddled in her chest all day.

But if she didn't call, the note would get bigger and bigger, until it crowded out everything else. She clenched her teeth, dialed the number.

"Sargent residence," said an older woman's voice.

"Hello. Is Mr. Sargent available?" Abby asked.

"May I ask what it's regarding?"

She wasn't prepared for the question. "I'm, ah, interviewing people for a job, and I heard he had information about one of my candidates," she improvised. "Zan Duncan. Could you mention the name to him?"

"I'll tell him." The woman sounded doubtful. "Hold on."

Abby waited, stomach congealing to cold lead.

"Who wants to know about Zan Duncan?"

The brusque voice made her jump. "Ah, hi. My name is Abby Maitland. I was given your name as a person who could tell me more—"

"Yes, yes, my wife told me. Zan Duncan, huh? That's a name I haven't heard for years. Surprised he's still alive. Where should I begin? Grand auto theft? Drunk driving? Drug pushing? Manslaughter?"

"Manslaughter?" she repeated, her voice faint.

"So you want to start with that? Yes, he hit a man with a car. To be more precise, he hit a man with *my* car. Killed him, too. When the cops brought him in, they found cocaine in the trunk. Worthless punk didn't even do time. His dad was some cop hero, killed in the line of duty, fatherless boy, out come the violins. He should be rotting in jail."

"Oh, God," she whispered.

John Sargent paused. "Miss? This isn't about a job interview, is it? You're romantically involved with Zan Duncan, aren't you?"

Abby hesitated, but there was no reason to lie. "Yes."

Sargent went on, his voice gentler. "You sound like a nice young lady. I don't know you, but I'm sure that you can do better than that loser. Whoever told you to call me did you a favor, honey. Count on it."

"Thanks." She hung up and sank heavily into her chair.

Unbelievable. It was an evil joke. She'd made a formal list of things to avoid in a lover, and point for point, Zan embodied it.

Fate had made a blithering fool of her once again.

What you are is a sum total of where you've been. If you deny it, you're cutting off your own strength.

His words echoed in her mind with the ring of a universal truth.

After all, she had unsavory events in her own past. It would be hypocritical to judge him for something that had happened decades ago.

Screw it. She couldn't fight this feeling. The world could rub her nose in the awful truth all it wanted. She wanted Zan anyway.

She tried dialing Zan's number, for the twentieth time. His phone was still turned off. She looked around hopefully as she hurried to the bus stop, just in time for the last bus. No locksmith van anywhere to be seen. She was getting spoiled by those surprise rides home, with the yummy, naughty, sexy strings attached once they arrived.

A light was on in her apartment, she noticed as she climbed the stairs. Maybe Zan had left it on. The phone rang as she fit the key into her new lock. The answering machine clicked on. She paused in the kitchen and listened to it. Dovey. His voice was gratingly cheerful.

"Abby, are you home? I tried to get you alone today to chew the fat about Mr. Perfect with his big sexy dangling moneybags, but Bridget was breathing down my neck. You know that buying a twenty-thousand-dollar table was for your sole benefit? I can smell it when a man is trying to impress a girl. And then begging you for a dance in front of all of us, ooh-la-la! Anyhow, call me! We need to discuss what you're going to wear to the gala, now that you finally have a hot date. Ciao!"

Abby sank down into one of the kitchen chairs, shrugged off her blazer, and kicked off her shoes. She stared at the blinking message machine and pushed the button, in case there might be other, better messages. There weren't. Dovey's message began to play again.

She stabbed DELETE right after the bit about Lucien's big sexy dangling moneybags. Eeww. Not that she'd been hoping for a message from Zan. He'd never called before. Or even asked for her number.

"So tell me about the dangling moneybags, babe." Zan's soft voice floated eerily from the shadows of the living room.

Abby almost jumped out of her skin.

Zan was sprawled on her couch, Sheba draped across his chest.

Abby's knees quivered so badly, she slid down the wall and thudded to the floor on her butt. "My God, you scared me. What the hell are you doing here?" Her shock was quickly turning into fury.

Zan dropped Sheba gently onto the carpet. "Petting your cat."

Her jaw dropped. "You mean you've been here all day?"

"In and out," he said.

"In and out?" Her voice cracked with anger. "This is my private space, Zan! Mine! I pay the rent here! And I did not give you a key!"

Zan shrugged. "I pinned up your locks myself, remember?"

"You made yourself a spare?" She struggled to her feet, outraged. "That is so inappropriate!"

He got up from the couch. There was an expression in his eyes she had never seen before. A glittering hardness. "You tell me all about the dangling moneybags. Then we'll discuss how inappropriate I am."

"He's nothing!" she yelled. "Just a silly matchmaking idea of one of my friends at work, but he is absolutely nothing to me!"

Zan sauntered into the kitchen. "No? Is that a fact? Twenty-thousand-dollar table? What the fuck is that all about?"

"For the gala. The fund-raising ball, to inaugurate the new wing and launch the new exhibit." She was babbling as if she were in the wrong. "He bought a table for his administrative staff. That's all."

"That's all," Zan repeated. "Twenty thousand dollars, and you say 'that's all.' Wow. It must take a hell of a lot to impress you, sweetheart."

Abby reached out to touch his face, but he caught her wrist in his hand before she could make contact. "You impress me, Zan."

"Yeah? Oh. That's nice." He moved closer, tilted her head back. "That's sweet, Abby. Were you thinking how much I impress you this morning when you were exchanging phone numbers with Moneybags?"

She wrenched away from him, bewildered. "What do you mean?"

"How about when he started sucking your fingers?"

Abby's back fetched up against the wall. She wrapped her arms across her chest. Her throat was too dry to swallow. "You were watching me? You followed me? *Spied* on me? That's crazy, Zan. Why?"

His eyes were intensely cold. It started to dawn on her just how angry he really was.

"So what's Moneybags's name?" His voice was deceptively casual.

"None of your goddamn business. You shouldn't have spied on me! That's creepy stalker behavior, and I won't put up with it!"

"Right." He grabbed her purse, rifled through it, and found the embossed card. "Lucien Haverton. Haverton White Foundation."

She lunged for it, but Zan held it out of her reach. "Give me that!"

"Executive director, no less," he went on. "Wow, check you out. The big cheese himself. You never do things halfway, do you, Abby?"

"I hate you when you're sarcastic!" She was trembling, on the verge of tears. "Stop it! You're scaring me!"

He held it out. "Take it, then. If it's so fucking important to you."

She crumpled the card and flung it to the floor. "Why are you doing this?" she shouted. "It's so unnecessary! This guy is nothing!"

He passed a shaking hand over his face. "Jesus, Abby. You tell me you've got a date to go to a black tie party with a rich asshole who is publicly trying to buy you with his money, and then say it's *nothing*?"

"I did not 'tell' you anything! You overheard a private message!"

"So you would never have even mentioned this hot date to me?"

"You made up the rules, Zan!" She flung the words at him. "No strings, no spectators, no regrets. Remember?"

"Oh, great," he snarled. "Call me fatuous and stupid, but I thought we were past all that calculated bullshit!"

"Me too!" Abby yelled back. "But I wasn't counting on you cutting yourself a key and moving yourself into my apartment uninvited! Or that you would spy on me where I work! That's bad! If that's what happens when we suspend the rules, then we have to rethink this!"

She yanked her purse out of his hands and tossed it on the table. She stalked into the living room and flipped on a lamp. She was acutely aware of Zan's big, catlike body following her into the quiet room.

"Sounds like I've just been put in my place," he said.

Abby shrugged. "If you want to interpret it that way, you can."

"So you'll go to the ball, flirt and network with Moneybags, eat at his twenty-thousand-dollar table, let him kiss your hand. Then you come home, wipe off the makeup, and wait for me to sneak in your window to fuck you till you scream. Is that the plan, Abby?"

She covered her shaking mouth with her hand. "You'd better go," she said. "You're way out of my comfort zone."

He slid his fingers into her hair, gripping her scalp. "I don't care about your comfort zone. Comforting you is not where my talent lies."

"Don't do your silly Dominator crap on me. I'm not in the mood—"

Her words were cut off by a demanding, ruthlessly sensual kiss. "Don't tell me about your moods. I've got you nailed," he said. "I know what makes you hot, what makes you nuts, what makes you come. And I know you don't want me to go. No matter how pissed you are."

"Don't flatter yourself, you arrogant boob. You're acting like a—"

"I'm not invited to the fancy ball. Why bother to behave myself? That's not what turns you on." He wound his hand into her blouse. "You like it when I go crazy. Admit it."

Abby grabbed his hand. "Don't even think about ripping this blouse!" she hissed. "It cost me a hundred and eighty-five dollars!"

"I'm not impressed with the blouse. I'm more interested in the tits underneath," he said. "They'd look great framed by shreds of silk."

"Stop it," she fumed, prying his hands off. "You already destroyed one of my nice blouses today!"

"Take it off, if you care about it," he said.

"I have no intention of encouraging this kind of behavior by stripping for you!"

"But my bad behavior makes you so wet," he said. His hand tightened, stretching the delicate fabric to the limit.

Abby hastily unbuttoned the cuffs. "I shouldn't do this, but I don't feel like sacrificing more of my wardrobe to your piglike excesses," she grumbled. "I should just smack you right now, you overdramatic jerk."

He shoved the garment off her shoulders and tossed it away. The cool air made her nipples tighten. The ivory satin bra was the front-clasping kind. Zan made short work of it, flinging it to join the blouse.

Abby crossed her arms across her naked breasts and shook her hair over herself. It felt warm and ticklish sliding over her shivering shoulders. The low-slung miniskirt and the stockings made her feel more provocatively naked than if she had on nothing at all.

Zan stared at her body, his color high. He shook his head.

"What?" she snapped.

He slid his hands under her skirt, hooked her panties, and wrenched them off. "Just contemplating my next round of piglike excesses," he said, pushing her down onto the couch. "Open your legs, and I'll show you what I have in mind."

He pushed her thighs wide and stared down at her cleft, his breath raggedly audible in the quiet room. His hand rose up, tracing the tight swirl of ringlets, her sensitive, swollen labia. His finger slid inside her, thrusting in one deep, slow, liquid caress, up to his knuckle.

Abby moaned, clenching around his finger.

"I knew it." His voice was triumphant. "You're ready for me. Right now. You love my piglike excesses, don't you, baby?"

No, I don't love them, you big silly jerk. I love you! She wanted to scream the words at him, but in his present mood he wouldn't believe her anyway. She felt too vulnerable to risk being shoved away.

He stood up, peeled off his shirt, shucked his jeans. He knelt before her, naked, and started kissing his way up her inner thigh.

She pushed at his face. "Wait," she said breathlessly. "This is too weird for me. I . . . I thought you were furious with me."

"I have to taste you anyway. I need my fix of Abby juice. Those luminous pink bits inside your slit, long sleek hidden treasure, silk and sea salt and sweet nectar, oh my God, I can't stop licking it. And your clit, all swollen up like a pearl, waiting for me to—"

His words cut off as he closed his warm lips around her clitoris, his tongue rasping tenderly back and forth. He'd learned her body so well, he turned her on so fast, she was already dissolving into her first climax. He laughed, his mouth tickling her tender flesh as it shuddered through her, and tugged her down until she was lying on her side.

He propped her legs up and rose onto his knees, his cock rising up in front of her face. "Suck me, Abby."

There was no command in his voice, just shaky pleading. She reached for him, eager to absorb his passionate energy and coax back the wonderful closeness they had shared the night before.

He gripped her hair, head flung back, eyes closed. She loved it that he couldn't keep still. Three times he almost came, going stone hard and hot. Each time he backed it off, holding her head still while the pulsations throbbed beneath his balls, under her caressing fingers.

She was squeezing her own thighs together to top the crest of pleasure that kept beckoning and teasing, and Zan slid his hand between her thighs. "Squeeze my hand," he said. "While you suck me."

Her eyes fluttered open. "But don't you want to—"

"Not yet."

"You never let me make you come," she complained. "You are such a control freak. Relax, already."

He shook with breathless laughter and nudged his penis against her mouth again. "Shh. Squeeze around my hand. Pump those muscles as fast as you can. Harder . . . oh God, baby, *yes* . . ."

A throbbing rush of pleasure pounded and crashed over her.

When she stirred, he was ready with the condom, stroking his heavy erection. When he saw her eyes open, he rearranged her body. She made no resistance as he positioned her for his pleasure. He stacked her sofa pillows behind her back so her bottom was right at the edge, and pressed her thighs high and wide.

"Watch me," he said.

It didn't matter how tired she was, the contact electrified her, brought her into painful, trembling eagerness. He prodded himself inside her with teasing thrusts, swiveling to catch every sensitive bit, and lavishing hot, caressing contact on all of them with each skillful stroke. She came to life again, moved, lifting her hips, offering herself.

His movements grew faster. They stared down, mesmerized by the pulsing rhythm, by the broad gleaming shaft disappearing inside her in a long, delicious lunge, dragging out in yet another sensual caress.

Abby let out a whimpering gasp with each shock of contact. The lovely swell was rushing toward her again, huge and inexorable.

Zan put his hand down to caress her clit. She looked into his eyes, but he tilted her face down. "Look at us," he said. "When you're dancing with Moneybags, think of how it felt when I was inside you."

"No!" She tried to shove him away, but she was too far gone. She felt like she was going to faint. She didn't want this. Didn't want to fall apart while Zan watched her with that cold look in his eyes.

"Every time he touches you," he whispered. "Every time he looks at you. Think . . . about . . . this." He punctuated each word with a driving plunge of his hips.

She couldn't hold the climax back. It wiped her out. When she dared to open her eyes again, he was still staring. Eyes still cold.

"You bastard." She licked her dry lips. "Why did you do that?"

"I wanted to make a point," he said. "I think the point was taken."

She hauled her arm back and whacked him in the face.

He didn't even try to avoid the blow. He pulled himself out of her body without a word, and slid the condom off his still-erect penis. He padded into the dark kitchen and rustled around, getting rid of it.

Abby slid off the couch, tried to get to her feet, and ended up in a shaky crouch, her hot, tear-blinded face pressed hard into the sofa cushions. Zan came back into the room and began to pull his jeans on.

"That was mean," she whispered. "Really awful, Zan."

"Yeah, well. In any case, you came. Like crazy. You loved it, babe. What a complicated girl you are. A guy has to watch himself with you."

That hurt so badly, it made her breath stick in her chest like something heavy and solid. "You pushed me," she accused him. "You shoved me to the edge, and then messed with my mind when it was too late for me to stop. It's unfair to make me feel dirty for that."

He shrugged. "Hey. Life's not fair. I've been reflecting on that sad fact myself. All afternoon."

She got up, standing as tall as she could. Just like Dovey said. Shoulders back, chin up, tits out. She had nothing to be ashamed of. "Just go," she said. "Leave the keys you made here. Don't come back."

He groped in his pocket. Laid two keys on the shelf by the stereo.

It was the first time she'd even looked in that direction. She hadn't even noticed the table. Tall tapers, flickering over a bacchanalian feast. Heaps of assorted fruit, plates of cheese, roasted meats, a dish of some sort of pasta, salads. Wine, decanted and ready to pour. Some goopy dessert item, heaped with whipped cream and drizzled chocolate.

"Oh my God," she whispered.

"Never mind," Zan said, shrugging into his jacket. "Just put it out with the trash." He walked out the door.

The strength that had held her up drained away after the door thudded shut. She sank down to the carpet, hugging her knees, and lay there, rolled into a ball. She heard wet smacking sounds at some point. Her opportunistic cat had leaped onto the table to sample Zan's feast.

Abby didn't have the strength to scold her. She just lay on the carpet, watching the shadows dance on the walls until the candles burned down, guttered in their pools of wax, and went out.

Chapter

17

". . . on Sunday afternoon at St. Mary's, and we're all going to chip in to buy some . . . Abby? Abby, are you OK?"

Abby rubbed her eyes and blinked until the sparkles in her eyes resolved into Cathy's face. "Yeah?" she asked blearily. "What did you say? Sorry. I'm kind of wiped out."

"Are you coming down with something?" Cathy asked anxiously. "God, I hope not, the day before the gala! Bridget would have kittens."

Abby shook her head. "Just not sleeping much."

Cathy perched on the edge of Abby's desk. "OK," she said doubtfully. "Anyhow, as I was saying. I just got a call from Gwen, Mrs. Clayborne's secretary. Elaine's funeral is Monday afternoon at five. I'm making sure everyone knows, and we're all chipping in ten bucks apiece for the flowers. I'm doing the collection now."

Abby pulled her checkbook out of her purse. She scrawled the check. "Here you go. Monday afternoon?" She sat up straighter. "Oh, wait. If the medical examiner released the body, they must have done the autopsy. Maybe they know more about the bastard who killed her!"

Cathy winced. "Uh . . . maybe."

Some perverse impulse prompted Abby to ask, though she already knew the answer. "Do you think she committed suicide, Cathy?"

Cathy's eyes slid away. Abby suddenly had a sense of what all those hushed conversations that faded abruptly into nervous silence when she walked by had been about. Poor Abby, going off the deep end.

"Never mind," she said. "Didn't mean to put you on the spot."

"Abby, it's not that we don't believe you," Cathy said earnestly. "I believe that you believe, get me? But the facts don't lie. She was taking long lunches, coming in late every day, she'd lost weight, and she was so distracted. I was having a hard time covering for her. That's one of the signs of clinical depression, you know. People stop caring about their job and lose interest in their normal activities. I read a list of the symptoms in a brochure at my therapist's office. Elaine had them all."

They were also signs that a woman was having an intense secret love affair, Abby thought. The bleak irony was so un-funny. God knows, nobody had to tell her about the symptoms of depression.

"I think maybe I read that brochure, too," she muttered.

Cathy looked relieved that Abby seemed to be coming around to a more officially sanctioned point of view. "Well, I better hurry. I have to tell everyone about Monday, and call the florist. Let me know if there's anything I can do to help, Abby. Anything. Really, I mean it."

"Thanks, Cathy. You're sweet," Abby said.

Abby stared at the door after Cathy shut it. She felt so tired. So heavy. That nightmarish episode with Zan had been the final straw.

It was better this way. Of course. It would have been crazy and self-destructive to get passionately involved with a jealous, suspicious, controlling lover with a secret criminal past. To say nothing of the skill to let himself into her apartment at will. Very scary stuff.

But his face was stamped on the inside of her eyelids. His gorgeous grin. His hands, touching her. She jerked out of her helpless reverie when the phone rang. She snatched it up. "Abby Maitland."

"Hello, Abby. It's Lucien."

"Oh!" She had to struggle to switch gears from thinking about Zan, which always melted her brain into mush. "Uh, hi. How are you?"

"Well, thank you. Just wondering if you'd given any more thought to my invitation."

She hadn't, having had more compelling things to stress about. She thought about it on the spot. It would be embarrassing if she didn't have another date as an obvious excuse to turn him down. She might earn a few kiss-ass points with her bosses that could count toward saving her job. It was weird and inappropriate, yes, but what the hell? She'd survive. She didn't have to marry the guy, or sleep with him.

Just a dinner, a few dances, some conversation. She could deal.

Every time he touches you. Every time he looks at you. Think . . . about . . . this. Me, inside you. Fucking you.

She sprang to her feet, trembling with cold chills. Whoa. Zan must have put some evil spell on her. "Yes!" she said. "I accept."

"Excellent! Where shall I pick you up, and at what time?"

"I'll meet you at the museum," she said. "I'll be here all day."

"Very well. By the way, how goes your murder investigation?"

Abby's stomach clenched. "Nowhere, at the moment," she said. "Let's avoid the subject. No offense. It's just painful, that's all."

"Of course, I understand," Lucien said. "Till tomorrow, then."

Abby laid the phone down. She'd been so caught up in her own stupid love problems, she'd barely thought of her so-called investigation.

Guilt stabbed through her. How silly and self-absorbed she was.

She stared down at the seating chart for the gala that she'd been thrashing out over the past several hours. It was like solving an insanely complicated puzzle, and it still wasn't perfect, but she'd managed to keep bitter ex-wives seated relatively far away from their ex-husbands' new trophy wives, and acrimonious business rivals at a safe distance from each other. She'd called the caterers, given a last-minute head count, worked out a setup plan for tomorrow. The goodie bags were ready, the decorations were done, the speeches written and timed.

Everything else could wait a little while.

She stepped out of her office, glanced down the hall. Nobody was looking. She slipped into Elaine's office. Bridget and Peter were already interviewing people for Elaine's job, but nobody had bothered to clean out her office. There was something awful about that. They should have made a solemn ceremony of collecting Elaine's things and taking them . . . where? To her mother? Something should be done.

She might even feel a bit better if she could find something to do, no matter how small or symbolic. Who knew? Maybe she would find something significant that had been overlooked before.

Elaine's drawers were full of tidily organized office supplies, the shelves loaded with reference books. A silver-framed photograph held pride of place on the desk: a shot of Elaine and Abby at last year's gala, looking very fine in their sexy evening gowns, arms around each other's shoulders, glowing with champagne. That had been a really good night.

Tears were clogging her throat again. She swallowed them back as she rifled through the drawers. The bottom one held a purple gym bag, full of neatly folded workout clothes. They'd worked out together two days a week. Three, when they were being rigorous and good.

No blubbering. She rubbed at her face with her sleeve. She had no idea what she was looking for, but somebody ought to be looking, and since no one appeared to be doing so, she would damn well start looking herself. Cell phone? Organizer? They must have been in her purse. The police would surely have taken them. Unless Mark had.

There were some books in the drawers. A self-help book that promised to teach you how to "release your inner energy and transform your life," and a Spanish-English phrase book. The receipt was still tucked inside. It had been bought a week before Elaine's death.

Odd. She'd never known Elaine had an interest in Spanish.

She jerked open the zipper of Elaine's gym bag and began packing things into it. Books, the photos, her fountain pen, her emergency stash of Godiva chocolate, two pairs of gold earrings, a cashmere cardigan.

No tears. She'd cried for so long, her head felt hollow, and the muscles in her belly hurt, and her nose was sore. She tucked the photo of herself and Elaine at the gala into her pocket.

Bridget's voice crescendoed as she advanced down the hall. Abby scurried behind the door. ". . . don't care how hard a time she's having! If she can't handle her job, she should find work that's less demanding. I don't like to be a hard-ass, but after that shocking outburst the other day, even Peter had to admit that we simply cannot risk our . . ."

Bridget's voice faded as she turned the corner into her own office. So it was official. She was going to be fired.

Abby glanced at her watch. It was almost seven. She'd been there since six that morning. Had stayed till three in the morning the night before, trying to make up lost ground and prove her dedication.

It would seem that her efforts were useless.

Well, hell. She was too tired and depressed to face getting fired tonight. They could fire her tomorrow, if they felt like it.

No reason to fuss about how to excuse herself from the office if she was getting canned anyhow. She picked up Elaine's duffel bag and marched out of the museum without even bothering to be sneaky.

The clouds were heavy, threatening rain. Twilight was already well advanced. Abby stood on the steps, contemplating her next move.

She would take the things to Elaine's mother. Maybe the woman would know some more about the results of the forensics exams. Her hunger for news about that bordered on desperation.

Elaine's mother lived on the penthouse floor of an exclusive waterfront condo, and Abby regretted not calling a cab by the time she got there. The bag was heavy, she was chilly in her cotton blouse, and rain had begun to plop down. The blustery wind had whipped her French roll into a frothy halo of wisps. She looked like a rumpled waif.

So what? She wasn't trying to impress the woman.

Abby waited for a long time in the lobby before the doorman permitted her to get onto the elevator. Her next shock was when it opened directly into the apartment. She'd been trying to fix her hair in the mirror, and wasn't prepared to see Gloria Clayborne in front of her as the doors rolled open.

Gloria looked frail and lovely. Her face had a faintly martyred expression. "Abby Maitland? Elaine's little friend from the museum? You're the one who called the police, aren't you? I never thanked you."

"It's OK," she said, flustered.

"How nice to see you." Somehow, she succeeded in embracing Abby without actually touching her. "Elaine thought so highly of you."

"I thought highly of her, too," Abby said. "I wanted to tell you how sorry I am for your loss. She was such a wonderful girl."

Gloria's eyes looked faraway. "That's very kind of you, my dear."

There was a flat, stupid silence after the interchange. Abby was appalled at herself for being so tongue-tied in the face of the older woman's genteel suffering. "I, um, brought Elaine's things," she blurted. "From her office. Her personal things. Pictures, jewelry, and all that."

Gloria's eyelashes fluttered. "Did you, now? How very thoughtful of you. Thank you. You can put them in here." She slid open a long, mirrored door, revealing a closet filled with hanging coats. "I'll see to them later."

Abby put the bag into the closet, where it disappeared beneath the shadows of the hanging coats. Gloria slid the door smartly closed.

Abby felt an absurd urge to drag the door open and rescue the cheerful purple duffel bag from the closet. The last little piece of Elaine that she had, and it was buried under a bunch of old coats.

And she was a childish idiot, freaking out over a silly gym bag. Who could blame the woman for trying to avoid reminders of her grief?

"I better be going," she said hastily. "I don't want to keep you."

"No, come in. Have a cup of tea with me," Gloria said. She led the way into her apartment. The place was white. Walls, furniture, even an arrangement of white roses. It felt cold and funereal.

Nowhere to run, nowhere to hide. Gloria Clayborne was one of those women who had to do the proper thing at all costs. *Don't whine*, she lectured herself. Nobody had ordered her to come here.

"Thanks," she said, forcing a smile.

Minutes later, shortbread cookie in one hand and a cup of tea in the other, she was still tongue-tied. She'd always been good at finding things to chat about, but Gloria Clayborne's mournful, martyred eyes short-circuited that ability. She put her hand over the photo of herself and Elaine in her blazer pocket and clutched it like a talisman.

Gloria finally took pity on her. "Was there something in particular that you wanted to say to me, Abby?"

She seized the moment. "Yes," she said. "I was wondering if you'd heard anything from Cleland on the status of the investigation."

Gloria's face went blank. "Investigation?"

"The murder investigation," Abby prompted. "I figured, since the funeral is scheduled for Sunday, that they've already done the autopsy."

Gloria shook her head. "I don't think there are any doubts about what happened," she said. "And the police have no doubts, either."

Thank God. Finally, some good news. "Of course not," Abby said. "It's obvious that Mark is the murderer. I'm glad to hear it, because I'd gotten the feeling they weren't taking me seriously when I . . . what?"

For Gloria was shaking her head slowly back and forth. "No, Abby," she said gently. "There was no murder."

Abby's hand tightened. Her cookie exploded into buttery crumbs all over her lap. "What? What do you mean?"

The other woman's surgically retouched face seemed as hard and smooth as porcelain. "I don't know how well you knew my daughter."

Abby covered her mouth with her napkin. "I knew her well," she said. "When I moved here three years ago, she was incredibly nice to me. She introduced me to her friends, included me in everything, made me feel so welcome. She's . . . she was the sweetest girl I've ever met."

"Sweet, yes." Gloria's smile took on an ironic twist. "Strong, no. Perhaps you have no idea quite how fragile Elaine really was, Abby."

Abby wanted to head her off before she could say something unfair about Elaine, who could no longer defend herself.

"She was such a sensitive child," Gloria continued. "Incredibly imaginative. She had imaginary friends, as many children do, but she kept hers until she was in her teens. She didn't outgrow them, Abby."

"Ah, yes," Abby said. "But what does that have to do with—"

"She wrote letters to herself, when she was in high school. From imaginary boyfriends. She even mailed them to herself. I think her imaginary relationships were more satisfying to her than the real ones. Less problematic, less demanding."

"She had a real relationship with me," Abby said. "She was a wonderful friend. And not just to me. She was nice to everybody."

Elaine's mother leaned forward and patted her hand. Abby had to force herself not to snatch it away. "I'm grateful that Elaine had such a loyal friend," she said. "But you're going to have to accept the truth. Only then will you be able to let her go."

"Let her go?" Abby was getting desperate. "Mrs. Clayborne, you can't think that Elaine would actually hang herself. She wasn't depressed or suicidal. On the contrary. She was finally starting to—"

"She'd attempted suicide twice before," Gloria said.

Abby's mouth opened and closed.

"Once, when she was thirteen," Gloria continued. "She ate a bottle of sleeping pills. Again when she was nineteen. Pills again. She spent a good amount of her adolescence in mental institutions. I'm surprised she never told you. If you were such a good friend as you say."

Abby's teeth sank into her lower lip in a ruthless effort to keep herself from saying something unpleasantly rude. She stared around the pristine, sterile perfection of Gloria Clayborne's apartment.

"I imagine she felt ashamed," she said. "For not being perfect."

Gloria's eyes hardened. "My daughter had been medicated for severe depression for the last eighteen years. She had the best care that money could buy. The best doctors, the best institutions. The absolute best of everything. I did everything I could think of to help her."

Except for appreciating who she really was, you cold, stupid bitch.

Abby held the words back with a huge effort. "The day that she was killed, Elaine told me she'd hired a detective to do a background check on this man she was involved with. The detective had told her that this Mark was an alias. That he apparently did not exist."

The older woman's delicate eyebrows lifted. "Yes. Just as I said."

"No, you don't get it! Elaine was devastated that he had lied to her. She intended to confront him. He was walking in the door when I called! She called him on his lies, and he killed her! Don't you see?"

Gloria shook her head sadly. "Abby. There's no way to make this less painful for you. The background check turned up blank for the very simple reason that the man truly does not exist. There is no Mark. There never was. He was a wishful figment of Elaine's imagination."

"But I . . . but he . . ."

"Did you ever actually see him, Abby?"

"No, but . . ." Abby thought furiously. "No, wait. I heard him talking to her when I was on the phone with her. And I saw her order a romantic dinner for two that she intended to eat with him."

"Which she billed to me, yes. I know all about those romantic dinners for two," Gloria said dryly. "And what you heard could very easily have been a recording of some kind."

"No! That's ridiculous, Mrs. Clayborne. Elaine wouldn't fake something like that! Not to me. That's so convoluted and . . . crazy!"

"Yes," Gloria said, very softly, very sadly. "I know."

Abby wanted to slap that pitying look off the older woman's face.

"There is no Mark," Gloria said, her voice harder. "It was all an elaborate hoax. I don't pretend to understand why she did that to you. Maybe she felt she had to impress you. Maybe it's because of a lack of a father figure for so much of her life. I imagine at this point, we'll never know." She paused. "I'm so very, very sorry," she added deliberately.

Abby's mouth tasted bitter, like metal. "I bet you are. And you told the police that? The suicide attempts, the imaginary boyfriends?"

"Certainly I told them." Gloria's face had become once more a blank, serene mask. A white plaster statue of the suffering madonna.

Abby got to her feet. "I don't accept that," she said.

Gloria lifted her slim shoulders in a little shrug. "Then you will suffer even more than you have to."

"So be it," Abby said. "I'm going." She headed for the elevator. Her face felt numb, but it didn't matter. She no longer felt the slightest necessity to smile at that woman.

Gloria caught up with her. "Wait. I have to call the elevator for you," she said. "You have to have a key to operate it."

Abby stepped inside the elevator and turned to face Gloria Clayborne. "Elaine was murdered," she said flatly. "I am going to find out who did it. And when I do, you're going to feel rotten for turning your back on her. But I see that it's not the first time you've done that."

The doors closed just as the mask on Gloria's face crumpled.

Abby covered her own crumpled face with her hands as the elevator descended. She felt no satisfaction for having scolded the woman. What was the point? She wouldn't be able to make good on her arrogant pronouncements anyway. Like she had the faintest clue how to investigate a murder. She couldn't even hang on to her own damn job.

God, it hurt to imagine how Elaine must have felt, having a mother who had been so embarrassed for her. All the way to the bitter end. She walked out onto the street and wandered down the sidewalk, feeling shellshocked and lost. She turned at the sound of her name.

"Yo, Abby? Hey! That you?"

It was Nanette, the espresso cart girl. Today she was a platinum blonde with glittering eyelids, a silver bodysuit, and shiny black lipstick.

"Nanette! Where have you been? This isn't your usual spot."

"I moved," Nanette said cheerfully. "I make more money down here. More tourists. Plus I took a few days off because of my rehearsal schedule. I'm about to go to my last rehearsal now. The final dress. We're opening tomorrow. It's so exciting. Want your regular?"

"What the hell?" Abby said. "What are you rehearsing?"

Nanette packed espresso into the machine, looking pleased and embarrassed. "*Romeo and Juliet.*"

"Oh, really? I heard that the Stray Cat was doing that one this year. What part do you play?" She tried to imagine Nanette without face jewelry, decked out in a Renaissance gown. It boggled the imagination.

"I'm Juliet," Nanette said, batting her glittering eyelids modestly.

Abby's mouth dropped open for one brief, unguarded moment. "Nanette, that's . . . that's fabulous! How exciting for you!"

"Yeah, I know. It's a totally cool production. Extremely hip," Nanette confided. "Want to come?" She looked at Abby with big, hopeful eyes, twirling one of her silver eyebrow studs.

Abby blinked. "Uh . . . I . . . I'd love to," she heard herself say.

"Really? That's so excellent! I'll get you a great seat! Friday night, Saturday night, or the Sunday matinee?"

"Sunday is best," Abby said. "I've got the gala on Saturday night."

"No problem! Totally cool! I'll get you the best seat in the house!"

"I can't wait to see it," Abby said warmly.

"Oh, and would you do me a favor? I told Elaine, and she wanted to come, so I got her a ticket for the matinee. I've been meaning to give it to her except that she's, like, totally disappeared off the face of the earth. Would you give her the ticket and remind her about the show?"

Abby promptly fell to pieces.

A few seconds later she finally focused enough to hear Nanette's anxious voice. "... Jesus, Abby, are you OK? Should I call somebody?"

"No." She shook her head, wiped her eyes. She took the cup Nanette held out, and took a gulp. It was scalding hot. She coughed and sputtered. "Sorry, Nanette. It's just that . . . Elaine is dead."

Nanette's painted eyes went blank for several seconds, and then got huge and somber. She opened her mouth, closed it again.

She grabbed Abby's hand, led her to a nearby bench and pushed her down onto it, then sat down next to her. She grabbed Abby's hand, squeezing it and patting it with her other hand.

Abby's eyes welled up again. It was the nicest, realest thing anyone had done for her in days. She stared down at the complex, swirling henna designs on Nanette's hands. The girl's black-lacquered fingernails had glittering rhinestones glued to the center of each one.

"How?" Nanette asked, her voice very small.

"She was murdered," Abby said. "They're calling it a suicide, but that's bullshit. Elaine would never hang herself."

"Hang? Oh my God." Nanette's hand tightened. "That is so awful. And here I was, thinking that things were finally looking up for her."

"Why did you think that?" Abby ventured another cautious sip.

"It was when I saw her coming out of the hotel with Mr. Perfect, you know? I figured, great. She's finally getting a little afternoon delight, and it couldn't happen to a nicer girl, you know?"

"Mr. Perfect? You mean, you saw Mark? With your own eyes? Oh, God." Abby's heart pounded. "At this hotel? The Sedgewick?"

Nanette blinked at Abby's intensity. "Yeah. What about him?"

"Was he really good-looking?"

"Yeah, he was, as a matter of fact. I remember thinking, wowie zowie, you go, girlfriend. Then I decided that he looked like trouble."

"What sort of trouble?" Abby demanded.

"Oh, too good-looking to be for real. Tall and built, all that salon-treated blond hair. Guys like that are closet gays, or else they think they're God's gift, or whatever. There's always a catch when a guy dresses that well." She stopped, lips pursing into a black O. "You think this guy was the one . . ." Her voice trailed off. "Oh, jeez."

"Would you recognize him if you saw him in a police lineup?"

Nanette looked thoughtful. "Well, I could rule out ninety-nine point nine percent of the rest of humanity, that's for sure."

"What day were they at this hotel?" Abby asked. "What time?"

Nanette pondered. "It would have been Wednesday, after lunch. I was wearing my poison-green leotard. I remember drooling over that guy's leather coat and wishing I'd worn something warmer."

Abby pulled Nanette's slender form into her arms and gave her a tight, grateful hug. "Thank you so much," she said fervently.

"Don't worry about it," Nanette said, flustered and pleased. "Wait just a second, Abby. I've got something for you."

She went over to the espresso cart, dug through a big black bag behind it, and came back over with a small envelope in her hand.

"This is, ah . . . this was Elaine's ticket," she said hesitantly. "Why don't you take it? And I'll dedicate Sunday's performance to Elaine."

Abby hugged her again, and they both got very soggy.

She headed for the hotel once she got herself under control, stopping when she caught sight of herself in the glass. Yikes. She dug lipstick out of her purse and slicked some on, realizing too late that it was the Russian Red. Not a good choice. It made her seem too pale, à la Vampira, and accentuated the red around her eyes. Oh well. Too late. She tucked up her wisps as best she could and headed into the lobby. She assessed the staff and chose her prey. Young, male, chinless.

She unbuttoned the top two buttons of her blouse, took a deep breath, and stuck her chest out to strain the remaining buttons across her bosom. She headed toward him with a dazzling smile. The guy goggled, and peeked behind himself. His name tag read BRETT.

"Can I help you?" Brett asked timidly.

"Hi, Brett. I certainly hope so." She made her voice warm and soft, playing up her Southern accent. "I have a couple questions for you. I'm looking for a friend, trying to track down where she's been, and I think she was recently here. Have you seen this woman?"

She pulled the photo out of her pocket and showed it to him.

Brett stared at the photo, his pimply brow furrowed. A surprised look dawned on his face. "Yeah. I remember her. She was in here the other day. I checked them in right before I went on my lunch break."

Her chest fluttered with excitement. "So she was with someone?"

"Yeah," Brett said, eager to oblige. "A guy."

She whapped him with another high-wattage smile, and followed up with gentle prompting. "What kind of guy? Could you describe him?"

"Tall," Brett offered. "Long hair, I think. A big guy."

Abby felt dizzy. "Did they check in under his name or hers?"

Brett was gathering his wits for a reply when a heavyset older woman with iron-gray hair marched over. Her name tag read FRANCES, and under that, MANAGER. "Can I help you?" she asked.

"Actually, Brett was already helping me," Abby said.

"With what?" Frances's eyes narrowed.

"I'm looking for information on one of your—"

"We don't give out information about our guests," Frances declared. "Under any circumstances." She gave Brett a fulminating glance. He cringed, and pushed the photograph back toward Abby.

"Sorry," he whispered miserably, to both of them.

"Brett, come on into my office." Frances's voice was ominous.

Brett turned gray. Abby felt a stab of guilt, but desperation stiffened her spine. "Frances!" she called.

The other woman turned, still scowling. "Yes?"

"Is this hotel lobby equipped with a security video camera?"

Frances stuck out her chin. "Miss, we do not gossip about our guests. They mind their business and we respect their privacy."

"I'm not asking about your guests. I'm asking about your security," Abby said. "Do you have a camera or don't you?"

Frances shrugged impatiently. "Yes! So?"

Abby put her hand to her heart and exhaled a shaky breath. Her eyes were welling up again. Of all the silly times for that to happen.

"Thank you," she whispered, meaning it with her whole heart.

She walked out into the street, dazed with triumph. The police had the right to demand that tape from the hotel staff, even if she did not. And when they did, this Mark bastard would be all over it. Bingo.

She dug her cell phone out of her purse and the detective's card out of her wallet. Her fingers shook with excitement as she dialed.

"Cleland here," the man said curtly into the phone. "Who's this?"

"Hi, Detective, it's Abby Maitland," she said.

"Ah. What can I do for you, Ms. Maitland?"

"I have a lead for you," she announced.

He made a noncommittal sound. "Hmm. Is that a fact?"

"Yes. Solid proof that this guy Mark actually exists," Abby said. "I have an eyewitness who saw him. He checked into the Sedgewick Hotel with Elaine last Wednesday. They have a security camera. I even know the approximate time. You can see exactly what this guy looks like."

"Ms. Maitland." Cleland's voice was calm and measured, as if he were dealing with a fretful child. "You are aware, I hope, that it is not a crime to check into a hotel with a woman."

"Yes, I know that!" she snapped. "But being as how you dismissed this guy as a suspect because Elaine's mom told you that he didn't exist, I thought that his actual existence might be relevant to you."

"I don't appreciate the sarcasm." Cleland's voice had a hard edge. "Even if he does exist, he's not a murder suspect, because there was no murder. Elaine Clayborne hung herself. It's tragic, but there it is. No foul play. The district attorney has ruled it a suicide. Case closed."

She wanted to shriek with frustration. "But that's not possible! I told you, this guy was walking into her house when I—"

"The evidence techs were extremely thorough. No evidence of

violence of any kind was found in the autopsy. No cuts, bruises, abrasions; no drugs in her system; no blood, skin or hair under her nails; no broken blood vessels in her eyes to suggest suffocation. The marks on her neck are consistent with the placement of the rope. Blood was beginning to pool in her feet, indicating that the body was not moved after death. Doors and windows were not forced—"

"I told you that the guy had keys! He had *my* keys!"

"And were your keys on a yellow plastic shark keychain?"

Abby stopped short, mouth agape. "You found the keys?"

"In Ms. Clayborne's purse." Cleland's voice was clipped.

Abby's jaw flapped, but she rallied quickly. "He could have put them there," she argued. "Just to throw you off the track."

Cleland grunted. "Besides, there's no motive for a homicide. She had no enemies, no one benefits financially from her death—"

"But I gave you the motive!" Abby wailed. "I handed it right to you! He had to shut her up because she uncovered his false identity!"

"It is quite possible that Ms. Clayborne was sexually involved with someone," Cleland said doggedly. "But this does not necessarily mean that this hypothetical lover murdered her and then expertly covered his tracks by making it look exactly like a suicide, and I do mean *exactly*."

"No evidence except for what she said to me on the phone!"

Cleland was silent for a moment. "I don't know a gentle way to tell you this, but your friend was an extremely troubled young woman."

"You're telling me that she lured me to her house with a pack of convoluted lies and then killed herself just to spite me? That's sick!"

"Yes," Cleland said. "It is. That's my point. The forensics evidence, together with her past suicide attempts and her psychiatric history—"

"No, wait. Mrs. Clayborne said Elaine used pills, those other times," Abby broke in. "She wouldn't have changed styles if she were going to kill herself, which she absolutely wasn't, but just for the sake of argument, if she were, she would never use a rope! If you knew her, you'd understand. She hated for things to be ugly. She would never—"

"She bought the rope herself."

Abby sucked in a sharp breath. "She . . . she what?"

"We found the plastic packaging lying on the floor. Her prints were all over the plastic. The receipt was in the bag. It had the name of store, the time and date, even the purchase price. I checked the tape on the store's security camera. There was a three-minute interval of your friend, waiting in line to buy her rope."

"That's—that's still not proof," Abby faltered. "There are a million reasons she could have bought a . . . a length of, uh, rope."

Her voice faded into a dismayed silence. Yeah. Right. Hardly.

"I promise, Ms. Maitland. I have been doing my job," Cleland said heavily. "Please don't continue with this amateur murder investigation. It's not a good use of your time." He waited for a moment for a reply, then grunted again. "Have a good evening." He hung up.

Abby's phone hand dropped to her side. Rain pattered onto the sidewalk. She shuddered as cold drops snaked their way into her collar.

Chapter

18

bsessive.
O Zan didn't see himself that way. He was a pragmatic man. He didn't get carried away by lust or anger to the point of being obsessive.

Not until this moment, anyway.

He would have laughed, if his chest muscles were capable of moving. He'd been congratulating himself for getting out, tending to business, no more sulking in his lair, licking his wounds.

He'd walked out of the computer supplies store and there she was. Sitting on a bench, having an intense conversation with that bizarre-looking coffee cart girl. She'd lost weight, and her eyes looked huge and shadowy. As usual, her blouse was plastered to her body by the rain, thereby showing the world the perfect shape of her tits.

It was like being sucker punched. His whole body reacted. His belly fluttered, his heart thudded, he broke out in a sweat. It was a massive adrenaline rush, carefully crafted over millions of years of evolution to give him the surge of sheer brainless nerve necessary to chase her down, pick her up, and carry her off to his cave.

Where he knew just what he would do with her.

Unfortunately for his hormones, that kind of behavior was frowned upon in today's society. It was creepy and illegal to follow a girl around after she'd formally told him to fuck off. If he had any dignity, he would slink away now, before he did something he would regret.

She got up and ran across the street, tits bouncing. She stopped outside the mirrored window of the bank to freshen up her lipstick and fuss with her hair, then headed into the Sedgewick Hotel.

At seven thirty in the evening. His body went into a sick boil of anger. There was only one reason that a woman would go into a hotel in a town where she had her own place.

A hot rendezvous with Dangling Moneybags.

So what if she was? the cool voice of reason asked. Abby was a free woman. She could meet whom she pleased, when and where she pleased. He had no right to object. Or even judge, for that matter.

He couldn't move. He stood in the door, blocking other patrons from entering and exiting, immobile as a statue. Staring at the facade of the Sedgewick. Imagining his Abby in a hotel room with that smirking asshole. So much for dignity. It was all he could do not to throw up.

He was both puzzled and passionately relieved when she burst out a couple of minutes later, looking agitated. Her blouse gaped, showing miles of shadowy cleavage. She pulled out her phone, maybe to bitch the guy out for making her wait. Had a heated argument into it.

Then she just stood there for the longest time, eyes wide and lost-looking. So at least her new love affair was not running smoothly.

Cold fucking comfort, that.

Abby lifted her arm and flagged a cab. Zan sprinted for his van. He was in gear and tailing her cab before he knew what he was doing.

She took him for a sicko stalker anyway, and he'd bungled their last encounter so badly, he hadn't gotten a chance to explain himself.

He was living up to the label for real, but what the hell? Abby would never know. This was just to satisfy his own unhealthy curiosity.

He had to see if she'd rescheduled her rendezvous. See what luxury car the dickhead drove.

Before he hotwired it and rolled it off a cliff.

Yeah, right. He might fantasize about childish shit like that, but that was as far as it went. He wasn't Alex Duncan's son for nothing.

Zan's burning eyes fixed on the cab's taillights in the gathering dark. He was almost there before he realized where it was taking her.

Elaine's house.

Zan parked before the turnoff to Margolies Drive. He walked into the rhododendron bushes that screened the houses from the road. The cab turned around in the cul-de-sac and accelerated past him.

Abby stood on the street, staring up at her dead friend's house.

Rain pounded down. She just stared at the building as if waiting for it to say something to her. She didn't turn, or sense his presence. She wasn't thinking about him. She wasn't meeting Moneybags, either. She could care less about the whole fucking lot of them.

She was grieving for her friend.

His throat started to ache. He felt embarrassed for his angry, selfish thoughts. As if his lust and his hurt feelings meant jack shit when they were measured against what had happened in that house.

He wanted to call out to her, but he didn't want to scare her. She'd had enough adrenaline rushes lately. He pulled up her number on his cell. She jerked slightly as it rang, rummaged in her purse, and stared at the name that showed up on her display.

It kept ringing. She kept staring. Three—four—five—six times. If it got to ten, he would hang up and fade away into the bushes. Forever.

Seven. Eight. She pressed the button and put it to her ear.

"Hi," she said softly.

He was so surprised that she'd answered at all, he just sputtered for a while. "Uh . . . hello," he finally managed. "It's, uh, me."

"I know it's you."

He was at a loss for anything else to say. "Are you OK?"

He heard a soft, whispery laugh. "You always ask that."

"Sure. Only because you're always in trouble," he told her. "Always a drama. One damn crisis after another. What do you expect?"

"I have absolutely no idea what to expect from you." She looked up at the sky, as if just now noticing the pelting rain.

He felt guilty for sneaking around in the bushes. "Where are you?"

She looked back up at the house. "At Elaine's."

The sad, remote sound in her voice made him nervous. "What the hell are you doing there?" His voice was harsher than he meant it to be.

"Just thinking."

"Why can't you go and think someplace warm and dry and safe?"

He heard that whispery laugh again. "If you have to ask, there's no point in explaining it to you."

"You must be soaked," he said.

"How do you know I'm outside?" she asked.

"I'm not there to pick the lock, so I assume you're outside."

She wiped rain from her forehead with her sleeve. "Oh, I'm dry enough," she lied through her teeth. "I'm under a tree. No problem."

Yeah, right. No tree, no coat, no car, no decent shoes, in the rain and the dark. The cab was long gone, the house looked like something out of a horror flick, and for some reason, he felt responsible for all of it.

"Aw, fuck," he muttered. "Stay right where you are, Abby."

He raced back to his van and drove into the cul-de-sac. Abby gaped as he jerked to a stop. He got out and pulled his jacket off.

"You've been following me," she accused.

"So?" He draped the jacket around her shoulders. "What of it?"

"What of it, my ass! That's called stalking," she lectured him. "It's illegal, Zan. And creepy. And unsexy, I hope you're aware."

He preferred the rosy indignation on her face to the lost, faraway look she'd had before. "You shouldn't loiter in the rain on dark, deserted streets with no jacket and no ride," he countered.

"That has nothing to do with anything. It's also not illegal!"

"Nah, just stupid," he said. "What the hell were you thinking?"

"About Elaine," she said simply.

That little zinger cut off the tirade he was winding up to. He looked at the house. The memory of what he'd seen there made him queasy and sad. "Is that a good idea?" he asked.

An ironic smile flitted across her face. "Probably not."

He pulled the jacket around her shoulders. "You're chilled. Get into the van."

She looked worried. "Zan. Please. We shouldn't even start. We'll just crash and burn, and I can't take it again. It's just too awful."

"Just get in." He tried to soften the edge in his voice. "You're shivering." He put his arm around her shoulders and helped her up into the van. He got in and started up the motor.

She grabbed his hand on the gearshift as he put it into first. "Hey! Just where do you think you're going?"

"Anywhere." He pulled out. "This place is bad for you."

"I'll decide that for myself!" She flung open the door.

Zan screeched to a halt and grabbed her arm before she could scramble out. "Jesus, Abby! That's dangerous!"

"Do not push me around, Zan!" Her voice shook. "I have had a really shitty day. I won't put up with it. I'm warning you."

He yanked up the emergency brake and threw up his arms in frustration. "Goddamn it, Abby, you shouldn't be moping here. I know it's hard, but you have to put this behind you and move on!"

"I can't!" Abby yelled. "She was my friend! And nobody else seems to give a damn, not even her mother! Everyone's decided that Elaine had a bad day and decided to hang herself, out of nowhere, and that she made up this story about the psycho sadist boyfriend just to mess with my mind. Bullshit! This guy exists, and he killed her, and he's going to get away with it! So don't tell me to move on! Not you too!"

He killed the engine and reached out for her hand. He waited for a few moments before he dared the next question. "What did you think you were going to accomplish, standing around in the rain?"

She huddled into the black shell of his jacket. "I don't know," she admitted. "I wanted to poke around. See what occurred to me."

"Look for clues? Like Nancy Drew?"

She squinted at him. "Don't you dare make fun of me."

"OK, I won't," he agreed. "So how were you planning to get in?"

She fiddled with the battered cuff. "I hadn't gotten that far," she said, her voice small. "I was considering my options."

"Breaking in? The cat burglar in the miniskirt and the gartered hose and the three-inch heels? You always think ahead, Abby."

"Oh, shut up," she said crossly. "For one thing, this isn't a miniskirt. It's just a few inches above the knee. For another, these heels are two and a half inches. Measure them if you don't believe me. Three, I didn't plan on coming here today, or I would have dressed differently. And lastly, I wouldn't be burglarizing anything. No one lives here. It's not even a crime scene anymore. It's just a sad old empty house now."

He snorted. "It's still against the law."

"So's stalking," she shot back.

"Hmm." He gazed out at Elaine's house, drumming his fingers. "So what's your plan? Break the window with a brick?"

"I hadn't really made a plan. But since you've so fortuitously shown up . . ." Her voice trailed off suggestively.

"Ah. I see," he said. "A low-life stalker like myself should have no scruples about breaking the law, right?"

She looked disgusted. "Stop whining. This is not a whim. If it bugs you, leave. I was standing here minding my own business, and you pop up out of nowhere and start throwing your weight around—"

"Let's skip the finger pointing and get down to business," he said. "What'll you give me if I do?"

She pondered that. "Double your usual fee?" she offered. "I wouldn't worry about the lawbreaking part. Nobody seems to care."

He shook his head. "I don't want your money, Abby."

She stared at him, eyes widening with outrage. "I cannot believe you even have the nerve to imply it, Zan. If you think you have a chance in hell of getting into my pants after the other night—"

"Sorry about that," he was astonished to hear himself say. "It was mean and stupid. I've been wishing ever since that I hadn't done it."

She tilted her head and studied his face. "Hmm," she murmured. "Is that a fact?"

"Yes." He realized the moment he spoke that it was true, and that it felt good to say it. "I've been feeling bad about it. Would you like me to grovel? Plead your forgiveness? Should I wallow in the mud at your feet?"

"Yes," she said promptly. "Please do. Go right ahead, Zan."

He was taken aback. "Uh . . ."

"There's a sloppy puddle over there, in the corner of the yard."

He studied her face. Her mouth was tight, quivering from trying not to smile. Euphoria fizzed through him until he felt like levitating right up off the seat. "You're glad to see me," he said. "Admit it."

"That's not groveling," she said primly. "That's called gloating."

"You didn't deny it, though."

She shrugged. "A locksmith is handy in these situations."

He picked up a tangled lock of her hair and twirled it around his finger. "It's nice to feel useful. But if you want me to break the law and risk my livelihood, you'd better make it worth my while."

She rolled her eyes. "I've had enough of your kinky sexual mind games," she said crisply. "I'll figure out something else, thanks."

"OK. Call some other locksmith. Ask him to do this for you. I'll stay and watch the show. Should be entertaining."

"Are you deliberately trying to piss me off?" she asked.

"Maybe," he admitted. "I'd rather have you pissed off than sad and mopey. Pissed is comfortably familiar. Sad and mopey scares me."

She made a disgusted sound. "If my emotions are so frightening to you, maybe you should just leave me and my emotions alone."

He blew out a violent sigh. "Yeah, right. Tell it to my dick."

Her eyes flicked to his crotch. "I'll pass, thanks," she said demurely. "Your dick isn't all that talented a conversationalist."

"He's got lots of other great qualities," Zan offered hopefully.

She muffled laughter with her hand. "I know what you're doing, Zan. You're trying to control this thing between us by reducing it to an economic bargain. But you can't. It'll just blow up in our faces."

He barely even heard what she said, he was so thrilled with himself for making her laugh. He kissed her hand. "Psychoanalyze me all you want, baby. It'll have absolutely no effect on my hard-on."

"I'm on to you, Zan," she said gravely. "I see right through you."

"Whoa." He whistled. "You terrify me, babe."

"Oh yes. I know I do," she said dryly. "So let me explain what's going to happen here. I'm going into the house to take a look around. If you want to help, that would be lovely. If you'd rather not, bye-bye. I understand. Have a nice life. I'll manage nicely on my own."

"But I—"

"I do not promise sexual favors in return for services rendered," she said. "It might happen, but then again, it might not. It depends on how you act. How I feel. You know me and my wacky mood swings."

He reached out to touch her hair again, but she grabbed his hand and held it out away from her. "I am not a sure thing, Zan," she said, enunciating every word with icy precision. "Get that into your head."

He nodded. "I never thought you were."

She wiggled out of his jacket and laid it on the seat. "Thanks for getting me all worked up," she said. "I needed the energy boost."

"I'm glad that I'm good for something," he said sourly.

The smile that hovered around her lips was infinitely mysterious. "Aw. You're good for lots of things, Zan." Her low voice brushed across his nerve endings like fine fur. She leaned one slender hand on his shoulder and kissed him, soft lips lingering against his. The faint, flirtatious flick of her tongue made desire roar through his body.

Her hand stroked his thigh and gave his throbbing cock an indulgent little *pat-pat-pat*. "Be good, now," she murmured. "Bye."

She got out and started across the lawn. Hips swaying, back elegantly straight, though each wobbling step made her heels sink into the soggy turf. Shit. She'd called his bluff. He was so fucked.

He cursed viciously under his breath, leaped out of the van, and sprinted after her, laying the jacket over her shoulders again.

"Put this on before you catch pneumonia," he growled.

The smile she gave him was so luminously beautiful, it hurt him.

"Oh, good," she said. "I'm so glad you decided to stay."

He was an idiot and a chump, but she knew just how to play him. Witchy woman. He couldn't resist her wiles.

He threw his arm over her shoulders, shielding her from the pelting rain and the oppressive darkness that oozed from that house.

Chapter

19

Keep it together, you crybaby dork. Bursting into tears of gratitude would totally destroy her purely symbolic upper hand. Still, she'd have given anything at that moment for two seconds of privacy and a tissue.

She was pathetically glad that he hadn't left her alone. He was so strong and sexy and yummy. His presence gave every cell in her body a jolt of energy. He was a bad idea, sure, but today she didn't care.

I'll manage nicely on my own. Like she'd been doing so brilliantly so far. Soggy, depressed, and probably fired too. She had to keep Rule Number One in mind. Desperation was not sexy.

Unfortunately, it appeared to be her default setting lately.

Warm shivers of pleasure rippled through her from the contact of his arm over her shoulders. The rain had plastered his T-shirt to his shoulders. "Would you like your jacket back? You're getting wet."

He shot her an ironic glance. "Go ahead, Abby. Emasculate me with a few well-chosen words."

"Gosh," she murmured. "I had no idea your masculinity was so fragile."

He crouched in front of the door and gave her a quick grin. "Keep the coat, baby. You're not wearing enough clothes."

He pulled out his little leather envelope, unrolled it, and chose two of the tools. He inserted them delicately into the lock mechanism. His eyes looked a million miles away. The lock yielded in four minutes.

"That was quick," she commented. "Quicker than the last time."

"Last time, I was scared. This is a Medeco four-pin pop lock. If it takes me four minutes, that means it's a good lock."

"I didn't know it was so easy," she said.

"It's not. I'm just good. Your average thief doesn't invest the time I have learning to pick these. It's quicker to break the glass."

She stared into the yawning dark beyond the open door. Zan clasped her shoulder and pulled her gently back. "Me first."

"It doesn't matter now," she said. "There's no one here."

He gave her an expressive grunt and pushed his way past her into the entry hall. She flipped on the hall light.

"Is that a good idea?" Zan said. "We are breaking and entering."

"No one cares." Her voice sounded hollow. "I would almost be gratified for Elaine's sake if somebody did make a fuss."

"Not me," he muttered. "I'll pass."

The crime scene tape was gone, but the place still felt different. The scent of Elaine's potpourri had been replaced by the sharp smells of strong industrial cleaning fluids. It was no longer Elaine's pretty house, full of color and pottery and knickknacks. It was violated and sterilized. A corpse of a house, empty of all that mattered.

Abby stared around, at a loss. She didn't have a plan, just a blind impulse. Maybe Elaine's ghost would nudge her in the right direction.

That spooky thought raised shuddery goose bumps on her skin.

She forced herself to walk slowly and systematically through the dining room. The rope was gone, the room starkly neat. A mirror on the far side of the room reflected her pale face, her startled-looking eyes.

The table had been pushed back to its original spot, under the chandelier. She stared up at it. "I wish I knew why she bought the rope."

"She bought it herself?" Zan's mouth tightened. "That's bad."

She pushed past Zan without meeting his eyes as she walked into the hall. She didn't want to see his expression. She was no brilliant private eye, to find a shred of overlooked evidence to rub Cleland's nose in. But she was all Elaine had. She would just have to do.

The artificial cleanliness of the house pushed her that much further away from Elaine's final minutes. She moved through the downstairs rooms, trying to keep her mind empty and receptive. Zan followed her without comment.

Memories of Elaine kept broadsiding her. A painting Abby had given Elaine for her last birthday, framed and hung in the hallway. The Mexican rug Elaine had bought at a conference in Santa Fe.

No clues here. Just memories that made her chest ache and burn.

She gazed for a few minutes at the old-fashioned bedroom, at the long shelf crowded with antique dolls, then at the adjoining room that had been Elaine's home office. She leafed through the tidy drawers. There were piles of lists: gifts to buy, things to remember, notes to self for future exhibits, ideas for self-improvement, lists of positive affirmations, inspirational quotes, all written in Elaine's old-fashioned script. A ceramic holder for a box of tissues in the shape of a fat tabby cat sat on the desk. Abby grabbed one and pressed it against her nose as she flipped the lights off. She elbowed past Zan and hurried down the stairs.

That left the kitchen. It gleamed with frigid, perfect order. Elaine had never used the place. She'd lived on yogurt, fruit, and takeout.

A wad of menus was clipped to the fridge by a magnet in the shape of a hot fudge sundae. Elaine had adored sweets. Abby leafed through them. Greek, Italian, Indian, sushi, Chinese, and . . . wait.

That wasn't a menu. That was a credit card bill. Elaine had stuck it on the fridge, probably as a reminder to pay it, and the menus had covered it up. She checked the date. Months old.

Abby pulled out her phone. Maybe no one had thought to cancel it yet. She dialed the 1-800 number, and waited on hold until an agent came on line. "Hello, my name is Mrs. Simpson," said a bored sounding woman. "May I have your card number, please?"

"Sure." Abby rattled off the number on the bill.

"Will you verify your first and last name, please?"

She crossed her fingers. "Elaine Clayborne." A shiver went up her spine, as if impersonating her murdered friend cast a ghostly shadow over her.

"How can I help you, Ms. Clayborne?"

"I want to check my most recent charges, please," Abby said.

"For security purposes, would you verify your date of birth, your home telephone number, and your mother's maiden name?"

She rattled off the birthdate and number while frantically trying to remember if she had ever known Gloria's maiden name. Elaine's middle name was Carter. It was her best guess. "Gloria Carter."

There was a brief pause. Abby held her breath, groping for a pen. Zan placed one in her hand.

"There's a charge to Cape Voyager, for two thousand twenty dollars, dated June sixth. There's the Crown Royale Suites Hotel, one hundred ninety-seven dollars, dated June third. There's a charge for seventeen dollars at the Ace Hardware store, dated June second. Also on June second, one hundred ninety-five dollars at the Hinkley House. Then there's a charge on June first for the Sedgewick Hotel, for two hundred and thirty-five dollars," the agent droned

Abby scribbled the items madly on one of the takeout menus.

"Do you want me to keep on going to last month's charges?"

"No, that's good for now, thank you." She hung up and stared at the notations she'd made. "What's Cape Voyager?"

"A travel agency in Cascade Springs," Zan said. "I've seen their ads. A chunk of money that big has got to be a plane ticket."

Some travel agencies were open later in the evening. It was worth a try. Abby called information for Cape Voyager's number, and dialed it.

"Cape Voyager," answered a chirpy female voice. "Can I help you?"

Abby crossed her fingers. "Hi. My name is Elaine Clayborne," she said, in her best breathy, ditzy bimbo voice. "I bought a plane ticket from you guys, and this is so embarrassing, but my purse got stolen, and the ticket was in it. Everything is gone. I'm not sure what to do."

"Was it an electronic ticket?"

'I don't remember. I'm such a space case. Could you check?"

"Who helped you?" The girl had the forced patience in her voice that characterized people who dealt with the public all day.

"Gee, I'm so out of it," Abby mumbled. "The paper I wrote the travel agent's name on was in my purse, too. Could you ask around?"

"Hold on, please." The phone clicked, and she was listening to Muzak. Her eyes fastened on Zan's. His eyes were thoughtful. He grabbed her hand. She hung on, grateful for the contact.

The phone clicked. "Ms. Clayborne? This is Maureen. I helped you last week. I understand you've lost the paperwork for your ticket?"

"That's right. I just wondered if you could repeat the itinerary to me so I can, uh, tell the car when to meet me," she improvised wildly.

"OK. Flight 605 with TransOceanic Air, leaving from Sea-Tac on June twenty-first at eight fifty AM, changing in Chicago for flight 3262 at two thirty PM for Barcelona."

Barcelona? Abby gaped, then forced a brisk, unsurprised note into her voice. "OK, Flight 605 for Chicago, then 3262 for Barcelona. Coming back when?"

Maureen paused. "It's a one-way ticket."

"One way?" The words popped out before she realized how stupid they must sound.

"That's news to you? Look, miss, whoever you are, you'd better come here before I tell you anything else. I'm not going to repeat the authorization code until I see some ID from you."

"Uh, sure. Thanks," Abby said, dazed. "I'll . . . I'll come by."

She hung up the phone and stared into space. "A one-way ticket," she repeated. "To Barcelona."

Zan looked down at her scribbled list. "Those hotels are upscale B&B's or luxury hotels. The only one in Silver Fork is the Sedgewick. The other two are about twenty-five minutes away."

"I went to the Sedgewick today," Abby said. "Nanette told me she saw Elaine there last week with her new boyfriend."

"What kind of dickwad makes the lady pay for the room three times in a row?" Zan asked.

"A dickwad who didn't want to show up on any paperwork?"

Zan shrugged. "Yeah. Maybe."

The relief that swept over her was so intense, it made her knees buckle. She sat down in one of the kitchen chairs. "You believe me?"

Zan's face tightened. "I was choosing not to have an opinion, since it's none of my goddamn business."

"But you've changed your mind? Please say that you have, Zan."

He shrugged. "I didn't know Elaine Clayborne, so I can't speculate about her. But I know you. It looks like you were a real friend to her. I overheard her phone call, too, and it sounded genuine to me. If you say she wouldn't mess with your mind, I'm inclined to believe you. And buying a ticket to Spain does not strike me as suicidal behavior. So I think that you're on to something very weird. For what it's worth."

"It's worth a lot," Abby said fervently. "Thank you, Zan."

His brows drew together. "That does not mean that I think it's a good idea for you to run around trying to track this asshole down, however. If he actually did kill Elaine—"

"What do you mean, if? Don't start with 'if' again, for God's sake."

"If," he repeated heavily. "If he did, then you're talking about an ice-cold professional killer who knows how to cover his tracks well enough to fool the police. You need to stay as far away from a guy like that as you possibly can. Give this to the cops, Abby. Don't be stupid."

"I tried!" she yelled. "I've already given what I thought were fabulous clues to the detective, but they've ruled it a suicide and closed the case! I would need something more flashy than a plane ticket for them to take me seriously. Cleland already thinks I'm a hysterical idiot."

She walked over to the window and focused on the gold Renault in the driveway. She flipped off the kitchen light and headed for the door. "I want to look in that car."

Zan made a frustrated sound and followed her. "I don't suppose you have the keys?"

"If you don't want to open it, I'll just break a window. Elaine would understand." She poked around the shrubbery until she found a half-buried brick and headed purposefully toward Elaine's car.

Zan lunged at her and held her upraised arm. "Hey. Hold on."

She brandished her chunk of masonry. "Let go of me," she said shakily. "I have to do this really quick, or I'll lose my nerve."

"Put it down," he snarled. "I'll open the fucking car for you, OK?"

She tossed the brick into the bushes and doubled over with a shaky sigh. "Thanks," she whispered.

He stalked off to his van and came back with the duffel bag she'd seen the night he opened Reginald's car. "Don't thank me," he growled, pulling out his tools. "This is emotional blackmail, and I don't appreciate it. Don't stand here while I'm working. You distract me."

Abby backed away, biting her trembling lip. She almost regretted not breaking the window. It would have felt good to shatter something.

The door popped open after a couple of minutes. Zan gathered up his things and made a be-my-guest gesture with his hand.

Abby slid into the driver's seat and looked around. The car still smelled new. The glove compartment held a flashlight, registration, maps. Back in the dear old days when she had owned a car, it would have been a cluster of clues for a curious searcher, full of receipts and mementos from everywhere she'd recently been. Not neatnik Elaine.

There was a Heavenly Beans paper coffee cup in the front cupholder. Abby stared at the coral lipstick smudge on the edge of it.

She clamped her hand over her mouth. She could not start to cry. Not with Zan waiting outside in the rain, fuming. She stuck the cup back in, and noticed a scrap of paper stuck inside the cupholder.

She fished it out. It was a receipt from a parking garage on Bellavista Drive. Times and dates were stamped on it. Elaine had parked there at 10:00 PM, four nights before she'd been killed. She'd left at 8:50 the following morning. Abby grabbed the flashlight and searched the front seat more carefully. She was rewarded by another parking receipt that had slid down into the well of the emergency brake.

It was dated a week before Elaine's death. Same garage.

Mark had insisted that Elaine park in a garage five blocks from his house. Abby's heart began to race. She got out, and held the receipt out to Zan. "Would you give me a ride to this place?"

He took the slip of paper and stared at it. "You shouldn't get any deeper into this," he said. "It's starting to feel dangerous."

"You've finally noticed?" she said. "It certainly was dangerous for Elaine." She snatched the paper back. "Don't worry. You don't have to. I'll just call my car service." She pulled out her cell phone.

He caught her around the waist and pulled her back against himself. "I hate it when you blow me off like that," he said roughly.

She was startled at his vehemence. "I don't mean to be rude," she said. "I'm just on a roll, and I can't stop, or I'll lose my momentum."

"Go get in the van, then. Don't waste your precious momentum."

He was being a bad-tempered bear; but somehow even his snotty, sarcastic comments had the effect of cutting the creepiness of the situation. Everything he said either made her angry or made her giggle, and either option was way better than being sad, lonely and terrified.

She forced herself to ignore the anger that radiated off him. When he parked in front of the garage on Bellavista, she pulled out her compact and freshened up her lipstick. She unwound her messy bun, fluffed up the damp strands as best she could, and adjusted the snug blouse. "Wait here," she said. "I'll go talk to the attendant."

He stared at her, incredulous. "You think I'm letting you go in there alone with your shirt hanging open? Get real, Abby. Better yet, get dressed! Button your shirt, for fuck's sake!"

"My shirt is not either hanging open," she protested. "I'm perfectly decent. I never button those two top buttons."

"Decent, my ass!" he snarled. "You can see right into your bra!"

"If you're an inch from my face, looking down! Please, don't follow me. I'd rather talk to whoever's in there without you glowering at me."

"Dream on, sweetheart." He slammed the door shut, spun her around and buttoned her blouse right up to her neck.

She pulled away, teetering on her heels, and marched down the slope into the garage. She headed toward the attendant's booth and gathered what was left of her energy to shine high-potency charm out of every pore. She hit him with her thousand-dollar smile at ten paces.

The guy blinked and leaned forward for a closer look. "Can I help you?" His eyes flicked doubtfully up to Zan's face. Zan glared back at him.

Abby dug a vicious elbow into Zan's ribs. "I sure hope so. I'm looking for information about a friend of mine." She pulled the photo out of her pocket and handed it to him. "Have you seen her recently?"

She knew, from the flicker in his eyes, that he had. Elaine had been a beautiful girl.

"Yeah," the man said. "She's been in and out of here the past few weeks. Gold Renault, this year's model?"

"That's her." Abby's stomach fluttered with excitement. "Did you ever notice anyone with her? A tall blond man?"

The guy shook his head. "Far as I saw, she always came alone."

So much for nailing down the make of Murderous Mark's car. She took another tack. "Did you see where she went after she parked?"

The guy shook his head. "Could have been anywhere."

Abby tried to think of another stratagem, but she was too tired and sad to come up with any more crafty ideas. "She was murdered, you know," she said flatly. "Someone hanged her."

The guy's jaw sagged. "Uh . . . shit. Really?"

"Eight days ago." Abby fought for control of her trembling chin. "I'm trying to figure out what she did the last few days of her life." She fished out the garage receipt. "I found this in her car. It's all I've got to go on. Please. Anything you might have noticed could help. Please."

The guy stared down at his feet for a moment. "The first night she parked here, she asked me which way to turn to get to Otis Street."

Abby waited. "Well? Which way is it?"

"Right," he said. "Walk four blocks, bear right, and you dead-end onto the Cliffside City Park. That's Otis Street. That's all I know."

She nodded her thanks. Zan followed her out onto the street.

"You could go door to door," he suggested. "First tall blond guy that answers the bell, you can bash him on the head with your purse. Better yet, just unbutton your blouse again. When he blows a blood vessel, we can throw him into the back of the van and haul him in."

Abby clambered into the van. "Oh, shut up, wiseass," she muttered. "Sarcasm doesn't help."

"Dinner might," he observed. "I'm hungry."

She ignored him and pulled the crumpled takeout menu out of her purse, staring at the list of charges. "He lived here," she murmured. "Five blocks from here, on Otis Street. That narrows it down to just a few blocks. There's got to be a way to narrow it down even more."

Zan got into the driver's seat and started up the engine. "Back to the mundane," he said doggedly. "We've passed a Chinese restaurant, a barbecue place, and an Italian bistro. Got a preference?"

Something flashed across her mind, like a tickling, glancing touch. She turned over the menu she'd scribbled the credit card charges on. "Italian," she said softly. "Oh my God, Zan. Italian."

"OK, Italian it is." He put the van in gear.

"No! Wait. Look at this!" She unfolded the menu.

Zan leaned closer and peered at it. "Café Girasole," he read. "Fine Italian cuisine. Cool. I could use a big plate of pasta."

"No, you doofus, it's a clue! I came into Elaine's office the day before she was killed, and she was ordering dinner. To be delivered."

He shrugged. "So Elaine liked pasta. What of it?"

"A romantic dinner for two, Zan," she explained.

Comprehension dawned in his eyes. They stared at each other.

Abby pulled out her phone and called the number on the menu.

"Café Girasole," said a woman's voice.

"Hi," Abby said. "I'm Gwen, Gloria Clayborne's secretary. I need to order dinner for her tonight. We have a standing account with you."

"One moment while I check . . . ah, yes. We do have that card number," the woman said. "Go ahead. What would you like?"

Abby opened the menu and picked items at random. "I'll have an order of, ah, artichoke pastries, black truffle ravioli, tagliatelle with wild mushrooms, pine nut salad, and, ah, fruit tart with crème Chantilly."

"The usual Cabernet? And Prosecco for your dessert wine?"

"Uh, yes, that would be fine," Abby said. "That'll be all."

"That comes to three hundred and twelve dollars, with the delivery charge. Which address shall we deliver it to?"

Abby whistled silently at the price, and crossed her fingers again. "Well, actually, I have a bit of a problem," she said. "Maybe you can help. I'm not sure which address I'm supposed to have the meal delivered to, and my boss isn't here to ask. All I know is that it's the same address that you delivered to last Tuesday, the seventh. I'm not sure if that was West Ash Avenue, Margolies Drive, or Otis Street."

"One moment." Abby waited on hold in agonizing suspense. *Click.* "The address in our files for Tuesday the seventh was 284 Otis Street."

"Excellent," Abby said. "Deliver it there. Thank you very much."

She put the phone back in her purse and glanced over at Zan. He was giving her a very strange look. "What is it now?" she demanded.

"You lie really well," Zan said.

"Is that a compliment?"

"I'm not sure yet," he said. "It makes me kind of nervous."

She snorted. "I've never lied to you."

"No?"

She swatted his arm with the rolled-up menu. "I don't fake, if that's what you're wondering."

"Thank God," he said dryly. "That puts me right at ease."

She held out the piece of paper. "Will you take me to 284 Otis Street?" She waited. Silence stretched out. "Or do I have to walk?"

He stared at her for so long, she began to squirm.

"Yeah." His voice was hard. "Then what'll you do, Abby? Break in with another brick? And if Mark shows up, what's your getaway plan? Call your car service? Chat the guy up while you wait for it to show? Sprint through the rain in your stiletto heels?"

She looked away before he could see the chill of fear his words invoked. "That's not your problem, Zan. It's mine," she said.

"That's no longer true," he said. "If I hadn't helped, you would never have gotten this far. Which makes it my responsibility."

She bristled. "Do not underestimate me."

"Don't underestimate me, either," he retorted. "I'm feeling more and more jerked around and manipulated as the evening drags on. I think we need to renegotiate our agreement."

"What agreement? I wasn't aware of any agreement."

"Think about it. See if you can figure it out." He drove the few blocks to the park and turned onto Otis Street, reading the house numbers. There it was. Number 284. Zan stopped in front of a large, blank-looking house. It was dark, the driveway empty, the grass shaggy.

He looked over at her. "So? How are we going to play this?"

She blew out an impatient breath. "Don't tell me we're back to the same stupid sexual bargaining crap. I already explained I'm not—"

"I know you're not. But my sense of humor is wearing thin, so I'll just tell it like it is. I cannot drive away and leave you here alone, on foot, in the pouring rain, to smash a murderer's window with a fucking brick. I am not capable of doing that."

"Oh," she said, flustered. "Well, thanks. I appreciate—"

"Don't thank me." His harsh tone silenced her. "If I stay, if I open that door for you, then be aware, Abby. It's a done deal. You're spending the night with me. With everything that entails."

She stared into his bright, clear eyes, staring at her with such focused intensity, she felt dissected. "But I told you. I'm not—"

"Not a sure thing, I know. I'm the sure thing, Abby. Not you. Me."

She licked her suddenly dry lips, her hands twisting together nervously. "This is not a time to play your silly dominator games."

He shook his head. "This is not a game. This is just how it is."

She felt both trapped and deliciously excited. Her own body was betraying her. She craved him. His strength and power made her feel so safe; his desire made her feel so beautiful, so female. She wanted to claw his clothes off and devour him. God, it was so hard to play it cool.

"And if I don't want to?" she asked.

"I'll take you home. No more breaking and entering. No more taxi service. I'll call my brother Chris, the cop, and tell him what you're up to. Just in case you're suicidal enough to try this shit on your own."

She gasped. "You bastard. You wouldn't do that to me."

He just looked at her. "I know you don't want to do this alone."

She was too flustered to think of a dignified response. "You want to spend the night . . . where, at my place?"

"I don't care," he said. "Anywhere's fine. Your place, my place, the van. The beach. Bent over the hood of a car. Let's leave it open-ended."

"Leaving it open-ended doesn't strike me as very smart."

Zan gestured at the bulk of the house that loomed behind the swaying trees. "Babe. Neither does this."

She looked at the house. She looked into Zan's glittering eyes, and wondered why she was putting up all this silly resistance. Her pride seemed less and less important as the minutes went by.

"Oh, whatever." She flung open her door. "Let's get it over with."

Chapter

20

Zan hauled her along beside him, making her scurry over the wet grass and rotten leaves to keep up. This whole scene was starting to seriously unnerve him. The only solution was to get it done with, and get Abby to someplace safe. With a big, comfortable bed.

He pulled his flashlight out of his work bag and peered into the garage. "It's empty," he said. "Looks deserted."

"Spooky," she whispered. "It's so cold."

Zan pulled his leather gloves out of the bag and put them on. No signs of an alarm system. Just a standard KABA microswitch-cylinder lock, nothing fancy. It took him a minute and a half, because his fingers were cold. The door sighed open to utter darkness. It smelled stale.

Abby tried to step in. He barred her with his arm. "No fucking way. Me first. Don't touch anything. And stick to me like glue."

He walked inside, letting his eyes adjust. The carpet was some sort of gray or beige. He flicked his flashlight around. Floor-to-ceiling windows screened with vertical hanging blinds looked out over a side patio. The furniture was both luxurious and generic, like a fine hotel suite. No pictures on the walls.

Abby started up the stairs without waiting for him. He hurried to follow. She went into the bedroom at the head of the stairs and flipped on the overhead light before he could stop her.

"Oh, Christ, Abby," he growled. "You can see that from outside."

"It'll just be for a minute," Abby said.

They stared at the room. It had just a dresser and a stripped four-poster bed. Abby crouched at the head of the bed and reached behind the mattress. Her hand came up holding a strip of fabric that was knotted to the bedpost. Pale green silk, with a faint pattern of leaves.

"This is Elaine's scarf," she said, her voice very small. "I bought it for her, two years ago."

Zan's unease sharpened. "That would explain the rope," he said.

Abby looked up at him, startled. "How's that?"

"You told me that this guy was into bondage, right? Maybe she bought that rope to please him."

She dropped the scrap of silk as if it were a live snake and stumbled away from the bed. "You're right," she said.

Abby combed through the room with a systematic thoroughness that made him want to scream *hurry up, goddamnit.* The bathroom was empty. The other rooms were empty. She headed back down the stairs.

Zan followed. "Can we go now?" His voice vibrated with tension.

Briiiiing. They leaped into the air at the doorbell. Zan put her behind him and backed up. *Back door,* he mouthed.

"Wait!" Abby whispered. "If this were Mark, he wouldn't ring the bell. He would have a key. He'd just come on in."

Briiiiinnng, the bell rang again, a long, insistent buzz. Zan cursed under his breath and yanked her toward the back door. "Do you feel like explaining your presence in this house to whoever is behind that door?" he growled under his breath. "Because I do not."

He flicked open the locks on the inside door and carefully pushed it open. There was a faint rustling noise from the left side of the house.

He put his hand over Abby's mouth, noting with part of his brain how smooth and fine her skin was, how delicate the bones in her jaw.

"Shhh," he breathed into her ear, then moved, cat stealthy, to the edge of the patio. Right . . . about . . . *now.*

He brought the guy down the instant he cleared the corner, slamming him to his knees and pinning him on the wet grass, arm locked across the guy's throat. "Who the fuck are you?" he hissed.

The guy made a terrified gurgling sound. Zan eased up on the pressure until he could speak. "Food delivery!" he gasped out. "I'm just the takeout guy! Don't hit me!"

Zan let go. The guy fell forward onto his face, coughing and choking. He rolled over, stumbled up onto his feet, and ran away in an unsteady sprint. Zan finally saw the white paper bags lying on the overgrown grass. "Takeout?" he repeated. "What the hell?"

"Oh my God." Abby clapped her hand to her forehead. "Café Girasole. I pretended to order dinner to get this address, but . . ."

"Yeah," Zan said. "How would they know you were pretending if the credit card works?"

Abby propped up the bags. "That poor guy. Here he was, expecting a forty-dollar tip, and instead he gets clobbered by a madman."

Zan grunted. "So? He startled me. Come on. Let's get out of here."

"No, wait. Not yet." Abby looked around the patio. There was a big garbage bag dumped at the edge of it. She dragged it back in through the back door into the kitchen. Zan followed her in and watched, dismayed, as she grabbed an empty plastic shopping bag that lay on the kitchen counter. She put it over her hand like a glove, pried the tie on the bag open, and dumped the contents out onto the floor.

Zan jumped back barely in time to keep from getting splattered by rotting food. "What the *hell*?"

"All detective novels have the hero sift the garbage," Abby said. "It's a great place to look for clues."

"Oh, for God's sake. Can't we look for clues that aren't covered with stinking slime?"

"You're making me pay through the nose for this favor, so I'd better make it count." Abby slopped still more garbage onto the floor. "Wait outside, if your stomach's too dainty. But if you want to make yourself useful, get out your flashlight. Shine it on this stuff for me."

He trained the flashlight on the disgusting mess she was stirring with her hand. "This is getting more surreal all the time," he observed.

Abby ignored him, turning all her attention to the garbage. Wow. He had to hand it to her. The woman had nerves of steel. That stuff was so ripe, it made his eyes water, and she was rooting around in it as if it were nothing. She peered at the label on a champagne bottle, prodded little hockey pucks of espresso coffee grounds, examined a soggy box of water crackers. There were takeout containers with the Café Girasole logo, the insides thick with mold; a bottle that had once held Cabernet. Orange peels, plastic bags, a bottle of Italian mineral water called Orionte. A jar of Russian caviar.

"Expensive tastes," she said.

"You're a fine one to talk, sweetheart," he said.

She shook the bag, ignoring him. Strips of paper tumbled onto the floor. Remnants of a sheet of photographic paper, with the photos cut out. The colored edges of the photo still showed on the bottom strip. She smoothed it out. Zan trained the flashlight onto the stained, crumpled strip of paper. "These were photographs of Elaine," she said.

Zan leaned down to look, trying to breathe through his mouth. "Uh, Abby? There's no way to tell who this was. The faces are cut out."

"Don't condescend to me," she snapped. "I know what I'm talking about. Look, see that green splotch on the black strip on the bottom?"

Zan looked. "Yeah. So?"

"That's Elaine's scarf," she announced. "The one that's ripped into shreds and tied to the bedposts upstairs."

Zan looked again. "It's a very small splotch," he said doubtfully.

"I know the color. I know the way she knotted it. She always wore it with her black turtleneck Prada sweater," Abby said. "I'm dead sure."

She sifted through it again, picking up a fuzzy clotted wad of what appeared to be a pale bird's nest. She prodded it. "This is human hair."

He peered at it. "Looks that way," he said. "Elaine was blond."

"Elaine was ash-blond," Abby said. "This is white-blond. Nanette said Elaine's guy had long blond hair. I guess he doesn't anymore." They contemplated the pile of garbage for a moment. Abby let her makeshift plastic glove drift to the floor. "I don't feel obliged to put his garbage back in the bag, being as how he murdered my best friend."

"I agree with that sentiment with all my heart," he said.

Abby alarmed him once more by disappearing onto the patio again. He hurried after her, cursing under his breath, and found her with her arms full of the bags of takeout food. "Let's take these and go."

"You have got to be kidding," he said. "I'm not eating that stuff."

She gaped at him, outraged. "Are you nuts? You propose leaving a perfectly good three-hundred-dollar meal for the squirrels to gnaw?"

"I don't relish the thought of a dead woman paying for my dinner."

Abby blinked. "Oh. Well, it's Elaine's mother's account, actually, but I'll arrange to pay for it myself. In fact, I should go to the restaurant right now and make it right with that poor guy."

"Oh, brilliant," Zan said. "Confess to several witnesses that you misrepresented yourself on the phone, charged an expensive gourmet meal to a credit card not your own, and then broke into an abandoned house where you proceeded to snoop around and throw rotting garbage on the floor. Why not just invite the delivery guy to press charges against me for assault, while you're at it?"

"Smart-ass," she grumbled. "Serve you right if I did, the way you blackmailed me tonight. I will make it right, though. After it's all over."

"So, babe, what else is on your agenda?" he asked. "Got any more crimes to commit? Innocent people to attack? Want to set fire to something? Spray-paint graffiti on a public monument? No problem, I'll take it in stride. All in a night's work for a guy like me."

"Nope," she said. "I'm all out of ideas, smart-ass. For now."

"Thank God," he said fervently.

They eyed each other. Heat built between them in the eloquent silence. Zan shook himself and grabbed the bags of food from her.

"Come on, then," he said gruffly. "Let's get the hell out of here."

The buzz of the cell phone annoyed Lucien. He'd been studying the exhibit map, running through the heist choreography in his head. He believed in the power of visualization, but it required intense concentration. Difficult, when one was constantly interrupted by incompetent idiots. He checked the display. It was Neale.

He hit the decoder function. "This had better be good."

"Uh, boss? We've got a situation here."

"Talk fast," Lucien said. "I'm busy."

"Uh, yeah. Well, the girl met up with the locksmith, and they—"

"That's not an emergency, Neale," he said, through gritted teeth.

"Uh, yeah. But they met at Elaine's house," Neale said. "He picked the lock for her. Let her in to the house, the car, everything. The bitch is snooping around, looking for clues. And guess where they are now?"

"You ever play coy with me again, Neale, I'll cut off your balls."

"Sorry," Neale said hastily. "They're at the Otis Street house."

Lucien was astonished. He felt a cold sensation in his body. Not a stimulating buzz. This feeling was unpleasant.

"What are they doing?" he demanded.

"She just dragged a bag of garbage from the back patio into the kitchen," Neale told him. "I guess they're going through the garbage in there. Yuck. After eight days, it must be pretty pustulant by now."

"Garbage?" Lucien sprang out of his chair. "What garbage? I told Henly to clean the place out. I told him not to leave a single hair!"

"He, uh, did," Neale said hesitantly. "He put it all in a trash bag, but it looks like he forgot to haul the bag away."

"Idiot," Lucien hissed. His mind raced in circles, but he came to no conclusions, just uncomfortable possibilities. Not that there was any danger. Elaine's death had been ruled a suicide, the case closed. Anyone inquiring into who had leased the Otis Street house would quickly lose themselves in a maze of fictitious names and shell companies. Nor were his own DNA or fingerprints in any criminal database. He was unthinkable as a suspect, twinkling-eyed philanthropist that he was.

No one had ever had a clue about his secret hobby.

But neither had anyone ever wiggled their way so close to it before. He had no idea how much more Duncan and Maitland knew. What their sources were, or how much closer they might get. After the cup of coffee with Abby, he'd written her off as sexy fluff, no threat to his plans. A good pawn. He had miscalculated. Badly.

"Uh . . . boss?" Neale prompted. "Whaddaya want me to do?"

He decided to cut his losses. "We need to take them out," he said. He grabbed another phone, punched Ruiz's beeper number into it. "Henly and Ruiz are already in her apartment, so I'll just keep them in place in case they're headed back there. You stay at Otis Street."

"What for?" Neale whined. "I wanted to—"

"The garbage," Lucien said, his voice steely. "Make it disappear."

"I'm not the one who fucked up! Let Henly clean up his own shit!"

"Shut up, Neale. Henly's busy. I'll deal with him later, and you won't envy him when I'm done."

"You're going to have Ruiz and Henly take 'em out tonight, then?"

Lucien hesitated. "It doesn't matter when Maitland dies. No one will find her body. But the locksmith has to die after the job goes down. We'll have to keep him alive, and in one piece. Up at the cabin."

"Then you wouldn't mind if we, er . . . indulged?" Neale hinted.

"In the woman, you mean?" Lucien hesitated, irritated.

He'd planned to seduce Abby himself, at the gala. Luring her with his money, involving her emotions, fucking her on several different levels at once. The fantasy had excited him more than anything in recent memory, particularly after studying Ruiz's photos.

Such a beautiful body. So flexible and lush. So sluttishly eager to please her lover's every whim. Such a bad, bad girl.

She deserved to be punished. A slow, long, sexy, complicated punishment. Culminating in the ultimate betrayal.

But it would all be different, after Ruiz and Henly attacked her and tied her up. She would be sullen, frightened, angry, guarded.

There was nothing particularly stimulating in that scenario.

He had to be practical. He might as well pass her on to his men at this point. She had no further use to him as a game piece.

"Very well," he conceded. "Do whatever you like with her, after you deal with the garbage at Otis Street. Just you and Ruiz, though. No goodies for Henly. He can watch, but he can't touch."

Neale whistled. "Ooh, boy. He's going to be one unhappy puppy."

"Only way to communicate with an idiot like that. Reward and punishment. Like Pavlov's dog."

"Yeah, if you say so, boss. Gotta go. They're coming out."

Lucien fumed as he waited for Ruiz to call him back. He was furious at himself for having brought Elaine to Otis Street. Elaine had broken her promise to keep his existence secret. He was angry enough to kill the stupid cow. Irritating that she was already dead.

Abby was still alive. She would do nicely as a substitute.

Chapter

21

Zan parked, sitting for a few moments before he spoke. "Abby?"

"Uh-oh." She peeked at him. "That tone makes me nervous."

He ignored the sarcasm. "I admire the fact that you're all gung ho about finding out what happened to Elaine—"

"You mean, finding out who *killed* Elaine," she corrected him.

He plowed doggedly on. "I hope someone would do as much for me if I got offed." He blew out a slow, measured breath. "But there's a reason cops do this stuff for a living. They're trained. They're armed. They're aware of the risks. You're not, Abby. God, look at you."

"No." She held up her hand to stop him. "Don't."

"My dad was a cop," Zan said relentlessly. "A good one. Smart, brave, heroic. He got shot in the chest in the process of doing his job."

Abby shook her head. "I'm sorry, Zan, but it's not relevant to me. Let's not talk about it anymore."

"Oh, great," he said bitterly. "All we need. Another taboo subject."

"I'm just trying to avoid conflict," Abby said.

"Avoiding conflict?" His voice got louder. "Is that what you were doing while you ran all over town, lying through your teeth to everyone, jerking me around, breaking into houses? Avoiding fucking *conflict?*"

"I was doing what I had to do!" she said savagely. "You don't have to tell me how unprepared and incompetent and ridiculous I am. Believe me, I know. So please. I don't want to fight. Things are weird enough between us as it is. Let's talk about something else. Please."

He was wary of the tremor in her voice. If he pushed her, it was going to lead to tears. Seriously unproductive. Time to switch gears.

"So," he said thoughtfully. "You don't want to fight. We can't talk about what happened tonight. We can't talk about Elaine. That leaves only one thing to talk about that's either interesting or important."

She rolled her eyes. "Oh, don't tell me. Let me guess."

"Yep," he said. "You guessed it, babe. Sex."

Her mouth flattened as she tried not to smile. "Nonsense," she said briskly, gathering up the bags of take-out food. "There are lots of things to talk about besides sex."

"Yeah? Such as?"

"Art? Culture, music, literature, movies?" She got out of the van and started briskly up the walk toward her staircase.

Zan slammed out of the van and loped to catch up. "Nah," he said. "We'd have to see it or listen to it together to have anything intelligent to say about it. And secret lovers don't get taken out into polite society. They don't get to go see the symphony or the theater or the film forum. They have to stay put in their cages until the deepest dark of the night, when their special skills are called for."

She giggled. "Oh, stop it. How about food? Let's talk about that."

"Food and sex are inextricably linked," he said.

"Yeah. Right." She set down the bags and dug through her purse for her keys. "Let's unlink them long enough to set the table and pour ourselves a glass of wine. I'm starving."

It was hard to say when his neck started to prickle. He'd been thinking up silly things to say to make her laugh, his eyes following the key in her hand, gleaming bright and new as she inserted it into the—

The faceplate. That lock was too new to have those scratches.

Snick, the key turned and she pushed the door open before he could react. He jerked her back and tossed her to the side as a black figure hurtled out her door like a mad bull. "Run!" he screamed, which cost him that zillionth of a second necessary to parry the big fist that plowed into his solar plexus. *Wham.* Oh shitfuckouch, the man's momentum knocked him back against the porch pillar.

He grappled with the guy, gasping for air. His opponent was horribly muscular and strong, like a big, crushing python. The nylon stocking over his face looked like a condom, Zan thought, with a detached part of his mind. Made sense. The guy was a dickhead.

Bam, a blow to the temple, and stars were spinning, he was falling off into welcoming darkness—

Abby. He couldn't leave her here alone. He fought his way back up to consciousness by sheer, desperate force of will.

He opened his eyes. They watered copiously. He could tell, even through the stocking, that the guy was gloating, and that he'd let down his guard. He lifted up his big hammy black-gloved fist, brought it down in horrible, surreal slow motion to finish Zan off.

Some remnant of all those years of training brought Zan's knee up to slam into the guy's balls. He shrieked, stumbled back. Abby swam into his field of vision, lifting a chunk of driftwood. She bashed the guy on the back of the head. Of course, she hadn't run. As if she would.

Another guy barreled out the door, and Zan got busy evading kicks and punches. The second dickhead was smaller, but quicker. The flurry of darting, stinging blows disoriented Zan, with his head still ringing from the first guy's monster whack to the temple. He blocked and parried, noticing out of the corner of his eye that the first guy was on his feet again. He'd gotten Abby's chunk of driftwood away from her.

The big guy jumped on her. They went down. She heaved and bucked under his mountain of a body, barely budging him.

Terror gave Zan a jolt of energy. He blocked a slashing blow aimed at the base of his neck, managed to catch and hold the guy's leather-gloved hand, and pinched deep into the base of the thumb.

He twisted, torquing tendons to send electric agony flashing up the guy's arm.

Dickhead II screeched, crouching to lessen the pain. Zan followed up and brought him down, slamming the guy's head onto the warped floorboards of the porch. A hollow, nasty thunk, another, and another.

Then he hurled himself at the guy hulking over Abby. She was still kicking and yowling like an alley cat, thank God. The asshole was too slow to make it to his feet before Zan jabbed a vicious side kick to his ribs. He tripped over his partner's prone body, hit the banister, and fell down the stairs, bumpity bumpity thud, grunting all the way down.

A flicker of movement brought Zan whipping around. The second guy was on his feet again. Tough son of a bitch. Blood stained the nylon over his face, creating mottled, pinkish spots.

And aw, suffering Christ. He was holding a switchblade.

Abby was struggling onto her knees. Way too close to that knife.

"Get out of the way," Zan barked. She scrambled away on her hands and knees as he and Dickhead II started circling. The guy feinted to test him, but Zan was tuned in to him. If no one else intervened, he was reasonably sure he could disarm him. He'd done it countless times with a wooden knife. Real ones as well. But always in a dojo, never in a real fight. It was different when there was something precious at stake.

Abby. She was huddled up at the end of the porch. He couldn't even turn his head to see if she was hurt. No time to think. The guy's knife had made him overconfident. He lunged, stabbing for Zan's midriff. Training took over; block and turn, grasp and twist.

The knife dropped, flashing as it hit the floor and spun. Zan sank to his knees, using the guy's momentum to send him sailing headfirst over the porch railing into the dark.

A guttural howl was cut short by a series of thuds, crackling, and rustling. The guy had landed on a steep slope covered with scrubby bushes and ivy. Zan leaned over the railing. He was rolling up onto his feet already, loping away in a limping run. No sign of the first guy.

A car engine revved, seconds later. Headlights sliced the night. A vehicle pulled away with an angry squeal of tires.

So much for chasing them down. The dickhead duo had flown.

Zan's legs gave way. He sagged onto his knees and leaned his throbbing forehead against the porch railing. So close. So fucking close.

Abby limped over to him, barefoot. "Are you OK?"

He started to laugh helplessly. "That's my line. Oh, Abby."

"You do not have exclusive rights to that question," she said.

He dragged her close, pressing his face against her belly. She hung on to him, draped over him and clutching his head and shoulders with her arms. He looked into her face. "Are you hurt?" he asked.

She gave him a tremulous smile. "That big guy landed on me like a ton of lead, and my elbow and wrist got scraped up. No big deal."

"No big deal, she says." Zan started laughing again. This time he couldn't stop. He hid his face against her shirt, shoulders shaking.

He looked up after he'd gotten himself back under control to check out her arm. Her sleeve was stained with blood.

"Aw, shit," he said, dismayed. "You're bleeding!"

"Nah. Those guys hurt you a lot worse than they hurt me. Where did you learn to fight like that? I saw you clobber Edgar, but tonight, wow. You were amazing."

He grunted. "Hardly. I let them take me by surprise, I let them skin your elbow, and I let them pound the shit out of me. Plus, I let them get away. I would not call this episode a resounding victory."

"Oh, for heaven's sake." She hugged him. "We're alive, right? I thought you were fabulous. You saved my butt, big time."

He grabbed her back. "Thanks. This is all very gratifying, but let's get the fuck out of here. You can express your gratitude later."

"Shouldn't we call the cops?" she asked doubtfully. "Again?"

"You decide," he said. "It's your apartment. I doubt that this is a coincidence. It's a message from Mark. I hope you're listening."

Her face stiffened. She lunged for the door. "Sheba!"

He grabbed a handful of her shirt. "Don't go in there. Me first."

She pulled away. "Those assholes might have hurt my cat!"

He followed her in. Abby flipped on the light. Sheba yowled angrily from the top of the refrigerator, making them both jump. "Oh, thank God," Abby said weakly. "It's OK, kitty. Come on down."

Zan reached up and grabbed the trembling animal. She struggled and clawed in his gentle grip. He passed her to Abby. "Stay here," he said. "I'll check the place out. If I yell, run."

She frowned. "Zan, I don't think—"

"For once in your life, do me the favor of saying, 'Yes, Zan,' he snarled. "It's been a tough night. Indulge me."

She shook with giggles and buried her nose in Sheba's ruff, her eyes big over the billowing puff of fur. "Yes, Zan," she murmured.

"God, that was good." He shivered in mock rapture. "My wildest, most improbable fantasy fulfilled. Do not move your ass from here."

No bad guys. He was back in less than a minute. "All clear," he said. "They didn't rip the place apart, as far as I can tell. Take a look."

He followed her as she walked through each room, cuddling her cat. The routine felt familiar. It was exactly what she'd done at Elaine's house, and Otis Street. She spent a long time picking through the stuff on her dresser. She set the cat on the bed, looking puzzled.

"Strange," she said. "They didn't take the TV or the stereo, or my jewelry. But random things are missing."

"Such as?" he demanded.

"My hairbrush. The round one I use for blow-drying. Some lipsticks that were on the vanity. My silver pen that always stays next to the message pad. Nothing particularly valuable."

"Could you have misplaced them yourself?" he offered.

She looked dubious. "Maybe." She flung her closet open, and gasped. "My clothes! Those rotten bastards! They stole my nice clothes!"

He peered over her shoulder into the closet, which was, in fact, almost empty.

"Huh," he murmured. "So they did. Very weird."

"They took my purses!" Abby's voice was outraged. "My scarves! That's nuts! Why would they want my used clothes?"

"Got me. Those guys didn't strike me as cross-dressers."

"This is not funny, Zan!"

"I don't think so either." He rummaged on the shelf above the clothes rack for a small duffel bag. "Get some things together. Let's go."

She packed, grabbed her cat, and stopped in the bathroom. She flipped on the light. There was a long silence. "They took my toothbrush." Abby's voice floated out the door, hollow and quavering.

He leaned in to investigate. "Huh? How's that?"

"My toothbrush," she repeated. "Why would anybody . . ." Her voice trailed off, and her throat bobbed. "It feels almost like someone wants to do some strange voodoo spell on me."

He met her eyes in the bathroom mirror. Her face was white, lips pressed together. Her eyes looked huge, smudged with mascara and shadowed with exhaustion and fear.

She was right. It was spooky. His skin was crawling. He felt a surge of rage at those assholes for scaring her. Messing with her mind, killing her best friend. She was a good person. She didn't deserve this.

Abby shook her head. "I can't tell the cops that the scary bad guys stole my lipstick, my Dior, my Coach bags, and my toothbrush. They'll send the guys in the white coats to take me away. I'm already the laughingstock of the police department. I just can't face it."

"Then don't," he said. "You can use my toothbrush, sweetheart."

He tried again to drag her toward the door, but of course it wasn't that simple. They had to collect the cat toys, wet food, dry food, the cat carrier. Even when they finally got out the door, his arms full of writhing feline, Abby tugged on his arm. "No, Zan. Wait a second."

She started gathering up scattered cartons from Café Girasole.

"Dinner," she explained. "The salad got smeared all over the porch and the Prosecco bottle broke but the Cabernet's fine, and everything else looks good."

"Whatever." He bundled her into the van, passed the cat to her. "I just want to get someplace safe."

Abby tried to soothe the yowling Sheba. "And where is that safe place?" she asked as he climbed in the driver's side.

He put the van in gear. "My apartment," he said. "High-security electronic locks, state of the art alarm system, plus two of my brothers."

"Are your brothers as good at fighting as you?"

"Better," he said. "Jamie's the kung fu wonder kid. He's won every championship there is. Then there's my baby sister Fiona. She has a black belt in three different disciplines. She's hell on wheels."

"Wow," Abby said, her voice envious. "Lucky her."

"Chris can take me, about half the time we spar. He's the cop in the family, so he works the hardest at staying sharp. But Jack, my oldest brother, can kick our combined asses with both hands tied behind his back. He's ex-army Ranger. Among other things."

"Wow. How statistically unlikely is that? A whole family of warrior ninja types." She shot him a teasing glance. "Makes you wonder."

He shrugged. "My brothers and I got heavy into it after Dad got killed," he said. "Mom encouraged us. The discipline was comforting, and it kept us more or less out of trouble. Fiona was little. She just wanted to do whatever her big brothers were doing."

They were quiet for the rest of the drive. He pulled into his spot next to the freight elevator and killed the engine. "Be real quiet until we get up to my apartment, OK?"

She gave him a nervous look. "How come?"

"Granddad," he explained. "Ground floor. He never sleeps. He's a great old guy, and he'd be thrilled to death to meet you, but then we'd have to have a beer with him, do the whole heavy-handed teasing routine. I can't face it tonight. So let's tiptoe like little mice."

He breathed a sigh of relief when the battered elevator doors clanged shut. The mechanism began to drag them laboriously upward.

He tried to remember how messy the place was. He'd been in I-don't-give-a-shit hermit mode. It wreaked havoc on his housekeeping, never stellar to begin with. The door creaked open to his apartment, and he preceded her in, laying down the cat carrier, the duffel, the takeout bags. "So," he muttered self-consciously. "This is, uh, my place."

She spun around, Sheba's fuzzy head tucked under her chin.

The moonlight that spilled in the bank of arched windows illuminated the big room and made Sheba's white fur glow. One side of the building looked out over the sea. The other looked out over the long sweep of city lights twinkling along the curve of the bay.

"My God, Zan," she murmured. "This place is incredible."

Yeah, right. Until he turned the lights on and she saw what a slovenly bachelor mess it was. He shrugged. "It suits me."

"It's so big and gothic. It's like the Bat Cave."

He laughed. "Yeah, except that I'm not a superhero."

She turned around, gently placing her cat on the floor. Sheba arched and stretched. "Speaking of which," she said. "Let me see where those guys hit you. Turn on the light, Zan."

"No," Zan said. He grabbed her shoulders.

"But I want to see if they—"

"No." He swallowed the rest of her protests with a reckless kiss.

He was all instinct, strung out on adrenaline. He couldn't wait, he needed her now. She gasped when her back hit the brick wall, and he froze, muscles trembling with the effort to control himself.

"What?" he demanded, breathless. "Did I hit a sore spot?"

"N-n-no," she quavered. "I was just, ah, startled."

He slid his hands up her hips and cupped her ass, brushing his fingers over the warm scrap of satin that covered her cleft. "If you have requests, get them in quick, because my heartbeat's getting louder by the second. It's already like ocean surf in my ears."

She wrapped her arms around his neck. "Anything," she said.

His fingers dug into her hips. "You really mean that?"

She nodded. "Do whatever you want," she said. "I want you. I trust you. I love everything you do to me. It's all great."

"I'm taking you at your word," he warned.

"Do that," she said.

He groped in the pocket of his jacket that she still wore, looking for the condom that had been in there since the night he'd put her locks in. His hand closed around the velvet box that held the necklace. He'd been hauling the thing around, just to torture himself. Putting off going back to the jeweler's.

His chest tightened. Maybe . . . *Not yet.* He couldn't tear his chest open and offer his heart to her yet. He would fuck it up for sure. He groped until he found the condom, stuck it in his jeans pocket, and shoved the jacket off her shoulders, letting it thud to the floor. Her soiled, tattered blouse gaped open, showing off her cleavage again. He grabbed the edges of the collar.

"First thing on my agenda," he said. "This blouse. It shows off your chest to any drooling idiot who cares to look. And when they do, I want to gut them. I find this stressful."

She seized his fisted hands. "Zan—"

"It goes." He wrenched it open with a vicious snap of his wrists. Fabric ripped, threads snapped, buttons flew.

She squawked. "Hey! But you've already wrecked my—"

"I'll take you shopping for a new blouse tomorrow," he said, wrenching her cuffs open. "A better one. One that stays buttoned."

She sidled out from between him and the wall. Her laughter had a breathy, nervous sound. "The dominator has been unleashed."

He whipped his shirt off, sending it flying. Kicked off his shoes. He advanced on her. "I let you manipulate me into putting you in danger. My dick overriding my brain. No excuse for it. You could have been killed, Abby. It was so fucking close. I don't think you even realize."

"I—I'm sorry. I didn't mean to—"

"And it would have been my fault," he went on grimly. "Do you have any idea how badly that scared me?"

"Oh, Zan." The fullness of her tits gleamed, highlighted by moonlight, brushed by velvety shadows. Propped up on her bra, they were a blatant provocation. She placed a cool hand against his chest. It skittered away at the contact with his heat, then gently came to rest again. Right over his pounding heart. "I'm sorry that happened," she said. "But you take too much on yourself. I'll take responsibility for my own poor judgment, thank you very much. Don't punish me for that."

"I'm not. Just being honest." He pressed his face against her cleavage, sucking in deep, hungry breaths of her delicious perfume. "Every guy who saw you today dreamed of doing this, you know that?"

"Oh, please." She swatted at him. "Don't be silly."

He pulled out his pocketknife and flicked the blade open. The cups of her bra were held together by a twisted filigreed cord that gave way after one twist of the blade. It fell open.

"You're being overdramatic," she told him. "Cutting off my underwear with a knife is really over the top."

"We haven't gotten anywhere near the top yet." He unhooked her skirt, let it fall around her ankles. She almost tripped over it, trying to back away from him, but he grabbed her arm to steady her, herding her in the direction of his king-sized bed. "Get your panties down."

She hit the bed with the back of her knees and sat down with a little thud and a startled gasp. "Zan, I—"

"You're too slow." He grabbed the fragile satin garment, tugged it away from her body. "And you talk too much." Two quick flicks of the blade, and he threw away the scrap of cloth. He stripped her stockings off, her shoes. No need for sexy props or games. He wanted her naked.

He fell to his knees and shoved her thighs apart, putting his face to her muff. It was already puffy and slick with copious lashings of girl juice. He could just lick and lap it up forever. He slid his finger inside.

"Oh my God," she quavered. "I thought that you . . . that we . . ."

"You need to be really sopping wet and soft for me to fuck you how I want to fuck you," he told her, between long, rasping strokes of his tongue. She tumbled onto her back, whimpering.

He worked on her silently, sighing with pure satisfaction at the fluttering clasp of her cunt around his finger at her first climax.

When the ripples had died down, he slid his gleaming hand out of her body and pulled her onto her feet. He turned her around, cupped her ass and pushed until she knelt on the bed. He pushed some more until she was poised on her hands and knees.

She turned her head to look at him, and arched her back, raising her ass high in the air. "Do you like me like this?"

There was nothing submissive or passive in her voice. On the contrary. She was temptation personified. Sound wouldn't come out of his throat, it was so dry. He unbuckled his belt. "Yes," he said hoarsely. "I like you in every way there is. Like's too weak a word."

Love would be better.

The words almost slipped out, but he cut them off. Now was not the time. Now was the time for fucking until they were too sated and limp to move. Then they could discuss . . . love.

If he had the balls.

He rolled the condom on, guided himself into her shadowy cleft, and worked himself inside. He tried to give her time to get used to him before he started to move, but his good intentions melted away, and in no time he was hunched over her, muscles rock-hard, bucking like a wild thing. She lunged back to meet each stroke. They were slick with sweat. The bed creaked in tempo with their gasps, and it wasn't going to last, he couldn't hang on. An avalanche was crashing down on him.

He lifted his head some time later, realizing that he'd knocked her flat down onto her belly on the bed, and that she was wiggling beneath him like an eel. "You OK?" he asked drowsily. "I can move—"

"Do *not* move," she said savagely. "Do not even think of moving, Zan Duncan. Not until I . . . oh God . . ." She jerked and shuddered, the small, tight muscles pulsing delightfully around his still-erect cock.

He was startled. "Wow," he muttered into her neck.

"Uh, yeah. Wow." Her tone was snappish. "That was building up the whole time you were doing the pillaging-barbarian act, driving me crazy. If you hadn't let me finish, I would have had to kill you."

He kissed her neck, nuzzling her hair and licking away her sheen of cooling sweat. It was delicately salty. "I told you, Abby," he reminded her, sinking his teeth lightly into her throat. "It's not an act."

"Yeah, yeah," she scoffed. "You're very big and bad and hard to handle. I'm convinced, OK?"

"Can I move?" he asked. "Am I still in danger of imminent death?"

"Yes, you may move," she said primly. "The danger has passed."

Zan grasped the condom and pulled out, loving every fraction of that clutching pull. He couldn't cuddle up to Abby and doze off until he took care of the condom, so he struggled to his feet and wandered into the kitchen to dispose of it. When he turned, he found Abby behind him. Her curvy body was silhouetted against a nimbus of moonlight.

"You never let me see your bruises," she said.

"It's nothing," he told her. "Don't worry about it."

"I won't buy into that macho crap," she said. "I saw those guys punching and kicking you. Turn on a light and let me see."

Her tone was stern. She wasn't going to back down. Zan sighed, led her over to the couch, and flipped on a lamp. "Go ahead," he said.

Abby circled him, hissing under her breath as she touched the red, swollen marks on his ribs. More on his forearms, his thighs, his chest. More than he'd expected. Adrenaline was a kick-ass painkiller. So was sexual desire. He was just starting to feel the pain now.

"Ouch," Abby murmured. "Have you got some salve?"

"Bathroom medicine cabinet," he said. "Put some disinfectant on your elbow, while you're at it." He stared at her gorgeous backside as she disappeared into his bathroom. A few seconds later, he admired her equally stunning front side as she hustled back, hands full of tubes.

She pushed him down onto the couch, dabbed ointment on him, and rubbed it in. The inevitable physiological reaction ensued.

"Ah, your rude brute is showing an inappropriate interest in my massage," Abby said. "Down, boy. This is not a hand job, if you please."

"Hey. I go for naughty naked-nurse fantasies," he told her.

"Lift your arm," she said sternly. "Let me rub this on your ribs."

He obliged her. "Rub me anywhere you want, baby. There's just one small problem."

Her hands stopped circling. "And that is?"

"I don't have any more condoms," he admitted.

The silent laughter that shook her had a really interesting effect on her tits. "Oh, you poor man," she said. "You've got to be kidding."

"The rest of the box is on your bed stand," he said. "I didn't think to grab them. This one in my jacket pocket was just, you know, an in-case-I-get-insanely-lucky-someplace-unexpected condom."

"That's a tragic state of affairs for your rude brute."

"It doesn't have to be," he said.

Her hand stopped moving. "Meaning?" she said warily.

"If you really want to make me feel better, just mount me," he said softly. "Sink down onto my cock. Bathe me in your sweet healing balm."

"Without a condom? Dream on, buddy. You just got laid, what, fifteen minutes ago? Isn't that enough? At least for a little while?"

"No," he said simply.

They stared at each other, and he stroked her face with his fingertips, smiling. She tried several times to form the words. "Um . . ."

"We've already had the safe sex conversation," he said. "And you know that I come when I decide to come. You always bitch about what a control freak I am. Take advantage of it, sweetheart. Put me to the test."

"I would have to be insane to let you do that."

"Just look at these terrible bruises." He lifted his arms and blinked piteously. "They hurt, Abby. Comfort me. Distract me. Please."

She couldn't stop herself from smiling at his nonsense. "You clown," she said. "You're messing with me, Zan."

"I've been studying with a master," he said. "Now it's my turn to guilt-trip you into doing crazy things against your better judgment."

She was tempted. He could tell, from the flush on her face, the hot glow in her beautiful eyes. He was reeling her in, slowly but surely.

"But what about you?" she asked doubtfully. "How will you—"

"I'll come in your mouth," he said. "After."

She pulled her full, flushed lower lip between her teeth. "Oh."

"Please," he coaxed. "I've never wanted anything so badly in my life." It was the naked truth, and he wasn't just talking about the sex. He wanted to seduce her, compromise her, whatever it took. It was part of the charm he was weaving. Higher stakes, deeper trust, higher risk.

He grasped her hips and tugged, a pleading gesture.

She let out a hiccupping sobbing sound. Slowly and hesitantly, she clambered on top of him and reached down to hold his cock at the correct angle to nudge it inside herself. Just the tender clasp of her hand almost set him off. Then she sank down, forcing him inside her.

Oh, yeah. He sucked in a sharp breath. She stopped, looking worried. "What? Zan? Are you OK? Am I hurting you?"

"No. Yes. I'm fine. Don't stop," he pleaded.

She was so tight and slick, squeezing his whole cock. He shuddered with the sensation as she wiggled over him, forcing him deeper. She stopped, her eyes doubtful. "Are you sure you'll be able to not come? You look like you're right on the edge."

"Yes," he lied. "I'm sure. Don't worry."

He tried to stay still, let her guide, but it was his own feeble will pitted against the vast, inexorable impulse of desire. He grasped her hips and drove himself into her lush body from below.

She grabbed his shoulders and hung on, sharp claws dug deep into his shoulders, meeting every stroke with a jerk of her hips.

He'd thought having just had a blow-your-head-off orgasm only minutes ago would have taken the edge off, but where Abby was concerned, the rules of nature were suspended. It was torture, shocking pleasure bordering on terror, a tightrope of self-control with each hot, wet, licking thrust and glide of her body. He couldn't last much longer. Certainly not bareback. He had to make her come.

He shifted her, changing the angle so he was dragging himself over her clit, stirring her around with slow, swirling strokes. He backed off from his own orgasm while he worked her up into a creamy explosion. He felt like a god as she went off.

He grabbed her wrists to keep her on top of him, she arched so far. She cried out. The column of her throat, the contours of her chest, were the most heart-stoppingly beautiful thing he'd ever seen.

She sagged forward, her lips red and blurred. "Did you, ah . . ."

"No," he said, his voice strangled. "I'm pretty fucking close, though. You'd better get off. Slow . . . and careful."

He hissed at the tight, slick drag of female flesh around him as she slid off. She stared down at his gleaming penis, breathed in the humid scent of their sex. He grabbed her hand, pulled it to his lips.

"So?" He kissed it. "You going to have mercy on me?"

"Oh yes." She slid down between his thighs. Just a few skillful, voluptuous strokes of her hands and her mouth, and he was sucked into a vortex. He whirled and spun and burst into a million fragments.

Which made him feel, paradoxically, whole.

Chapter

22

Abby gently unwound his hands from her hair and laid them on his thighs. He sprawled, unmoving. Gleaming with sweat. He was limp and beatific, eyes closed. It was the first time she'd ever seen his penis soft, she realized. Partly soft, anyway. It curved smoothly over the thick, springy thatch of dark hair. A rush of tenderness made her lean forward to gently kiss it. The rude brute, finally laid low. How adorable.

She got up, swaying and stumbling, and headed back into Zan's bathroom. She washed her hands, rinsed her mouth, and stared at herself in the bathroom mirror. Wow, what very big hair. She needed some time with a comb, some cotton balls and cold cream.

She looked around the beautiful room, admiring the iridescent sheen of the floor and wall tiles. What was it she'd accused him of? Living in an abandoned warehouse? What an ass she was. And while she was on the subject of silliness, well. She'd done stupid things in her time, but never had she let a man persuade her to have sex without protection.

He was just so seductive, so convincing. She was under his spell.

Then again, she hadn't eaten in forever. Of course she was woozy and wrecked. She grabbed a terrycloth bathrobe off the door hook and draped it over herself. Food. Now. She had to ground herself.

She had to turn a few times to orient herself in that cavernous place. It was dimly lit with soft golden shadows from the single lamp Zan had lit in the living area. Ah, there it was. The entrance, the red cat carrier sitting beside it, the white splotch of the takeout bags.

She retrieved them and poked around in the kitchen till she found glasses, forks. Laid her bounty on the coffee table in front of the couch.

Zan sprawled, unmoving, as she rummaged through the bags. She was charmed to find a pair of candles, ceramic candleholders, and a book of Café Girasole matches. Nice touch. Then again, for three hundred and some odd bucks, one should expect some extras.

She lit the candles, melted some wax, and set them in the holders. A sweet smell like burnt sugar wafted up. "Hope you don't mind the food cold," she said. "I'm too hungry to bother heating it."

"I'm not fussy," he said. "I just don't think I can handle a fork. You'll have to hand feed me, sweetheart."

She laughed as she pried the cover off the artichoke pastries. "You're pushing your luck."

"And I'm just going to keep on pushing it. Right up to the wall."

She froze as she opened the Cabernet. "What's that supposed to mean?"

A smile twitched the corners of his mouth. "Whatever I want it to mean," he said. "I'm hungry. Get over here, babe. Feed me."

The cork popped out. She poured the wine. She should be resisting his wiles, but she couldn't quite remember why. Zan flicked off the lamp, then slid off the couch and sat cross-legged on the carpet, smiling. Waiting to be pampered and served by his love slave in the flickering candlelight, like a spoiled pasha.

Well, hell. After what the man had done tonight, he deserved a little pampering. No, make that a whole lot of pampering.

She rose up onto her knees, took an artichoke pastry in her hand, and popped it in his mouth. She passed him a glass of wine.

He chewed, sipped his wine, and twitched the bathrobe open, his finger trailing down between her breasts. "Delicious," he said. "Don't close the robe, though. I want you naked while you feed me."

She blushed. After all their wild antics, she was still giggling like a teenage girl. She forked up a plump ravioli and put it to his lips.

They devoured the meal like that: alternating bites, one for her, one for him; a sip of wine; a long, sweet, unhurried kiss. She wanted to make it last as long as it could. He played along, accepting every bite she put in his mouth with moans of exaggerated appreciation.

The adventures of the evening had pounded the strawberry tart with crème Chantilly into a puddinglike goop, but it still looked great when she pried the lid off. Abby scooped some up. "Try this."

His face changed as his lips closed around the spoon, a flare of heat in his eyes that made her gaze dart down to see if—yes.

Sure enough. His penis was lengthening. Indefatigable.

Zan grabbed the other spoon and scooped up a bite for her. It was lovely: creamy and gloppy with hints of fruit and liqueur, and lots of crunchy, buttery crumbs of delicious crust scattered through it.

"Oops, you've got cream on your lip." He swooped down, catching the back of her head in his hand, and gave her a sweet, sticky kiss. He scooped up another spoonful and let it dribble between her breasts.

"Oh no," he murmured in mock dismay. "Gotta fix that."

He pushed her onto her back and had at her with his tongue, with long, hungry swipes. She grabbed his shoulders. Everything inside her, outside her, was shivering and soft and hot. She loved him, she wanted to wrap herself around him, she wanted to give him everything.

And she appeared to be doing just exactly that. He spread her legs, folded them up, and laid her bare feet against his hot, muscular chest. He nudged himself between the folds of her labia, pushed.

"Zan, wait. Not without . . . what do you think you're doing?"

He thrust into her with one hard lunge. "Pushing my luck."

"I can't," she said, even while her body betrayed her by arching and writhing to accommodate more of him. "I can't risk this."

"You already did," he said. "Trust me, Abby."

She stared up at him and the words of protest fragmented in her brain as their eyes met, locked. She was transfixed by the sensual rhythm of his powerful body, by her desperate need for his strength, his tenderness. His pounding hips jarred her closer and closer, then right into it; the long, throbbing pulsation of pleasure. Zan jerked out of her, gasping as his seed spurted across her belly.

He sagged over her. "God," he said hoarsely, after a minute of stunned, panting silence. "What the fuck are you doing to me, woman?"

"Hey." She grabbed his chin and forced him to look her in the eye. "Get it straight, buddy. This time, it was something that *you* did to *me*."

He grinned. "Yeah. You liked it, huh?"

"That's not the point!" She shoved at his chest.

He rolled off her obligingly. "It's the only point I'm interested in."

She looked down at herself. "I don't want to play word games."

"Come into the bathroom with me, then. There are lots of other fun games we can play."

She started laughing. She couldn't stay stern. "I am not taking a shower with you. You are a sex maniac. You should be chained up."

He blinked innocently. "You're sticky, Abby. Let me wash you."

"I can bathe myself, thanks." She stormed into the bathroom in a mock rage. It would be such fun to take a shower with Zan, she thought, as hot water pounded down on her exhausted body. To just relax and let him do anything he wanted. Loving her up with slippery soap and his big, skillful hands. It made her almost faint to think of it.

But she felt so fragile every time she let herself wonder if this new level of intimacy meant that they were a couple now. She couldn't bear to find out that it was all just a sexy game to him.

Better to skirt around the issue, keep her mouth shut. Keep things as light as she could and hope for the best.

Zan was waiting outside the door with a kiss for her as she came out. He went in to take his own shower, leaving her alone to pour herself another glass of wine and wander around his apartment.

His bed was huge, set in an alcove right underneath one of those fabulous arched windows that looked out over the sea. What sunsets he must have. Amazing. She felt like a sorceress in her magical tower, curled up on Zan's bed, sipping wine and looking at the waning moon.

Zan joined her a few minutes later. There was an odd tension in the set of his shoulders as he stood by the bed, looking down at her. He held a small object in his hand as if unsure what he should do with it.

"What have you got there?" she asked.

His fingers closed, as if to hide it. "Abby, I wanted to ask you . . ."

She was starting to get alarmed. "What? What is it?"

"Let's leave town." The words seemed to burst out of him.

She was bewildered. "Ah, when?"

"Right now. Or tomorrow morning, if you want some sleep."

"But . . . to go where?" she asked.

"Anywhere," he said. "Mexico. Canada. Things are strange here. I can't keep you safe. Let's take a road trip. The Banff Jasper Highway is great this time of year. Or we can go south, find a beach to lie on."

Her heart thudded with terrified joy at all his offer implied. "Zan, I would love to. But now is not a good time. I have to find out who—"

"Killed Elaine," he broke in. "Yeah. We both saw what happens when you start poking around in that dark closet. What if I'm not with you the next time the monsters jump out?"

Abby shivered, and set her wine down on the bed stand. "It's not just that. There's my job. I think I'm about to be fired anyway, but even so, the gala is tomorrow, and it would be unprofessional of me to bag out with no notice. I should at least show up and make an effort—"

"Hold on," Zan said. "Are you going to the gala with that guy?"

Abby felt like a bird who had fluttered into a room and could not find the window to fly back out. "I—I—"

"You are," he said, his voice soft with incredulity. Whatever Zan had been holding in his fist broke with a snap. He tossed the two pieces onto his dresser. "Fuck me. You *are*."

"It's not like that," she said quickly. "You've got the wrong idea."

"I do? Explain it to me."

His expressionless tone chilled her. "It's just a courtesy thing, Zan, not a real date," she explained. "The guy's a big-shot donor, and Dovey set me up, and everyone put me on the spot, and I—"

"And you said yes."

She threw up her hands. "Yes!" she yelled. "I did! So shoot me! I thought I was monumentally single after that horrible fight we had the other night. Who could blame me?"

"I'm not blaming you. I'm just letting you know that you're not single anymore," he said. "In case you haven't noticed."

"Oh, I've noticed!" She scrambled off the bed and grabbed his arm. "I want to be with you, Zan. After tomorrow, I will never—"

"Not good enough," he said. "Call the guy. Call him right now. Tell him it's off. You already have an escort. Me."

She was dismayed. "But . . . but I can't do that! It would be so awkward and humiliating for him—"

"You think I give a shit about his poor tender feelings?"

"You should give a shit about my professional dignity!" she shot back. "It's such a meaningless thing, Zan, I don't understand why you're making such a big huge deal out of—"

"After everything that happened between us tonight, you're still going to the fucking gala with Moneybags as your escort," he repeated.

He was as unyielding as a stone. She wanted to shriek with frustration. "You're taking this way too seriously!"

"How far are you willing to go for your job, Abby? That must be one mother of a donation. Do they expect you to fuck him, too?"

Abby jerked backward as if she'd been slapped.

She felt like the air had been sucked out of the room. Her chest ached, ice cold. Empty.

Suddenly, being naked in front of him felt very bad. "It's happening again, isn't it?" she whispered.

He shrugged. "Looks that way."

She backed away from the stony anger radiating from him, and stumbled through the dark apartment to the entrance. She found her bag, rummaged for underwear, T-shirt, jeans. She dragged everything out of her purse to find her cell phone, and punched in the number for her car service. "A-Line Limo," a bored voice said.

"Hello," she said. "I'd like a car to meet me at, ah . . . at . . ."

"Seventeen Pearl Alley," Zan supplied from across the room.

She repeated the address and hung up. Trying to breathe.

"Where do you think you're going?" Zan asked. "You can't go home. You can't leave here if you don't have someplace safe to go."

She ignored him, punching in Dovey's number and praying that he was home. He picked up, his voice confused and sleepy. "Hello?"

"Dovey? Hi, it's Abby."

"Abby? Good Lord, girl, it's almost two in the morning."

"I know, and I'm so sorry to call so late. Can I come stay with you tonight? My apartment got robbed, and I'm scared to stay there alone."

"Oh my God! You poor baby. Of course, come right on over. Did you call the police?"

"Not yet," she hedged. "Long story. I'll tell you when I get there."

She hung up the phone. Sheba. She had to find her cat. She started calling. "Sheba, kitty? Where'd you go? Kitty, kitty?"

"Abby."

Zan was standing behind her. Sheba was draped over his hands. He handed the cat to her. "I'll wait with you downstairs for the taxi."

"That's not necessary," she said. "I can—"

"Shut up," he said harshly. "It's necessary."

He loaded himself up with the cat carrier and her duffel bag. The ride down was awful, both of them staring away from each other. When the heavy door creaked open, the taxi was already waiting, thank God.

Zan packed her stuff into the trunk and opened the car door for her. "Be careful, Abby," he said. "Don't get killed. That would suck."

The tone in his voice made her want to scream. "How do you do it, Zan?" she asked him. "You have such talent. You tear my guard down, and that's when you stab in the knife and start turning it."

His eyes were bleak. "Funny," he said. "I was thinking the exact same goddamn thing myself, about you. Have a great time at the gala."

He slammed the car door shut. The taxi pulled away.

Zan stared after Abby's cab until the taillights faded from sight. He kept staring, frozen in place. Maybe he would stand there forever.

It was over. Hopelessly and definitely over. After all their adventures: the attack, the sexy meal, the laughter, and the perfect, magical fusion of their lovemaking, it was all reduced to *I don't see why you're making such a big deal out of it, Zan. It's so meaningless.*

Meaningless, his ass. He swallowed bile.

"My, what a positive attitude," drawled a gravelly, familiar voice.

Oh, shit. The pipe smoke wafting out the window over his head hit his nose. "You shouldn't eavesdrop on private conversations, Granddad," he said tonelessly. "It's rude. You taught me that yourself."

"And what do you call tearing down the guard of a pretty young lady, sticking in a knife, and turning it, hmm? I do believe that's ruder."

It took all the respect for his elders pounded into him since childhood not to say something ugly. "You don't know anything about it," he said.

"Saw it with my own eyes," Granddad said. "Hurt her feelings so bad, she had to call a taxi. And you didn't even offer her a ride." He shook his grizzled head. "Very poor, Alexander. You were raised better."

"Don't worry about her," Zan growled. "She's got other fish to fry."

"Oh! So it's jealousy, eh? The green-eyed bitch." Granddad nodded sagely. "May the best man win, then."

"Back off," Zan warned. "I've had a shitty night."

Granddad puffed his pipe. "I think I just saw my last chance to get me some great-grandbabies get into a taxicab and leave in a huff."

"Forget about her. She's going to the museum gala with some richer-than-God butthole," he snarled. "What am I supposed to say to her? Hope he's a great kisser. Don't have him get you home too late."

"So you beat your chest, said rude things? God save us, boy."

"What the hell do you expect me to do?" Zan yelled.

"I expect you to use the brain God gave you," Granddad snapped. "The museum gala, you say?" He leaned out over the windowsill, eyes brightening. "My lady friend Helen is going to that gala. Her daughter's on the board of directors. Tickets cost eight hundred bucks. Each."

Zan let out a short, bitter cough of laughter. "Hell of a party."

"I bet it will be, with you there to kick up a fuss. I'll ask Helen if her daughter can get us another ticket." Granddad's voice was brisk.

"What?" Zan gaped. "Are you out of your mind? Pay eight hundred bucks for the privilege of watching her dance with another man?"

"And you're just going to lie down and let it happen? Too chicken to let her see the two of you side by side? Bwawk, bwawk, bwawk!"

"Do not start with me, Granddad—"

"It's the only way to get you off your ass, Alexander!" the old man bellowed. "Don't be a such damn sniveling coward. Go get her!"

Zan turned his back on him and walked away. There was no shutting Granddad down once he got himself worked into a state.

"You can get your tux at Eddie's Big & Tall, down on Greeley," Granddad shouted. "You'll need dress shoes. And a goddamn haircut!"

Zan ducked into an alley and pointed himself down toward the docks. He wished he knew where Mark's dickhead goons were hiding. He would hunt them down and cheerfully rip their limbs off.

Too chicken to let her see the two of you side by side? Bwawk, bwawk, bwawk!

Granddad's barb made him squirm. Being provoked beyond all bearing was not necessarily an excuse for acting like a raving asshole.

After all. His whole future was at stake. He could sacrifice it for his stupid macho pride if he wanted to. Hell, it was a free country.

Aw, shit. Maybe he should check out this shindig, after all.

"A knife," Lucien repeated. "Against my orders, you pulled a knife on the man and tried to stab him to death. Then, to compound your idiocy, you dropped the knife. It leaves me breathless, Ruiz."

"The pig practically broke my wrist!" Ruiz protested. "I had to—"

"Enough," Lucien said.

Ruiz held up the ice pack to hide his swollen face. "The guy was a fucking fiend, boss," he whined. "He practically ripped my arm off. He ruptured Henly's balls. He would have killed me if I—"

"This is the heart of our misunderstanding, Ruiz," Lucien said. "I really don't care if you're killed. In fact, as your incompetence reveals itself, I care less and less. If the locksmith dies before the job goes down, my plans are ruined. If you ruin my plans, I will be very angry. Are you listening?" Lucien grasped the man's elbow and gave it a vicious upward jerk. Ruiz shrieked and moaned. "You understand?"

Ruiz's head bobbed. Lucien let go of the man's elbow. He drooped until his face hit the tabletop, moaning. "You're being paid very well to risk your lives," Lucien said. "Both of you." He jerked his chin in Henly's direction. Henly opened one swollen eye a slit, groaned, and turned away. "You too, Neale," Lucien added, for good measure.

"I wasn't even there," Neale said defensively. "Don't blame me."

Lucien sorted through the plastic bags. Maitland's passport, small items with smooth surfaces that held fingerprints well: spoons, makeup. Her hairbrush and toothbrush to provide genetic material for the police. At least Henly and Ruiz had managed that much.

"The job goes down tomorrow," he said.

The moaning and muttering stopped. "Uh . . . isn't tomorrow the gala?" Neale asked. "The museum will be packed with drunken VIPs."

"We can't wait any longer. We can't afford to let those two run around loose, knowing whatever they know. The woman will be easy. We'll get Boyle to help lure the locksmith in, since you two can't manage him by sheer muscle. It requires intelligence. Which you both lack."

Henly groaned again. "Fuck," he muttered.

Lucien looked at the far side of the room, where a young blond woman was rummaging through a pile of clothes that lay on the couch.

"Crystal?" he called. "Are you finding anything that will fit?"

"Oh, totally," Crystal said. "All this stuff'll fit me real good."

Lucien winced at the girl's flat midwestern vowels. Nothing like Abby's husky Southern lilt. No matter, though. Crystal was just a visual prop. "What about your hair?" He frowned at her wispy blond waif cut.

"Oh, Lucy had a wig made for me. It's styled like your girl, and it looks great," Crystal assured him. She pulled out a plastic container and shook out a silky auburn coil of hair. "See? Real human hair. I have brown contacts, too, and sunglasses. Hair is easy. It's build and bone structure that are tougher to match. But don't worry. Once I put on the wig and clothes and do my makeup, I'll look exactly like her."

"Hmph." Lucien gazed at the girl's body, revealed in every splendid detail by the formfitting spandex. Neale was looking too.

"I bet you'll look real good in that," Neale said wistfully.

Crystal held up the fluttery black cocktail dress to herself and flicked him an indifferent glance. "Yep," she said. "To die for."

"I don't suppose you, uh, might be interested in, ah . . ."

Crystal's eyes flicked over Neale. Her pretty face hardened. "Lucy's contract stipulates sexual availability for the guy whose name is on the contract. Anybody else has to come to a private agreement with me. When my services aren't required by the boss, of course."

Neale turned big, hopeful eyes magnified by his Coke-bottle glasses on Lucien. "Uh, boss? Are you, uh . . ."

Lucien sighed. The man thought of nothing but sex. He looked over Crystal's spectacular body, and the glossy auburn wig that dangled from her hand. He contemplated the turbulent emotional unrest inside him. So disturbing. He needed an outlet for it, so he could think more clearly. "Sorry, Neale," he said. "Crystal's busy tonight. Another time."

He looked around at his men. "Rest while you can," he said. "We cannot afford any more mistakes. From anyone."

No one would meet his eyes. That angered him, too.

Lucien grabbed Crystal's arm and dragged her up the stairs to the master bedroom. She made a distressed sound at the way his fingers bit into her arm. He flung open the door and shoved her into the room.

She backed away, her face fearful. "Hey, mister. Don't—"

"Shut up," he said.

Her blue eyes blinked rapidly, like Elaine's. It annoyed him. He flipped off the light. "Put on your wig," he ordered. "Then strip. Scream if you want, but do not say one word."

Chapter

23

The gala was a glittering success.

Abby looked around at the crowd. She felt detached and dream-like. She'd also drunk more wine than she should have. It hadn't helped. On the contrary.

She should be proud of what she had accomplished. The exhibit hall was a multimedia art installation on its own merit. Her tropical underwater theme was gorgeous. Blue and green textile hangings commissioned from local artists waved above their heads. A stage designer at the Arts Institute had created a sunken galleon for the center of the room, surrounded by sprays of colored coral. A revolving projector was mounted on its figurehead. Images of brightly colored tropical fish spun in lazy, ghostly circles around the walls and the silken hangings, creating a swirling, dynamic light show.

Everything had gone perfectly. A baroque ensemble from Portland had played eighteenth-century dance music during a delicious dinner. A troupe of costumed dancers had performed with them. Before the speechifying, everyone had been charmed and tickled by a swashbuckling cutlass duel between two actors costumed as pirates. And when they cut the ribbon to the new exhibit hall and let in the crowd, the Pirates' Hoard collection had taken everyone's breath away.

The after-dinner dance band was red-hot and blazing. Abby had smiled and mingled and schmoozed. The museum might have made its funding goal, or exceeded it, but she couldn't for the life of her remember why she'd thought it was so important last night.

It was just a big party. These people didn't appreciate her. They were going to fire her. She could have been halfway to Mexico with Zan by now.

"Abby? Are you all right?"

She plastered on a smile for Lucien. Nice of him to ask. Nobody else did, except Dovey. Everyone was keeping a careful distance from her since she'd landed in the doghouse. "Fine, thanks," she said.

He touched her cheek. She resisted the urge to rub the touch away with her hand. "Are you thinking about Elaine?" he asked.

None of your freaking business what I'm thinking about, buddy.

She forced another smile. No need to be snotty. The guy was trying to be sweet and sensitive, and any such effort on the part of a man should be duly rewarded. "I, ah, suppose I am," she said.

The band was launching into a slow, dreamy number, and Lucien maneuvered her smoothly out onto the dance floor. "Dance with me."

She didn't want to dance with him. His touch made her twitchy. His gentle, pleasant, super-attentive smile bugged her, too. It looked like it was stamped on his handsome face. Sort of like a live Ken doll.

But even the handsomest, kindest, most perfect man in the world would annoy her right now. It wasn't Lucien's fault that he wasn't Zan.

Zan was jealous and controlling and rigid. She ran through the litany in her head for the thousandth time. He didn't respect her work or her professional dignity. He wouldn't meet her halfway. She couldn't live that way. Just couldn't. No and no and no. No matter how madly she was in love with him. No matter how miserable she was without him. She forced a bright rictus of a smile onto her face.

"You look beautiful tonight," Lucien said. "Red suits you."

She nodded her thanks. Her burgundy taffeta dress was, in fact, fabulous. An aggressively engineered corset hoisted the goods up to maximum height for clearer viewing, and a long, billowing skirt swirled around her legs. She and Elaine had chosen gowns reminiscent of the eighteenth century. Elaine's was deep blue taffeta. They'd had such fun designing them. They had meant to be perfect foils for each other.

She couldn't let herself think of it. It would send her straight down the wormhole. She'd have worn a different dress altogether, but the thieves had taken the rest of her clothes. This gown had escaped only because she'd left it at the seamstress's studio for the final fitting.

"How is your investigation going?" Lucien asked.

She tried not to wince. "Better than I'd hoped," she admitted. "I tracked down the murderer's house last night."

His eyes widened in startled admiration. "How on earth?"

It was a relief to have found something to talk about with him. By the end of the dance, she'd told him the relevant details of last night's adventures: her search at Elaine's, discovering the Otis Street house.

"Unbelievable," he said. "Elaine was lucky to have such a friend."

"I don't know," she mumbled. "I just did what I had to do."

"Have you thought about my offer to help? I have an excellent private investigator I could put on this. Getting the security videotape at the hotel could be discreetly managed, providing the right incentives."

"What do you mean, incentives? Large sums of money?"

He looked charmingly sheepish. "Money produces very quick results," he said. "The temptation to use shortcuts is irresistible sometimes, and I think you deserve some shortcuts. I would be proud to help. We could discuss it tomorrow, at lunch. If you're free."

She struggled to come up with an excuse, but was distracted by a shark image that wiggled across Lucien's smiling face. The answer came to her when she saw one of the baroque dancers, still costumed in her elaborate period gown. Oh boy, of course! Nanette's play. Bingo. Saved.

"Thanks, but I've got another engagement," she told him. "I'm going to see the matinee performance of a friend's play tomorrow."

"Oh, really? What play is that?"

"Romeo and Juliet," she told him. "At the Stray Cat Playhouse."

She was relieved to see Dovey bearing down on them, snazzy in his tux and rhinestone-studded bow tie. "There you are!" His chubby face was flushed with champagne. "You are a vision, Abby. And how are you, Mr. Haverton? Enjoying the evening?"

"But of course," Lucien said. "The company is so charming."

Dovey slid an arm around her waist. "Abby, I'm so sorry, but I've come to drag you to Bridget's side. I'll bring her back soon," he said to Lucien, tucking Abby's arm into his and steering her into the crowd.

"You're kidding," Abby said. "Bridget's not even speaking to me."

"It was an excuse, silly," Dovey said, sounding suddenly much less giddy. "I'm not taking you to Bridget. I just wanted to warn you."

"Of what?" Abby froze into place.

"Your locksmith lover," Dovey said. "He's here. After all those hairy stories you told me last night, I thought you should be prepared."

"Oh, no. You're kidding." Her bones turned promptly to water.

"Nope," Dovey said. "I almost didn't recognize him at first. He's a stunning sex god in a tux, but he still manages to look like a wild panther somehow. He's cut his hair. Wait'll you see. I'm not sure I approve, but those intense yellow panther eyes just give me chills."

"Oh, God." She stumbled on suddenly rubbery ankles.

Dovey grabbed a glass of champagne off a passing tray. "Drink up. Your guy looks like a volcano about to blow, so . . . well, you haven't got much margin for error right now, so try to avoid a scene, OK?"

"Dovey," she whispered helplessly. "What am I going to do?"

"Aw, honey." Dovey hugged her, and sucked in a breath as he looked over her shoulder. "Heads up. He's on the move. Coming around the galleon. Staring at you with the eyes of his soul."

Abby turned slowly. Their eyes met. All the sound in the room went away. She only heard her heart pounding.

Zan looked utterly different, as well as quintessentially himself in the tux. His dark hair was cropped severely short. He looked exotically perfect in classic evening wear. A small gold hoop gleamed in his ear.

Zan saluted her with his glass of champagne, drained it with one gulp, and set it on a passing tray. Abby grabbed Dovey's arm, so as not to sink down to the floor in a billowing crimson taffeta cloud.

Zan tugged uncomfortably on his bow tie. It made him feel hot and strangled. Abby stared back, eyes wide and scared. No smile of welcome. Not that he expected one, after his performance last night.

That dress was outrageous. Blatant, in-your-face sexual provocation. Her gleaming hair swung long and loose. Every inch of his skin remembered how it felt, swishing and sliding over him.

He started to sweat. Should have laid off the champagne, but it had been easier to lurk in the corner with a drink in his hand.

The little chubby guy threw his arm around Abby's shoulders as Zan approached, his cherubic face worried.

No need. He'd resolved to be supremely civilized. He would demonstrate total self-control. He'd even waited until Abby moved away from Moneybags before he approached her. Getting hauled into jail for assault would not improve his chances of getting Abby back.

Dancing couples swirled and rearranged, leaving an empty clearing in front of them. It would feel so good just to keep moving and pull her right into the circle of his arms, where she belonged.

He stopped a yard away, held back by an invisible force field of fear and doubt. They stared at each other.

The chubby guy cleared his throat delicately. "Abby, love," he murmured. "I'll just, ah, be off. If you think you're OK alone."

"Thanks, Dovey," she murmured. "You're a sweetie. I'll be fine."

Dovey ducked into the crowd with an airy wave of his fingers.

Abby's white throat bobbed. "What on earth are you doing here?"

"Supporting the arts," he said.

She rolled her eyes. "Yeah, right."

"OK," he admitted quietly. "I wanted to check out the competition."

She looked wary. "I wasn't aware of any competition. I thought you'd crossed me off your list forever."

He brushed the back of his knuckles gently across her velvety soft cheek. "No. You're the only name on my list, Abby."

She pressed her fisted hands against her mouth. "This is cruel," she said. "I can't let you get close to me again. You tear me apart."

He grabbed her hands and bowed his head over them, pressing them against his forehead. "I'm sorry," he told her.

"You can't keep being mean and horrible, and think that saying 'I'm sorry' will fix everything," she told him. "That only goes so far."

"I know." He kissed her hands. "But what else can I say?"

"I don't know." She wouldn't meet his eyes, she had tears sparkling on her lashes, and she was sniffling. But she wasn't pulling away. It gave him a burst of hope. He kissed her hands again. And again.

She looked him over; the haircut, the tux, the earring. "Wow," she murmured. "You look very fine, Zan. You went all out, didn't you?"

"I did," he said. "Speaking of which. That's one hell of a dress."

She flinched. "Here we go again. You hate it, don't you?"

"Not exactly," he said. "You know how I feel about your evening wear. It's more like a love-hate relationship. I want to rip down one of those hanging things and wrap you up in it. Then I want to drag you off someplace and fuck you senseless."

"Keep your voice down." She draped her hair over her chest.

"No, don't do that." He twitched the heavy fall of hair back over her shoulder. "Go ahead, baby. Don't be shy. Display the goods."

She slapped his hand away. "Oh. So you didn't come here tonight because you want me. You just want to punish me some more."

He winced. "No, Abby. Sorry. I didn't come here to make trouble. Watching you dance with Moneybags was hard on my nerves, that's all."

"I told you already!" she said in a fierce whisper. "That man is nothing to me! How many times do I have to tell you that?"

His jaw ached from clenching his teeth. "I don't know," he said starkly. "Tell me again. Keep telling me. I'll let you know when you can stop."

The band launched into a romantic ballad. He held out his arms. Abby hesitated, but the pull between them was as inexorable as gravity.

Both of them sighed as she melted into his arms. It was soothing and sweet, but laced with a thrill of hope. A kiss for his whole body.

And his soul.

Zan slid his hand across the smooth warmth of her back, bent to nuzzle her hair. The other dancers instinctively made room for them. They swayed inside a glittering cocoon of perfect intimacy, rocking on the waves of the sensual old jazz standard. As the last long, poignant note faded away, Zan lifted his head from her shoulder and looked down into her eyes. A bright tear welled up, hung on her lashes, dropped onto her cheek with a glittering flash. He kissed it away.

"Please, don't," she whispered. "Not here. People will see."

Like he cared, but now was not the time to insist. He fingered the key necklace in his pocket. "I have something for you."

"Really?" She sniffed, wiped her eyes. "What's that?"

"Find me someplace private, and I'll show you."

She rolled her eyes. "Oh, please, Zan—"

"No, I'm not being a clown. I'm serious. I wanted to give it to you last night, but we hit the wall before I got the chance."

She looked hunted. "Zan, is it . . . could it wait?"

"No," he said simply.

She bit her lip. Her eyes darted around. "Come with me, then. But this has to be quick. And I mean, quick. Like, three minutes, OK?" She spun around with a swish of her pouffy red skirt and cut through the blur of tuxes, sequins, décolletage, and endless swirling fish images into the administrative wing. It was silent and deserted.

Abby led him to her office and flicked on the light. "Here's a private place. But I have to get back, right away. I'll be missed. And I'm right on the edge of being fired already, so I don't want to push my—"

"Abby." He put his hand in his pocket, hesitating in a final agony of doubt. Too bad about the box, but he'd smashed the hinges last night. He opened up her hand. Laid the pendant in it.

She stared down at it. It gleamed, heavy and rich and sensual, like the pirate gold. "Oh my," she whispered. "Zan, are those, ah . . ."

"Real rubies? Yes. Who knew you'd be wearing red tonight?"

"Oh, Lord." Her voice was high, almost squeaky. "It must have cost a fortune. Zan, you're crazy."

"I know," he agreed. "I just wish it were a ring."

She opened her mouth, closed it again. "I—I, ah . . ."

"I bought this over a week ago," he confessed. "At the time, I thought it was too soon for a ring. I didn't want to scare you away. But things have moved so fast. It's been a wild ride, baby."

She touched the pendant with her finger. "Yes, it certainly has."

"I'd feel better if you were wearing my ring, but this . . ." He took it out of her hand. ". . . is going to have to do. For now."

He clasped it around her neck. It nestled into her shadowy cleavage. It looked perfect. "Do you like it?" he asked anxiously.

She wiped tears away, trying not to smear her makeup. "It's the loveliest thing I've ever seen. But I shouldn't accept—"

He cut off her protests with a kiss. "Think of it as a memento of all our strange adventures together."

"But I don't have anything for you," she said.

He shook with ironic laughter. "Oh, but you do, sweetheart."

"Don't be crass," she said tartly. "It must have been so expensive."

"Abby. Baby." He leaned down to kiss the velvety shadows above the pendant. "I don't know any delicate, classy way to say this, but the necklace didn't break me. I'm not hurting for money."

"Yes, I noticed that," she said. "I saw your apartment."

"I'm glad that's clear. I'm not loaded like Moneybags, but I—"

"Don't!" She put her hand over his mouth. "Every time we talk about him, you morph into someone I don't recognize. So don't."

"OK," he murmured against her palm. "No more talk."

He kissed her instead. All over her face, down her throat, her shoulders. Her cheeks were wet with tears, and he kissed them all away, following the tracks of moisture to get every precious, salty drop.

He pulled the low-cut bodice down. Her breasts popped out.

Abby gasped. "Zan, don't wreck my dress! I have to walk out of here in that! And people can see in that window!"

He flicked the light off, scooped her up, and perched her on the edge of the table.

"Zan. Please. I can't afford to do anything stupid tonight," she pleaded. "My bosses are watching me like hawks."

"I don't see your boss here, Abby." He pushed her down onto the table until she was flat on her back.

He cupped her breasts in his hands and pressed his face to them, kissing and licking and worshiping them. Wallowing in her silken softness. He loved the way she trembled, how vulnerable and open she was. The soft, hitching pants of her breath.

He settled his body against the voluminous folds of crinkly fabric, and lavished all the feelings he was too afraid to put into words with his hungry kisses, his lashing tongue, his warm, pleading lips.

He lifted his head, stared into her eyes. "You're my woman?"

She nodded.

"Say it," he demanded. "I need to hear you say the words."

She closed her eyes, her breath jerking between her lips. "I'm . . . I'm your woman," she whispered.

"Good," he said. "It's a done deal, then. Show me that you're mine, Abby. Lift your skirt up for me."

"Oh, please. You are such a manipulator," she accused him.

"Yeah, I'm terrible," he agreed, dragging the crinkly dress up over her knees, then her thighs. He wadded it over her belly into a big rustling wad—and stared down, startled.

She wasn't wearing any stockings. And her panties were not the seductive, skimpy scrap of lace that he had come to expect from her.

They were just plain white cotton briefs.

She wiggled self-consciously. "I wasn't expecting anybody to look under my skirt tonight, so I didn't bother," she said in a small voice.

He kept staring, stupefied and moved.

She swatted him. "What?" she demanded. "Do my boring cotton panties completely wreck the vibe of your conquering hero fantasy?"

"Oh no!" he burst out. "God, no! These are the most beautiful, sexy panties I've ever seen in my whole life."

"Oh, stop it." She tried not to smile. "They're awful."

"No, no, no. They're perfect," he said, meaning it with all his heart. He started to tug them down the silky length of her legs.

"No!" She whacked at him. "Stop that! No way, Zan. Forget it!"

He cupped her round, silky warm bottom with trembling hands, aching with the need to touch her everywhere. "God, Abby, please—"

"No!" She wrestled his arms down. "Not here, and not tonight. I would be too tense to enjoy it anyway. Back off and listen to me, for once! Show me you respect who I am and what I do, if you're for real about wanting to be with me. I am dead serious, Zan. Read my lips."

He could see from the steely look in her eyes that she was.

Keep it together, bozo. He couldn't fuck up now. Not with the shining prize almost in his grasp.

He forced himself to step back, wiping his damp brow with the sleeve of his tux. "Aw, shit," he muttered. "Whatever. Sorry. Again."

She stuffed her gorgeous tits briskly back into her bodice. "By now, the gala is almost over, and very likely my career along with it. I'm going to go out there and act professional, and you are *not* going to bug me, in any way. Is that understood?"

"I'll be as docile as a sweet little lamb," he promised.

And he meant it, with all his heart.

Abby yanked the door open. Light streamed in from the corridor, illuminating the flush on her creamy cheeks, the excited glow in her eyes. The necklace looked like a million bucks, nestled in her cleavage.

The sight of it made his heart thud with triumph.

His. All his. His bride, his love, forever and always. He'd won.

She shook her finger. "No scenes," she repeated. "I mean it, Zan."

"Sure you do, babe." He batted his eyes innocently, willing his hard-on to ease down to socially acceptable proportions, and followed her back out into the party.

Chapter
24

Abby plunged right back into work mode, smiling and chatting with patrons and donors. Part of her attention was constantly aware of Zan's hovering presence. Another part was occupied with staying well out of Lucien's line of sight. She didn't like to imagine what would happen if the two men should collide.

Finally, the guests began to leave. The kisses and thank-yous lasted another eternity. At last the room began to clear out. She leaned against the wall for a moment, dizzy with exhaustion.

Zan's arm slid around her waist. "Third time's the charm," he said.

"What's that?" She looked over her shoulder into his eyes.

"I've saved you from two bad dates. If I save you from number three, you're mine forever."

"You don't need magic, you silly man. I'm already yours." She patted his hand. "Be good," she whispered to him. "This is almost over."

She could hardly believe it. They'd gotten through this with no train wreck. They were almost home free. It made her want to float right up off the floor, buoyed by giddy, terrified hope. Maybe this could work.

"Abby. There you are!" Abby winced at Bridget's acidic voice.

"Lucien has been looking all over for you!" Bridget's voice was an accusing whisper. "It almost looks as if you've been avoiding him!"

"Sorry," Abby murmured. "I've just been working the crowd. I didn't mean to be rude to him."

"He's in the exhibit hall with Peter. Make an effort to be charming, hmm?" Bridget's eyes slid over Zan, and widened. "You! The young man who installed our locks!"

"The very one," Zan said calmly.

Bridget examined him with deep suspicion. "You look quite different. I had no idea that you were a patron of the museum, Mr. . . ."

"Duncan," he supplied. "Yeah, isn't life surprising sometimes?"

"Wait here for me," Abby told him sternly. "Do not move from this spot, Zan. I'll be just a minute." She hurried toward the exhibit hall.

Lucien was chatting with her boss, leaning over the pearl and gold encrusted cameos of the Byzantine Caesars. Lucien's eyes lit up when he saw her. To her horror, he rushed toward her and hugged her.

"Thank God," he exclaimed. "I was just telling Peter about that sinister-looking man I saw following you. Then you vanished, and I got nervous. Did he bother you?"

"Oh no," she said, flustered. "I'm fine. I just—"

"I'm not the one who's doing the bothering."

Zan's voice from the doorway was soft, but it cut right through the chatter in the room, silencing it instantly. All heads turned to stare.

Lucien thrust Abby behind him. "That's him! That's the man I was referring to! Someone call security, please."

"Oh, no, no, no!" Abby said hastily. "He's OK, Lucien. He's—"

"Stand back, Abby." Lucien's chest was puffed out, and his handsome face was grave and stern. "Let me deal with this man."

"Yeah, sweetheart. Step aside." Zan made a little beckoning gesture to Lucien. "Deal with me, then. I live for this."

Bridget gasped dramatically. "Someone call the police!"

Abby stepped between them. "Don't," she hissed to Zan. "Please."

Lucien pushed her aside and seized Zan's arm. "Shall we take this outside like gentlemen?" he suggested, in a fake-pleasant voice.

"If you want to keep your hand, take it off me," Zan said softly.

Lucien gave him a thin smile and jerked him toward the door.

The scene shifted into a scuffling blur, a chaos of flailing tuxedo-clad limbs, shouts and thuds and grunts. Lucien twirled. Splat, he sprawled facedown. Zan crouched on top of him, folding up his arm. Lucien struggled. Zan applied pressure. Lucien shrieked, flopped.

Abby dove at them, shoving Zan off Lucien's body. "Have you gone nuts?" she yelled. "Get off him!"

Zan got to his feet and brushed off his tux. "He provoked me."

Lucien struggled to sit up. He lifted his head. Blood streamed from his nose, horribly red against his white shirt. Everyone gasped.

Lucien looked up at Zan, his bright, pale eyes oddly unruffled.

"You are going to regret this," he said.

Zan stared back at him, and glanced at Abby. "I know," he said.

"Yes, he most certainly will!" Bridget shouldered forward self-importantly. "The police are on their way right now, if you should have any plans to attack anyone else!"

"No, ma'am," Zan said. "I'm satisfied with this one guy, thanks."

Lucien struggled to his feet. Bridget and Peter rushed to help him, but he swatted their clutching hands away. He straightened his clothes, pressed a napkin to his nose, and gazed at Abby, looking betrayed.

"So this man is your lover, Abby?" He let out a self-deprecating laugh. "My goodness. I certainly have made an ass of myself, haven't I?"

"Oh, God, no!" Bridget put a hand on his arm. "Mr. Haverton, we're mortified at what's happened. Please don't think—"

"No." Lucien wrenched away. "I have had enough. Enough."

"But—"

"Not another word," Lucien said. "This place is a madhouse. Just let me out of here, for God's sake." He stalked out.

A roar of horrified chatter swelled in his wake.

"Abby?" Peter tapped his cane fiercely to get her attention. "Is it true? You actually brought this person here to the gala, tonight?"

Abby's mouth opened. She looked at Zan, helplessly. Zan stared back at her, his face stark and rigid. "I . . . I . . . ah . . ."

"I know you've been under terrible strain after Elaine's death." Peter's voice vibrated with fury. "It pains me to do this. But if you cannot conduct your private life without humiliating the most generous patrons of our organization, then you do not belong here. Just go. Don't come back. You'll be paid your two weeks' notice, plus severance pay."

"Peter, I—"

"I don't want to hear any explanations," Peter said. "It's late. And frankly, I don't have the stomach for it. Just go, Abby. I'm sorry."

Abby nodded. She felt floating, disconnected.

"And you." Peter stuck his pointy beard in Zan's direction. "Leave the premises immediately, young man. The police are on their way."

Zan nodded. "Yes, sir," he said. "Sorry for the trouble." He cast an eloquent glance at Abby and walked out.

Abby looked at Bridget's and Peter's furious faces. Dovey had his hand over his mouth. He looked like he was about to cry. Everyone else was wide-eyed, awaiting the closing scene for this melodrama. A terrible secret revealed, or her head spinning around on her shoulders, maybe.

She didn't have the energy to oblige them.

She turned, and drifted through the hall of spinning fish. She was swimming through a grotesque aquatic carousel, around a sunken wreck of a ship. She knew exactly how that ship felt.

She retrieved her wrap and bag from the cloakroom. Zan waited at the foot of the steps, his face taut with misery. She stared down at him. The wind off the ocean made her hair whip around her face and her gown flap wildly around her knees.

"Abby," he said. "I don't know what to say."

"Don't try." Her voice felt faraway. "There's nothing you can say."

"I'm sorry," he said.

She nodded. "Of course. I'm sure you are. I've never doubted your sincerity, Zan. You're always sorry."

His mouth tightened. "I didn't mean to do that to you."

She clutched her taffeta throw around her shoulders, shivering. "This isn't the first time this has happened to me," she said, her voice expressionless. "Jimmy, an ex from Atlanta. I was working in a gallery. Jimmy got jealous. Went nuts on me. Attacked my boss. Really hurt the poor guy, too. It was just awful. I was fired, of course."

"Abby, no. This isn't like that," he began. "I—"

"No, Zan. It's worse. It's much worse." Her voice began to shake. "That gallery job wasn't an important job for my career, like this job is. Or was, I should say. And I didn't care about Jimmy the way I c-c-care about you." Her voice broke. Her chin was beginning to vibrate.

Damn. She had to be tough. No blubbering. She threw her head back, staring up at the dark sky, blinking madly until the tears cleared.

Zan reached for her. She shrank back. "No. Do not touch me."

"You'll find another job," he said, his voice pleading. "You're talented, smart. That hag makes your life hell. You deserve better."

"Maybe so," she said. "But I'm the one who has to make that call."

He shook his head, threw up his hands in mute frustration.

"I don't want to be with a man that I'm afraid to take out in public for fear he'll do something terrible and embarrass me," she said.

"Christ, Abby." Zan looked hunted. "I'm really not like that. My back just keeps getting shoved up to the wall. I swear, I'll never—"

"Yes, I'm sure. You'll never," she said. "That's like 'I'm sorry.' I've heard it before. Several times. I don't think I care to hear it again."

There was a dreadful finality to the words. Zan's face was white to the lips, a muscle pulsing in his jaw. His eyes burned.

She wanted so desperately to take it back. To throw herself into his arms, tell him it didn't matter. Drive off into the sunset with him.

But it did matter. It did. Her throat was too tight to speak.

"I guess I, uh, better go then," Zan said dully. "Before I wreck your life any more than I already have."

"That would be tough," she said. "There's nothing much left for you to wreck. I'm down to scorched earth at this point."

He stared down at the ground. "Good-bye, Abby," he said.

He strode away. She followed him with her eyes until he turned the corner of the new building and disappeared.

Some time later, she became conscious of her surroundings again. The people trickling out of the museum were giving her a very wide berth. She realized, faintly amused, that she had no ride.

Such a mundane detail after all the high drama. There was always Dovey, but dear and kind as he was, he was such a chatterbox. She couldn't bear to hash over what had happened tonight. Nor did she want to put her friend in a strange position with Peter and Bridget.

Best to keep her distance. Better still, just disappear. Poof.

She turned, on impulse, and headed into the bushes that lined the old museum grounds. Behind the building, there was a footpath that zigzagged in switchbacks down the cliff to the public beach.

She picked her way down, clutching the handrail and wobbling on the fragile sandals. The roar of the surf got louder as she descended.

Not loud enough to drown out the echo of what she'd said to Zan.

Lucien's hands shook as he drove back to the hotel suite the Haverton White Foundation had leased for the week. He kept touching his sore nose. His face was tacky with drying blood. He'd stalked through the crowd at the museum with his face streaming crimson, to make sure that everyone would scurry to find out what had happened.

He veered between elation and fury. That scum had dared to physically *attack* him. Him, Lucien Haverton VI, heir to a corporate empire, with a personal fortune of over three hundred million. Such a thing had never happened to him. He was so unsettled, his legs shook.

On the other hand, though, it was perfect. His plan had taken on such a gorgeous, organic spontaneity. He couldn't have made it more believable if he'd scripted it down to the last detail. Everyone who was anyone in Silver Fork had witnessed Abby Maitland and her unbalanced lover making a scene. Abby had certainly been publicly reprimanded by her boss, maybe even fired. A disgruntled, humiliated employee. It would be obvious to everyone who had pulled off the heist.

He parked near a security camera in the hotel garage, and made a big thing out of staggering to the elevator, clutching his nose. He chose a route that brought him past the reception desk, letting everyone get a good, long look at his gory face. Best to get the gossip cross-referenced.

Once in his suite, he shucked his tuxedo, washed the blood off his face and hands, and sat down naked on the stool in front of the bathroom vanity mirror. His nose was puffy, his eyes stinging. He was going to have two black eyes. How very unpleasant.

He peeled off the plastic backing and carefully applied the fake tattoo, an exact copy of the one on the locksmith's neck. Then the contact lenses, as his own piercing blue gaze was too striking to pass unnoticed. The contacts turned them to a muddy hazel. Close enough.

He pulled on the clothes: black cargo pants, black boots, a black turtleneck sweater, a black leather bomber jacket. He would have preferred to use Zan's actual clothing and gun, but staging a burglary of Zan's apartment was too logistically difficult at this late date. Too bad.

Then again, the locksmith was intelligent enough to procure an unregistered weapon like the Glock 9mm that Lucien shoved into the back of his pants. Black leather gloves, a ski mask, and his outfit was complete. He pulled the mask over his face. It made his nose hurt. He took it off and tugged the turtleneck up to cover the tattoo. No need for the mask until the last moment. Everything else was in the car. He went out onto his second-floor balcony and leaned over it. That was Ruiz's signal.

Pop, there it went. A tinkling explosion, and Ruiz's airgun shot out the bulb of the security light, casting the side of the building into deep shadow. The man was an excellent shot, whatever else might be said about his competence. Lucien arranged the coil of rope with the slender black thread attached to it, a metal weight at the end of the thread. He dropped the weight over the edge, felt the thread swing free.

Then he climbed over the balcony, dangled from the bottom, took a deep breath, and dropped. It was a long drop, but he made hardly a sound as he hit, sinking down like a black spider. He reached up, groping. There. The black thread dangled, just within reach. He could pull his ladder down and enter his room after, electronic alibis in place. Everything had been planned to the last detail.

He went loping through the trees to the car. Every step jarred his sore nose and shoulder. His mouth watered at the thought of what he would do to them once he got them up to the remote cabin.

He could not torture the locksmith, since the man had to ostensibly die from a pistol shot to the back of the head, and his death had to be timed, for forensics purposes, to a few hours before Crystal's plane left for Mexico City. But that was fine. When it came to torture, Lucien preferred psychological to physical. More bang for the buck. Any witless fool could make another human being writhe and scream, but to utterly destroy a soul without leaving a mark . . . that took artistry.

To that end, he had Abby to toy with. It was clear that the man was desperately in love with her. He smiled as he ran. He had no restrictions on how quickly or how slowly Abby Maitland had to die.

He could let his imagination run wild.

Chapter

25

Zan braked at the corner, startled by the pounding on the side of the van. For one brillant, shining instant, he thought that it might be Abby. She changed her mind, decided to forgive him.

Matty's flushed, shiny face appeared in the window. Not.

Disappointment made him even more twitchy and furious. Matty yanked the door open and climbed in without asking permission.

"Yo. Dude," he gasped, breathless. "Favor to ask."

"Get out, Matty," he said. "I've got no favors to give tonight."

"My car is parked down at the office." Matty mopped his forehead, which gleamed with sweat. "I rode up with one of the guards, but his shift isn't over till eight. C'mon, it's on your way home. Gimme a ride?"

Matty's eyes had that bright, unfocused glow that Zan knew all too well. He was stoned. "I'm not going home. Call a cab," Zan said.

"Please?" Matty wheedled. "It's just a couple of minutes. What, you going out somewhere? A bar? Wanna go get hammered with me?"

Zan floored it. It would take less time and energy to drive Matty to his car than it would to argue with him. "I'm not good company."

"Yeah, buddy, I saw that scene in the exhibit hall." Matty's giggle sounded almost shrill. "Smooth move, man."

He braked. The van screeched to a stop. "Out," he said.

"Sorry," Matty said hastily. "Champagne makes me into an asshole. I'm serious about going out drinking. Wanna tie on a few?"

He'd sooner drown himself than go out drinking with Matty.

"Not with you," he said.

Matty tittered, as if Zan had said something funny. He fidgeted, flipping down the visor, buzzing the window down, humming, giggling to himself. He was monumentally fucked up, which made it Zan's civic duty to make sure he didn't drive.

"You're loaded," he said wearily. "Forget the fucking car, Matty. I'll just drive you home."

Matty's laugh was a wheezing cackle. "Thanks, Mr. Pure. Do you think I'm going to plow into somebody again, turn 'em into ketchup?"

Zan sucked in a sharp breath. "So. You do remember that night."

Matty's manic smile faded. He fidgeted, twitching the lapels of his tux. He wouldn't meet Zan's eyes.

Neither of them said a word for the rest of the ten-minute drive.

Zan pulled into Matty's long driveway and drove up to the house. He killed the engine and waited for Matty to speak.

"You hate my guts, don't you?" Matty asked. "You think I'm pus."

"No," Zan said. "It hurt, to get fucked over by my best friend. Took me years to get over it. But I'm over it."

Matty's eyes looked wet. "I'm really sorry, man. For everything. Really. Here." He pulled a silver flask out of his pocket and uncapped it. "Go on." His voice shook. "Have a shot of this stuff."

Zan looked at the gleaming flask. At Matty's shaking hand, his bloated, shiny face, his desperate eyes. "No, thanks, Matty."

He leaned over Matty, unlatched the door, and shoved the man out.

"Hey! Wait a sec!" Matty groped for the door handle, but Zan slammed the door and locked it. He shook his head when Matty hammered on it. Every line in the guy's body spelled desperation.

It hurt to look at him. He needed a friend so badly.

Oh, fuck. He couldn't be Matty's friend. The guy made his skin crawl. It was too goddamn much to ask of him. Besides, he himself could give anyone a run for their money when it came to desperation.

He pressed down on the gas and watched Matty's figure shrink in the rearview mirror until he couldn't see him anymore.

"What do you mean, *lost* him?" Lucien slammed his gloved hand down onto Matty Boyle's kitchen table, his voice razor sharp.

"He just drove away." Matty's tone was vague and sullen.

"Drove away? Your job was to draw him in and neutralize him! We needed him out of circulation! Now he's out there, drumming up God knows what alibis. Boyle, you incompetent piece of shit!"

Matty shrugged. "I couldn't stop him."

"The drug I put in that whiskey would have stopped him!"

"He wouldn't drink it," Matty said dully, sinking down into a chair. "I couldn't make him. It doesn't matter. He won't have any alibis tonight. He'll want to sulk. Alone. That's what he does when he's upset."

A car pulled up. Lucien twitched aside the curtain. Neale and Henly walked up to the door. The hangdog set of their shoulders made Lucien go tense. He shoved open the door. "The girl?"

Neale's froglike face was tense and apologetic. "Ah . . ."

Lucien's sense of being favored by destiny began to erode. "An unarmed girl in a ball gown," he said softly. "And she gave you the slip."

"She disappeared, boss," Neale said, his voice defensive. "I was covering the museum, and Henly had the parking lot. She turned out of my line of sight, and I ran to catch up, figuring Henly'd nab her on the other end. But she fucking evaporated." He stared at Lucien, his heavy lower lip protruding. "You wanna, uh . . . put this off?" he suggested delicately. "Until we rope those two in? Tonight is not shaping up to—"

"No!" Lucien snarled. Tonight was the night, damn it. It had to happen while that dramatic scene was fresh in everyone's minds, when the conclusions that people leaped to would stick the fastest, and have the bare minimum of thought and reflection applied to them.

"Henly, Ruiz, get the locksmith. Wherever he is. Use the GPS locator. Do not damage him. Is that understood?"

Henly and Ruiz exchanged alarmed glances. "How the fuck are we supposed to do that?" Henly asked. "The guy's a fuckin' ninja maniac!"

"Go dig your balls out from under the rock where you hid them and earn the money I'm paying you. Neale, Boyle, let's go."

Neale and Boyle were too cowed to bother him with mindless chatter as they drove over. Lucky for them. Before this job, he'd welcomed extreme emotions, even anger or fear. No longer. He'd had quite enough. From now on, he was scaling back his criminal activity to jobs he could accomplish on his own. No more incompetent fuckups.

The first part of the heist went just as they'd drilled it. They left Boyle at his home office to slip the bug into the clever back door that Neale had painstakingly coached the man into coding into the museum's security software months ago. The bug knocked out the control box that processed the signals gathered from the thicket of sensors that protected the installation. The sensors still functioned perfectly—but the information they gathered fell upon deaf ears.

A brief text message signaled that it was done. That left the video surveillance intact, which was part of his plan. Lucien pulled on his mask, tugging it up to show the damning strip of tattoo ink. He used the master key Boyle had provided, punched in the security password. All of which the locksmith could have bullied or tricked out of Boyle.

A hypothesis that Boyle would soon be far too dead to deny.

Once inside, it was easy. He just had to be Zan Duncan. He'd thought it through for the vid cams. The man was violent and deranged, yes, but he was no professional thief. His movements would be jerky. His hands would shake. His gaze would dart from right to left, his shoulders would hunch guiltily. He would scuttle like a rat, fumble and drop things as he shoved them into the bag.

The loot glowed against the black leather of his gloves. Jeweled baroque-style necklaces and earrings, heavy gold chains, golden coins, jewel-encrusted candlesticks, reliquaries, golden crosses of the orders of various knighthoods—the goodies went on and on. Lucien sincerely regretted treating it so roughly, but it would be out of character for the locksmith to show care or finesse. If items were damaged, *c'est la vie*.

"Hey! Hold it right there, or I'll shoot!" a guard howled.

Lucien's movement was smooth and automatic. *Pfft*, the silenced bullet spat at the man's shoulder.

The man twitched to the side, as luck would have it, and the bullet that should have perforated his shoulder plowed sideways into his chest. The man spun, hit the wall, and slid heavily to the floor, leaving a thick, viscous black-red streak in his wake. He made sucking, bubbling sounds as he struggled to breathe. He'd hit a lung. Shit. The idiot.

Lucien had to leave at least one witness alive to nail the ident. This one was meat. Time to go looking for the other.

"Hey. Rod? What the hell is—" The other guard stopped as he ambled into the exhibit hall, eyes going wide.

Pfft.

This time the bullet hit the man's thigh, knocking him off his feet. Lucien kicked the gun away from the man's hand. He stared into his terrified eyes, aiming between them. The man was bleeding, but not copiously. He'd missed the femoral artery. He would live.

He turned his head, a slow, neck-craning gesture that exposed another centimeter of tattoo. He looked back, noting that the man's expression had changed. He'd seen it. Very good.

He kicked the man in the head, made sure he was unconscious. Plucked the walkie-talkie off the guard's belt, ground it beneath his heel. He searched for the man's cell phone, gave it the same treatment. He did the same with the dying man's equipment.

Then he grabbed his heavy bag and ran.

Voices attacking his head like buzz saws. Coming in and cutting out. "Thanks for telling us, Freddy." *Granddad?*

"Shit, didn't know what else to do. Found him under the dumpster. Thought he was dead, at first. Gave me a real nasty shock."

"Oh, God. He looks like shit." *Christian.*

He ventured a squint, but a laser bolt of light seared the tender, mushy, bruised stuff inside his skull. He closed his eyes up tight again. Pain. "Uh," he grunted.

"Should we call an ambulance?"

"No, from the smell of him, I think he just needs some coffee and a cold shower. Zan? Wake up, boy! Enough of this crap. He went to that goddamn party at the museum last night, see. Got himself into trouble."

"Mmph." He managed to emit a low, croaking sound.

"Come on." It was his brother Jack's voice. "Help me get him up."

"Leave him where he lies," Chris said. "That's what he deserves."

"We can't leave him under Freddy's dumpster," Jack growled. "Grab his arm, you lazy bastard."

Arms grabbed him, hauled him into a sitting position. He was fully conscious now, and seriously regretting it. Shivering. Cold, damp, pain. Every place he'd been thumped or punched or kicked in the last ten days hurt like a son of a bitch. He felt like a live punching bag.

Barely alive, rather.

He located something that might or might not have been his head, it was so painful and huge. He located his hand, placed it protectively over his eyes, and peeked through his fingers.

The faces peering down were distorted and wavering. There was Granddad. Jack, his oldest brother, wearing a shirt that was so white, it caused an explosion behind his eyes. Freddy, an itinerant guy who squatted in an abandoned warehouse nearby, peering through his bushy gray beard. Christian, looking disgusted. As usual.

Zan widened his field of vision, and a fresh wave of pain stabbed through his skull. He was lying in the street, under a dumpster.

He vaguely recalled parking the van at the liquor store, buying his booze. Then came the problem: where to drink it. Going back to his apartment carried the risk of running into Chris, Jamie, Granddad.

He'd drunk it down on the docks. The plan had been to creep home via back alleys, so as not to risk human interaction.

That brilliant plan had landed him under Freddy's dumpster.

"Yo, Zan? Wake up!" Chris swatted his face.

He flinched, slapping his brother's hand away. "Ouch! Fuck!"

"I hope you bought that tux, not rented it, because ain't nobody taking that stinking awful rag back," Granddad warned. "What the hell happened to you, boy? You've got blood on you!"

"Not my blood." He glanced down at the spatters on his cuffs.

"Aw, Jesus, Mary and Joseph," Chris said, his voice grim and soft. "Don't tell me. Let me guess."

Zan opened slitted eyes long enough to glare at him. "Bite me."

"A drunken loser passed out under a dumpster is always a tragic sight," Jack said. "But a drunken loser wearing a tuxedo passed out under a dumpster seems particularly poignant."

"Yeah? Are you moved?" Zan asked sourly. "Try not to weep."

"You could have changed your clothes before sinking into a morass of stinking depravity," Chris lectured. "You'd attract less attention. But it's not your style. You just have to make a splash, huh?"

Zan struggled up onto his knees. "What are you talking about?"

"I'm talking about the call I heard about last night. The fight up at the museum. The psycho who freaked out and beat the crap out of some rich big shot in a tux. Granddad told me you were going to that party. Guess who came into my mind as the perp?"

"Oh." Memory of last night's awful events flooded back in a nasty, unwelcome rush. It made him nauseated. "Yeah. That. It sucked."

"I take it you didn't get the girl." Granddad's face was long.

"Nope." Zan rubbed his sore, gritty face. "I got her fired, though."

"Oh, dear me." Granddad's voice suddenly got more cheerful. "That's terrible, Alexander! That poor little lady no longer has any means of support. Better make it right by proposing to her, quick."

"Oh, I did," Zan admitted wearily. "She'd rather die a horrible death than ever see me again." He heaved himself up onto his feet, and waited an agonizing endless moment for the nausea to pass.

There was an appalled silence. He avoided everyone's gaze and concentrated on not vomiting on their shoes.

"Shit," Jack said, with cautious sympathy. "That bad, huh?"

"Women." Freddy shook his bushy head. "Getcha every time."

"All righty, then," Granddad said, with false heartiness. "Nothing like a good distraction when a woman rips your heart out. Let's get you into the shower. We got time to pump coffee and aspirin into you, and then we gotta go, or we'll be late."

"Late?" That alarmed Zan enough to open his eyes, despite the laser bolts that smashed into the back of his skull. "Late for what?"

"Jamie's play," Jack said. "The matinee, remember? That's why I'm here. Slashing throats, gouts of blood, sounds just right for your mood, bozo. C'mon, let's go. Curtain time's in forty minutes."

"Fuck, no." Zan rubbed his throbbing head. "Once was enough for that massacre. Tell Jamie I'm sure he was great, but I can't deal."

"That's enough of your sulking," Granddad rapped out. "I'm sick of it. Jamie worked hard on that show, and the least you can do is plant your lazy whining ass in a seat and watch it. Get him by the arms, boys. Jamie's got us comp tickets for front and center seats, and we're all going to be there for him. Every last goddamn one of us."

Zan groaned as his brothers grabbed his elbows. "Great. With my luck, we might even be close enough to get spattered with blood."

"This had better be good news," Lucien snapped into the phone. "Uh . . . uh . . ." Henly's voice dribbled off.

Lucien sighed, slumping lower into the car seat. He was parked near Abby's apartment, and she still hadn't reappeared. At this rate, the police might very well get to Duncan before they did, which would ruin everything. "Spit it out, Henly. What have you fucked up now?"

"Nothing, boss. We found the van, but he wasn't there. I stayed with the van and Ruiz covered his building. He just got home."

"And you didn't nab him? You failed? *Again?*"

"His whole goddamn family was there!" Henly protested. "He looked like he spent the night in the gutter. There's two brothers, big bruisers just like him, and his old coot grandpa, too. You want us to just waste the rest of 'em and bring him in now? No witnesses, right?"

"Henly," Lucien said slowly, articulating with exaggerated care. "Do me the favor of not trying to think for yourself."

"Uh, yeah," Henly muttered, his voice sullen. "Whatever."

"Keep on him," Lucien ordered. "Do not 'waste' anyone until I tell you to do so. Do not let yourselves be seen. Bring him in as soon as you have an opportunity with no witnesses. Undamaged. Is that clear?"

Lucien barely heard Henly's mumbled reply as the flash of claret-colored fabric caught his eye. Abby, tottering up the street. Her makeup had run, giving her haunted raccoon eyes. Her hair had been whipped into a froth of wild elf-locks. Even bedraggled, she was magnificent.

His penis tingled. Time to pounce.

He froze in the act of getting out of the car, letting the door fall closed when an old lady charged out of the ground-floor apartment. She shook the spade she held, and harangued Abby at some length.

Abby barely reacted. She looked dazed. She nodded and headed wearily up the stairs. The old lady stared after her, shaking her head.

And then, damn her, she stayed in her yard. Lowered herself creakily to her knees and started digging in her fucking flower beds.

Lucien willed her to get up, creak right on back into her house. Failing that, a catastrophic stroke would be fine. He was tempted to just kill the old bitch himself, but there were too many windows looking on.

Damn. *Damn.* Lucien forced himself to wait.

One foot in front of the other. Right. Left. Right. Her skirt swung, heavy with saltwater, gritty with sand. Her feet were frozen from walking through the surf, watching the foam churn between her ankles.

She hadn't been home since she and Zan had been attacked. Less than two days ago, but it seemed like decades. Her apartment didn't beckon like a safe haven anymore, but at least it had hot water, warm socks, coffee. The sodden dress made her self-conscious. Hey, everyone, there goes the scarlet woman of Tremont Drive, strutting the sidewalks on Sunday morning in the Saturday night Dress of Shame.

The people hustling spit-shined kids into SUVs to go to church were all giving her the hairy eyeball. As well they might.

That's right, folks. There goes the neighborhood.

But the hairy eyeball didn't really bother her. She was too cold, too numb, ears deafened by hours of pounding surf.

She looked at her apartment, almost surprised to find it still there. The ground-floor door burst open. Mrs. Eisley, her landlady, marched out. "Abby? Is that you? You must have had . . . quite a night!"

You intemperate slut being the obvious subtext.

Abby was too exhausted to take offense. "Yeah, it was a doozy."

Mrs. Eisley stared for a moment, then remembered her grievance.

"Some strange things have been happening to my garden," she said, shaking her spade. "First, someone drove over my pansy beds last week! Then, yesterday I go to trim my ivy and I find it all torn up! Like a herd of wild pigs was rooting through there! What on earth?"

"Not a bad description of those guys, actually," Abby commented.

Mrs. Eisley's eyes narrowed. "You think this is funny, missy? I don't know what kind of men you've been bringing home, but you keep that trash out of my garden, or else find another place to live, hmm?"

Abby nodded. No problem there. She had no intention of bringing any more men home, wild pigs or no. Enough, already, thank you.

She turned, having nothing more to say, and climbed the stairs.

She dropped her sandals into the kitchen garbage. Limped into the bedroom, unhooking the bodice. Let the dress fall with a wet *plop* to the floor and flung her panties on top of it, leaving her naked but for Zan's ruby necklace.

She hadn't dared to take it off, though its sensuous weight had seemed to burn her. She'd been afraid she'd drop it on the sandy beach. That would be awful. She ought to send such a precious thing back.

She tried to undo the clasp, but her fingers were too cold, and her eyes kept welling full of tears. Hell with it. Later for that.

She wound her snarled hair into a knot, thawed herself in the shower, then dressed in jeans and a blouse the thieves had evidently thought too boring to steal. She put on sneakers, a tattered gray sweatshirt. Raggedy comfort clothes.

Coffee was next on her agenda. She stumbled on Sheba's bowls, and had a flash of longing for her cat. She had to get her kitty back from Dovey. First, coffee. Something about that tickled her memory. . . .

Oh, God. Nanette's matinee. Doomed love and double suicide. Lovely. She would have preferred to lie facedown on her bed with the shades drawn, but Nanette had dedicated this performance to Elaine, and Abby damn well ought to be there for it.

She grabbed the phone, checked the clock. If her car service was zippy and the curtain rose late, she just might make it. Exhausted as she was, she felt jittery, strange. Very relieved to have something to do.

She had an uneasy feeling that she ought to keep moving.

Chapter

26

Abby inserted herself into the stream of people pushing toward the green room, hiding her goopy nose behind her hand. She should have brought an entire box of Kleenex. The deluge had started when Nanette dedicated the performance to Elaine. Then the tragic death scene had finished her off. She'd been forced to use her sleeve. Nasty.

The lady behind her handed her a tissue.

"Wonderful show, wasn't it?"

Abby honked and nodded. She would tell Nanette she was fabulous, go home, eat a pint of ice cream, and cry all afternoon.

After that, she would take stock of her life and act grown-up.

"Abby! Hey, Abby? Over here!"

She couldn't believe it. It was Lucien. The skin under his eyes beginning to turn purple, but his smile still looking like a Ken doll's plastic grimace.

She forced herself to smile back, then resented the energy the effort cost her. She'd been fired, for God's sake. It was no longer her duty to kiss up to him. She could be flat-out rude, if she liked.

Still, he hadn't destroyed her life deliberately. He'd even been trying to defend her, however misguided the attempt. She gave in to social conditioning. "Hey, Lucien. How's the nose?"

His lips twitched. "Hurts," he said, with charming candor.

"Sorry to hear it," she said. "What are you doing here?"

He shrugged. "I wanted to see you."

"Me?" Her belly tightened in alarm. "Why? I would have thought I'd be the very last person you would want to see."

"I was worried about you," he said gently. "I heard what happened last night after I left. About you losing your job. I felt terrible."

Aw, how sweet, a cynical voice muttered inside her.

"Yeah, it was bad," she said flatly. "I'm handling it, though."

"I think you could handle just about anything."

Her smile curdled at his admiring tone. Was it conceivable that this guy was actually still trying to flirt with her? No way.

"Would you excuse me, Lucien?" she asked. "I have to—"

"I could speak to Peter on your behalf, if you liked," he said earnestly. "I'm sure that if I explained to him that you—"

"No!" She backed away. "I do not need to be rescued, and I do not want that job back. I will manage just fine, thanks. Don't interfere!"

He jerked away, looking hurt. "I've offended you again," he said. "All I wanted to do was help. I understand if my presence makes your, ah, boyfriend nervous, and I don't want to create difficulties for—"

"No," she cut in. "Not an issue. I don't have a boyfriend."

He blinked. "Good God, Abby. So I ruined your love life as well as your professional life? In one fell swoop?"

It was so ridiculous, she actually started to laugh. "Later," she said, turning away. "I've got to go see one of the actors, Lucien. Bye."

She pushed her way into the green room and spotted Nanette, still gory from her death wound. Nanette's eyes lit up. She hurried over.

"Abby! You really did come!" she cried. "Did you like it?"

Abby sniffed eloquently and nodded.

Nanette's goopy eyes opened wide. "It, like, made you cry? I really felt the power today, you know. It was Elaine, I think. She helped me."

"You were just wonderful, Nanette," Abby said, in a wobbly voice.

Nanette grabbed her, and they both started to bawl.

By the time the sob fest eased off, Abby looked like one of the actors herself, with all the fake blood that was smeared over her blouse. She zipped her sweatshirt up to her neck. So much for her very last blouse. But whatever. It seemed symbolically appropriate, somehow.

Nanette grabbed her arm and pulled. "C'mon, I want you to meet the others. Martin, my Romeo, is way cool, and Jamie, that hot guy who plays Tybalt, is to die for. C'mere. Jamie! Meet my friend, Abby!"

Abby hastily wiped her face with her sleeve and focused on the clot of sweaty, bloodstained actors. Her smile froze. The world stopped.

Zan. Everywhere she went, everywhere she turned, there he was. He looked haggard and pale, and oh, so not happy to see her.

Nanette was shaking her arm. "Earth to Abby! You OK?"

"Uh, sure," she whispered. "I'm fine."

"This is Jamie, our Tybalt," Nanette said, indicating a tall, muscular guy with dreadlocks and wild makeup who had still seemed oddly familiar, for some reason. She sucked in an incredulous breath.

Of course. Duh. The fight rehearsal. He was Zan's little brother.

An elderly man stood next to Zan. He had the same cheekbones and heavy, slashing brows, though his were gray. The men standing behind them had similar features. Tall, broad, darkly handsome.

Whoa. She was surrounded by Duncan males. The testosterone level was overwhelming. She dragged her wits together. "You were just wonderful," she said, shaking Jamie's hand. "The show was great."

"Thanks," Jamie said graciously.

"Hi, Abby," Zan said.

Zan's brothers and grandfather exchanged startled glances. She hated to think how she must look with her wispy bun, her leaky nose, the apocalyptic remnants of last night's makeup still smeared under her reddened eyes. And his necklace. Dear God. She still hadn't taken it off.

Zan's eyes flicked down, registered it. His gaze was so cold.

"Abby? You mean, you're *that* Abby?" Curiosity lit Jamie's eyes.

"What Abby?" Nanette asked.

"The Abby my brother's gone totally nuts for," Jamie explained to the room at large. "He's been frothing at the mouth since he met her."

"Shut the fuck up, Jamie," Zan muttered.

"Lemme take a look at that girl," the grizzled old man said, pushing his way to the front. "I'm the boy's grandfather."

He stuck out his hand. Abby took it. His gnarled fingers closed over it tightly, and squeezed. "How do you do?" she asked.

"I'm fine, thanks." The old man's keen eyes bored into hers. "So you're the tart who wants to marry money, eh?"

"Jesus Christ, Granddad!" one of Zan's brothers hissed, horrified.

A burst of laughter exploded from her chest. For some reason, the old man's rudeness made her embarrassment vanish.

She shook her head. "Nope. It doesn't seem to be working out."

"Hmph. Well, you are a pretty thing. I see why the boy lost his head." The dimple that carved itself into the old man's wrinkled cheek was exactly like Zan's, Abby noted with a pang.

"Don't flirt with her, Granddad," Zan said. "There's no point."

"Don't be grumpy to the ladies, Alexander," the old man said.

A heavy arm circled her shoulders. It was Lucien. Grabbing her, right in front of everyone, as if he were her boyfriend. The clueless jerk.

She pulled away. His arm tightened until it was almost painful.

"You shouldn't have to listen to this kind of abuse," Lucien said, with pompous stiffness. "Come on, Abby. I'll take you home."

"Lucien, I'm *fine*," she hissed. "I don't need to be rescued!"

The old man's eyes narrowed as he took in Lucien's bruised face. "Oh, ho, ho!" he cackled. "You must be that richer-than-God butthole my grandson pounded the crap out of last night. I heard about you!"

"Shut up, Granddad," the other Duncan brother said.

Lucien dragged her so close, she was practically smothered against his chest. "Let *go*, Lucien!" she protested. "I'm fine!"

One of Zan's brothers fished for a beeper. He frowned at the display. "Gotta go," he said. "Emergency. Duty calls."

"Me too. We're out of here," said the other one. "Later, Jamie. You kicked butt on stage. Don't let Zan kill anybody." The two men took their grandfather by the arms and towed him firmly toward the door.

"Pleasure meeting you, miss," Granddad called back. "You're cute as a button, but you should have picked my grandson! He's a prize!"

An agonizing silence ensued. Nanette, bless her heart, broke the spell. Her sharp green eyes settled onto Lucien, and a small frown creased her blood-spattered brow. "Hey. Don't I know you from someplace?" she asked him.

Lucien's Ken-doll smile appeared. "I very much doubt it," he said. "I'm just passing through. You were excellent on stage, by the way."

"Thanks," she said slowly. "It's funny. You look so familiar."

Zan stared at Lucien, his eyes bleak, then turned his gaze on Abby. "Incredible," he said. "You move so fast, it makes me dizzy."

She shook her head. "Zan, I'm not—"

"Don't flaunt your new lover in front of me, babe," Zan said. "Not if you want to keep him in one piece."

He's not my lover, she wanted to shriek, but it felt like one of those dreams where she was desperate to run but couldn't move.

Jamie slid between his brother and Lucien with a big, placating grin. "Hey. We're cool. Zan was just leaving. Zan? Beat it, dude. Out."

It was like being slow-roasted, the look of contempt in Zan's eyes. But what did it matter if he thought Lucien was her lover? What would it change if she tried to explain? It was still over. Still hopeless. Fate just kept flinging her at the same old brick wall, over and over.

She wrenched away and ran out of the green room, bumping into people, walls, doors. She barely made out the red blur of the exit signs.

She sank down on one of the benches outside the Performing Arts Center, and hid her hot face in her hands.

"Abby? Are you OK?" It was Lucien's voice, gentle and worried.

God, give her patience. She took a deep breath. "Yeah."

"I know this may seem like the worst possible time, but my lunch invitation is still open," Lucien offered. "And if you'll excuse my saying so, you look like you could really use a distraction."

"Lucien, I don't want lunch," she said bluntly. "I'm wrecked."

"Just to discuss your investigation of Elaine's death," he coaxed. "I've got some ideas that might help." He sat down next to her. "It's a platonic invitation, I promise. I admire your courage. I'd like to see you get some satisfaction. Or at the very least, some answers. Please, let me help. I caused you such problems last night. I want to make amends."

She chewed her lip. The guy made her uncomfortable. He was so incredibly, ickily *nice*. Bleah. It was cloying . . . but hardly a crime.

She might as well have lunch with him. Lucien might be annoying, but he was also very rich and powerful, and he had offered to help. Finding Elaine's murderer was the only thing she could think of that was worth doing. For Elaine's sake, she could swallow her pride and endure some discomfort. Hell, she'd squeeze the poor bastard as dry as a bone. She shrugged. "OK."

Avenging Elaine was her last obligation to anyone on earth.

After that, she was in free fall.

Hats off to the woman. She'd done it again. Waited till his guard was down, stuck in the knife, and turned it. And he'd felt like utter shit even before seeing that godawful, depressing, blood-soaked play.

The rock band that had played the Capulet party had threatened to split his head open like a rotten melon. Watching Jamie get his throat slashed was no more enjoyable than the last time he'd seen it. They hadn't gotten splattered with blood, but they'd come damn close. Then Abby waltzes in with her new flame, still wearing his necklace.

Talking about turning the knife in the wound.

He would just get into his van and point it out of town. It was the only way to get that girl out of his face. He would come back when he didn't care anymore. Or maybe he just wouldn't come back at all.

"Abby! Abby!" A girl was screaming the name in a panicked voice.

Zan jumped as if he'd been stuck with a pin. It was Nanette, the blood-drenched girl who had played Juliet, sprinting out the stage door, her fluttery black Goth rags flapping about her. She grabbed his arm.

"Where's Abby?" she demanded, breathless and wild-eyed. "Did you see her leave with that guy? Tell me she didn't leave with that guy!"

"She left with that guy," Zan said bitterly. "Why should I lie?"

"Oh, shit," Nanette moaned. "Oh no. This is horrible. Do you have a cell phone? I gotta call 911, right away."

Zan's stomach dropped like a stone. "Why? What's wrong?"

"That guy! I can't believe I didn't recognize him right off! He's shaved off the goatee and cut his hair, but he's got those icy cold eyes, you know? You can't mistake those eyes. At least not unless you're a self-absorbed pinhead like me, so freaking dumb and slow—"

"What the hell are you talking about?" Zan bellowed.

"Mark!" Nanette wrung her blood-smeared hands. "That guy with Abby was Mark!"

Zan's mind went utterly blank. "But that's . . . that's Moneybags. That's Lucien what-the-fuck's-his-name. That can't be Mark. No way!"

"Yes! Way!" Nanette wailed. "It's him! I swear! He's Elaine's Mark! Murdering Mark! Hurry! Call her, call the police! Call everyone!"

Zan punched her number up. A recorded message began to play. "She's turned it off. But she wouldn't answer me anyway, since she hates my guts." He held up the display to Nanette. "Memorize her number," he ordered. "Go find another phone and keep trying to call. I'll call the cops." He sprinted to his van, pulling up Chris's number.

"Zan? What the hell?"

"Problems," Zan said, panting. "That asshole glomming on to Abby at the theater? Lucien whatever-his-name? I've got to find him. Quick."

"Didn't you hit him hard enough the first time? Grow up!"

"It's a long story and I'm in a hurry," Zan said. "I've got to find this guy. I think he's a murderer. And he's got Abby."

"The museum was robbed last night," Chris said baldly.

Zan screeched to a halt at the light just in time. "Say *what*?"

"The Pirates' Hoard. Gone. Alarms disactivated. Two guards shot. One of them is really bad. They don't think he's going to make it."

Zan's gut ached with dread, and the tormenting sensation of a larger design that continued to elude him. "Shit. That sucks, but this murderer who's got Abby takes precedence, so my problem is bigger."

"Your problem is huge," Chris said grimly. "One of the guards came to. He got a look at the perp. The guy wore a mask, but the guy remembers one thing. He keeps repeating it to everyone who will listen."

"Chris, goddamnit, I don't have time for—"

"A tattoo, Zan. On the left side of his neck. A Celtic cross."

Zan was incapable of speech for a minute.

"Chris?" he ventured. "Get real. You know that I'm not a killer."

"Of course I fucking know that! But a dumpster is a shitty alibi, Zan! How do you do this to yourself? It's that girl, right? You tried to pull her bacon out of the fire, and this is what happened?"

"Chris, please. I've got to find Abby," Zan repeated, desperate. "This guy could kill her. He already killed her friend Elaine."

"I suggest you start concentrating on saving your own sorry ass. Not hers. You don't have a whole lot of time for either one. You get me?"

"Yeah," Zan said. "I get you."

Zan hung up and stared out the windshield with burning eyes. His brain was buzzing, but with frantic anxiety, not any sort of useful cerebral function. The only people who might know where Lucien was were museum people. He didn't even know their last names.

But Matty would. He pulled up Matty's number.

"Huh?" Matty croaked. "What the hell?"

"You've got to help me," Zan said. "That guy that I slugged last night? I've got to track him down. The museum people might know where he's staying, right? The little fat guy, what's his name? Dovey?"

"Dovey Hauer," Matty said. "Like any of them would be crazy enough to tell you where he was staying after what you did last night."

"That's where you come in," Zan said through clenched teeth. "The guy's a murderer. He killed Elaine. And now he's got Abby." Matty was silent for a long moment. "Christ, Matty, wake up!" Zan exploded.

"I know where you can find Haverton," Matty said tonelessly.

"You . . . you what?" Zan was stunned. "How? Where?"

"Come pick me up," Matty said. "I'll take you right to him."

"I don't have time to fuck around! Just tell me where!"

"I don't remember the street address," Matty said. "I'd have to see the area to remember my way."

"So tell me the general area, and meet me there!" Zan snarled.

"No car. Remember? If you want Haverton, you gotta come here."

Zan flung the phone down. The van accelerated. He had a strange feeling about this, but no other cards to play. If it turned out Matty was blowing smoke up his ass, he would tear the bastard limb from limb.

Chapter

27

"Unbelievable," Lucien murmured. "Social engineering at its best."

Abby squirmed on the squishy couch. She got up and twitched aside the drape to look out over the manicured hotel grounds.

Lucien's fawning compliments annoyed her. She didn't need to be petted and praised. She wanted ideas, brainstorming. Real help.

She shouldn't have agreed to lunch. Bad call. She felt strangely stupid, talking about her investigation with him. Almost as if Lucien were making sly fun of her with his gushing, overdone praise. Nor was she happy to find herself in his hotel room. She'd expected him to lead her to the restaurant, but she'd found herself in his private suite.

For privacy, Lucien said, all innocence. *It's a sensitive subject, not for all ears. We can order room service and talk more freely this way.*

True enough, but she still felt itchy and odd about it.

Lucien got up with a big smile. "I'll make us some coffee."

Thank you, God. The first useful or intelligent thing the wretched man had said so far. "That would be lovely," she said sincerely.

He headed off into the kitchen corner. Abby wandered around, too restless to sit. She peeked at his luggage, which sat in the middle of the room. Black leather rolling bags. Two enormous suitcases and a carry-on. A butter-soft leather coat was draped over one of them.

That made her think of Zan, who blew all standards of male beauty straight out of the water with a pair of faded jeans and a T-shirt.

"You're traveling?" she called out, to distract herself.

"Yes. Taking off today. That's why I was so insistent about seeing you. I knew it was my last chance to talk to you for a while," he called back.

She heard the loud hiss of an espresso machine. Odd thing to have in a hotel suite. Maybe he'd brought one with him.

Something fluttered across her skin, like wind rippling the surface of a lake. She stared at the luxurious coat. The enormous suitcases.

There's always a catch when a guy dresses that well.

Oh, please. As if, she lectured her fluttering tummy. Her overstressed brain was playing tricks on her. She saw bogeymen in every corner. So Lucien was well dressed. Big whoop. Lots of men were.

Still, she opened her purse and rummaged for her phone. That prickly rush on the back of her neck made her want to feel connected.

It rang the second she turned it on. She thought instantly of Zan. Her stomach plummeted when she saw the display. It was Bridget.

She could ignore the call, of course. She was no longer obliged to tolerate Bridget. Still, she had no reason to hide from the woman.

She clicked the talk button. "Hi, Bridget."

"The museum has been robbed," Bridget announced.

Abby's jaw sagged. "Uh . . . what?"

"The Pirates' Hoard is gone. Every last piece. Two guards were shot. One of them may be dying. Is that locksmith with you, Abby?"

"No," Abby said. "Of course he isn't. I'm not involved with Zan anymore, Bridget. Not after last night's scene."

"Last night's scene," Bridget repeated. "Yes. That scene couldn't have been more vulgar or ostentatious if it had been . . . planned."

Abby went stone cold. "What exactly are you implying?" she asked.

"I knew you were unhappy in your job, and resentful of me, but I would never have dreamed you were capable of something like this!"

"Bridget, you're insane." Abby flipped the phone closed. Her hand shook. She had to warn Zan. She had no time to waste on this useless lunch date. She headed for the kitchenette, composing her brush-off.

Her eye focused on the bottle of spring water in the refrigerator as Lucien put the milk back. Orionte. She blinked.

The cup Lucien presented her was heaped with whipped cream, dusted with cocoa. A single chocolate coffee bean was perched on its fluffy apex. "Triple shot of espresso, vanilla syrup, one sugar, and lots of whipped cream." He grinned bashfully. "I remembered."

Abby shivered as she lifted the beverage to her lips and sipped. *He memorized how I take my coffee. Every detail. He's like that.*

Elaine's words rushed through her mind like a flash flood. She tried to stop herself from swallowing. Too late. She coughed, sputtered.

The liquid she'd already swallowed left a bitter taste behind.

She looked into his glittering, icy eyes. At his fake, plastic smile. He knew that she knew. There was no need to pretend.

She spat the coffee out onto the carpet. Wiped her tongue on her own sleeve. Her mouth felt thick. Her tongue was buzzing. Her blood pressure was dropping.

"Hello, Mark," she said.

Zan jerked his van to a halt, yanked the emergency brake, and left the engine running. He bolted for the front door, hoping that Matty was sober and ready to roll. He had a sickening feeling of time draining away too fast. Doom, speeding toward them like a huge killer wave.

Abby. He pounded on the door. "Hey! Matty? You ready to go?"

"Come on in," Matty sang out, from the back of the house.

Zan slapped the door open. "Get your ass out here. I'm in a big—"

Whap. Pain, exploding.

He fell down into a deep hole. So deep, consciousness was just a pinhole miles above him.

Abby, a voice as soft and as huge as the wind in the grass murmured, and he was flying up toward that pinhole. It got brighter. He slammed into his own body again with a force that made him groan.

"So this worthless shithead is awake?" someone said.

The toe of someone's heavy boot hit his thigh. Zan sucked in air, tasted hot, salty blood. He'd bitten his own tongue.

"Good," said another, faintly accented. "We can have some fun."

A huge weight that had been crushing his back shifted, wrenching his arms behind him. He felt the metal bracelets being snapped around them. The wrench of duct tape being unwound. They bound his legs until he felt like spider bait, wrenched them back, taped them to the cuffs. He was helpless. Wide open. It scared him to death.

They kicked him onto his back. He finally dared to open his eyes.

Two guys. Dickheads I and II, from the looks of them. Both held guns, but he couldn't focus well enough to tell what kind. Semi-automatic pistols, maybe. The smaller guy's face was grotesquely swollen and bruised. The big blond guy didn't look much better.

"Let's have some fun," Dickhead I, the blond guy, said. "Scumbag owes me some teeth. And a couple of ribs. My balls, too."

"Lucien says no damage," Dickhead II said.

"Lucien's an asshole. He wants to gloat. That shit messes you up. I say, you wanna kill somebody, don't dick around."

The darker one shrugged. "We could tell Lucien we had to do it, you know, rough him up some, to bring him down," he suggested.

"Wait." Matty shuffled into the room like a zombie. He stared at Zan with eyes that were frozen wide. "Lucien said don't touch him."

Zan stared up at his ex-friend. "You're in on this thing?"

The smaller guy laughed. "Wow, big fuckin' genius, huh?"

"You helped that guy rob the museum? And kill Elaine?"

Matty shook his head frantically. "No! I never hurt Elaine!"

Zan stared at him until Matty's eyes darted from side to side.

"Remember what I said last night?" Zan asked. "About how I don't hate you anymore, because I'm all over it?"

Matty tensed visibly. "Yeah? What about it?"

"I've changed my mind," Zan said. "I think you're pus."

The two other guys hooted and slapped their thighs with glee.

Matty's face hardened. "Guess what? I've changed my mind, too," he said. He turned to the others. "Go ahead. Hit him."

"I was starting to think you'd never figure it out," Lucien said. "I thought I would have to simply tell you. You were so blind. All that magnificent courage and determination. So little intelligence to guide it."

Abby was too frightened to be insulted. She backed away, stumbling, almost falling. He advanced casually, keeping pace with her.

"You killed Elaine?" she whispered.

His shrug was offhand. "She was a glitch in my plan."

"A glitch," she repeated, voice shaking. "In your goddamn plan. She was a flesh and blood woman. She was my friend."

"Yes, I know. I'm sorry," he said. "Most unfortunate."

His tone was solicitous, but his eyes were blank. There was nobody home in there. Just a cold, dead void. Oh, her sweet Elaine. "You stole the Pirates' Hoard?" she asked. "And shot those guards?"

He held up his hands modestly, fluttered his fingers. "*C'est moi.*"

She shook her head, then regretted it, the way the world was spinning. "Why?" she asked. "You're filthy stinking rich already!"

"True," he said lightly. "I did it for fun."

There was an ocean inside her body, stomach heaving, briny and bitter, billows rising and falling. She was bobbing like a cork. "The coffee," she tried to say, but her lips were too thick to form words.

He understood, and nodded. "Yes. You took only a sip, but I dosed it heavily enough so that a sip would do it. If you'd chugalugged the whole thing, you'd be dead to the world." His smile widened. "Literally."

"Zan," she said, as if invoking his name would give her strength.

"Ah yes. Zan. Don't worry, your lover will share your fate," he said cheerfully. "The two of you are the best scapegoats I've ever had. You've staged it so well, I barely needed to do a thing. I don't even have to worry about an autopsy, so I can use drugs. So much simpler."

"Autopsy?" she echoed.

"Oh no," he assured her. "Nobody will find your body. Or if they do, it'll be bare bones, decades from now. Brrr." He mock-shivered.

His cell phone rang. He put it to his ear. "Yes?" He listened for a moment. "Excellent. We'll see you shortly." He clicked the phone shut. "My men have finally landed your lover. Now we can proceed."

With what? she wanted to ask, but she was beyond speech now.

"Crystal? Come on out. It's time," he said.

A door opened. A woman stepped out. Abby wondered if she was hallucinating. The woman looked like her. She even dressed like her. That looked exactly like her orange chiffon blouse and her . . .

Oh. Yeah. Duh. Her doppelganger moved closer, and Abby began to see the differences between them, the heavy makeup that masked them. The girl stared into her face, looked her over from head to foot.

"Honey, you look like shit," the woman said, her voice hard.

"You will leave the hotel in the clothes she's wearing," Lucien said.

Crystal pouted. "Aw, c'mon. All those cute outfits she's got, and you make me wear her scuzzy old sweatshirt?"

"Shut up." Lucien unzipped Abby's jacket with a brisk jerk. He and the woman stared, puzzled, at the blood on Abby's blouse.

"Yuck," Crystal said. "You can't expect me to wear that. Gag me."

Lucien undid Abby's jeans and shoved them down over her hips. "Just wear the sweatshirt and jeans," Lucien said. "Put your hair up like hers. The camera has to see her walk in, and see her walk out."

Crystal got into the jeans, tucked the blouse into them, and pulled the sweatshirt jacket over it, zipping it up with a grimace of distaste. She knelt down and pried Abby's shoes off. "Can't believe it," she muttered. "Dirty sneakers. And I could be wearing her Manolos."

Abby struggled to stay conscious. It was a losing battle. Things were getting soft and fuzzy. Sounds were cutting in and out.

"Step along, my dear, right . . . here. Yes, that's good. Thank you."

Lucien led her, shuffling, until she found herself standing in one of the suitcases. He pushed on her shoulders. She crumpled like a puppet.

"Time to take the luggage out to the car," he said. "Bye-bye. We'll have fun later, pretty Abby." He fluttered his fingers at her.

The zipper closed her into darkness, and the world went away.

Chapter

28

He felt so heavy. He just wanted to let go and fall endlessly. Pain was the thread that he dangled from. He pulled himself up, hand over hand, on that thread until he managed to open his eyes.

Dirty cement floor. Dimness. He smelled mold, dust, and rot. Cobwebs. He was disoriented, off balance, as if he'd been turned inside out and upside down. He was dangling from the wall, arms cuffed behind him at such a height that he could neither stand nor sit; only dangle at that excruciating angle, as he'd been doing, or struggle into an awkward half crouch. Difficult, with his legs taped together.

His handcuffs were hooked to a metal ring bolted into the brick wall. He looked for the source of light. A high grated window, so filthy it barely glowed. He looked around the room.

His heart seemed to stop.

Abby lay on a bed, on a bare mattress. Her white blouse was drenched with blood. She was half naked, feet and legs bare. In that cold, dim light, she looked like a beautiful wax doll.

He tried to shout. Only a harsh croak came out.

She didn't move. Her arms were drawn up, wrists handcuffed to the wrought-iron head of the bed, hands dangling limply. He stared at her chest, trying to detect a rise and fall. If she'd been stabbed or shot, there would be more blood, he told himself. And there was no point in handcuffing a corpse to a bed. She had to be alive. Had to be.

"Abby!" This time the name came out, a rough plea for mercy.

She moved. The first time, he thought it was wishful imagining, but then she shifted for real, moaning. Moved her head slowly from side to side. He shut his watering eyes, his chest shaking with convulsions of relief. "Abby," he tried again, his voice shaking dangerously.

"Zan?" Her eyes fluttered open. She wiggled, discovered that her hands were bound up above her head. "Dear God. What the hell . . ."

"Are you OK?" he burst out. "What the fuck did they do to you, baby? Are you hurt?"

She looked around the room until she located his dim corner. Her face stiffened with horror. "Jesus! Zan! What did they—"

"I asked my goddamn question first," he said harshly.

"I, ah, think I'm OK," she faltered. "My arms hurt, and I've got a headache from whatever Lucien drugged me with. But that's all."

"What's that blood from?" he demanded. "You look like somebody stabbed you through the heart."

She glanced at her chest. "Oh. It's fake blood. The girl who played Juliet stabbed herself, remember? And she gave me a big hug after."

"Oh, Christ." He dissolved into the painful, convulsive laughter again. "Fake blood," he gasped out. "Fuck me. Not again. I almost pissed myself, sweetheart. I thought you were dead."

We will be soon.

The unspoken words vibrated between them in the silence.

No, he thought. They could not afford to freak out, give in to fear.

He took a deep breath and gave her a big, shaky grin. "Hope that shirt's synthetic," he said lightly. "That stuff stains like crazy."

"Nope. It's pure cotton," she said, gratefully following his lead.

"It's history, then," he informed her. "Kiss it good-bye."

"It's practically the last garment that I own," she said glumly. "And to think that horrendous bitch has all my nice clothes."

"What horrendous bitch is that?" he asked.

"My evil twin," she murmured. "It's a long, weird story."

Her voice choked off as they heard a muffled thumping behind the door. The thunks and clinks and rasps of locks and latches opening.

The door creaked slowly, heavily open, and Lucien came in.

He smiled like the host of a garden party, a gun in his gloved hand. A Glock 9mm, Zan noted. He looked relaxed, his color high.

"And how are my honored guests doing?" he asked, his voice jolly.

They stared at him, motionless, as if he were a poisonous snake.

He checked his watch. "I've got a few details to attend to before I devote my full and undivided attention to you two," he said. "But I thought I'd pop in, see if you'd woken up."

"Oh, please. Take your time," Abby said.

"It won't be long now," he assured her. "Neale is about to drive Crystal to the Portland airport. Abby Maitland is fleeing to Mexico City. You charged the plane ticket to your credit card this morning. You'll wear your gray Dior. My choice. Very classy. The woman who finds body doubles for me is incredible. After her makeup job, Crystal really does look exactly like you. Except, ah, somewhat better." He chuckled. "No offense, Abby, but today, you're just not at your best."

"Oh, gee," she mumbled. "I'm so crushed."

"When I give her the go-ahead, she'll head to the airport, and shop in the airport mall in clear sight of the video cameras. It'll be easy to pick up your trail. Evidently you're not a very canny fugitive, Abby."

"Evidently not," she said. "So the Pirates' Hoard goes to Mexico?"

He chuckled. "The Pirates' Hoard stays in my suitcase. Selected smaller pieces go to a dealer in Mexico City, others go to Paris, the police will be duly tipped off, and the global hunt for the wicked Abby Maitland will be on—half a world away from me and my lovely shining stash of pirate treasure. And my private buyers certainly aren't going to be calling the police. They all have their own reasons to be discreet."

He clearly expected her to say something admiring. She swallowed, and nodded. "Ah. I see," she croaked. "Very, ah, creative."

"Oh yes, it is. It's stimulating, creating a convincing story for the police to piece together. You get to be the double-crossing villainess, Abby. I hope you're flattered. It cuts way down on expenses to have a single villain. I have to create a false trail for only a single person."

"What did I do?" she asked. "According to your story?"

Lucien sat down next to her on the mattress, with a relaxed, companionable air. She flinched and shuddered as he stroked her leg.

"You used your sexual wiles to seduce Mr. Duncan into helping you steal the Pirates' Hoard, and then"—he waved the gun—"you shot him." He gestured toward Zan. "You let your dick do your thinking. Trusted this conniving bitch just because she gave such good head."

"Shut your filthy mouth," Zan said. "Get your hands off her."

"You should be more polite, considering," Lucien said. "Besides, I have photographic evidence of how well Abby performs fellatio. My man was in a tree outside your window about a week ago. Remember that fiery night? Ruiz certainly will never forget it. The photos are incredible."

Zan declined to reply. Abby curled up as tightly as she could.

"Anyhow, you"—Lucien indicated Abby with the gun—"shoot him in the back and run off with the loot. In fact, now would be a good time to take care of some little details, before things get all messy with blood and whatnot." He put the gun up to Abby's hand. "Grip this. Firmly, please. Squeeze the trigger a few times."

She shook her head violently. "I am not touching that thing."

"In that case, let's play a fun game." He pulled a cartridge out of his pocket, slapped it into the gun, and pointed it at Zan. "I use him for target practice until you change your mind."

Abby's face froze in blank horror. "No."

"The psychiatrists will have fun analyzing the parts of his body that you plugged full of holes. What made her such a sadist, they'll wonder. What childhood traumas twisted her so? They'll write books about you. You'll be mentioned in criminal psychology texts for years."

"Don't," she said. "Lucien, stop."

"Shall I go for a hand? A foot? Or something more catastrophic, like his spine? Would you like him to die quickly, or slowly?"

"You are so twisted," she whispered.

"Oh yes, I know. So? Do you leave your prints on the gun? You have five seconds to decide. Five . . . four . . . three—"

"OK!" she yelled. "Fine! Give it to me!"

He popped the cartridge out of the gun again. Abby uncurled her trembling right hand. He pressed it against her fingers. She gripped it.

"Squeeze the trigger," he directed. "Several times."

She clicked away at it, jaw clenched.

"Good, that'll do, thank you." He pried the gun out of her stiff fingers, slipped the cartridge in, and slammed it up with a sharp ratcheting sound that made her jump. "It's handy that the police took your fingerprints last week. It's coming together so smoothly. You had me worried when you were poking around, but it's all perfect now."

"Where were you planning to leave my body?" Zan kept his tone casual, as if he were asking about the weather.

Lucien looked blank. "Oh, right here is fine. But I'm not going to drill you quite yet. I want to have some fun with you two first. I need something to compensate me for all the trouble and stress you caused."

"What happens to Abby?" Zan's voice was starting to waver and shake. He tried to breathe, to calm it down, but air wouldn't go in.

Lucien's eyes raked the length of Abby's gorgeous body. "Hmm. I haven't quite decided yet. I was thinking of just letting ideas come to me as they will. You'll watch. Then I'll bag her in plastic, weigh her down, and sink her into the lake. And boom, put you out of your misery."

Abby's eyes were frozen wide. Zan wished he hadn't asked.

"If you hurt her, I will rip your entrails out of your body and strangle you with them," he said. He didn't know how he was going to accomplish this, but the promise vibrated with raw sincerity.

Lucien beamed. "Oh yes, this works for me." He petted Abby's hair with his black-gloved hand, then grabbed a thick handful and wrenched her head back. "Killing her means so much more if I do it in front of somebody who cares. Otherwise, there's a sameness to it. Blood and body parts are all pretty much of a muchness, after all."

"You want relief from boredom, just undo these handcuffs," Zan offered. "I promise you, asshole. I will rock your world."

Lucien chuckled. "Aren't you a clever boy. Exploiting my vanity?"

"Aren't you up to the challenge?" Zan asked. "Can't take me?"

"Now you're going for my pride." Lucien shook his head. "I already took you, idiot, or you wouldn't be here. And I'll take your woman, too. Right in front of you. You are whipped."

"Just trying to keep things entertaining," Zan murmured.

"Oh, I'll be entertained by what I have in mind for you two." He stroked Abby's hair again, almost tenderly. "It'll be great."

She shuddered. Lucien got to his feet, pushed the door open, and leaned out. "Boyle? Come down here. They're awake," he called.

There was an uneven stumbling sound on the stairs. Matty walked into the dim room. He stood and stared at Zan, at Abby, his face blank. He looked down at Abby's long, shapely bare legs.

"Stunning, hmm?" Lucien said. "If you're good, I'll let you have the first piece, before Henly or Ruiz get their turn. I have a feeling that might bother Mr. Duncan. Which would amuse me no end."

A muscle in Matty's jaw twitched. His face was dead gray, and wet with sweat. He glanced at Lucien doubtfully. "In front of Zan?"

"Of course," Lucien said. "That's the beauty of it."

Matty's eyes darted back and forth between Abby and Zan.

"Take this time to say your good-byes," Lucien said. "Boyle, lock them up when you leave. Henly is keeping watch at the top of the stairs, so don't bother having a change of heart. Just think about . . . her."

The door swung shut. Matty looked as if he'd been left in a trap. "So," he said to Zan. "Recognize our dungeon full of snakes and rats?"

"Yeah. The basement of the Wilco Lake cabin," Zan said.

"What dungeon?" Abby asked. "Which cabin?"

"This is Matty's dad's fishing cabin. Matty and I used this cellar in our games of make-believe," Zan said. "You've got to help us, Matty. I know you hate my guts, but you have to help Abby."

"There's nothing I can do," Matty said dully. "It's too late."

"Get these cuffs off her," Zan said. "Give her a fighting chance. Come on. You can't do this. This isn't you, Matty."

"You think you know what's me? You don't know shit."

"I know what you're not," Zan said quietly. "I know you're not a psycho like this freak Lucien. What rock did you find him under?"

"The Internet. He's my business partner. He needs me to—"

"He doesn't need you, Matty," Zan said. "He's going to kill you."

Matty's eyes flickered. "I knew you'd say that," he said stiffly.

"Think it through," Zan said. "He's going to leave my body right here, at this cabin. How could he do that unless he plans to whack you, too? How does he expect you to explain my corpse?"

"Just shut up, Zan. You don't understand jack shit."

"He doesn't expect you to explain," Zan continued. "Two corpses, killed with the same gun. Abby's the only one he's set up a double for."

"Do I really seem like such a femme fatale?" Abby asked.

"Yes, you do," Zan said flatly. "Two corpses, Matty. One villainess. It's the only way his plan will work."

"Shut up. I can take care of myself." Matty turned to Abby. "And you. You stupid bitch. I didn't want this to happen to you. You just couldn't keep your hands off him, huh? I tried to warn you."

"Warn me?" Abby tried to puzzle it out. "Was it you who left me the note to call John Sargent? To scare me away from Zan?"

"I wanted to keep you out of it!" Matty yelled. "And now it's too late, goddamnit! Now I can't help you! I wanted you! I *loved* you!"

"Loved . . . who? Loved *me*?" Abby stared at Matty in horrified dismay. "Matt . . . I . . . I never knew that you . . . oh, God."

Matty's face twisted. "Yeah, go ahead. Say it. I know the line by heart. You're so sorry, but you're in love with Zan, and you just don't feel that way about me, so can't we just forget it and be friends?"

"Actually, Matty, 'can't we just be friends' is a lot to ask of a woman who's handcuffed to a bed," Zan said. "How about you cut her loose and then see if she still wants to be friends?"

"Don't make fun of me, or I'll cut your throat."

"Sorry," Zan murmured. "I didn't mean to insult you."

"Your whole existence is an insult," Matty fumed. "I exist on this earth just to make you look good by comparison. I bet you told Abby all about how I ruined your life with the Porsche thing, huh?"

"No, Matty," Zan said quietly. "I didn't do that."

"Tell me what?" Abby asked. "What are you guys talking about?"

Matty glanced from Abby to Zan and back. "You never told her?" Zan shook his head. Matty began to laugh. "You kill me, Zan."

"Tell me what?" Abby almost shrieked with frustration.

"That it was me." Matty started to laugh. "Everything John Sargent told you, about stealing the car, the coke, running that guy over. That was me." Matty shook his finger at Zan, gasping hysterically. "Blood everywhere, and Sir Lancelot here has to stay to hold the guy's hand while he croaks. Fucking typical."

Abby looked at Zan. "You took the blame for that?"

He shrugged, as much as his bound arms would allow. "Matty's dad fixed it so that no one believed me."

"Do you know how it feels to ruin somebody's life?" Matty stormed on.

"Uh, I never really thought about it," Zan said. "At the moment, I'm more concerned about—"

"It sucks!" Matty yelled. "Everybody stops talking when you enter a room. And my dad, with that look in his eyes. Like, would you believe the shit luck I pulled, pulling this loser out of the hat? So I figured, I'm already the bad guy, right? Got the name, might as well have the game."

"I'm not asking you to save us," Zan said quietly. "I'm asking you to save yourself. This guy will fuck you over, Matty. And you know it. This is your chance to do the hard thing. The right thing. Please."

Matty backed up till he hit the wall, his jaw twitching. "Can't," he said shakily. "Don't have the key, anyhow."

"You don't need the key," Zan said quietly. "Use the toothpick on my pocketknife. It's in the boot sheath. Right boot."

Matty leaned over, prodding at the hem of Zan's mud-caked jeans, and pulled out Zan's all-purpose pocketknife. He stared at it.

He wiped sweat off his forehead with his sleeve and shook his head. "No. Too late." His eyes flicked to Abby. "Sorry," he muttered.

He put the knife in his pocket, wrenched the door open, and left. The thuds and scrapes of the locks echoed in the silence that followed.

Matty doubled over outside the door once he'd finished locking it.

The pain in his belly was no longer just a nagging discomfort. It had evolved into a full-blown, horrible pain. Ulcer, maybe, with his luck.

He pulled the string for the overhead bulb to light up the stairs. The light revealed cryptic markings dating back to their childhood games; all conceived, directed, and starred in by Zan, supporting roles played by Matty. Aliens, buccaneers, cowboys, samurai, visigoths.

And pirates. Crossed cutlasses carved into the sheetrock.

He glanced at his hand. The blank space on the web of his thumb looked like a scar. Was a scar, in fact. He stared at his thumb for so long, the door at the top of the stairs flew open. Henly scowled down at him. "What the fuck you doing down there, Pimple?" he growled.

"Nothing." Matty hurried up the stairs. "Where are the others?"

"Neale and Crystal left to go to Portland. Ruiz is on guard duty. The boss went up onto the hill to get better cell reception. He's gotta call Mexico, some shit like that." Henly rubbed his ribs. "I need morphine."

"Hurts, huh?" Matty reached into his jacket, fumbling till he came out with a silver hip flask. "Have a shot of this. Warm you right up."

Henly eyed the flask hungrily. His gaze flicked out the window to check for Lucien. He shrugged. "What the fuck. Boss ain't lookin'."

He took it, uncorked it, and took a long, glugging swallow.

The flask fell. His face took on a flat, surprised look. He toppled heavily to the floor. Matty picked up the silenced automatic pistol Henly had carried. It was warm from the other man's hand.

He stepped out the door and went looking for Ruiz.

Chapter

29

"So." Abby attempted a bright tone, even though her teeth were chattering. "That was unfortunate. On to the next brilliant escape plan."

Zan stretched around until he could see her better. "You work out hard, don't you, babe? That's why you've got such stunning legs."

"Only you could make comments about my body at a time like this, Zan."

He ignored her words, his eyes burning into hers with manic urgency. "Can you grip the top rail of that bedstead with your hands?"

She wriggled around until she almost could. "Sort of."

"Can you kick up and reach the wall behind you with your feet?"

She tried it, and realized what he was getting at. She kicked up both tied legs, braced them against the wall, and pushed.

The bed didn't move. It was awful. The angle was absurd. She couldn't get any leverage. Every muscle in her body trembled like jelly.

"Harder," he said.

"Easier said than done," she snapped. "I was kidnapped, mauled, and drugged by a madman today, if you please."

"I got you beat. I was kidnapped, tied up, and pounded by Mark's goons," he said. "Push harder. Get that bed away from the wall."

Abby gripped the top rail of the bedstead. The angle made the metal of the cuffs cut hard into her wrists, and her head throbbed with each heartbeat. She pushed as hard as she could.

The bed jolted, screaked on the cement floor. Immensely heavy. She collapsed, soaked with sweat, gasping for air. "Damn," she hissed.

"Do it again," he said. "Your panties are stunning, by the way."

She glanced down at her pink tap pants. "Don't even start with my panties," she warned. "You can make lewd comments another time."

"Can I hold you to that after?"

Her laugh was more like a sob. "You think there will be an after?"

"I don't know. I do know one thing, though."

She almost shrieked with the effort as she pushed again, gained another quarter of an inch. "And that is?"

"If we live through this, you're mine."

She caught her breath. "Uh . . . meaning?"

"What do you think I mean?" he said impatiently. "Everything. Forever after. You'll be my bride. You'll share my bed. We'll have kids together. You'll grow old with me. I'll honor and cherish you all the days of my life, et cetera, et cetera. The traditional package."

"That's what you want?" she said shakily.

"That's what I want. But right now, what I want is for you to push that fucker away from the wall. With everything you've got. *Move!*"

"You have such a romantic way of proposing," she grumbled.

She pushed, grunting with effort. The heavy frame scraped across the floor in torturously small increments. She pushed and pushed, body rigid with effort, her wrists bleeding from the pressure of the cuffs.

"I can't," she gasped. "Too heavy. This bastard weighs a ton."

"And you're strong," he said. "Very strong. Any woman who would dog an icy-hearted killer all by herself while the whole world told her she was crazy, she's strong enough to push that bed around."

She sobbed silently, shaking her throbbing head. "Zan—"

"Any woman who would break into a house and pick through rotting garbage for clues about her friend's murder while a smart-ass punk like me stood by making unhelpful remarks, that's one tough woman. An iron bedstead is nothing to a woman like that."

She dragged a hitching breath into her lungs. "Damn you, Zan."

"Push the fucking wall, Abby." His voice was as hard as steel.

Another huge, gut-wrenching shove, and the bed let out a rusty shriek and shifted against the concrete.

"Again," Zan said.

"Let me catch my breath," she gasped. "I have to—"

"No time. Do it again. *Now*."

She used all her fury and desperation, yelling her frustration with each push. Again and again, gaining an inch or a fraction thereof.

Finally she lay on the bed, muscles trembling. "Now what?"

"Now you pull yourself up and over the railing like you're on the parallel bars, and you'll be standing on your feet," he said.

"I'm no gymnast," she snapped. "I hated the parallel bars in PE."

"And if you used the energy you use resisting me to just do exactly as I say, we'd be a lot further along."

She poised herself again, shoved again, gained a few more inches, and with a convulsive jolt of effort she shifted her center of gravity over the top and toppled over, panting and trembling.

"I'm still chained to the damn bed, Zan," she said.

"Yes, but you're on your feet and you're facing forward," he said. "You can push with your weight behind you. Can you get the bed pulled around so you can reach my hands?"

It seemed to take years, and it made such a racket, she couldn't understand why the bad guys didn't rush down to stop them. Inch by torturous inch, she shoved the bed from behind. Then she wrenched it around to the side and had to pull the bed behind her.

Zan kept up a steady stream of annoying banter, provoking her constantly. Keeping the dread and fear at bay. She got herself to a point where, if she slid her handcuffs all the way to the extreme end of the bedstead, she could reach his hands.

He studied her snarled hair. "Got a hairpin, sweetheart?"

She ran her hands over her hair, crunching and squeezing. She'd put her hair up that morning, but a lot had happened since then. She was beginning to despair when she felt one, and fished it out. "Here!"

"Ah. I can't imagine a woman I'd rather be chained to a wall with."

"Stop sucking up and tell me your plan," she said. "Like, just how do you intend to pick the locks if your hands are handcuffed?"

"I'm not, love," he said. "You are."

She squinted at him. "I swear to God, Zan, I'm not deliberately cultivating a negative attitude, but I've never picked a lock in my life."

"Let me worry about that. Move closer. Can you reach my cuffs?"

She shuffled and groped. The hairpin fell from her trembling fingers. It hit the mattress, bounced, fell into the shadows by the bed.

She couldn't bend down; neither could he. She tried to reach it with her groping foot. She couldn't. She screamed with frustration, flailing at the bed. "Goddamn it!"

"Abby? Stop banging your hands. You'll get bruises."

"What difference do bruises make now?"

"They make a difference to me," he said. "I love you, Abby."

She stood there, mouth opening and closing like a deranged goldfish. "Zan," she squeaked. "Now you tell me? I just dropped my hairpin. We're going to die horribly. What do you mean, you love me?"

"Bummer about the hairpin, but I still love you," he said. "I figure, if we're doomed, I better tell you now. Just so you know."

Her throat began to shake. "I love you, too," she whispered.

Zan grinned, slow and blissful. "Ah. That's great. Since you've finally declared your love for me, I guess now I can tell you that you've got another hairpin dangling behind your left ear."

She groped for it, her face hot. "Why didn't you tell me before?"

"Because I'm an opportunistic bastard, and I wanted to hear you say you loved me," he said. "Don't you dare drop this pin, though, babe. Nibble the plastic bulb off. Break it into two pieces."

She did so, trying not to notice the blood on his beautiful face.

"Look at the bottom of the body of the cuff," he said quietly.

"There's a little hole. It's the locking pin. Slip the tip of the bobby pin into the keyway, and lever it to push down the pin . . ."

Zan's voice was a hypnotic drone, describing, never getting frustrated with her clumsiness, repeating himself endlessly, patiently.

It took her what felt like hundreds of fumbling tries.

Finally one of the bracelets yielded, and Zan sank to the floor, ripping the duct tape off his legs. He shook blood and feeling back into his hand, and grabbed the hairpin she clutched in her shaking fingers.

He started in on the cuffs that bound her to the bed. They opened in seconds. He grabbed her, held her tight.

"Now what?" Abby said. "We're still locked in."

Zan groped in the long snapping side pocket of his pants and pulled out a screwdriver. "Lucky me," he said. "Mark's goons were so busy pounding me, they didn't bother to empty my pockets. Let's look for a rock, a brick, anything heavy and hard."

A broken cinder block, half buried in mud and cobwebs and various bits of trash, fit his requirements.

"Hold this door in place for me while I tap the hinge pins out," he said triumphantly. "We'll just take the hinges right off the fucking door."

Her mouth dropped open, and she started to laugh helplessly. "I can't think of a man I'd rather be chained to a wall with, either."

Lucien clicked his phone shut with a pleasant sense of accomplishment. It was like the well-oiled snick of perfectly machined pieces falling into their proper, ordained places.

He'd worked hard, and now it was time to indulge.

He slipped the phone into his pocket and waited for the blazing, blood-drenched sun to slip over the edge, leaving a roiling sea of coral-tinted clouds. Magnificent. He pulled out the walkie-talkie they were forced to use for communication up here. "Ruiz? Respond."

Ruiz did not respond. Lucien tried again. Still no answer.

He tried Henly. Nothing. Again. Still nothing.

It could be equipment failure. The wretched devices never

worked as they were supposed to. He squinted, trying to find Ruiz in the place to which he'd been assigned, the vantage point overlooking the switchbacks of the single rough road that led up the mountain.

He couldn't see him, but of course, Ruiz wore camouflage. He chose a path toward the house that swung around near Ruiz's guard post. There was no one there. Just the wind in the grass.

Lucien was irritated. That idiot couldn't follow the simplest order. They were wide open with no one watching the road. The man's incompetence was stunning. When Lucien got his hands on—

He tripped, fell headlong with a startled grunt. He struggled to his knees, and realized that he'd tripped over Ruiz's booted foot.

The man's prone body had been almost hidden in the tall, waving grass. There was a small red hole in the nape of the man's neck, right beneath his perfectly trimmed black hair. Powder burns around it.

The perfectly machined pieces in Lucien's head flew into hideous disarray. He sprinted toward the house, groping for his gun.

Abby followed Zan up the cellar stairs. She crept on her bare feet, still managing somehow to make more noise than he did. He pushed the door. They both sighed with relief when it opened.

The room was empty, filled with the shadows of gathering dusk. They picked their way silently to the door. A huge blond man lay on the floor, his meaty face grotesquely squished against the kitchen linoleum.

Zan stepped over him with exaggerated care, held his hand out to steady her as she did the same. They tiptoed out onto the porch and into the muddy clearing.

"That was weird," she whispered.

He nodded, and shot a dismayed glance at Abby's naked legs and feet. "True to form, baby. I see you're dressed for the occasion."

She winced as she stepped on a thistle. "I wore jeans and sneakers out of the house this morning!" she shot back, stung. "Is it my fault they were stolen off my body by a psychotic maniac?"

"Only you, babe. You're like those chicks in adventure flicks who get thrown into snakepits in their evening gowns. Stay behind me."

A shadow from the porch roof made them glance up. The sky fell on her, smashing her down to the muddy, rain-soaked pad of pine needles with bone-wrenching force. She had no breath to scream; it was all knocked out of her. A cold, hard circle was shoved beneath her ear with a force that made her eyes water. Her hair was wrenched up.

"I've lost my sense of humor," Lucien said, panting. "You're too goddamn much trouble for my tastes, Duncan."

Zan's face was rigid. "I'm honored to hear it."

"Don't be smart with me." Lucien wrenched Abby's hair again. His hand shook. "Not unless you want me to blow her head off right now."

"No," Zan whispered. "Don't do that."

"Any last words?" Lucien taunted him. "I'll write my memoirs someday. I might even immortalize you. If you're interesting enough."

"No words for you," Zan said. "Just for her." He looked down into Abby's eyes. "Sorry, baby," he said simply. "I tried. I love you."

Her eyes overflowed. She couldn't nod, but she blinked at him.

"Oh, please. So predictable," Lucien complained. "People get so banal when they face death."

"Those were *your* last words, you festering piece of shit."

Matty's quavering voice came from the other side of the clearing. The silenced gun he held spat out a bullet—and missed.

Matty fired again. Lucien started to laugh. He lifted the Glock, squeezed off two shots, and had the barrel in place under Abby's ear in barely a second. Matty flew backward and thudded heavily to the ground, clutching his belly. His gun spun uselessly away into the dirt.

Blood poured between his fingers. He stared at it, and started to laugh. A helpless, wheezing giggle that must have hurt him terribly.

"I fucked you," he said, his voice halting. "You fucked me, too . . . but I fucked you . . . worse. I hid the gold. Where you'll never find it."

Lucien's body stiffened.

Matty's gasping giggles turned into sobs. "Asshole. Who's the . . . big man now, huh? Yanking on your dick. Feeling so . . . smart."

"Where is it?" Lucien shrieked. "Where did you put it? I'll cut off your balls and shove them down your throat. Where is it?"

Matty spat blood in his direction and grinned with bloody teeth. "Fuck you. You'd have to . . . let go of Abby. Zan would tear you apart. I'm dying anyway . . . and you're still fucked."

"Where is it?" Lucien shrieked again.

Matty's eyes rolled in Zan's direction, ignoring Lucien. "Sorry, man. Just wasn't . . . cut out to be a . . . pirate. Know what I mean?"

His eyes went blank. His body went still.

Lucien sidled toward Matty, eyes fixed on Zan, dragging Abby with him in a hideously tight embrace. He nudged Matty's body with his foot. It flopped limply. He began to kick it. A strange sound came out of him, rough grunting howls like some monster from the depths of hell. Each blow jammed the gun up into her neck with bruising force.

Abby shut her eyes and tried not to faint with horror.

Lucien's eyes were wild when he spun around. "Let's get this over with," he said. "Turn around, Duncan. Show me your back."

"I know where Matty hid the gold," Zan said.

Lucien's eyes narrowed. "You're bluffing."

Zan shrugged. "Only one way to find out."

"Get it, then." He wrenched Abby's hair back so hard, it felt like her neck would snap. "Now."

"Let her go, and I will," Zan said.

"Try to bargain with me, and I shoot her in the face," he warned.

Zan nodded. He was bluffing, of course. Abby was as sure of that as she was sure that they were both going to die, but still, she was so grateful to Zan for buying her another few seconds.

She'd never wanted so fiercely to live. Never realized what a miraculous privilege it was. The world glowed with holy perfection. The fragrant evening wind cooled her sweaty hair, ruffling the water of the lake, which caught the light of dusk and turned a lambent silver-white. An eagle swooped down, bearing solemn witness to the terrible scene.

Every exquisite detail of it burned into her mind. She tried to hold them all, to love them all as they deserved. As she loved Zan. Her heart ached for the life they would have lived together. The children they would have had. She loved it, longed for it, mourned it, all in one collapsed, poignant instant.

She put her hand up to the burning ache at her neck . . . and felt the ruby-studded golden key, warm against the hollow of her throat.

Her hand tightened around it, snapping the delicate chain.

Matty's limp arm jerked, driving something into Lucien's calf. Lucien shrieked, pulled the gun away to point it at Matty, and Abby's terror-locked muscles uncoiled like a spring. She jabbed up with the point of the key between her fingers, aiming wildly for Lucien's eye.

Lucien jerked. The stabbing blow became a raking tear. He shrieked again as blood spattered and flew from his torn eyelid.

Zan was already in the air, spinning, leg coming around.

Crack, the gun flew from Lucien's hand, twirling high in the air, turning as it came down. Both men dove for it as it dropped.

Abby landed on the ground and stared at the writhing knot of limbs. The two men struggled, making hoarse, heaving gasps and grunts of effort, and then Lucien was on top, and oh dear God, no—

The gun went off. So did the top of Lucien's head.

It evaporated into a pinkish cloud above his surprised-looking, blood-rimmed blue eyes. He slumped on top of Zan.

Abby's heart tried to beat its way right out of her body. She tried to yell Zan's name, but her throat was swollen from screaming, and all sounds were silenced anyway.

Zan moved, finally. He shoved Lucien's body off and sat up, in slow motion. He wiped blood and chunks of pink tissue off his face with his forearm. *Abby?* His lips formed the word, but she heard nothing.

She tried to get up, but fell right back down again, her legs were shaking so violently. She crawled over to him, grabbed him, held him.

She was shaking apart, but he was solid. Trembling, spattered with blood and worse, but solid and warm and real. She smelled the sharp, salt tang of his skin, felt his heart pound, felt the desperate strength of his arms as he held her too tight to breathe. Her valiant, magnificent Zan. So precious, she thought her heart would explode.

The world crept back into the chinks in Zan's mind. The hollow cry of an owl, the coldness of the wind, dusk that was almost night. He and Abby were glued together with blood and mud. Abby was almost naked. They needed to get warm and dry. To come back to the world from this distant place. He stumbled up onto his feet and looked down at Matty's body. His old friend stared into the sky. His face looked peaceful.

He crouched to straighten Matty's legs and fold his arms over his chest. "We used to play at dying when we were kids. Matty always had to die in a blaze of glory."

Abby nodded. Her grubby fingers dug into his shoulder.

"He did," Zan said. "He came through for us. He stabbed that bastard in the leg. With my goddamn pocketknife. He was a hero."

Abby's arms circled him from behind. There was no time to cry for the tragic waste of Matty's life. Later. He had to take care of Abby.

"Now what do we do?" she asked hesitantly.

"We find a phone. We call Chris. My cop brother," he said. "But we find that gold first, or they might end up blaming us for real."

"You weren't bluffing? How could you know where the gold is?"

"Matty told me when he said the word 'pirate.'" He took her hand and pulled her toward the lake. "I'll show you."

They found a rowboat at the dock. The cold water slapped against the boat with each rippling wave. Memories superimposed themselves on everything he saw. That lake had been a magical place when he was a kid. The tiny, rocky island turned into a peninsula in the summer when the water level dropped. A fallen cedar still clung to the rocks, branches reaching up to the sky with feathery needles, though the trunk that dipped into the lake was white as bone.

He and Matty had walked the plank from that tree.

Zan stepped out into the water to yank the boat up onto a pebble-strewn beach. "Wait here," he said. "I'll be quick."

Abby nodded. He scrambled over tumbled boulders until he found the opening behind the roots of the cedar. The cave opening was so much smaller than he remembered. He wormed into it. A black suitcase was wedged between two stones. Zan unzipped it. Saw the gleam of gold.

He and Matty used to use gunnysacks loaded with pebbles, marbles, bottle tops for pirate treasure. It made him double over with something like laughter, except that it hurt. A dry, silent shaking.

All this cruelty and horror, for some metal and colored rocks.

Chapter

30

Abby floated on rubbery legs down the corridor of the hospital emergency room. It occurred to her that she had no money. No purse. In addition to no pants or shoes. She was wearing a pair of green hospital scrubs that a kindly nurse had scrounged up for her.

She'd been examined, patched, disinfected, and pronounced free from serious injury, though the doctor had urgently recommended a good psychotherapist. She'd been interrogated by the police, too.

Zan was sitting on a bench near the door, his head leaning against the wall. He was asleep. Bandages and patches all over him. Her heart thudded in her chest at the sight of him.

He looked beautiful, and awful. So pale and bruised and exhausted, but still alive. *Zan.* Her whole heart whispered his name, though her throat was too hoarse from screaming to produce sound.

He woke instantly, turned his head, and smiled at her. His eyes were bloodshot and shadowed, but their clear golden color was still beautiful. "Hey. There you are. Finally."

"Hey yourself." She forced the scratchy, hoarse sound out. "Shouldn't you have been admitted? They beat you up so badly."

"Aw, I'm OK," he said. "I just hurt all over, that's all. I'll heal."

"Did they give you anything for pain?"

He shrugged. "Yeah, but I haven't taken it yet."

She frowned at him. "Why the hell not? Macho idiot."

He shook his head. "I wanted to drive you home first."

But you're my home, she wanted to say. The words stuck in her throat behind the sore, ragged lump. Maybe he'd changed his mind. The icy needle of fear stung through the tangle of other feelings.

"Come on." He put his arm around her as if she were made of blown glass and led her out to his van. "I talked to Chris," he said as he helped her in. "They nabbed your evil twin at the Portland airport. She rolled over right away. Confessed everything she knew, which wasn't a lot, but it was enough to pull our asses off the grill. She had pieces of the Pirates' Hoard in her carry-on bag. Along with your clothes."

"Oh. Well, that's good." She knew she ought to be passionately relieved, but having their innocence proven seemed an insignificant detail compared to whether or not Zan still wanted to be with her.

"Same with that dickhead we found asleep in the kitchen," he went on. "He woke up and started talking. So we're home free."

"That's wonderful," she said.

The drive was quiet. He pulled up in front of her apartment. She looked at him, and let the silence speak for her.

"Uh, Abby . . ." His voice trailed off, unsure.

She reached across the seat and grabbed a corner of his jacket. She tugged, and he slid closer. Their hands twined together.

"Are you going to ask if I've got someone to come and be with me tonight?" she asked. "Because the answer hasn't changed."

"I want to be that person for you," he said. "I want it more than anything else in the world."

"Thank God," she said. "So what's the problem?"

He lifted her hand to his lips and kissed it. "All that stuff we said today, about love and marriage and babies? I can't hold you to it. Christ, Abby, you were chained to a bed, under threat of torture and death. Not conditions under which to propose marriage to the woman of your dreams." He let out an explosive breath. "So I'm letting you off the hook," he finished, in a strangled voice. "If you want off, that is."

She shook her head.

He gave her a wary look. "What does that head shake mean?"

"I like being on your hook," she said.

He grinned. "A smart-mouthed, dirty-minded lout like me could do a lot with that statement."

The smile started deep inside her. A sunrise that flushed her entire being with clear, pure light. "I was counting on it," she said primly. "Since I handed it right to you. On purpose."

"Yeah? OK, then in that case my hook is all yours, baby. Every hot, hard, aching, throbbing inch of it."

The giggles were a big mistake. They made every muscle in her body hurt like hell.

"All silliness aside, Abby," he said earnestly. "I mean it. I'm not going up those stairs with you tonight unless it's forever." She opened her mouth to reply, but he rushed on. "I will try to do my best for you, because that's what the woman I love deserves. When you get your next big, important job, I'll be the perfect trophy husband. Supportive, classy, charming, attentive. I'll even try to be a sharp dresser, if you help me out with it. You'll be the envy of all your female colleagues."

"Zan, I—"

"You'll be able to take me out in public anywhere," he promised. "I swear, I won't freak out and slug people. That's not me. Not unless I'm being goaded by a psychotic maniac, that is."

She lifted her grubby, scratched hand to his face. "You're magnificent," she said softly. "You're so fine, Zan. You're exactly what I want. And you are mine. You hear me? Mine, mine, mine. If I have to handcuff you to a bed to keep you, I will."

His eyes gleamed. "Uh . . . yikes. Really?"

"Oh yes. And I'll be smart enough to bolt the bed to the floor first, too," she added. "I will leave absolutely nothing to chance."

He laughed. "I don't want to look at a pair of handcuffs for a long time, sweetheart. It's gonna be pure vanilla sex for this boy."

"That's fine," she said graciously. "Whatever you prefer, Zan. Vanilla sounds just great to me. Any flavor is fine, as long as it's you."

A thought occurred to her, and she started to laugh despite her sore muscles. "I'm locked out of my apartment," she said.

He whistled. "The hell you say."

"I had my keys this morning, but my evil twin stole my purse, the bitch." She jumped out of the van, picking her way barefoot over the damp wooden walkway that led up to the stairs.

"Only you." Zan followed her up, and pulled his pick and wrench out of his tool roll, grinning hugely. He knelt down. The usual look of total concentration came over his face as he got to work on the lock.

"By the way? Zan?" Abby said.

"Yeah?" Zan murmured back absently.

"You haven't proposed to me properly yet," she informed him. "This afternoon, I was too stressed to appreciate the romantic nuances."

His hands stopped moving. He looked up at her. "You want romantic nuances from me? Tonight?"

She shrugged. "It would be nice."

"Isn't it all just, you know . . . understood?" he asked plaintively.

"Nope," Abby said.

"I thought the women went for the strong and silent act."

"I prefer the strong yet eloquent act," Abby told him.

"Ah. Hmm. Eloquent, romantic nuances." He turned back to the lock. "Well, in that case, I could tell you the raunchy sexual fantasy I had when I opened your door for the first time."

"Oh, please. Men are such dogs. Do I want to hear this fantasy?"

"You prefer the strong and silent act?"

"That's not fair," she grumbled.

The skin around his eyes crinkled. "Take me as I am, babe."

She sighed theatrically. "Fine. Zan's raunchy sexual fantasy number one. Roll film."

"OK. It starts out slow, with lots of smoldering eye contact."

"So far, so good," she said.

"I'm on my knees beside your door, picking your lock with amazing skill while sneaking peeks at your fabulous, strong legs."

"Hmm. Typical," she said.

"Then you move closer," he said. "Slowly, so it seems unplanned."

She nudged closer. "Like this?"

"Yeah. Close enough so that I could see what color thread your

miniskirt is hemmed with. The pattern of the lace on your stockings."

"I'm not wearing stockings today. I'm wearing surgical scrubs."

His hot hand slid around her leg, closed over her calf. A sparkling,
ticklish rush of pleasure raced over her skin. He put his hands back
up to the lock. "That doesn't affect my fantasy. So anyhow, I'm
sniffing your delicious woman smell when the lock opens." Her lock
clicked open at that moment. "And then there's this riff where
you're admiring my incredible lock-picking skills, what a turn-on it
is, blah-blah."

"Ooh, you're so good, baby," she crooned. "Like that?"

"Yeah, except more sincere. Then you invite me in."

She walked into the apartment. "I have to write your check."

"Right." He followed her in. She didn't bother to turn on any
lights. She turned to face him and threw her tangled hair back.

"So, are we back to our kinky themes of economic exchanges?"

He reached out to cup her jaw with a tender hand. "No," he said
simply. "In my fantasy, we've already forgotten the check. I'm not
interested in barter. I don't want to get anything from you."

"N-no?" she faltered.

He pulled her closer. The tips of her breasts poked against the
fabric of her grubby, bloodstained shirt, tingling as they grazed his
chest. "No," he said. "On the contrary. I want to give everything to
you."

Her mouth opened, but she couldn't exhale. Her chest was so full
of emotion, it felt like pain. The sweetest pain she could imagine.

"Everything I have," he said. "Everything I am. In my fantasy,
you look at me and recognize me as if you've known me since before either of us was put on this earth. As if we were made to be together."

He began delicately unbuttoning her shirt.

"For your information," she said shakily, "this shirt is beyond all
hope of redemption. You are free to rip it to shreds if you feel like
it."

"No," he said, brushing the shirt off her shoulders and reaching
behind to unhook her bra. "Tonight, I touch you like you're some

rare flower that only blooms every hundred years in the light of the moon."

She sighed with delight as he stroked her, bending to kiss her shoulder, her throat. His hands slid into the waistband of the scrubs and her panties, tenderly pushing them down until he was kneeling in front of her. "A magic flower," he murmured against her belly. "A holy flower whose scent will bring the dead to life, make the blind see, any miracle you can dream up, that's what you are to me. I want to worship you with my body. I want to be a part of your heart."

Her wobbly knees gave way, and she sank down and pressed her face against his neck. "Oh, Zan."

"I want to make you happy," he said, his arms tightening around her. "I want to be a better man for you."

"You're perfect the way you are," she sniffled. "I already told you."

"Better," he insisted. "Kinder. Braver. Less grumpy and sarcastic. I want to save you from dragons and burning buildings."

She laughed at him. "You already did."

"Like hell. You saved me, too," he said forcefully. "I would never have gotten out of that death trap without you, babe."

He pulled her to her feet, scooped her into his arms, and carried her into the bedroom. The moon glowed through the window as he pulled off his clothes and flung them away.

Abby held out her arms to him, gasping with pure satisfaction at the burning heat, the marvelous weight of his body. There was no question of finesse or skill or control, just fumbling tenderness, naked honesty. Hunger and need and acceptance. Joy and passion, too.

They flung themselves into it together and rode out the wild, rushing course of it without fear, hearts pounding, lungs heaving.

Hands and lips and hearts and lives, entwined forever.

Please turn the page for a preview
of the next book in Jessica Inclán's
marvelous, magical trilogy,
REASON TO BELIEVE,
a Zebra trade paperback
available right now.

Fabia opened her door, quickly running down the hall and stairs and then pushing out onto the street. The temperature had dropped even more than the report had predicted, Fabia's cheeks flushed from the slick slap of cold air. Rubbing her gloved hands together, she walked toward the man, slowing as she neared him.

"Hello," she said softly, blinking against the streetlight.

He stared at her—no, past her—his face expressionless. His face was smudged with dirt, a deep, dark red scratch running from temple to jaw, one eye blackened. Blood swelled the skin under his eye and hung in a painful purple moon over his cheek. As Fabia moved closer, she realized that his hair wasn't so much matted from the wet, dank air as from dried blood. There was a clear, perfect circle of reddish broken skin around his neck, and she noticed now that the dirt she'd seen under his nails this morning was actually blood.

Whatever had happened, he'd fought back. Whoever he'd fought with probably looked as bad as he did.

"Are you all right?"

The man turned to her, tried to look up, and then took a deep breath, his mouth trying to move. He was trembling, his arms tight against his body now, his black eyes filled with fog and sadness.

Again, she tried to reach for his mind, but the iron wall was still there, planted solidly.

What do you think? Fabia asked Niall without even meaning to.

All that blood, Niall thought. *Maybe it's not his.* Moyenne *are messy murderers.*

He hardly looks capable of a right killing, Fabia thought.

True. He didn't do his level best, there. So he might be on the lam. Injured from the barbed wire he crawled under, Niall thought. *Just call the police.*

Fabia stared at the man, ignoring Niall for a moment. Maybe she couldn't read the man's mind, but there was something about him. Something kind even in his quiet, painful desperation.

Bloody bleeding heart, Niall thought. *But just be ready to escape. Be prepared to step into the gray, okay? Hop back to your flat.*

Yes, sir, Fabia thought, shaking her head. But Niall was right. It was easier to extend this kindness knowing that if the man grew strange or crazy or even dangerous, she could disappear in an instant, traveling through matter to the police station, where she could report the crime she'd just escaped. The *Moyenne* she worked with at the clinic were always amazed that Fabia would go to flophouses and tenements and dark alleys looking for clients. What she couldn't tell them was that she was protecting them by doing so, keeping them away from danger from which they might not be able to escape.

Fabia bent down, trying to attract his gaze. But he wouldn't look at her, and she could feel the tension radiating from inside him.

"Hi, there," she said. "My name's Fabia Fair. I live at a flat just down a bit."

He didn't move his eyes, but he blinked, once, twice.

"Would you like to come with me?" Fabia said, crouching down farther and looking into the man's desperate, searching eyes. "How about a wee bit to eat?"

He licked his lips, breathing in, scanning the ground as if he'd dropped some change. *Not drunk,* Fabia thought. *Schizophrenic.*

Perfect, Niall thought. *Go from Cadeyrn to just another crazy. Get yourself into another fankle.*

Haver on, man! Would you mind affording me some space here? she thought back. *Go watch your bleeding telly.*

Fabia closed her mind to her brother and moved closer to the man. He was shaking, his knees hitting together. Again, he moved his mouth, but then shook his head, tears streaming from the corners of his eyes.

Fabia watched him, trying everything she knew to get inside his mind, but there was no opening, as if the block was put there on purpose. And not by the man, who clearly was in no shape to create or even maintain a block, even if he were *Croyant*, magic, like her. And there was something about him, even with his quaking gaze and his long, thin, dirty body. Fabia couldn't read his mind, but she could feel . . . kindness.

"All right," Fabia said. "That's it. Please, come with me."

She stood up straight and held out her hand. The man breathed in, looking at her hand and then her face, her hand, her face again, and then slowly, he lifted his dirty palm from his knee, studying his movements with surprise as if he'd never moved before. His fingers quivered, shook, and Fabia took them in her small gloved hand, feeling how cold he was even through the leather and wool.

Shit, she thought to herself, hating how *Moyenne* treated their castaways, knowing that in her world, the world of *Les Croyants des Trois*, this man would have food and a bath and a bed, no matter what was wrong with him. Adalbert Baird made sure of that, finding places for the damaged and weak. The only people who escaped his care were the ones who disdained it. Like Caderyn Macara. Like Quain Dalzeil. *And what will happen if Quain wins?* she thought.

We'll end up like this poor sod, Niall thought.

Shut it, thought Fabia, and clutched the man's hand more tightly. "Come on," she said. "Don't be scared."

But the man was scared. More than scared. She felt his fear in the energy coming off his body, in the sizzling whites of his distracted eyes, in his stiff, hesitant walk. Who had done this to him? What had happened?

"It's all right," Fabia said, her hand holding his as they walked slowly to the door of her building. "You'll be fine."

He turned to look at her, his black eyes so dark she couldn't see the irises. His forehead was creased with worry, his face gray with cold and hunger and fear. Despite the filth on his clothing, the blood on his head and body, and his clearly distressed mind, Fabia wanted to stop, pull him to her, and comfort him.

Please turn the page for an exciting
preview of Erin McCarthy's
YOU DON'T KNOW JACK,
also available right now from Brava.

dle a man whose personal assets added up to more than his T-shirt collections and a carton of Marlboro Reds. Since the thought of both breaking her leg and meeting a man who wore a suit or something crazy like that gave her cold sweats, she had pushed the prediction to a back corner of her mind.

It was going to happen sooner or later, she was convinced, but if that time was *now*, why couldn't she be looking cuter? As it was, she probably resembled a Brillo pad with eyes.

"There's no time frame on destiny," Beckwith said with great dignity.

Nor was destiny something she sat around and thought about on a regular basis. It certainly hadn't been in her thoughts that day at all. And at the moment she just wanted to get home and pull a pint of ice cream out of the freezer and inhale it. Then she could meet the man of her dreams. After she'd gained five pounds from the mint chocolate chip. Shoot, that would make a bad situation worse. If her fated soul mate saw her and ran screaming, she would be humiliated on top of everything else. Maybe she should skip the ice cream and have a salad with low-cal dressing.

"I'm on my way home, you know. And I wasn't planning to do anything tonight but paint my toenails, so I don't see how I could meet anyone. Maybe the handbags interfered with your radar. Maybe I see him tomorrow." That would be better anyway.

Digging through her purse to put her swipe card away, she sensed movement and realized everyone around her was surging forward.

Dang it. The train was here and she would be the last one on. There was nothing worse than folding yourself into a full subway car and sharing your personal space with approximately thirty people of various ages and odors.

"Gotta go, Beckwith! I'll call you later, sweetie."

Running as fast as wedge sandals would allow her, she launched herself through the doors as they began to close and grabbed for the nearest available surface to hold on to.

Not fast enough. The car moved again with a frantic lurch and Jamie went stumbling forward, her handbag clipping the woman in the seat to her right.

"You're going to meet him today."

"Him?" Jamie repeated, this call finally starting to make sense. She had a pretty good idea of where Beckwith was going with this. The Tarot card prediction. Intrigued—no, make that freaked out—she stopped trying to shove her subway swipe card in her bag.

"It's been five months since your prediction and so far, nothing." Thank goodness. The problem with believing in Beckwith's psychic ability was now that he had predicted something she'd really rather he hadn't, she was stuck waiting for it to happen.

Why couldn't she be a total skeptic like Allison?

At first Jamie had been seriously on the lookout for Mr. Right, the dishonest dream man. She had walked cautiously past the melons in the grocery store and had scrutinized the deliveryman carefully when she'd ordered a veggie pizza twice. She'd even taken to using the stairs at work instead of the elevator like she normally did since movement had been integral in Beckwith's prediction.

Nothing. No scary accidents with men fated to make her happy. But Jamie was optimistic by nature. It served her well in social work. She had figured the man Beckwith had described would show up eventually, which did not thrill her in the least.

Not only was it a little unnerving to imagine accidents around every corner, she was absolutely certain she had no clue how to han-

"Watch it," the woman said.

But Jamie couldn't apologize. She couldn't speak.

Because the man she had collided with in her forward motion was *him.*

Him of the tarot cards. Him of the light brown hair, the minor accident . . . she looked at his chest. And the food—now crushed against him in a brown bag that was leaking some kind of oily sauce from multiple directions.

"Oh," she said. Beckwith had been so completely right. It was disarming, unsettling, weird, not as bad as she'd thought. It even felt a little . . . wonderful.

His hand was on her arm, gripping it firmly to keep her steady.

It was a strong hand. A warm hand.

Oh, my. Jamie stared up at him and smiled in spite of herself. "I'm sorry," she ventured, not exactly sure what she should say to the man of her destiny.

He smiled back, showing white teeth in a somewhat crooked grin. "I'll be all right, but I don't think my shirt will ever recover."

When he shifted the bag of food, she saw that he was now wearing red sauce on his white T-shirt. Her hand came up without thought to brush it, but he shook his head. "It's without hope. Don't bother."

"Aaaah. I'm such a klutz. I'll pay you for the shirt."

The train came to a stop and Jamie was pushed and jostled as four or five people moved around her to get off. She was pressed up against him, a blush starting to creep up her face.

They were close enough that if she were to tilt her head up, they could kiss.

He had a strong jaw and smelled like soap and tomatoes.

The need to fan herself was overwhelming. Either the air conditioning was on the fritz, or she was experiencing an explosive burst of lustful heat. Chances were it was the latter.

He shrugged, the movement drawing her attention to his broad shoulder. She fought the urge to squeeze his bicep muscle. Beckwith hadn't warned her about the sexy factor. This guy was built like a racing horse. No, that didn't sound right. He was . . . was . . . *lickable.*

Before Beckwith had spouted off about marriage, her original thought had been that she was destined for a rather fun affair, her first strictly steamy relationship. Looking at super-sexy in front of her, she thought he was probably capable of fun with a capital *F*.

Hopefully unaware of her lecherous thoughts, he said, "Don't worry about it. I mourn my ruined dinner more than my ruined shirt."

"Italian?" she guessed, thinking of the tomato scent.

A stale, hot pocket of air fluttered over her as he nodded. "Spaghetti and meatballs. With garlic bread."

Of course. A traditionalist. No trendy pesto for this guy. He probably didn't even own a suit, given how comfortable he looked in his jeans. And his eyes were blue, swimming with amusement and perhaps hunger. For his pasta.

"I'm so sorry about your dinner. I'd offer to take you out to replace it, but you could be weird or something." Weird? Oh, geez, why had she said that? Jamie wanted to groan. Followed by a mental kick in her sundress-covered behind. It was intelligent and important for a single woman to be cautious, but heck, she could have phrased that differently.

But he only grinned. "No weirder than anyone else in New York."